A STRING OF SERIOUSLY UNLUCKY EVENTS

VAMPIRE INNOCENT
BOOK FOURTEEN

MATTHEW S. COX

DIVISION ZERO PRESS

ISBN (ebook): 978-1-950738-46-5

ISBN (paperback): 978-1-950738-47-2

CONTENTS

1. Natural Enemies   1
2. So Much for Being Harmless   11
3. Quentin Freakin' Tarantino   16
4. F Bomb   27
5. Grand Theft Sarah   29
6. Seeing Red   33
7. Truth AND Consequences   42
8. Eternity is a Really Long Time   47
9. Urban Exploration   50
10. Vicious Creatures   57
11. Deep Philosophical Questions… and Kittens   61
12. Frosty Buns   70
13. The Bystander Effect   83
14. World Exploding Things   87
15. The Many Flavors of Luck   93
16. Fast Thinking   99
17. Six-Inch Fangs   106
18. Chloe   111
19. Deal with the Devil   118
20. To Grandmother's House   121
21. Full Contact   128
22. Surreal   131
23. Orphans, Girlfriends, and Vampire Wars   138
24. The Proper Feeding of Hellhounds   147
25. Daltoned   153
26. The Exact Opposite of Normal   160
27. The Dire Whims of Greater Powers   167
28. Early Registration   178
29. A Bit More Relaxed   186
30. The Girlfriend   199
31. The Suckitude of Responsibility   205
32. Experiment One   208
33. Acheron   214
34. Dragon Breath   221
35. It's Only Folklore Until it's Real   229

36. An Extra Helping of WTF   232
37. Meditation... or Something   236
38. The Mill   239
39. Time for Carnage   246
40. When Safewords Fail   253
41. Not Even Going to Monologue   259
42. What's Worse than Mercenaries? Undead Mercenaries   264
43. How To Make Ten Minutes Feel Like Ten Hours   272
44. Plot Device   282
45. Hot Flashes... to the Face   287
46. Chasing Forest Nymphs Always Ends Badly   294
47. Betrayal   300
48. Vrais Démons   309
49. Foolish Younglings   315
50. Tag   327
51. Weird is In   330

Acknowledgments   335
About the Author   336
Other books by Matthew S. Cox   337

NATURAL ENEMIES

Accepting things beyond my control isn't the easiest thing to do. Luckily, my ability to change my immediate circumstances has significantly improved over the past year or so. You know what they say: being dead has its perks. Wait, no one says that. Well, maybe vampires do... at least the ones like me who find it amazing. Don't get me wrong. I'm not one of those megalomaniacal types who will do anything for power, money, and influence. In fact, I don't even try to sneak a few extra bills of fake money out of the pile when playing Monopoly with my family. I just adore being able to fly. And hey, not getting old or sick or staying injured for too long is really damn cool.

Oh, and it's awesome being able to eat whatever junk I want and not have to worry about it all going to my thighs. Another thing about being a vampire no one really talks about I find absolutely amazing is not having to live in a constant state of fear. Being a girl is kinda like being a mouse living in a city run by cats. I can't remember exactly how old I was when I first noticed some grown man acting creepy toward me, but I was *way* too young. Thanks to my dad's skinny genes, I was a bit older than most girls before I started to attract that sort of attention. My friend Ashley is kinda scrawny, too, but she doesn't have Wright family genetics. Jerks started catcalling her in eighth grade.

Yes, there's a damn good reason girls learn early on to move in packs.

Being a vampire allows me to go out alone at night without fear. This is especially handy now since I'm walking down an unfamiliar street somewhere in Chicago. I'm not the least bit scared, though being somewhat lost might make me seem like an easy target for a creep.

I start mentally humming the theme from *Airwolf*.

That might seem random, but I have a father who never got over the Eighties. He's like really stuck on the decade, to the point he even looks back nostalgically on how he used to think nuclear war would happen at any moment. Movies like *Red Dawn* put him back in the same headspace. So, what does *Airwolf* have to do with me being in Chicago? Nothing. What the hell am I doing in Chicago? Ask Arthur Wolent. Better yet, ask why vampires over two centuries old refuse to use freakin' email.

Sigh.

I guess old people and technology are natural enemies or something, kinda like the way Great Uncle Hank says remote controls for televisions are a communist plot to make Americans lazy. As if having to get off the sofa to change channels would somehow keep us all in fighting trim for the day the Red Army invades.

Sigh part two.

Dad once told me grandma and grandpa wouldn't let him get a modem as a kid because they believed placing phone calls from a computer would just cost more than an ordinary voice call. Back in the dark ages before the internet, computers had to use literal telephone lines to reach the outside world. Yeah, I know, right? A computer making phone calls. Serious dinosaur tech. I gotta give it to elder vampires though. Fear of technology must get deeper and deeper the older someone is, or maybe it has to do with how far removed from one's childhood any given technology is. Anything that's relatively new or cool during a person's childhood and teen years is considered amazing, exciting, and great. Stuff that gets invented after you turn forty falls into a different bucket... a bucket of disdain. I imagine technology invented 200 years after you were born probably feels like the devil itself.

How much does a man have to hate technology to pay for plane tickets to send me in person to Chicago to hand-deliver a USB memory stick rather than send a stupid email attachment? Argh. But hey, what Arthur Wolent wants, Arthur Wolent gets. It's not like I'm subservient or anything to him. He's no Dracula to my Renfield. More like he's the boss and I'm a new employee. Sure, I think this is wasteful and stupid, but... guess who's in Chicago right now.

Oh, right. *Airwolf*. Why am I humming the music? For one thing, it was one of Dad's favorite shows as a kid. He made me watch it. Okay, 'made' is a bit strong. Not like he tied me to a chair and taped my eyelids open like that guy in *A Clockwork Orange*. The show was pretty cool if a bit cheesy in places. Anyway, so like the premise of it is some company made a military attack helicopter but disguised it as an ordinary civilian one. The Russians (Eighties stuff always used Russians for bad guys) wouldn't think it was a threat, then *bam*… guns everywhere.

Right now, I feel like the wolf in sheep's clothing.

I'm just some innocent seeming teenager on my own in downtown Chicago after midnight. It's really crazy and foolish of me to think, but I'm almost hoping someone tries to do something bad to me. How I react depends on what they have in mind. A simple mugger looking for cash is going to walk away alive. A *true* creep, I'd probably end up killing on the justification that if I hadn't been here, they'd have attacked some mortal girl who *can't* stop them. Also, if I let them go, they'll only hurt someone else. Sure, I'm still freaked out by the idea of casually killing mortals. Even a guy who wanted to leave me in a shallow grave somewhere after doing unspeakable things to me, I'd feel awkward about ending. Not guilty, just awkward. The same kind of awkward as going to a good Tex-Mex restaurant and ordering a cheeseburger.

A sudden weird idea hits me. Straight up killing a creep like that would be less awkward to me than how I felt when Ashley told me her mother found a dong in her bedroom. Cringe, right? The absolute worst part was Mrs. Carter having such a non-reaction to it, as if every woman had one; implying she, too, might have one hidden away somewhere. Ugh. Shudder. And, hey, don't look at me like that. I don't have one. There are Littles in my house… and Mom has like bionic senses.

Ugh. Focus, Sarah. I'm on the clock… so to speak. Yeah, if I'm thinking about Ashley and her adult toys, I must be anxious. This whole job had a strange unspoken hint of danger. No one said anything about risk, merely a simple trip to hand off some data. Maybe I'm becoming paranoid, or just used to the simplest tasks going wrong in the wildest ways imaginable. Whatever the reason, I've been on edge ever since almost dying at the airport a few hours ago.

Oh, my near splat experience had nothing to do with the job. Just some drunk jackass in a white cargo van not realizing a parking lot isn't where you're supposed to try to break land speed records. Dude almost ran me over while I was walking from where I parked to the terminal. Some people, I swear.

Anyway, that set the tone for this whole trip.

So far, nothing else weird has happened. Which means the Universe is gathering its energy for a high-powered blast from the BOHICA cannon.

What's that? See, Mom's dad is retired Air Force. She sometimes uses the phrase 'BOHICA' because he used it her entire life. As with everything in the military, it's an acronym. Means 'bend over, here it comes again.' When Grandpa Sheridan uses it, he's almost always talking about someone being dragged into a commander's office to get chewed out, reprimanded, punished, or given some undesirable assignment. Mom tends to use it whenever something goes wrong.

I'm expecting something to go wrong.

No particular reason, just my danger sense tingling… and it started way before I happened to be alone on the streets of Chicago.

I stop short when three big black guys come out of nowhere and approach me. They look kinda like gangbangers, but then again, I'm a white kid from the suburbs of Washington State. What do I know about Chicago street gangs? Normal me probably would've been terrified at the sight of these guys. Vampire me is calm. More so because I can see into their minds. They're worried about me being out here alone since this is 'not a nice area.'

They also think I'm like fifteen, and maybe a stupid runaway.

Sigh.

I talk to them for a few minutes, being friendly and thanking them for their concern. There really is no good reason for me to be out here at this hour on my own, so I don't even bother trying to come up with a lame excuse. All three of them get a memory implant that they found some random girl wandering around lost after her car broke down and helped her—me—get it running again and on her way home.

Leaving them in a derp trance, I hurry to the end of the block and round a corner out of sight.

Heh. Wow. Not what I was expecting from a city this big. It's refreshing to bump into genuinely nice guys, even if they do look kinda scary. Last time I ran into guys kinda-sorta dressed like that, I'd stumbled into the middle of a drug deal. I still feel awful about shredding most of them. Not my fault. I'm extremely allergic to sudden flashes of bright sunlight.

Speaking of that… apparently, I *am* getting better at tolerating the daylight. An Innocent's ability to come off as lifelike does seem to be a power capable of improving. Sam and Dad tell me I have to 'put skill points' into it, as if life is some kind of roleplaying game. Honestly, I probably would've been too chicken-slash-wimpy to try working on my sunlight tolerance. I had the good—bad—luck of pissing off a vampire who chained me to a tree in hopes of a sunrise roasting. Yay me, I managed not only to survive, but it toughened me up to the sun a bit. It only cost me a few hours of miserable, burning, inescapable agony so painful I kept on blacking out and waking back up, as torturous as if I'd been forced to watch a Dr. Phil marathon.

Here I am in Chicago.

Can't really object. Not like I have anything else to do during the summer. My 'vampire night job'—can't really call it a day job—is at least keeping me occupied when everyone is busy. Michelle's crazy. She's taking a few classes over the summer as well as still working. The girl doesn't have to work. Her parents are paying for everything, but she's gotten in the door at a law firm and is hoping to score brownie points. No, she's not doing anything legal yet, merely a file clerk, mail room person, or coffee-getter or whatever they need. But she thinks being around legal people will help her.

Ashley is still working at the same vet place and also dating this new girl she met last week, Raleigh Murphy or something like that. Dammit. Now I know why I'm so anxious. I haven't seen Ashley face to face in almost a week. We've both been busy on different schedules. This whole adulting deal really sucks. I'm super glad it's only a temporary thing for me. Being eighteen forever is perfection. I can be adult when I feel like it and fall back to being childish when the need arises. If the other vampires in Seattle want to think of me as a 'useless child,' I'm more than happy to exploit it and not subject myself to work or responsibility.

Yep. I think I'm either jealous or just having separation anxiety. We've never really spent this much time away from each other. Yeah, I got the scoop via phone call. Raleigh is our age. Well, almost. She's eighteen. Ashley is still eighteen for roughly two months. Her birthday is October seventh. I'm technically nineteen, but it doesn't count since I stopped aging less than a month after graduating high school. I forget if it's her mom or dad, but one of Raleigh's parents has a fairly high up position with either Amazon or Microsoft. VP or something. So, the girl has money. Not that Ash really cares too much about that sort of thing. They hit it off right away and Ashley's already wondering to me via texting storm if 'she's the one.'

This is Ashley after all. 'The one' doesn't mean she's wondering if they'll end up married and spending the rest of their lives together. For Ash, 'the one' means the person she finally dates where a relationship makes it past the three-month mark. So far, Ash only had that happen once and it ended in disaster. My best friend is cute, innocent, adorable, trusting, sweet, caring, feisty... and incredibly unlucky in the love department. Something always goes wrong. Yes, I'm biased, but it's almost always that she discovers the person is really a jerk. Ash is kind of a happy-go-lucky, submissive sort of personality. Wait... 'Submissive' is not quite the appropriate word. Accommodating is better. She won't just sit there quietly and accept being mistreated. The instant she gets a hint the person is a douchebag, she's out.

And sure, there's also the chance some people can't handle her peculiar mix of personality traits. Ash can go from acting like an oversized child squeeing at rainbow unicorns one second to Red Sonja the next. If something annoys her, she is *not* shy about letting her feelings be known. Hate to say it, but I think most of the people she's thus far ended up dating have been looking for a spineless wimp they could push around all the time or an obedient 'trophy girlfriend' who kept quiet and did as she was told. She's only submissive when she wants to be. It's like a weird Faustian thing where the seemingly innocent, weak person has all the power... or something like that. I mean, look at me. Not that I'm a super assertive person, but compared to her I am. Yet, anything she wants, I'm right there to do for her. All she has to do is start sniffling and I scramble to fix whatever's upset her.

A sudden car whooshing down the rain-soaked street nearly startles a yelp out of me. After the van at the airport, I'm a bit jumpy at fast-moving vehicles coming close. Granted, this one didn't pose any danger, just went past me on the street.

Yep. Vampire night job as a courier. Could be worse, I suppose. At least Wolent isn't sending me to kill anyone. It's not a bad job, really, working for him. It's usually less demanding than delivering pizzas. Alas the money isn't as good. Okay, the money's nothing. But hey, I get brownie points with the boss.

This year is setting itself up to be the lamest summer of my life so far. No, I'm not splitting the technical hair of it being my unlife. Like I said, Ashley and Michelle are kinda ghosts lately due to being so busy. Ashley's voice drifts around inside my head, replaying a past phone call. She's talking about Raleigh's high-end wardrobe and telling me the girl isn't status obsessed, just wearing the stuff her parents get her. It's not as if she's buying custom made designer duds like some Hollywood starlet, but still. I could fill half a closet for what it sounds like this girl's parents spend on one or two outfits. Ash is a little uneasy since Raleigh has thus far refused to bring Ashley to her house, introduce her to the parents, or even her friends.

My assumption—which Ashley shares—is that Raleigh isn't out of the closet to her family yet and doesn't want them to know she's dating a girl.

Ash can sorta sympathize. Mrs. Carter is absolutely accepting of her, but Michelle's parents… no way. If they ever found out Ashley was bi, we're all certain they'd instantly forbid Michelle from having any further contact with her. I honestly think they'd freak out more over that than learning I'm a vampire.

I start to get angry with them for imagining them hating on my best friend for no reason other than their religious crap, but the anger rapidly morphs into sadness. It's irrational sadness, though. It's only been eight days, eleven hours, thirty-two minutes and—I look at my iPhone—fourteen seconds since I saw her face to face. I'm not obsessed. Nope.

We're just close.

I'm not jealous of Raleigh monopolizing Ashley's time.

A 'no parking' sign almost smacks me in the forehead due to me not paying attention to where I'm going. As if it attacked me, I punch it— bending the metal. It takes me a moment to realize I just punched a sign in anger. Ugh. Okay, maybe I *am* jealous of Raleigh. And no, I know this sounds super messed up and weird, but I am *not* in any way romantically attracted to Ash. It's protective and possessive. Like we're enchanted elven twins or something who will waste away to nothing if kept apart too long.

Hi, my name is Sarah and I'd like to thank the Academy for the Most Melodramatic award.

I stop walking. Hang on. If there's something I've learned about being a vampire it's that sudden unexplained emotions mean something. Still haven't figured out why I got so nostalgic and maudlin over my childhood —which wasn't that long ago. Maybe my brain just needed to sort out such a massive change in my reality. Whatever. Me being so randomly possessive of Ashley is strange. Half of it is like big sister protector mode, the other half is not wanting to share her with anyone else. She's *my* friend, dammit. We hang out together constantly—except we're not hanging out together.

Not too long ago, I had to officially declare to the Seattle vampires Ashley Carter is my thrall.

Unless I have a serious sleepwalking issue, we have not done anything to make it an official thralldom. Ashley's not tasted a drop of my blood or been affected by any sort of vampiric mind altering powers. Merely saying 'she's my thrall' shouldn't establish any sort of mental link between us, right?

Hmm. Not so sure now that I think about the Transference.

The process of making another vampire involves three key components: death, blood, and desire. At the moment of—or *very* soon after—death, a vampire cuts themselves open and feeds their blood to the new prospective vampire. In order for it to work, the vampire has to desire to impart the gift. Merely dribbling blood in the person's mouth without wanting them to receive the gift doesn't do a damn thing but make a big mess. So, desire has real power. Same goes for closing a bite wound. If I just lick the blood off someone's neck or wrist, the fang marks remain. I have to want the holes to heal for them to do so.

Hey, vampires are magic. Science can't explain this stuff.

Dammit. Did I want Ashley to be a thrall? Do we have some kind of actual mind link going on now more than us simply spending damn near every waking moment of our lives together? And if so, am I feeling possessive and lonely or am I reading *her* feelings?

More cars going by startle me into walking again. There's no point in standing here asking myself questions I can't answer. I need to finish this handoff and go home. Even though I'm an immortal undead, my parents are worried about me being so far away from home. In their eyes, I'll forever be a kid who isn't ready for the world.

Well, I am frozen at eighteen for eternity, so maybe they aren't exactly wrong.

I keep walking, checking my phone map and trying to compare it to my surroundings. There's a rendezvous point I need to reach. Unfortunately, vampire elders don't like technology. They couldn't simply give me a geotag to find. Nope, they had to give me a Post-it note with a handwritten address. Problem is, the street name they used probably got changed sixty years ago.

My irrational sadness-slash-jealousy is distracting me from what I need to do. Hey, at least I recognize it's not rational. Probably not terribly healthy, either. I mean… in every vampire story, a driving sense of possessiveness is what leads to tragedy. Honestly, if my life was ever made into a vampire story, it would totally not be one of those overly emo, melodramatic horror stories. Nope. Not me. I'd wind up the lead character in something closer to one of Dad's Eighties comedy movies. Nothing too serious, moments of drama punctuated by plenty of silliness and bad luck with convenient comedic timing and plenty of 'dad jokes'.

I pause to wait for the pie to hit me in the face.

After a look around for sneaky clowns—and finding none—I resume trying to find this damn address. I'm no longer eight years old. There's no reason for me to cry my eyes out over Ashley having to go home and sleep in her own bedroom after we literally spent every minute of the last week of summer vacation together. Not exaggerating, she'd essentially moved into my room for a week that year. Not my finest moment when she finally had to go home—all of half a block down the street. I bawled like some mysterious 'they' hauled my best friend away and we'd never see each other again.

Okay, so I didn't have any other friends back then and Sierra was like two.

I'm being totally hypocritical here, getting jealous. Ashley's been completely cool about me spending time with Hunter. Why wouldn't she? We aren't tweens anymore. Dating is normal. I should not feel like this Raleigh girl is taking my best friend away from me. There's no way in hell I'm ever going to give Ashley the same kind of love as a romantic partner. I can't begrudge her wanting that from someone, just like she doesn't begrudge me getting it from Hunter.

Yeah, this is irrational. Something's up. Question is, what?

I can worry about it later.

Right then, on with it. It's exactly the sort of thing Dalton would say. I mutter, "Right, then. Let's be on with it," in an overdone English accent somewhere between Cockney and soon-to-be-out-of-work minor theater performer who's getting fired for their bad accent.

Back to the matter at hand. Old people vs. technology. Or more accurately, old people giving me crappy directions. No, I'm not digging on the elderly. I mean *old* people. Like… centuries old. It seems no one over the age of 180 trusts the internet. I squeeze the USB stick in the pocket of my jeans. Apparently, they don't trust FedEx either. No idea what's on this stick except for it being 'business' type stuff. Some things I overheard at Wolent's led me to believe the data is related to various companies owned or at least influenced by vampires. Someone getting their hands on it wouldn't reveal any secrets unless someone stopped to ask what all the companies in there had to do with each other. Even then, it's pretty unlikely any mortal person would make the bizarre leap of abstract logic to assume these businesses are all part of some shadowy vampiric power cabal.

It sounds so silly when I think it, even if it's true. No one would believe it.

It's a little after two in the morning when I finally arrive at the spot where the handoff is supposed to occur. Turns out, Wolent sent me to the corner of North Plainfield and Irving Park Road. I look around. Most of the buildings in this area are these narrow row-houses all crammed together. I'm standing in front of a Polish Bistro, across the street from Bob-O's hot dogs. I hear they take hotdogs super seriously around here.

Like, if you try to put ketchup on one, you can get thrown out of places... or punched.

The parking lot of a small auto-repair shop across the street from the bistro has a few cars in it, probably left there for service. No one is moving around that I can see. It's fairly quiet. The noise of distant cars whooshing along filters among the various buildings. Wow, they really love one-way streets here, don't they?

No sign of anyone, vampire or otherwise.

Uh oh. I almost forgot. This is me. Something is going to go wrong. I hang my head, staring down past my black Foamy the Squirrel T-shirt and jeans at my off-brand canvas sneakers. This outfit is majorly unassuming with a side of slacker. Most people wouldn't give me a second glance. By some miracle, I've managed to arrive at the designated spot neither too early nor late... and no one is here. Sigh. Yeah, something is definitely going to go wrong. Ten bucks says an hour from now, I'm going to be shot, stabbed, or on fire... and probably stranded somewhere naked.

Not that I want to go streaking, it just always seems to happen when I get into a fight. My vampire body is much tougher than clothing and vampires just *love* sharp weapons that rip things apart. Sigh. Old people and technology, werewolves and vampires, Sarah Wright and 'things going smoothly.' Yeah, all natural enemies. Well, maybe not so much werewolves and vampires. That feud is a BS Hollywood thing. We aren't intrinsically forced to fight like cats and dogs.

But me and things happening the way they're expected to happen? Yeah. Not likely.

I hold my arms out to either side and stare up at the clouds.

"Okay, fate. Hit me."

2

SO MUCH FOR BEING HARMLESS

I suppose tempting fate is a bad idea.

To clarify, I'm not trying to tempt it as much as give it a 'let's get this over with' nudge. College has a complication high school did not. Namely, how long do you wait when the teacher doesn't show up before you can leave? High school is kind of like prison with crappier food and fewer stabbings—usually. What I mean is, we're not allowed to leave whenever we want to. At SCC, the debate rages if it's ten minutes, fifteen minutes... if a professor happens to have a PhD, do they get twenty minutes?

Same thoughts rattle around my head. How long do I stand here on the corner looking like an obvious drug mule before going somewhere else? Like hey, this girl who's trying so hard to look inconspicuous is the exact opposite. If any cop—or nosy neighbor—sees me, they're either going to think I'm looking to buy drugs, sell drugs, or I'm a runaway who doesn't know what to do with herself.

All three assumptions would lead to confrontation and memory surgery. Problem is, if someone watching me from one of the nearby houses calls the cops, then watches the cops leave and I'm still standing here, they're going to call back. So, I probably shouldn't spend too much time here.

For about ten minutes, I pace around in a circle. Anxiety becomes impatience. To reduce my conspicuousness, I sit on the sidewalk and lean against the Polish Bistro, hoping it's more difficult to notice a lump on the ground than a person standing like a post out in the open. At the fifteen-minute mark, I reach for my phone to call Wolent's people and ask them if something changed.

In the midst of scrolling down my contact list, a flash of headlights catches me square in the face. They're painfully bright to vampire eyes. I gasp and cringe away, muttering something Mom would give me a stern look for saying. Hint. First word was "ow." Second word is something Samuel L. Jackson loves to say.

Yeah, Mom really hates that one. Even more than the C-word. I'm no Sophia—who is almost scared of swearing—but I generally try to avoid it unless pain or emotion gets the better of me. The squirrel on my shirt wants to stab someone in the eye with a really hot French fry. Fairly sure that wouldn't hurt as much as headlights—at least, not to me.

Thankfully, looking at my iPhone screen caused my eyes to dial back the night vision sensitivity enough to where having headlights slap me across the face doesn't leave me blind and seeing stars for five minutes.

I'm only helpless for about *two* minutes.

When I can see again, I blink away the laser-lines floating in my vision. The offending car—a dark silver Mercedes—has pulled into the parking lot of the auto repair place right across the street in front of me. Yeah, go me. Great idea to sit on the ground so my face is exactly at headlight level. The Mercedes came down the street between the auto place and the Bob-O's, pointing right at me as it turned the corner to my left.

Three younger guys—all early twenties—in expensive-looking suits are standing around the car expectantly. They look like newly hatched lawyers or, I dunno… as though Sophia magically animated the mannequins at a Men's Wearhouse. Seriously, they all have similar hair, perfect chiseled chins, and impeccable suits. Did some elder vampire like 3D-print these dudes? They definitely fit the description of 'well-dressed professionals' Wolent told me to expect.

I'd feel underdressed in jeans and a T-shirt, but if it hits the fan, joke's on them. I'm not the vampire who'll be out a few thousand bucks of wardrobe. Not to be too presumptuous here, but maybe a chance exists this meeting will happen without a problem.

The guys stare at me. It's not a creepy leering sort of stare, or even a 'look at the little peasant girl' condescending type stare. The mood they're giving off is a 'is that the person we're supposed to meet?' I mean, there's no one else out here and I'm totally out of place. In seconds, it's obvious to me they are all vampires. Confusion in their expressions makes me smile. They're having a difficult time telling if I'm a mortal or a vampire. Like I said before, *Airwolf.* No one sees me coming until the machineguns pop out the side pods. Or in my case, claws.

Okay. Game time.

I use a tiny bit of my flight power to effortlessly rise from seated on the ground to standing. It's subtle, but the unnatural smoothness of my motion is enough of a clue for the three GQ mannequins to realize I'm not mortal. They relax. The blond one can't seem to decide if he wants to give me a pitying look or a stupid grin. They walk toward me out of the parking lot and cross the street to the corner in front of the Polish Bistro.

"Hey," I say. "You guys are up late."

"Do your parents know you're outside at this hour?" asks the blond guy.

"Yes." I fold my arms. "They do." The guys think I'm kidding. I'm not.

The black-haired guy tilts his head, slightly raising his eyebrow like he's about to hit me with his smoothest pick up line. "They said you looked young. Looks can be deceiving."

"Okay, so you are..." Blondie gives me a genuine smile. "Wasn't sure if you were enthralled or not. Not like Mr. W to trust this sort of job to a pawn."

Oh, whoa. So he wasn't questioning if I was a child or old enough to be a vampire. The pity in his expression seems to have been from wondering if I'd been turned into a slave drone or something. He seems thrilled to see I'm a vampire. Yanno, it's weird to meet three guys this age and *not* immediately endure a bunch of cheesy attempts to hit on me. The energy these dudes are throwing off is total business plus a bit of elitist exclusivity, like we're all part of some special secret society.

Suppose we *are* part of something like that, being vampires.

Their attitude makes me like them right away.

We have a brief, friendly conversation mostly about if I had a pleasant trip here. The blond guy, Grayson, jokingly asks me if I've had a 'real hotdog' yet. He's obviously not serious and I don't bother commenting that I could, in fact, try one if I wanted to. Dylan and Andrew both wince at the idea of consuming actual food. Any vampire could, in theory, eat... but most don't find the subsequent vomiting worth the momentary enjoyment.

In only a few minutes, I get the distinct feeling they're keen on getting this over with and on with the rest of their night. They aren't looking to become best buds, hang out with me, or get in my pants—which is totally cool with me. Having grown up in the society we have, it's almost weird for three guys in suits to treat me like we're all on the same level. Can't even say it's a vampire thing since there are plenty of old school chauvinistic bastards among the undead.

It's beyond obvious I have located the correct people.

"Sorry to be so abrupt, but we are on a timer," says Grayson.

"Yeah, no problem. I kinda wanna get back home, too." I fish out the USB thing and hand it to him. "Mind if I ask a stupid question?"

"Ask away," says Dylan, the brown-haired guy.

I smile. "Why didn't they just email this stuff?"

The guys chuckle.

"Tradition, mostly." Grayson tucks the USB stick into his inner suit jacket pocket. "The data on this thumb drive is related to business entities largely controlled by our kind. The ones in charge like keeping it offline. That way, it is much more difficult for mortals to become aware of our involvement."

Considering the Persons In Black exist, I have to assume there are other mortals aware of us. I shrug. "Okay. Makes sense."

Grayson offers a hand.

I shake.

… and a bunch of gunshots go off from across the street, striking the wall of the Polish Bistro with pops, snaps, and high-pitched zings all around me.

Six dudes about the same age as these guys rush toward us out of the parking lot by the repair shop. They are *not* wearing nice suits. Nope. These guys look like a vampire biker gang. Three have already bared fangs. Without missing a beat, Andrew and Dylan pull silver handguns out from under their jackets and return fire. Grayson lifts one leg, draws a smallish gun from an ankle holster, and tosses it to me before going for a bigger one under his left arm.

"Damn. Left the Thompson in the trunk," mutters Andrew. "Thought it'd be quiet tonight."

"Eep!" I yell, reflexively catching the gun flying at my chest. "What am I supposed to do with this?"

"Shoot them!" yell Grayson, Dylan, and Andrew simultaneously.

"If I shoot at them, they're going to shoot me."

Grayson grabs my arm and drags me along with him as he and the other two guys run to the right. The gang vampires are between us and the Mercedes, and it doesn't look like my new temporary friends are interested in a six-on-three brawl.

"Yes," calls Andrew. "That's usually how this works."

"They're going to shoot you anyway," shouts Dylan.

I tuck my hand behind my back to hide the gun. My Innocent bloodline doesn't have even a tenth of the charm power Aurélie has, but it does give off a supernatural sense of harmlessness. Maybe if I don't do anything combative, they'll leave me alone.

Running, though, that's easy. I should probably fly, but for some stupid reason I don't, compelled by an unknown instinct to stay with the group. As soon as he realizes I'm keeping up with them, Grayson lets go of my arm. The guys twist back to shoot at the pursuing bikers every few seconds.

Incoming bullets ping off chain link fences in front of yards, strike cars, break windows, and clip a stop sign with a loud *clank* and sparks. Intermittent soft thumps tell me whenever one of the suits takes a hit. Something makes me look back. I lock stares with a bald, bearded, skinny, fanged biker right as he points the biggest damn hand cannon I've ever seen at my face. Holy shit that thing would dent a tank.

Know what's cool? The bullet time special effects in the *Matrix* movies.

Know what's *not* cool? Bullet time happening for real and having a slug the size of my thumb glide past my face as I power-lean to one side. I'm too frazzled to really tell if I evaded the shot or he simply missed. All I can do is stumble-run into the side of a parked car, setting off the wailing alarm. Yeah, I think I ducked with enough force to throw myself off balance. Gah! I push off the car and sprint to catch up to the guys.

So much for being harmless.

"Guess it doesn't work all the time," I mutter.

"Nothing ever does," yells Grayson while shooting over my head at the bikers.

A yowl of pain precedes the thumping scuff of a man going in an instant from a hard run to face-planting the sidewalk. Ooh, that's going to leave a mark. We whip around a corner to buy a few seconds of reprieve from bullets thanks to having a solid building between us and them. I glance down at the little gun Grayson gave me. I don't know guns well. In my hand, it doesn't look so tiny. Guessing it's a 9mm. Kinda reminds me of the James Bond gun.

It's definitely not the portable howitzer the guy pointed at me.

I sigh mentally. Screw it. I'm playing this round of paintball whether I want to or not. Might as well try to get some points.

3

QUENTIN FREAKIN' TARANTINO

Time and reality blur into a series of sprints from cover to cover while engaged in a running gun battle. I shelter in doorways, behind concrete porches, cars, a metal trashcan (not smart), and mini trees in huge flowerpots (also not smart). A few passing cars burn rubber making illegal U-turns to get away from us. Don't blame them. No cop in the world would ignore a raging shootout to issue someone a traffic ticket.

Even though my gun looks small compared to everyone else's, it's not significantly quieter. I *do* recognize Daryl's gun as a Beretta—mostly because Dad loves the *Lethal Weapon* movies. It sounds about the same as mine when fired, so yeah… Grayson threw me his backup 9mm. I fire all eight shots in this thing and run out pretty fast. I do, however, manage to put one of those eight bullets into hand cannon biker's neck. He goes down face first, still awake but paralyzed for a while. Ooh, he's gotta be pissed.

The guys fire about three times as many rounds as I do and hit with almost all of them… only the bikers don't seem to give much of a damn. Grayson's lost the use of his right arm, forcing him to fire with his weaker left hand. Dylan and Andrew have both absorbed quite a few slugs. Maybe my powers of cuteness are helping. Only the one dude appeared to be purposefully shooting at me.

While taking cover in an alley three or four blocks from where we met,

Grayson pulls a thin single-stack spare magazine from another holster strapped to his left ankle. "Here."

"Thanks." I grab it. Takes me a second to find the magazine release for this gun.

I manage to reload and chamber a round right as the bikers find us and charge into the alley.

Dylan shoots one in the kneecap. His leg emits a splintering crunch as the knee bends backward, hyperextending in the wrong direction. Screaming, he eats pavement, but keeps shooting from the ground. Dylan soaks up three bullets from him before Andrew puts a round in the dude's forehead, silencing him.

We have another big problem: sirens.

Of course, a roving shootout in a big city is not going to escape the notice of the cops. Amid a hail of bullets, we sprint down the alley. I get the bright idea to fly-jump over a dumpster rather than waste time going around it… and it gets me shot in the back. Son of a… I shriek in anger and pain at having a hot nugget of burning ouch stuck inside me. It hurts enough to send me into a stagger when I crash back down on my feet.

I clamp a hand on my side above my left hip—over the spot where the bullet would have come out if it had been powerful enough. Feels like it did. Feels like I've got a red-hot arrow skewered through me. Knowing the wound is going to heal keeps me from freaking out. Getting shot really isn't such a big deal for me anymore. It's comparable to stubbing my toe: hurts like hell for a while then goes away like it never happened. To be fair, pinky toe on bedpost actually hurts more than this bullet.

"Swear," I rasp. "This was supposed to be a simple delivery job. If I black out and wake up in a morgue cooler again, someone's going to end up with claw wounds in a sensitive place."

The guys all wince.

We stop shooting back and focus on running faster. At the end of the alley, we veer left and sprint as hard as we can push ourselves. Of the four of us, I'm the only one breathing loud enough to hear. The guys aren't even bothering to breathe at all. Hey, it's not on purpose. My body just does it, okay?

I risk a peek back. "Who the hell are these guys?"

The bikers are still chasing us, but they, too, have stopped shooting. Maybe they're low on ammo. Maybe they're trying to be quiet for a while to lose the cops. Hard to say.

"No idea," says Grayson.

"What?" I yell, gawking at him. "How can you not know? They obviously know who we are."

Andrew laughs. "To them, we're just 'the man.'"

"Traditionalists." Dylan jumps a fallen trashcan on the sidewalk.

"They really don't look like Traditionalists," I rasp between breaths.

"Not them. Us." Grayson leaps over a public bench as we round another corner.

I grab a streetlamp post and swing around it to keep from falling over from taking a turn at this speed. "Kidding. But really, who are they?"

"No idea," calls Andrew, presently in the lead. "This happens all the time."

Remind me *not* to ever move here.

More sirens close in on our position from the left. At least I don't hear a helicopter yet. Guess we haven't gotten up to three stars on the wanted meter. Probably stupid of me to keep the gun out in my hand while running and ducking like I'm trying to flee a hailstorm before having my head cracked open. A young woman running down the street wouldn't get too much attention from bystanders. Put a gun in her hand and suddenly everyone loses their minds.

At least it's after three in the morning now and there aren't too many people outside. Every time a shot from behind pings off cars, signs, buildings, concrete planters, porches, or whatever around us, I flinch and duck. Despite knowing bullets can't kill me permanently, running away from a pack of guys trying to shoot me is still pretty terrifying. All it would take is one bullet catching me in the head and out I go. It's not death that scares me, rather what might happen to my body between the time the bullet knocks me out and when consciousness returns. Photographic evidence of my corpse is bad. Getting embalmed is worse. It won't destroy us but, oh wow... picture being boiled alive for about six days straight. If someone decides to autopsy a vampire and remove the brain to weigh it, there's another eight to ten hours of sleepy time. I don't know what would happen if they keep the brain in a jar instead of putting it back inside the body.

Really don't want to find out.

"Chicago is a bit of a warzone at the moment." Grayson snarls while forcing his damaged arm to cooperate enough for him to reload. "There are over twenty different groups of anarchists fighting for power."

"Fortunately," says Andrew, "They go after each other as much as they attack us. Capone is still firmly in control."

Shocked, I absentmindedly slow my stride without realizing it. "Wait. What? Capone? Like *Al* Capone?"

The guys all nod at me like it's no big deal, continuing to sprint away from me.

"You must be fairly young," Andrew yells. "If you think he died."

His words have implications. Like, whoa. How many powerful or famous people actually became vampires?

My thoughts don't have too much chance to explore that concept right now. It's kind of a bad idea to daydream in the middle of people trying to kill me. One of the biker jerks decides to prove this to me by shooting me in the ass. Okay, not quite ass. Upper thigh, really. The bullet whacks me in the femur with a jolt as if a lightning bolt connected my hip to my big toe. I legit felt my skeleton shake inside my body. A *crack* reverberates around my skull as loud as if someone walked up to a bare skeleton and hit it with a crowbar.

"Ow, shit!" I yell.

The muscles in my leg give my brain a giant middle finger and quit working. This is a Charlie horse from hell. My turn to eat the pavement. I go down hard, but not badly enough to break anything. My awed disbelief about the Capone thing kinda stunned me down to a 'fast jog,' but being shot reminds me about the vampires chasing us.

Fear stomps on the pain in my leg. I shove myself up off the sidewalk, pulling a total Supergirl flying maneuver in hopes of catching up to the three guys who either didn't notice me go down or didn't care enough to stop. They're already a block away from me thanks to running way faster than mortals can. I have eyes on them for only a few seconds before a city bus picks this exact moment to come barreling by on a crossing street, forcing me to stop short and swivel my body upright.

Crap! This is a bigger road and there's a shocking amount of traffic for the hour. Time jolts to a standstill. I've got three possible choices and under a second to make a decision. Choice one: I fly over the traffic and risk someone catching me on a dash cam or cell phone video. In the dark, blurry, it would probably just end up being included in one of those 'creepy unexplained videos' on YouTube. Choice two: I dart left into this alley and run off in a different direction away from Grayson, Daryl, and Andrew. Choice three: I stand there like an idiot waiting for a gap in traffic and get shot a bunch of times.

One is probably a bad idea. Three is *definitely* a bad idea.

Alley it is. Without even thinking, I whip around in a ninety-degree turn and sprint. My sneakers hit the ground about six times before I realize

I'm hammering weight down on my left leg. It hurts, but the bullet didn't break the femur, just hit it. Adrenaline—or whatever it is a vampire has— is doing an awesome job trivializing the pain.

The echoes of shouts and footsteps in the alley tell me the biker vamps decided to keep chasing the guys and ignore me. Whew. Nice. Remind me not to complain about looking young and nonthreatening ever again. Relieved, I slow to a jog and peer back to make sure I'm in the clear.

A lone biker dude is jogging toward me, his footsteps drowned out by the crazy amount of police sirens blaring from seeming everywhere. He's a scrawny skinhead in jeans, combat boots, and a denim vest over an olive drab T-shirt bearing the words 'gun control means holding your weapon in both hands.'

Oh, he must be fun at family gatherings.

His 'gotcha now, bitch' manic-eyed grin is seriously Charlie Manson levels of creeptastic.

I let out a startled, "Gah!" and throw myself into another sprint. I'd fly, but the buildings around us are all shimmering in the purplish flicker of red-and-blue flashing lights. If I go airborne, the police are going to see me —and I'll become an easy target for this dude to shoot. At least down here, I have plenty of dumpsters, discarded refrigerators, trash cans, and unidentifiable junk to weave around.

Another awesome thing about being a vampire: we don't get tired. I can run forever. Well, not *forever*. It burns the same energy as using any supernatural power does. Eventually, the metaphorical batteries will run out and I will fly into an insane feeding frenzy… assuming of course, I don't stop pushing myself when I get hungry.

So, it's great I can keep running for hours without needing to stop. Bad part? So can he.

My sneakers hate me. They're not designed to run this fast or jink side to side so hard. I'm convinced at any second the rubber is going to shred right off the bottom of my shoes. Grabbing random convenient cardboard boxes and trashcans to throw at the guy doesn't do much to stop him, but it does keep him from getting a clean shot at me until we reach the end of the alley.

I cheat physics upon reaching the sidewalk on a crossing street, using flight to redirect my momentum to the side and sparing my shoes from destruction. A handful of people around me—including two cops in a patrol car zooming past—probably think they saw something unusual but can't quite explain what. Wait, no. A person making an instant ninety-degree turn while running at full speed like a Tron light cycle is totally and obviously weird.

The skinhead isn't ready for me 'noping' to the side so fast. Guy was pouring so much energy into trying to overtake me, he can't stop in time to avoid stumbling out into the street. Remember that cop car? Yeah. It finds him. Dude wraps around the front end like the cops hit a life-sized gummy bear. His head bounces off the hood while his feet are somewhere underneath the car. The police barely have time to realize they've hit someone before the scrawny vampire gang member slips down and they run him over. No sooner is the car off him than he springs upright again and comes after me.

Eek.

I dash to the next block and take the corner with this torn-up, bloody biker dude on my heels. The craziest—and scariest—part of this is the absolute lack of reason here. I didn't do anything to these guys and he's chasing me like I tried to kill his brother. Anyone who is this committed to hurting a complete stranger is a psychopath. If he gets his hands on me, I don't want to know what will happen to my body while I'm unconscious. For all I know, this is just some crazy vampire version of tag and he'll simply shoot me in the head 'for a point' and walk away laughing. Maybe, but I'm not gonna hold much hope it's anything so benign.

We weave around a few pedestrians and a guy dropping newspaper bundles on the corner from a big box truck. Neither one of us is shooting, but running around holding guns is enough for anyone who sees us to sprint away screaming, collapse in a heap screaming 'don't kill me,' or start calling the cops.

A flash of silver behind me—no matter what it really is—makes me think he's raising his gun to take a shot. In a panic, I dart to the right down the narrowest alley I've ever seen. Shit. This is a deathtrap. No way am I dodging bullets here. Skinhead overshoots the alley mouth, then backtracks to chase me.

Panic squeezes the back of my brain, but rapidly becomes anger. Why is it every time I think about not being afraid to be a girl outside alone at night anymore, I end up running for my life like an ordinary eighteen-year-old? I'm just about to slam on the brakes and try to give this guy a sound shredding when a door flies open in my face without warning.

I'm no physics geek, but one does not need to understand the intricacies of dark matter to contemplate a scenario of basic kinetic energy. A small, relatively light object—me—can inflict a seemingly great amount of damage comparable to its size and weight if given enough velocity. A tiny pebble in outer space striking the space shuttle, for example, can blow a massive hole in it.

When I crash into the steel door, mostly because it swung open right in my face—the person who opened it eats about the same amount of force as if a giant pro linebacker charged him. The door slams shut, then bounces back open so fast it hits me again. A huge crash of steel pots and cookware echoes from inside. A man lets out a wail of pain and a stream of cursing in what I guess to be Chinese. Skinhead grabs me from behind—since I more or less stopped cold on impact with the door and the alley is too narrow to get past it while the door is open.

"Good chase, but it's over now, babe." The man's breath is a hot blast on the top of my head. He starts raising his gun to my temple.

Before he can shoot me, I thrust my left hand back, claws out, searching for testicles. I get hold of something fabric-y and squeeze. He shrieks and shoves me away. Vampire claws inflict a serious amount of pain. Way more than blades their size should. His reaction is subconscious, like a person yanking their hand back from a hot surface. Dude flings me to the ground and staggers away, gawking at his stomach. Aww, pity. I missed. Instead of a sex change, I started to give him a C-section.

While he's caught up in the throes of wondering how the hell that hurt so much, I leap to my feet, swing my right arm up, and shoot him right between the eyes.

Or try to.

Nothing happens when I pull the trigger.

Shit. Safety's on!

He snarls and reaches for my hand. I duck, whip the door into his face, and dart to my right into the building, almost stepping on a middle-aged Chinese guy with a bloody nose. He's flailing about on the floor in a storage room, half buried under an avalanche of giant bowls, pans, a few woks, and enormous soup pots. Two somewhat younger women to my right are yelling at him. I can't understand a word any of them are saying, but tone and body language make me think they're mad at him for being clumsy. Ugh. Poor guy.

"My fault!" I yell while dashing across the room to a hallway. "Sorry!"

The women stop shouting at him. They stare at me in silence for a few seconds until Skinhead stomps in after me, gun pointed. That's when the screaming starts. Dude on the floor begins throwing cookware at Skinhead. One of the women runs after me, fleeing from the biker while the other charges at Skinhead with a meat cleaver. I skid to a stop. No way am I going to let this guy murder some random innocent woman.

He easily catches her by the forearm when she swings the cleaver at him, then palms her face, throwing her off her feet to one side. Oh, whew. He's not going to kill her. The other woman runs into me and shoves me forward. I have two choices: be trampled or run. Not a difficult decision. She darts into a little office a few steps later while I keep going to a kitchen. Two younger guys appear to be getting ready to start cooking. They both stop what they're doing to stare at me as I attempt to sprint across their work area. Problem. Oily floor plus flat-soled canvas sneakers. Fortunately, I know how to ice skate—and being able to fly helps loads.

When Skinhead stomps into the kitchen, growling at me and waving his gun around, the two cooks both scream and drop in place, hiding behind the row of woks on their gas burners. In here, biker vamp has me at a serious disadvantage. *I* don't want to hurt bystanders. Doesn't look like he cares if anyone eats stray shots. My newborn deer on ice routine comes to a sudden end when my sneakers hit a rubber trim strip separating the red tile floor from a short, carpeted hallway. I tumble forward a tenth of a second before Skinhead shoots at me.

Thank you, power of flight.

Not only do I avoid catching another bullet, my face remains free of carpet burn. Hope no one sees me hanging in midair for a few seconds like I'm on wires. The bead curtain at the opposite end of this tiny corridor clatters around me as I haul ass into the seating area of a restaurant. It's not a big place, only large enough for five booth seats along the left wall. Still dark out, but it has to be getting close to dawn if they're making preparations to open.

Shit.

How the hell long have I been running?

Expecting the door to be locked, I brace for impact and try to focus some power into strength. I hate breaking people's stuff, but they can fix a door more easily than they can fix themselves psychologically after having 'some random girl murdered in their restaurant.' A couple of early birds out on the sidewalk scream as I bash my way out the door in a hail of shattering glass and bent aluminum frame. They scream again when Skinhead fires. Not sure where his bullet went other than it didn't hit me.

He's out the door seconds after me. We sprint down the mostly deserted street. I think the only reason we haven't seen cops yet is they are turning too early, not expecting suspects on foot to be moving as fast as cars. Sirens and flashing lights remain close, but not *that* close. Three cross streets from the Chinese place, a convenient truck rumbles in behind me, forcing Skinhead to stop for a few seconds. Lucky! Hoping he can't see me through the truck, I dart left, go across the street, and head into a rather wide alley.

Unfortunately, it's a damn dead end. Barely fifty yards in from the street, it stops at a two-story-tall chain link fence. On the right, the alley expands into a courtyard abutting a small truck dock with two garage doors on the back wall of an industrial property. The left side of the courtyard ends at a six-story grey brick building with a rusty fire escape. Gotta be apartments.

I spin to look back. The street at the mouth of the alley is aglow in purple flashing lights, but no sign of Skinhead. Whew... Not being a complete moron, I don't just keep standing there in the open. Instead, I take cover behind a dumpster against the apartment building wall. Back pressed to the warm bricks, I finally look down at my gun and hunt for the safety switch. Not sure how it engaged. Must have bumped it while running.

Aha! I click it off and wait.

I know my luck. The idea of gliding up to the apartment building roof tempts me, but before I can overcome the worry I'll get seen or shot as soon as I break cover, the familiar tromping boot-steps of Skinhead fill the alley on the other side of the dumpster.

Come on. This is a dead end. He's going to just take a quick look, figure he went the wrong way and back off. Stay calm. Stay quiet. But... I raise the gun to my right, arm against the dumpster wall. If he keeps advancing, I have to ambush him. My shot femur decides to start throbbing again. Ugh. Bad timing. Worse, the bullet inside my left kidney picks now to pack up and move out. Holy mother of itch. Gotta stay quiet. He won't hear me breathing over the sirens.

What the hell, Sarah? A roving shootout across half of Chicago? How on Earth did I wind up in a freakin' Quentin Tarantino movie? Wait... no... I left the katana at home and the soundtrack is all wrong. Wailing sirens aren't artsy enough for a Tarantino flick. Somehow, I can still hear the soft crunch of Skinhead's cautious footsteps coming closer.

He's gonna go away, just wait.

Skinhead sniffs. "Here, mousey mousey," he coos in a gravely rasp. "I got somethin' for ya."

Crap. I hang my head. Dumbass. Of course he can smell me. I can smell people. He's a vampire, too. Bastard knows I'm here... just not my exact position. Big ass dumpster is likely an obvious hiding place. I doubt he's going to walk by and let me shoot him in the head. This is the first spot he'll look. I'm literally six feet away from the courtyard entrance behind the first big object. Yeah, way to go Sarah. Great choice of hiding place. Since I'm already hanging my head in annoyance, I can't do it again. But… I do end up staring at a rock next to my foot.

Oh hell. It works in movies.

I crouch, pick up the rock, and throw it at another bank of dumpsters catty corner to where I am, all the way on the other side of the courtyard near the truck dock. It hits the back wall of a green dumpster with an echoing metallic *boom*.

"Dumb bitch," mutters Skinhead.

Figures. He's not going to fall for something so Looney Tunes as throwing a rock to distract the bad guy. How freakin' stupid am I? Staying crouched feels safer, so I do, raising the gun in both hands at the corner of the dumpster I'm hiding behind. My only hope is that his first shot is going to be aimed for where he thinks my head is and he'll miss, since I'm ducking down. Any second now, he's going to whip around at blurry speed.

… and he walks right on by, staring at the green dumpster in the opposite corner.

Holy crap. Seriously? He fell for the rock toss?

Skinhead stalks past me, not even noticing me huddled against the wall. He sneaks toward the spot my rock went as if he absolutely believes I'm inside the recycle bin. It's a damn miracle I don't laugh out loud. Okay, so this guy isn't the sharpest knife in the drawer. All my fear and worry evaporates. I ease myself up to stand, then creep after him, taking aim at the back of his head.

Sorry pal. Nap time.

"Drop the gun!" yells a man behind me.

Ever have one of those moments where something scares the hell out of you so much time seems to just stop? Skinhead's right there with me. He freezes in place, partially leaning over the top of the green dumpster, gun up as if to shoot someone hiding inside it. I freeze, my gun still aimed at his head. Two police officers stand about twelve feet behind me at the spot where the alley meets the courtyard. Their cruiser is stopped at the mouth of the alley about sixty feet behind the cops—who are pointing their guns at me. Yeah, they totally see me holding a firearm like I'm about to use it on Skinhead.

My life is over. I'm going to jail. I'm never going to see my family again. I'm never gonna see Ashley again. Or Michelle. Or Hunter. If I get out of prison before Mom dies, she's going to kill me, and… and… what the hell am I freaking out over?

Follows Rules Girl just had a panic attack. I'm okay now. Really, I should be more worried about my mom grounding me for shooting a gun around bystanders than anything the cops will do.

I'm not going to jail.

Jail is for mortals.

4

F BOMB

So, here stands Follows Rules Girl pointing a gun at some guy's head in front of two cops.

When Mr. Zaleski, my guidance counselor at school, asked me during senior year where I saw myself in five years, being caught between three guns while simultaneously wanting to shoot a guy isn't exactly how I thought my future would go. To be fair, he's not a 'guy,' he's a vampire. Shooting vampires doesn't carry even a thousandth the emotional baggage shooting a mortal does.

However, this is still a bad situation. Like *really bad*. Last time I had such a 'my life is over' feeling, the red faerie came to visit me in the middle of chemistry class freshman year when I had on white jeans.

Sometimes, circumstances truly call for a certain four-letter word. Sorry, Mom, but the real world is not a Disney production. It really does blow off a bunch of stress to cut loose and shout an F-bomb at the top of my lungs. The only reason I'm not doing so right now is time. This moment of introspection is really taking place over about six-tenths of a second. Not enough time to even finish opening my mouth, much less scream a worthy F-bomb into the clouds.

I'm not sure if it's the existential wonkiness of a life-changing moment or my vampire reflexes that's responsible for slowing my perception of time down to a crawl. For anyone not a vampire, this is the moment where they would have to decide between never seeing the outside world again, or death. Everything they knew would be taken away no matter what choice they made.

The moment is powerful. One doesn't have a cop aim a gun at them and shout 'drop it' without feeling an emotional reaction. Well, maybe a sociopath would. Seriously, for three tenths of a second there, I went straight back to being a mortal girl about to get in an extremely serious amount of trouble. I'm not too proud to admit that if I'd consumed any non-blood liquids at any time over the past few hours, I'd almost certainly have wet my pants the instant the cop shouted at me. We're talking primal 'good girl who never did anything wrong going to jail' terror here.

It's something about cop voice. I swear.

Anyway... my adrenaline is spiked to eleven. My vampire reflexes can't go any higher. I'm pretty sure once the cops mentally process the sight of me pointing a gun at some dude's head, they're not going to wait for me to drop it. Figure I've got another three-tenths of a second before they open up on me. Unless they think I'm a juvenile *and* happen to be soft hearted, in which case, they might not want to shoot a kid and wait another second or two.

Don't feel like risking that.

On the other hand, I don't want the cops to die or even get hurt. The jerk who's been chasing me is going to shoot the cops, or me, or all of us. Good chance the cops are going to let us both have it. So, yeah. This moment is worthy of an F-bomb. Pity I don't have enough time to let one out, so I'll have to settle for dropping one mentally, an imagined shouting of the dreaded word so powerful that somewhere, a thousand miles away, my mother senses a disturbance in the force.

5

GRAND THEFT SARAH

One thing I can't do is stand here contemplating what to do forever.

I've got about another three-tenths of a second to react before we recreate a scene out of a neo-noir western. Or would that be a noir neo-western? Damn, wasted a tenth of a second debating semantic nonsense. Okay, someone's definitely getting shot here and I would very much prefer it isn't me. Honestly, I'll take a bullet or two if it means the two mortal police officers don't end up dead.

What I need is a distraction. Something neither Skinhead nor the cops would ever expect.

Ooh! Idea.

The last thing the cops would ever expect… is their suspect zooming straight up into the air. I pull the trigger, sending a shot spiraling toward the back of Skinhead's dome. Then, propelled by the power of my atomic mental F-bomb, I launch myself straight up with such a sudden blast of acceleration my sneakers remain on the ground and I nearly leap straight out of my jeans. My flight clears the distance from the ground past the edge of the six-story-roof faster than a bullet can travel the distance from the cops to where I'd been standing.

Good thing, too… since bullets are traveling that distance.

I flip over and land flat on my back atop the apartment building. My pants are around my knees, but it's way better than losing them entirely.

Whoever invented 'skinny jeans' has not encountered Wright family DNA. My body possesses an attempt at hips. Maybe I'm being overly self-critical there, but physics agrees with me here. Know that trick where someone yanks a tablecloth out from under plates and glasses without disturbing anything? Yeah, I almost recreated the same phenomenon with my jeans.

And ouch.

I think I sprained something. Not like a muscle… like a vampire power core or whatever we have. My chest hurts. We're not supposed to go from zero to 140 miles an hour in an instant like that. It's doubtful I can do it again just for kicks. Hurling myself upward as though I'd been shot out of a cannon was a product of extreme emotion. Not sure which emotion… probably all of them except for the good ones.

The rippling of rapid fire peters out a few seconds after my half-exposed posterior lands on the roof. Naturally, my underpants land in a puddle of rainwater. Because, of course they do. And I thought the worst feeling in the world was stepping sock-footed on a cold wet spot. Vampire reflexes come in handy for other things than combat. I float off the ground, pulling my jeans back into place as I roll over, then kneel at the edge of the roof to peer down.

The cops—a man and a woman—have apparently riddled Skinhead with about twenty shots between them. He's sprawled on the ground, out cold. Not sure why they shot him. After all, to their perspective, I had to seem like the aggressor, being behind the guy about to shoot him unaware. Maybe they saw he had a gun, too and had been so freaked out by the sight of me taking off they went primitive lizard brain and did the Zog smash routine. On the other hand, he's on the ground, not slumped over the dumpster. So, he probably tried to point his gun at them.

Whatever happened, I need to clean up a bit… and get my shoes back.

The cops exchange a glance, then cautiously approach Skinhead's body. Woman Cop pauses briefly to look down at my sneakers, almost like she's trying to convince herself she really saw a girl there. Once they pass by below me, I vault the edge of the roof and glide silently down behind them, draping myself between them with an arm around their shoulders like we're old pals.

"Guys, chill out. Nothing to be scared of," I say.

The man screams like a blonde bimbo in a horror movie. His partner only blinks at me, the woman not even making a faint squeak of alarm. I give them about a second to breathe before bonking them over the head with the derp hammer. It's *so* damn tempting to feed off them, but I can't—

GRAND THEFT SARAH | 31

no time. The sun's going to be up soon and the area is still swarming with cops. More will be here any minute now. If I'm lucky, there will be enough time for me to clean this situation up and get out of here. I can feed later.

While the two cops stand there staring into the Eighth Dimension, I recover my sneakers, then lug Skinhead across the lot and toss him into the giant blue dumpster I originally hid behind. If the cops manage to keep any memory of the dumpsters in front of them as being significant, they won't find him. I almost drop my gun in there with him, but decide to keep it. Mom would kill me if she found out I had a gun, but I'm not planning to keep it forever… just not ditch it here. Before I toss it, I've got to be sure there are no fingerprints on it. I'm still not sure if I leave them, but no sense being careless. Non-Innocent vampires don't leave fingerprints unless they've put their hands into some kind of oil, ink, or paint. Since I'm so lifelike, it's quite probable my skin behaves the same way as a mortal's. That means oil, which means fingerprints.

Okay. Follows Rules Girl is not freaking out too much. It's not like I shot a guy in the head, murdering him right in front of two cops. We're basically playing vampire paintball. I don't even feel guilty at all. He's already dead, being a vampire. And two, he's going to get back up… probably not until tomorrow night. The heavy black plastic cover on that dumpster plus the shade of a six-story apartment building ought to keep him safe enough from the sun. If the dumpster happens to get emptied before tomorrow night, he'll wake up in a stinky place. But he'll still wake up.

There's a third reason Follows Rules Girl is calm. It's best for everyone involved if these cops don't remember anything. Both of them will believe they thought they saw someone run down into this alley, but it turned out to be nothing. Empty courtyard. No one here. I'm fairly confident their patrol car is far enough away the dashcam isn't catching anything. To humans—and cameras—it's really damn dark here.

Once I'm done blanking the cops' minds, I leap to the roof of the apartment building for a high vantage point and survey the area. Police are still zooming around like someone walloped a hornet's nest. Wow. I totally feel like I'm playing *Grand Theft Auto* right now waiting for the 'police rage' meter to go down. When did my life become a literal video game? I waste a moment staring mesmerized at the pulsating lights of the cop car in the alley below. Drat. Wasted opportunity. I could've totally stolen a police car and gone joyriding. Hah. Who am I kidding? Follows Rules Girl would never do that.

Besides, in real life, it's *waaaaay* more difficult to reset five stars' worth of police aggro.

Time to get the hell out of here.

I pretend to drop a ninja smoke bomb, make a soft *pssh* noise, and glide silently into the night sky.

Yeah, I'm a dork.

6

SEEING RED

When I first woke up as a vampire, I didn't know what to expect.

To be fair, the confusion had been epic. I didn't even know where I was or how I got there. I didn't even remember the party, Scott, or anything more recent than about a week really. I'd been in this strange sort of time 'non-space' where I'd somehow gone straight from an indefinable point in my ordinary life to waking up in a morgue cooler with only a plastic bag and an ID bracelet on. To say it kinda rattled me is putting things mildly. One thing is for certain: not in my wildest dreams did I ever associate vampirism with being Jason Bourne. Or Jane Bourne. Wait, this is me we're talking about… maybe *Spy Kids*.

Sigh.

No, what happened in Chicago is definitely a bit more adult than *Spy Kids*. Not too bad, though. Much like playing a video game, no one really died. Some of the crazier vampires engage in what appears to the outside observer as gang warfare when in reality, they're just having fun. Yes, the damaged idiots think shooting each other is having fun. Maybe I'm looking at it from a too-mortal perspective. When gunshot wounds—even fatal ones—heal in a few hours, I suppose it really does get to a point where it's not a big deal.

People have soccer, football, and whatever else. Some vampires play murderball.

The concept wouldn't necessarily bother me if not for the possibility of innocent mortal bystanders getting caught up in it. There's also the problem of it drawing attention to vampires. Fortunately—though sadly— if no one 'respectable' is among the casualties, the media tends to treat gang members shooting each other as the trash taking itself out. People won't notice the nameless, faceless gang dude found dead is the same dude found dead three weeks in a row. And the ones that do will probably call him a 'crisis actor' and cook up some conspiracy theory about how the evil government wants us all to live in fear of gang wars.

Sigh.

I'm flying over Chicago still, about two miles at my best guess from the epicenter of where the giant ball of poop hit the huge fan. Call me a wimp, but I'm too scared to stuff the gun in the front of my jeans, so I'm holding it still. Been shot enough tonight, thank you. I really don't need to shoot myself, especially in the groin. Even though I'm a vampire, being around guns still makes me somewhat nervous. It's not possible to grow up with a mom who's terrified of guns and not inherit at least some apprehension about them.

Wonder what would freak Mom out more... knowing I am holding a gun and I shot people tonight, or if she caught me wearing shoes in the house? Damn. Hard call there. Mom's got plenty of stress from her job. I don't need to add to it. There's already too much guilt weighing on me for being stupid enough to get murdered last summer. Yeah, I know... not really my fault. Everyone says that. At this point, except for the mental damage it did to my mother, I'm over it. Being a vampire is awesome.

I've been cruising around in a circle searching for Grayson, Andrew, and Daryl. No sign of them anywhere. Cops are still all over the damn place, but the sirens are off. As far as I can tell from the sky, the police didn't find any inert vampires. Guess the dudes chasing us doubled back to grab their wounded and got out of there once the heat level rose too much.

Not much time left before sunrise. As a last-ditch effort, I go back to the meeting point thanks to the GPS app in my iPhone. Nothing on the ground looks familiar to me. Without this phone, I'd be totally lost. The dark silver Mercedes is gone... no clue if the biker vamps stole it or the guys got back to their car in one piece. Hopefully, the USB stick survived and didn't get stolen. No idea if the idiots who chased us even knew about it. The attack might have been anarchists going after Capone's guys—that still sounds so weird to think—or just a pack of idiots doing violence for the lols.

Now is not the time to care about the particulars of why. Figure there's about fifteen minutes left before I have a serious problem of the fireball-in-the-sky kind. So, I zoom off in search of somewhere to use as an emergency sun shelter. My mind races past ideas: hotel, breaking into a house, under a bridge like a damn troll, crawling inside a water tower. Dalton did that once as a last resort. Thinking about it is kinda scary. Even though I can't drown, there's just something about being stuck inside a giant tank of water that reaches into my primordial brain and terrifies me. It's the idea of being sucked into a pipe like a bug going down the toilet. Ack.

I end up following a river for a while to a somewhat crummy looking industrial district near some docks. A giant building catches my eye, mostly due to the smashed windows and generally abandoned look to the place. Fading letters on the wall say something like O'Hara Shipping. Looks good. I don't think anyone's been here since the 1980s. What makes me say that? Probably the 1984 Plymouth K-car parked behind the place. I'm guessing. I'm not a car girl. Don't know what year it really is, but it looks damn old... and like it's been there since 1984 without moving an inch.

Works for me. Any place *this* run down won't be likely to have visitors in the next nine-ish hours before I wake up.

The huge windows facing the water are all broken to some degree. I aim for the most damaged one, slipping between shards of glass and a bent steel frame piece. Inside, the air stinks like a million wet dogs live here. There isn't much left other than empty shelving and some pallets of cement mix, paint, and tools. Looks like someone planned to restore the place awhile back and gave up on it.

I cruise across the warehouse type room to a door, searching for the most sunless, protected spot inside the building. Let's just say a huge room with massive windows all facing east is not the best place for a vampire to shelter during sunrise. The rusty steel door opens with a horror-movie-worthy creak to reveal a bare concrete corridor that looks like it came from a ghost hunter video of people exploring an abandoned mental hospital. All that's missing are broken wheelchairs and gurneys. Wood paneling has rotted off the walls to land on the floor in decaying mold-covered scraps. The remains of wallpaper clinging here and there resemble the 'grandma tissue' that's been tumbling around a purse unused for twelve years—just in case someone needs a tissue.

Eww.

This place is so nasty. I don't want to touch anything, but... no choice.

At the end of the hall, another rusty steel door opens to a stairway down. Perfect. Strange basements used to scare me to death. Now, I kinda like them. Guess that makes me a card-carrying member of the monster's guild. There won't be anything down there scarier than me. At least, I'm pretty sure this basement doesn't contain Teletubbies or Jehovah Witnesses.

Talk about creepy as hell.

I'm right. No Teletubbies. Just plenty of junk, broken furniture and crumbling concrete. I feel like a human rat entering a hastily built maze. Fragments of walls still stand but all the doors and drywall are gone. Still, it is a basement and there's no chance of sunlight getting down here. I scurry past graffiti masterpieces, everything from crude penises like fourth-grade boys draw on their desks to band names to upside-down crosses over 666 marks. I'm not even close to being a mystic, but my senses are capable of picking up that sort of thing. This place feels as mundane as unflavored oatmeal. Not real ritual marks, just idiots who tried to be cool and edgy.

My senses tingle. I can almost hear a NASA-style countdown in my head as I rush toward a pile of cement mix bags in the corner of a basement storage room. Doesn't really matter what I curl up on, but they look softer—and drier—than the filthy concrete floor.

I'm SORTA TREADING WATER AT THE DEEP END OF A SWIMMING POOL, BUT mostly holding myself up by a one-handed grip on the coarse concrete edge. Ashley's right next to me doing more or less the same thing, lazily kicking and paddling. We're about ten years old and in almost matching green swimsuits. The pool belongs to Andrea Warren's parents. It's a nice in-ground affair with an attached Jacuzzi—I had no idea what a hot tub was at ten—and a fairly large backyard around it. Like thirty feet away, a dozen or so other kids play in the water. They're really loud. Ashley and I are the opposite of loud. We're still and silent, safely removed from the chaos and observing it.

Considering I'm not a child anymore, I'm immediately aware this is a dream. It isn't one of those dreams like a video game where I can do stuff. Nope, I'm just watching a movie, no control. If memory serves, it's Andrea's eleventh birthday party. She's invited a little more than half our class over to have fun. Even sent a note with the invitation that no one is expected to—or should—bring her a gift, she just wants to have friends over for a party. Andrea generally was nice to people, but we weren't

SEEING RED | 37

exactly close friends. No bad blood. Honest. The girl is merely way too extroverted for me.

Speaking of anti-extroverts, Ashley and I are basically sheltering from the noise at the deep end of the pool. Neither one of us had any interest in being picked up and thrown around by the boys, splashed by anyone, or pressured into climbing up on anyone's back for a chicken fight. Water Frisbee or tossing a volleyball around, fine.

Mrs. Warren, Andrea's mom, wanders around the pool on dry land to check on us, then assuming we're just being shy, shoos us into the chaos. To be fair, we *were* just being shy. Ashley gives me a resigned stare of 'she's not going to leave us alone, let's just get it over with' and starts swimming toward the Frisbee area. I follow. We aren't Sophia levels of shy. Pool parties are awesome. But we had some limits. Anything over eight kids exceeded our comfort zone.

Weird dream.

This boy I don't even remember the name of—haven't seen him since eighth grade—yells my name and whips the Frisbee in my direction. I jump up to catch it and the next thing I know, I'm sitting on a sofa with Ashley squished up against me. We're in her house watching a movie... and still both in our bathing suits, soaking wet. I'm still holding the Frisbee.

Ugh. Dream lag. Come on brain, update our avatars already.

As soon as I think it, my bathing suit transforms into a sweatshirt, jeans, and fuzzy purple socks. The Frisbee turns into a bowl of chips. Ashley's rocking an orange sweatshirt with a bedazzled jack-o-lantern, a bright pink skirt, and pale pink frilly socks. We're also dry. Much better. Did I mention my best friend loves pink stuff? I'm ambivalent to it. The color neither bothers me nor makes me feel 'girl power.' Sierra loathes pink. She loathes anyone who thinks 'girl stuff *must* be pink' even more than she hates the color. Sophia adores pink as much as Ashley does.

I remember this... it's October. We're watching a 'kid-scary' movie for Halloween. Ashley's clinging to me in fear, gawking at the cheesy special effect demon climbing out of the 'rift' in the backyard. Mrs. Carter must be baking since everything smells like pumpkin spice.

Ash gives a squeak of fright and squishes herself against me tighter, but keeps staring at the screen. She and Sophia are similar in that they both get scared easily by movies. The main difference between them is that Ash will scream, sometimes cry, and cling—but she'll keep watching. With Sophia, the instant something crosses her point of no return, she nopes out of there and refuses to keep watching. Another difference is how Ashley almost never gets nightmares after watching scary movies. If a movie sends Sophia running out of the room, she absolutely will have at least one nightmare.

I put a protective arm around Ash, which gets her to stop trembling. If she watched this same movie now, she'd probably be laughing at how cheesy it is. For some reason, my sense of protectiveness toward her blooms like an algae runaway in the ocean. As a kid, I'd never have dwelled on it but in this dream, I find myself thinking about how her dad left one day. You know that stereotype thing about 'dad went to the store to get a pack of smokes' and never came back? Mr. Carter didn't exactly chicken out that badly. He told Ashley and her mother directly he was done and intended to leave. I haven't seen the guy since around age eight when he took off. Don't remember all that much about him other than he's some kind of super nerd engineer at Boeing... and I never really liked him.

Kids have an instinctive sense about people. And no, I'm not saying Mr. Carter was a creeper or a danger to children. I think in his case, he just didn't like kids. Didn't want to be around kids. Had zero sense of humor and a barely-functioning emotion processor. I must've picked up on it and just stayed out of his way. Guy's one of those crazy smart scientist lab dwelling trolls. Not the best people skills. To give him a tiny bit of credit, he tried to tell Ashley that his leaving was not her fault and she didn't do anything wrong. Not sure it helped. Delivering what should be an emotional admission to your daughter in a tone of voice like you're reading an Ikea instruction manual for a new bookshelf isn't convincing... unless your kid's name is SMÅGÖRA. Even then, probably not.

And yeah, that's a kid bookshelf from Ikea. How do I know that? Sophia's got five of them. Guess what word Dad randomly kept blurting in Swedish Chef voice for weeks?

Anyway, after he took off, Mrs. Carter had to take on a second job to avoid losing their house, so Ash was like always over my place. My dream starts jumping around, showing me moments of Ashley and me hanging out together. There's no pattern to the scene switching, other than them being good memories. One moment we're loafing around in my bedroom talking about cartoon characters, the next we're older and loafing around in my bedroom talking about boys. Then, we're in the mall, or at an amusement park.

The dream takes an abrupt turn for the hilarious when I relive the time we went to play in the woods near the house—same woods where Sam and his friends tripped through a cave to Serbia, Croatia, or whatever a few weeks ago. Ash and I didn't encounter anything magical. Quite the opposite. We got attacked by a skunk. In our haste to escape, we jumped a fence at the edge of the woods into a stranger's backyard and discovered he had three huge dogs. The animals were friendly, but… you can imagine what keeping three big dogs in a backyard does to the lawn. Land mines everywhere. By the time Ashley and I got back home, we were covered in skunk stink and dog poo.

We spent the next two hours sitting in a bathtub together trying to get the smell out of our hair.

Looking back on it now, if it had happened to someone else, I would've been in tears from laughter. In the moment, we were both in tears for other, obvious reasons. Kinda funny to think about how Ashley freaked out so much at having dog poo all over her and now she works cleaning it out of kennels like it's no big deal.

I feel like we've spent our whole lives together, and it's giving me this overwhelming warm fuzzy feeling along with a serious momcat vibe. Weird. I mean, I've always been protective of Ashley, but becoming so acutely aware of that feeling usually only happens in direct response to something threatening her.

Maybe my brain is lagging and this is a delayed response to that jackass vampire addict trying to kill her last November.

The dream jumps again. We're in my bedroom hanging out. At first, it could be any of a million different days and I don't remember how old we are—somewhere around thirteen or fourteen I think—until I open my big fat mouth. Ashley's talking about wanting to go to the mall tomorrow and I say, "Umm, I kinda told Brendan I'd go on a date with him."

Ashley gasps at me.

I remember. We're fourteen, about two months (for me) away from my fifteenth birthday. It's the first time where I kinda wanted to hang out with someone other than Ashley. If it had been just friend stuff, sure, bring her along. Easy. But dates? That gets awkward. I wouldn't want Ashley sitting next to the bed doing 'sports commentary' as Hunter and I made love any more than she'd want me being third wheel if she went on a date with someone.

The moment I blurt about Brendan, Ashley's eyes redden and she looks like she's about to start crying. Initially, I feel like the world's worst friend and betrayer. Not romantically. She hadn't yet told me about being bi at that point—that happened at sixteen when she wanted my opinion on if she should ask a girl out. No, she's jealous about someone else getting to spend time with me when she can't. Speaking of Ash being bi… and talk about awkward. When I first woke up as a vampire, I thought my death messed her up so bad because she had a crush on me and she thought I died before she could tell me. As it turns out, I'd been kinda new at the whole telepathy thing and misinterpreted what I 'read' from her. She and I have the exact same kinds of feelings for each other. It's not a romantic crush from her side, but a love that goes beyond best friend and sister. It's hard to describe since most people can't comprehend the sort of love capable of making you give up on living if that person dies without it being sexual in nature.

That's one of the bigger differences between Ashley and me. When she thought I'd been killed last year, she wanted to curl up and die. If the situation had been reversed, I'd probably have tried to go kick the ass of whoever hurt Ashley... *then* wanted to curl up and die.

"Forget it." My dream-self shakes her head at Ash's reaction. "I'll cancel."

Ashley sniffles. "Great. Make me feel guilty. It's okay if you want to go. We're like *always* together. I can survive a few hours without you." She forces a giggle.

My present day adult—or as close to adult as I will ever get—mind wonders what might have happened if I insisted on cancelling the date not to upset Ash. Brendan wasn't a bad guy, but we didn't click. We had a more or less super awkward and totally normal first date for fourteen-year-old kids. Neither of us possessed the first clue how to act on a date, or what to do, and it ended up being about the same as going to a movie with a friend plus hand holding. Nothing bad happened. Like I said, we just didn't click. Then again, who clicks at fourteen? Okay... who clicks at fourteen except for Hunter?

The boy swears he fell totally and permanently in love with me the instant he saw me on our first day at high school.

Anyway, if I skipped the date to continue as normal with Ashley, probably not much would've changed. Eventually, a date would have happened. Ashley got over it fast, too. Also, what the heck is with the 'Ashley nostalgia trip'? Great... I'm going to spend the next few months trying to figure out what this dream means.

Eek...

Umm, I hope this isn't coming from something vampy like a premonition or warning. By now, the dream's shifted to replay a moment from one of the family road trips where Ashley came with us. A random noise in the woods scared her, so she squeezed into my sleeping bag. Fortunately, we were like nine and both on the scrawny side, so we had plenty of room. Wow, this dream is seriously shifting time gears without a clutch. I start whispering to Ash to calm her down and tell her there's no such thing as monsters when our tent flap pushes open.

Ash is too scared to even scream. Her fingers dig into my side like blunt knives. I remember this… a mountain lion poked its head into the tent. We both screamed bloody murder, Ashley in terror, me screaming at it to 'go away.' Fortunately, without even knowing it, we'd done the right thing. Mountain lions tend to run away from loud noises and don't generally attack humans unless they feel cornered.

In the dream, the mountain lion sticks its head into the tent. We lock stares with it… and things finally take a wild leap away from reality. Rather than roar, the mountain lion emits a tiny kitten 'mew.'

What… the… hell?

TRUTH AND CONSEQUENCES

Home is nice.

I am somewhat introverted. To me, being home is way more fun than going to parties. I get it's not everyone's thing, but whatever. Who cares what everyone does? My attachment to home is so strong it overpowered vampire tradition and resulted in me unliving with my family. Whenever something truly scares me or freaks me out, the thing I want most is to go home.

Chicago, ugh. So glad to be done with that 'simple' job.

According to the clock on my desk, it's 3:24 a.m. Still August, so no studying to worry about. I'm playing *Skyrim*. Yeah. I know. It's an old game. I've lost track of how many times I've finished it... but I still keep finding new stuff. Decided to make yet another stealth archer character, probably thanks to me getting the drop on Skinhead with an ambush from behind.

I'm not planning to go anywhere as evidenced by my lack of pants. My long, oversized T-shirt is super comfortable. Love these things. If going outside ever stops being a thing, I'd probably just wear these, have a whole closet full of knee-length T-shirts screen printed with graphics from 1980s movies.

Right in the middle of me stealthily making my way through a cave in the video game, it hits me that I can't remember how I got home from Chicago or what happened with the USB handoff. I mean, I remember handing it off to Grayson and the shootout, but I think it's been a couple days and my brain's drawing a blank trying to fill in how Wolent reacted. Pretty sure he'd be fairly pissed off at someone trying to shoot me.

While I sit there trying to figure out if the data successfully made it to Capone's people or not, my bedroom door opens. Considering I live with three siblings who have varying degrees of respect for personal space, plus an imp, someone walking into my room unannounced is not an unusual thing. It is, however, kinda weird for one of the Littles to be awake at three in the morning.

I turn to look... and raise both eyebrows in confusion. Ashley's strolling into my bedroom, stark naked, her right hand tucked behind her back as if she's hiding a surprise gift. A few alarm bells go off in my head. While Ash is, shall we say, a bit more 'adventurous' than I am, this is weird. I wouldn't put it past her to streak from home to here if dared. Not like anyone would see her at this hour, but it's still out of character for her to just go full wood nymph without someone egging her on.

There's nothing the least bit sexy about her demeanor or body language. Her eyes are anticipatory in the way they get right before she opens a Christmas present. This, too, doesn't fit with her suddenly showing up here at this hour in her birthday suit. It's not overly shocking to me. I mean, we've changed together to go swimming, shared baths a few times due to extenuating circumstances like skunks, dog poop, or extreme amounts of mud. We're comfortable enough around each other not to care much about nudity, but there's gotta be a reason for it... and at the moment, I can't think of one. This is just too weird. Is she drunk? High?

My only reaction is a gasp-giggle. "Ash? What the heck are you doing?"

"Woke up and came right over."

Okay, Ashley usually sleeps nude ever since she read something online about it being healthy. Easier for her to do since she doesn't have three younger siblings with no concept of personal space living in her house. I do it sometimes, too, but only when the mood hits. For Ash, it's routine—except if she sleeps over somewhere. Just too awkward and inappropriate.

So, yeah, her parading in here *au natural* is definitely an eleven on the 'something ain't right' meter.

"Umm, most people get dressed before they leave their bedroom... and definitely do so before leaving the house."

She shrugs. "I wouldn't want to waste good pajamas."

"What the heck are you talking about, Ash?"

"I've been thinking…" She smiles.

"Uh oh."

Ash sticks her tongue out at me. "Seriously. I've been thinking, and you know how we've like always been together? I don't want to lose that."

Concern grows. I get up from my desk chair and take a step toward her. "Why would we lose that?"

"I just spent the past hour crying because I randomly woke up and started thinking about how I'm gonna grow old and die and you're always going to be the same. I got sad thinking about how sad you're going to be when I'm gone. I want to stay with you, just like we are."

Ruin perfectly good pajamas. She means blood. I blink at her. "You… you're asking me to… you know I can't hurt you."

She tilts her head, all innocence. "I know you can't." She flashes this ditzy exaggerated smile like someone who's taken *waaaay* too much E. "I took care of it."

Before I can even think, she whips her hand out from behind her back. I realize the 'surprise gift' she'd been concealing is, in fact, a gun—right as she shoots herself in the chest. The bang barely reaches my ears, being all flash and little sound.

All I can do is scream my throat raw as the life fades from her face and her body falls limp, careening over backward to the rug.

"Ashley, no!" I shout, diving at her.

It's too late to do anything else… she didn't give me a damn choice. I hurriedly raise a shaking hand to my mouth and fang a gash into my wrist, not even feeling the pain. After prying her mouth open wider, I dribble my dark blood over her teeth, staining them crimson. Every ounce of my desire cries out to the Universe not to take Ashley away from me. I want her back. I want her with me forever.

"Please don't turn evil," I whimper. "Please stay the same."

Ashley's canine teeth grow out into vampire fangs. Her eyes pop open, bright and cheerful. She giggles. "Me? Evil? Are you serious?"

The gunshot wound in her chest is gone. Her blood smears over her super pale skin like cherry syrup on vanilla ice cream. It takes me a few seconds to process the reality of Ashley not being dead anymore. Overcome with emotion, I cling hug her and sob into her shoulder, belting out sorry after sorry that this happened to her.

"Please stop crying." Ashley squeezes me. "This had to happen while we are basically the same age so it doesn't get strange."

I sniffle back tears, and sprawl there, holding her, head spinning with guilt.

"Thank you." She makes a funny face while prodding her tongue at her fangs. "Wow, this is going to take some getting used to. They feel so weird."

"It does. You'll get used to it."

Ashley giggles again. "I'm sorry for the shock factor, but you never would have done it otherwise."

I pause, then glance at the computer. Wait. I can't remember how I got home from Chicago or anything that happened after other than having a super vivid dream about how strong a bond I have with Ashley... and Mom isn't banging on the door yelling at us for discharging a gun in the house.

"Ash?"

"It's okay. Don't be mad. You never would have done it..."

"Ash, I still didn't do it." I sigh. "I'm dreaming, aren't I?"

"How should I know?" She shrugs. "If you are dreaming, it must mean you really want me to stay with you."

"Umm..." I gradually start to rein in my wild emotions. As Dad would say, I roll to disbelieve. This isn't really happening.

Ashley looks down at herself. "Also, if you're dreaming, you imagined me naked as a symbol of purity and innocence... and now it's stained with blood. Part of you is still afraid being a vampire is something dark and evil and you're trying to protect me from it."

"I guess so." I wipe my eyes.

"Sare, I'd rather be a little bit dark if I get to stay with you. I don't wanna die. Remember when you told me you'd rather date Brendan than go to the mall with me?"

Ugh. Here comes the tears again. "Yeah."

"Same thing. Please choose me this time."

A loud clattering noise—like a wooden plank crashing down on concrete—comes from outside in the basement. It startles both of us into jumping. For the unlife of me, I can't think of anything in my basement capable of making that sound—unless Dad's decided to try apprentice carpentry and ran to Lowe's for wood earlier. Even still, it's incredibly difficult for lumber to clatter upon bare concrete in a fully-carpeted basement. Maybe something got into the water heater closet? I start to give Ashley a 'what the hell was that' stare—but she morphs into a giant contractor bag of cement mix. In an instant, my bedroom changes, becoming the stinky, abandoned building near the riverside in Chicago. I'm hugging a bag of cement mix, not Ashley.

Well, that explains the sound of a falling board.

Dreaming.

Sigh.

If someone knocked over a board, it means I'm no longer alone in here.

"Shit…"

8

ETERNITY IS A REALLY LONG TIME

Ugh.
I moan into the cement bag, then sit up, rubbing my face. What a dream. Oof. My hands are still shaking from watching Ashley shoot herself right in front of me. I don't think she'd ever actually do that. She'd be too worried about the emotional damage it would inflict on me. Question is, how much do I trust my memory? When I told Ashley about Brendan, she got upset and jealous, about to cry over a mere few hours apart from me.

That's kinda... umm, strange, right? Even twins aren't *that* clingy with each other. I've gotta be remembering it wrong. Of course, Ashley did used to cry when we had to stop playing so she could go home at night, but we'd been little then, and her dad just left. It makes sense how a little kid in her position could take those feelings of paternal abandonment and apply them to separation from her best friend even if it's only until tomorrow.

But now? It's not normal. And Ashley doesn't freak out if we don't spend every waking minute together. In fact, for the past couple of months, we haven't really had much chance to hang out. Our schedules are in conflict. As kids, we really were like twins, not wanting to do anything without the other, always side by side. We even used to sleep together all the time. No, not like *that*. More in the 'kids from a medieval peasant family piled in the same bed' kind of way.

After Mr. Carter ditched them and her mother had to work such crazy hours, Ash basically moved in with us. She'd sleep over three or four nights a week sometimes. Mrs. Carter would even come over to have dinner with us because Dad wanted to give her a break from having to cook after working fourteen hours.

Yes, Ash is clingy. She's kind of a weird mix of shy and fearless. Like, she'll never be the first person to start a conversation with a stranger, but once it starts, she'll talk to anyone. She'll sit with me in the corner of a crowded room, happy to remain quiet and unnoticed... but I swear, if Michelle dared her to streak the mall, she'd totally do it. Timid and shy one moment, bold and fearless the next. That's Ash. Around new people, she's quiet, but she can also be the stereotypical fiery redhead who possesses neither shame nor any sense of self-preservation depending on the situation.

I can't help but laugh at the time some guy we didn't even know thought it would be funny to sneak up on us at the beach while we sunbathed and steal her bikini top. To be fair, the guy didn't rip it off her. We'd both taken our tops off so we didn't get tan lines on our backs. The guy was around our age—meaning stupid teenager. As we lay there, face down on towels with our eyes closed, the dude tried to sneak over and swipe our tops without us noticing, probably on a dare or something from his friends. What did Ash do? Exactly what his buddies hoped one of us would do. She popped right up to chase the bastard across the beach. When she caught him, she kicked his ass. Well, slapped the hell out of him. The guy knew he screwed up and at least had the class not to hit her back. She recovered our tops and marched back to our towel, victorious.

And now I'm freaking the hell out.

Am I as clingy as she is? Did the dream I have mean I can't stand the thought of us drifting apart? She's going to grow up, get a job, have a career... and probably a wife or husband, kids. Will she even still want to hang out and do stuff when she's like fifty? Am I going to be able to cope with watching her become elderly? How is it possible this same girl that I used to go to the mall and pool parties with is going to turn into a rickety old grandmother before my eyes? Ashley will become wise, mature, lose interest in the things we once thought fun.

I'm never going to change, neither physically nor mentally. Whoa, is this sudden random upwelling of fixation on Ashley similar to the weird nostalgia I have for my childhood even though that's totally nonsensical. It's not like I'm in my mid-forties wanting to be a kid again—hi, Dad. I don't think my father genuinely wants to go back to being a child as much as he's tired of responsibilities.

I've become the ideal, having no responsibilities (at least like rent or job) and am neither a child nor an adult. Sigh. Yep. I'm a teenager. I'm *definitely* a teenager. I absolutely want Ashley to stay my best friend for eternity. Dammit. I've been lying to myself. The idea of us being separated upsets me way more than I've admitted to myself. But… I still can't do it to her. How much of a hypocrite would it make me to save her from that addict vampire only to do the same thing to her he almost did? The immature teenager in me has demands, but I'm either mature enough—or care about her too much—not to force what I want onto her life.

Ugh. I roll flat on my back, staring at the filthy concrete ceiling above. Long strips of peeling… something hang down. Looks papery. Might be insulation. Impossible to tell. No, I can't force Ashley to do what I want, at least not any more. Did enough of that when we were younger. She's so passive, always agreeing with whatever I wanted. To be fair, most of the time she didn't have any strong opinions on what to do, what movie to watch, what game to play and so on. Going along with me didn't matter when she truly didn't care what we did. I'm sure if I suggested giving her the Transference so we could stay BFFs—taking forever literally—she'd shrug and say 'okay' as casually as if I'd suggested we watch *Frozen* again.

She'd just walk away from her plans to become a veterinarian, get married, have kids, doing the whole normal life thing to remain a teenager with her best friend until the end of time—or something finally blows us up. But, honestly? Everyone does the normal life thing. How many people get to stay teenagers forever and hang with their bestie? Ugh. There I go again, rationalizing because I want something.

The more I think about it, the more I'm desperately terrified of going on without my best friend. Wanting her to stay with me sets off a shudder of guilt. I'm about to curl up in a ball and cry for being such a selfish, needy, horrible friend, but I don't.

Another random crash comes from upstairs. I'm definitely not alone in the building. Someone's tromping around up there. Crap. I pantomime opening a file cabinet drawer and stuffing my excessively emo moment away for later contemplation. Got more pressing issues facing me.

Time to go.

9

URBAN EXPLORATION

Sleep got me harder than it usually does.

When I sit up, two bullets roll down my front and collect where my T-shirt tucks into my belt. That little rock I'm sitting on? Yeah, not a rock. It's another bullet... probably the bastard that bounced off my femur. On a positive note, nothing hurts—no lingering aches. I managed to avoid being hit with vampire claws or fire. This also means my clothes survived a vampire fight. Go me! Yeah, my Foamy the Squirrel shirt has a few holes in it, but they're easy to hide. Also, it's a black shirt, so bloodstains aren't so obvious.

Another nice thing about being a vampire—we don't bleed much unless we want to. It's super creepy to watch. Vampire blood tends to collect in wounds like fluid in zero gravity. The only spray or blood loss we have to worry about is whatever gets physically blasted out of us by the bullet—with one big exception. Beheading a vampire tends to result in an epic geyser effect. My thought is the control center for the 'hey keep all the blood, that's food' is in the brain. So... when the brain is no longer plugged into the body, it leaks.

I tug my shirt up, fish out the bullets, and toss them aside. Not taking my jeans off here, so best I can do is stand up and do a weird one-legged shimmy until the little lead nugget makes its way down and out. Unlike my shirt, I'm pretty sure the pale blue denim on the back of my left leg is an obvious bloody mess. Anyone looking at me will know right away I've been shot or stabbed. Had it been closer to Halloween, I could've claimed to be in costume. However, the excuse of being an extra in a zombie movie might work. I'm not hurt and also not too proud to moon an overly concerned Samaritan to prove there's no bullet hole in my leg, at least until it's dark enough for mind control to start working again.

Wait. Is it still technically 'mooning' someone if you have underpants on?

More proof I'm a teenager: I impulsively hopped on a plane to Chicago without packing anything. No bags. No backpack. No change of clothing, toiletries, nothing. Didn't think I'd need it. Spending two days in the same clothes isn't a big deal, and I expected to go home the next day. In fact, I *still* expect to go home the next day. That day being right now.

Someone walks by overhead. I peer up at dingy, cracked concrete, strips of unidentifiable mung hanging overhead, frayed wires, mold patches… ugh.

I have a new problem. This whole building smells horrible, and that smell has no doubt seeped into my clothes. Vanity is not one of my vices, but it would be too embarrassing to get on a plane and have everyone staring at the 'stinky homeless girl.' Worse, this smell is probably bad enough to get passengers to complain to the point the airline removes me from the plane. Right. Before I go to the airport, I need to stop somewhere and clean up. Since it would be kinda rude to sit around naked in some strange person's house while my clothes tumbled in their washer and dryer, my best bet is to get new stuff, grab a shower, and cram what I'm wearing now into a plastic bag to trap the stink until I can wash everything at home.

How bad does it smell? I *think* the spot of floor where I slept hasn't been peed on. Operative word there being 'think.' I can't tell for sure. It's difficult to smell anything over the vomit plus mildew plus wet-dog plus stale cheese sprinkled with pee odor.

Someone is definitely moving upstairs. Okay, no big deal. Probably just some homeless person looking for shelter. We came to this building for the same reason. It's definitely not one of the gang vampires who tried to kill me last night. They'd all be deep asleep at this hour. It's a few minutes away from being five in the afternoon.

Crap. Overslept.

I hurriedly shoot off a few texts to the 'rents, Ash, Michelle, and Hunter to let them know I'm okay and merely slept longer than expected. Sounds completely mundane, doesn't it? Parental worry quenched, I stuff the phone in my pocket, get up, and navigate a minefield of debris down a long ass corridor. It's way longer than I remembered on the way in.

Imminent sunrise fear tends to make me hurry and not pay attention to details. I fly to the end of the hall, silently avoiding about ninety feet worth of junk-strewn hallway. Sunlight's visible in the stairway, so I land a couple yards away from it. You know that old cartoon where the gorilla with concrete wings is flying because he doesn't understand it's impossible? I think it's Bugs Bunny... as soon as the rabbit tells him he can't fly with concrete wings, he plummets like a bomb. That's about what happens to me if I fly into daylight. Instant off switch and a mouth full of dirt.

Thanks, I'll pass.

Hoping to avoid bumping into anyone, I creep up the stairs. Sunlight washes over me with a momentarily painful tingle like a swarm of fire ants. It ends before I can even gasp, leaving me uncomfortably warm. The sun is still capable of becoming so intense I have to hide from it, but usually only in places like Arizona or California. Okay, Seattle can sometimes get so sunny I still can't take it, but for the most part, I've completed peace negotiations with the sky fireball. Being outside on a non-rainy day is distracting, but doesn't hurt anymore. The whole time I'm out there, it's like I have to concentrate actively on not catching fire. People I interact with think I'm distracted by heavy thoughts, but it's generally mild unless the sun goes nuclear.

Today's a clear day in Chicago. Big cities can get damn hot, but it's not heat that's the problem for me, it's the UV. I should be fine. Fists clenched, I sneak up the remainder of the stairway to the upstairs hall, peek out—see nothing—and step the rest of the way into the corridor. My biggest problem at the moment is not being able to fly. I came in last night through the window, which leaves me clueless as to where the normal door is. Catching my plane on time doesn't leave me the opportunity to hide out in this building until dark. In fact, there's only about two hours left before takeoff. I may end up trying to clean myself up in an airport bathroom.

No, that won't work. Getting arrested while offline would totally suck. Hmm. Would some random woman call the cops on me if she caught me taking a bath in a sink? Meh. Not worth the risk, the awkwardness, nor the discomfort. If I can get access to a real shower, I will.

It's easy to get out of the big warehouse style room. The office area attached to it is a little more of a maze. I sneak about fifteen paces down the most 'main' looking corridor before a *thump* comes from a doorway up ahead. Follows Rules Girl has another heart attack at the idea of being busted for trespassing. I freeze like a damn deer in the headlights of an oncoming truck.

A man's voice comes from the doorway, talking about how there are rumors this massive, abandoned warehouse is haunted by the spirits of fifty or sixty workers who perished in a fire in 1981. He mutters something about no one's been able to make use of the property since then for various reasons.

"Yeah, you see all those construction materials?" asks another man. "They said the workers who came in to fix the place up walked off the site after seeing stuff they couldn't explain."

Still paralyzed by the dread of getting in trouble, I stand there motionless as a thirtysomething man steps over a debris pile in the doorway. He's carrying a moderately elaborate camera rig and wearing a headband with lights on it plus a vest of pockets loaded with I'm guessing extra batteries for various electronic components. He's kinda pasty-faced, rocking a dad bod.

"Such nonsense," says the guy in view. "People will believe anything."

Glim once gave me some advice somewhere between combat training and survival. He said most people's reaction to sudden light is to dive for cover. However, the better thing to do is freeze, especially in the woods or places with lots of visual clutter. The human eye goes to motion. Standing totally still makes a person *less* obvious than diving to the ground or darting behind a tree. His advice came from the context of Army training. This building doesn't have trees. I'm also a bit high strung during the day, back to being my formerly timid self. When the sun is up, I am helpless. Okay, not literally helpless, no more so than any other person my size. I mean in comparison to being online. No excessive strength or mind powers or flying. Just me. Sarah Wright, teenager.

And whoa. Glim's advice seems to work. The guy is standing outside the doorway facing the wall in front of him. If he turned ninety degrees to his right, he'd be staring directly at me. Dude ought to see me, since I'm just out here in the damn middle of the corridor leaning slightly forward, hands up, like some video game character's 'stealth posture' is going to help me.

Dude isn't reacting to me.

"… can't believe anyone could ever fall for nonsense like ghost stories," says the guy, shaking his head.

And that does it. The tiny back and forth motion of his head is enough to push me out of his peripheral vision into focus vision. He stares at me for half a second. All the color drains out of his face and he lets out this scream worthy of Sophia finding five live cobras in the bathtub right after she stepped into it. Hmm. I guess holding perfectly still and not moving at all made me seem unnatural and creepy?

It's unclear if the guy faints or jumps back through the door he came from. Follows Rules Girl is hit with instant guilt as if I did something wrong on purpose to him. Still, there's enough Sierra in my personality to trigger an initial urge to get away clean. I backpedal three steps and make for the nearest open doorway into what had once been a small cube farm. The sizable room contains the collapsed remains of about ten or twelve desks with workstations. It's all a mound of bland grey fabric at this point covering the rusted out husks of desks, chairs, and ancient computers.

"Dude, dude, dude!" yells the guy, hyperventilating. "I swear I just saw a little girl standing in the hallway."

Grr. Okay, I'm no longer afraid of getting in trouble. Now I'm mad. I am *not* a 'little girl.'

"Come on, Gabe," replies the other guy. "You know that stuff is nonsense. Why does every damn haunting always claim to have a little girl spirit? Because of the aww factor. It's super sad and little girls are innocence personified. Stories like that play on your emotions to bring people to check out the haunting."

Gabe continues rasping for air. "Swear, I saw her. Just… Isaac, go look."

A shoe crunches in the hallway. "Nothing there."

"Long, dark hair. Sunken eyes…"

Isaac chuckles. "You're talking about the kid from that *Ring* movie."

"Dude, I swear I saw something." Crunching and rustling get louder as if he's walking into the hallway toward the room I'm in. A Velcro rip follows. "Camera."

"It's probably just some squatter," says the other guy. "But let's be thorough and debunk your ghost." The guy clears his throat and calls, "Hello? Is someone there?"

Two sets of footsteps draw closer. I move away from the door, tucking myself into the front corner of the room, to the left of the door in. My heart pounds in my chest. Good thing I don't *need* to breathe because my throat's getting tight. People tend to do dumb or random things when they're scared. I'm no exception. Right now, I'm basically an ordinary girl and pretty much a wimp. I don't know these two guys or what they might do to me if they believe they've found a young woman in a place no one is watching.

I mean, they could be nice guys, but I don't know that. So yeah, scared. What dumb thing does my brain cook up in the last few seconds before they reach the door of the room I'm in? Well, the one guy said he thought his friend saw the ghost from *The Ring,* so… I whip my hair forward over my face, let my head tilt to one side and stand in a really odd, unnatural posture. Not being able to see leaves me too vulnerable, so I hastily pull my hair open just enough for one eye to peek out. Hey, that's probably even creepier than going full Cousin It.

My bright idea to scare them off so they don't hurt me is either going to work perfectly or get me shot.

Five seconds after I'm fully committed to my acting role as a vengeful spirit, the guy who saw me wanders in through the doorway. Somehow, I manage not to flinch and hold perfectly still. Again, the dude doesn't notice me standing right there. I'm about fifteen feet away from him in the corner to his left. Gabe raises his camera, aiming it at the pile of old cubicle parts, narrating his video about looking for signs of the supposed girl he saw. A black guy about the same age walks in behind him, also holding a video camera. He's a bit taller, a bit thinner, but also basically throwing off 'dad vibes.'

Neither look at me. Who'd have thought an exposed corner would be such a great hiding spot? Being this close makes them less scary. These guys look like older versions of the geeks at my high school who used to play D&D in the cafeteria after hours. Basically… my dad in his thirties with an extra fifty pounds or so.

Camera guy, who I assume to be Gabriel, pans to the right, staring at the little screen on the device. He's got his back to me for about ten seconds before he slowly swings around in a wide arc to record the whole room. Isaac leans back to peer down the hallway outside, evidently having heard something in another part of the building. Gabriel is fine until he finishes his sweep of the room and ends up looking straight at me. The instant he spots me on his camera's mini-screen, he recoils away with one knee practically to his chest, screaming like an overly stereotypical 1950s housewife seeing a mouse. He tries to run away so fast he trips over parts from the busted office cubicles and falls in a heap. Poor guy doesn't even bother trying to stand again; he just curls up into a ball and starts sobbing.

Isaac stares at his friend having a breakdown for a second before catching me out of the corner of his eye. He spins to stare at me, clutching his chest. Never in my life have I seen such an 'oh hell no' expression before.

I have a choice. I could keep standing there as still as possible, hoping they keep freaking out and run away. Or, I could snarl, raise my arms at them, act aggressive. Unfortunately, there's enough Sophia in my personality for me to feel like a jerk for nearly giving these guys heart attacks already. I can't make it worse. They are clearly not dangerous. Neither one of them set off my creep-dar. They're probably 'my people,' as in they enjoy video games and geeky stuff.

Option three it is.

I straighten my posture and pull my hair off my face. "Sorry! I didn't mean to scare you so bad."

Gabriel wheezes a few non-words.

After a few seconds of staring at me, Isaac's petrified face shifts to a 'what the hell is wrong with you' glare, then he cracks up laughing. At this, Gabriel finally uncurls and looks up from the ground.

"Hi. Sorry. No ghost. Just me." I flash a cheesy, apologetic smile.

"Girl, you scared the hell out of us," says Isaac. "What the hell you doin'? Damn, kid, you on the street?"

"No..." I stuff my hands into my pockets. "Really sorry for scaring you. I'm not from around here, and I got lost last night. Some creep started chasing me, so I ran in here to hide. Lost him. Fell asleep. Woke up and heard you guys. You kinda scared me, too."

The guys stare at me while I explain my idiotic plan to frighten them away as a defense tactic because I was scared of what two strange men might do to me. Ultimately, they're good sports about it and laugh it off. Turns out, they're just a pair of urban explorers who check out old, abandoned buildings for fun as a hobby. If I'm lucky, Gabriel is going to be too embarrassed over his meltdown to put any footage of me on his YouTube channel. I manage to slip away from them with the true excuse of needing to catch a flight home before either one of them can ask me to sign anything to grant them permission to use my face on their video feed.

Whew. Crisis averted.

I keep giggling to myself while hurrying down the hallway toward the exit. Wow, I could so totally mess with ghost hunters or urban explorer types at night. Imagine the kind of freaky stuff I could pull off? Like, let someone see me at the end of a hallway, then jump out the window and fly up to the roof so there's no body on the ground by the time they get there to look. Sounds hilarious... but I'm not mean enough to do that to anyone just for amusement. Besides, it's too much work.

I'd just give someone a fake memory of seeing a ghost.

Not that I'd ever do such a thing.

Honest.

10

VICIOUS CREATURES

Plans race across my brain as I hurry into what seems to be the last section of corridor.

The smell of the place isn't getting any better. In fact, pretty sure it's getting stronger. Entering this hallway is like walking into a swamp of rotting vegetation. Mold grows in veritable carpets up the walls. I can't tell if the slabs of grey material hanging from the busted drop ceiling used to be foam tiles or if they're inch-thick chunks of fungus. The building's entrance faces the river and most of the windows are smashed, which kinda explains why it's so damp in here. It's only slightly less humid than my bathroom when I'm in the middle of taking a shower.

The two urban explorers haven't followed me. Now that they've figured out they hadn't seen a ghost, but 'some kid' messing around, they're probably going to resume checking this place out. Got a feeling they're not supposed to be in here, either. Good chance it's why they aren't trying to make trouble for me.

So much crap fills this hallway, a combination of stacked up junk and the miasma hanging from above, it's dark enough for me to go online. Doesn't do me any good, though. I've got about thirty feet of darkness before I'm outside. This place is so damn nasty on the nose that for the first time in my unlife, I'd prefer to stay offline.

Extreme senses aren't always a good thing. Sure, a vampire having hearing, smell and eyesight better than most dogs comes in really handy when hunting human prey in the woods back in 1497. It's much less helpful in a suburban house while living with a dad who does things to the bathroom that are probably banned by the Geneva convention. It's equally cringe to have amped up hearing when the 'rents decide to get frisky.

Shudder.

There's a reason I keep my phone in arm's reach at all times. Music is my savior.

Speaking of amped up hearing, among all the various noises going on in the environment—distant traffic, boats, people outside walking, Isaac teasing Gabriel for how loud he screamed at 'that little girl', rats moving around upstairs, and so on... I hear kitten mewls.

Aww... they sound scared.

So, those plans rattling around in my head? Yeah, they're mostly me organizing my thoughts into how I'm going to get to the airport on time while finding a way to clean up and change. Being online makes it painfully obvious my clothing has absorbed the stink of this place. It might not be too bad outside, but in the confines of an airplane? People sitting next to me will throw up. I should have time to hit a store, buy some new clothes, and clean up. Maybe I'll sneak into a random hotel room to use the shower if I can't find a fitness center or something along those lines. Either way, I can get stuff done in two hours.

My plans also now include locating those kittens. The tone of the frantic mewling communicates to me on a level mortals aren't on. I can feel their fear. It's dread fear, like the poor babies know their lives are in immediate danger. Expecting to find them stranded in a muddy pothole or caught between traffic lanes, I rush down the rest of the hallway, tearing the hanging horribleness out of my way. My earlier guess proved somewhat incorrect. It's neither rotting foam tiles nor sheets of mold: it's moldy foam tiles.

Eww.

I finally make it outside to a street running along the riverside. This is, after all, some kind of commercial district, so the city didn't put too much effort into beautification. No benches, fancy streetlights, or whatever. There's also like no one here. Naturally, being outside in sunlight shuts me down. The loss of amped hearing is kinda like going underwater, a swooshy-drowny sort of toilet flush noise fills my ears and then I'm left feeling as though someone snuck up behind me and stuffed plugs in my ears I can't remove.

Concentrating on the mewls—which I can *almost* still hear—I turn in place, searching for the source. My gaze is drawn instinctively to motion.

A guy in a blue tank top shirt, gym shorts, and sneakers is fast-walking from a grey Nissan Pathfinder over to the concrete railing at the water's edge. Normally, I wouldn't waste too much time staring at a buff gym-rat, but this guy is carrying a pillowcase sack.

The sack is mewling.

Oh, shit... you bastard.

Before I can even think about what to do, I'm in a full sprint. Those kittens are seconds from drowning. Either the dude doesn't hear me coming as I zoom up behind him, or my anger is to the point I've metaphorically redirected power from shields to weapons, forcing myself online despite the sun.

Maybe a little of both.

There's only one way—during daylight hours—picking a fight with a dude this musclebound is going to end in any other way than me getting my ass kicked. I run up behind him and go straight into a field-goal kick between the legs as he swings his arm back in preparation to throw the kitten sack into the water. My foot mashes into his critical weak spot an instant before I grab the pillowcase, which he's obligingly extended back toward me. Dude doubles over while emitting a low groan. He lets go of the sack he's carrying to grab the sack that's dangling as he careens forward to slump on the railing. Unable to help my anger, I shove him. He flips over the concrete rail and falls out of sight.

A combination meaty *thud*-slash-sharp-*crack* precedes a splash—then a whole bunch of agonized screaming from down below.

Oops.

I peer over the railing, looking straight down. There seems to be some manner of dock here for the warehouse I slept in. This guy fell about twelve feet and landed on the concrete base at the bottom of one of the pylons holding up this extension I'm standing on. He's clinging to the pylon base, screaming. From the way he's positioned in the water—and that crack—it's kinda obvious his hip broke when he landed. Okay, he's not going to drown... at least not *too* soon. It is August after all, the water's not going to be deadly in five minutes. Considering this guy was about to murder a bunch of kittens, I don't feel too guilty. The guy glares up at me, but he's apparently in too much pain to curse me out.

Fury gets the better of me. I stab him in the brain with a mental compulsion to stay the hell away from animals. Tapping my powers during the day earns me a light scorching. Smoke billows around me, but hey, no open flames. And yeah, he doesn't remember what I look like. Since I'm in a hurry—and almost on fire—I don't put too much effort into blanking myself out. He remembers my clothing, but instead of my face, he sees one of those creepy, realistic horsehead masks. Have fun describing that to the cops, pal.

Owwie. This hurts. So worth it, though.

After stopping at his truck to dial 911 from the cell phone he left in the cup holder, I haul ass down the street. No reason the man needs to die. The police will find him down there before he drowns. Guy has a good grip on the pylon.

Smoke continues to peel away from me as I run, carrying the sack of kittens.

Yes, I am a dark and vicious creature of the night.

A few blocks away from the river, I'm confident no one saw anything and decided to chase me, so I duck into a secluded spot by some dumpsters. Speaking of vicious creatures, I tear open the pillowcase sack—no patience to untie the knot—and discover four fluffy kittens with patches of grey and white fur. One has a couple orangey-beige spots.

"Oh, you poor things..."

The kittens stop mewling and all stare at me, almost as if they know they're safe now.

A distant anguished scream echoes in the city behind me.

Not feeling any guilt over hurting that man could be an indication I'm giving in to the darker side of being a vampire. Honestly, mortal me would probably just have screamed at him and begged him to give me the kittens instead of throwing them in. But, I'm not so timid anymore. Makes me wonder if I always had it in me but hesitated out of fear. Chihuahua syndrome. Noodle-bodied Sarah Wright couldn't cash any checks her mouth wrote. This has changed. I could debate the moral implications of not feeling guilt over hurting that man, but...

I'm done with philosophy class.

Got an A, in fact.

11

DEEP PHILOSOPHICAL
QUESTIONS... AND KITTENS

I 'm not the only one in need of a cleanup.

Poor kittens were so scared they peed all over themselves. Swear animals know. I'm sure they sensed what that man was about to do to them. Pity I can't erase the minds of cats. Anyway, know what's amazing? The power of acting like you know what you're doing. I walked into this sports club type place not far from the airport and went right into their locker room as if I had a membership. No one stopped me or challenged me at all. Can't even credit it to the way my bloodline can make me supernaturally inconspicuous because the sun's up.

So, I took four kittens into the shower with me. Hey, the scratches are small. Tiny claws.

It's getting close to ten at night when I land in Ashley's backyard. I approach the back door to let myself inside. No, it's not breaking in. I have a key. The same way my parents have functionally adopted her, Mrs. Carter thinks of me as her 'other daughter.' I'm welcome here at any time.

Right as I put the key in, a mild twinge of pain gets me in the left butt cheek. I'd grab the spot but I'm cradling precious cargo. Kinda odd for mosquitos to bother with me these days, so it's more likely an aftershock from the bullet that cracked me in the femur. Between the squirmy bundle prodding me in the stomach and my eagerness to see Ashley's reaction, I brush it aside and hurry into the house. Vampire healing is weird. It might have simply been a bone chip sliding back into place.

Mrs. Carter is relaxing on the sofa watching an old movie. She glances over at me as I walk in from the kitchen hallway and gives me a weird look. I deserve it. Who wears a big long-sleeved sweatshirt in August with shorts and flip-flops? Don't judge. I had to buy clean clothes and didn't want to spend a ton of money, so I went cheap on the shoes.

"Hey," I say, waving. "Is Ash here?"

"Up in her room."

"Is it safe?" I grin.

Mrs. Carter nods. "Yes, she's alone. Go on up, hon."

"Thanks." I zoom past the couch and hurry up the stairs to the second floor like I've done a million times.

I sneak down to the end of the hall, the last door on the right—the only pink one in the house. For the most part, her bedroom has not changed much in décor for years. Anyone who didn't know the Carter family seeing the room would assume it belonged to a nine-year-old. It's an explosion of pink and unicorns. The plushie pile on her bed is big enough to be used as a cushion by movie crews for stunt falls off the roof of a ten-story building.

"Ash?" I ask.

"Hey," she chirps. "What's up?"

I step inside. She's sprawled on her overly fluffy pink bedspread, dressed in cute unicorn-patterned pajamas. My best friend is strange. She wears pajamas around the house to be comfortable, but takes them off when she wants to sleep. To her, PJs aren't 'sleepwear,' they're lounging attire.

She's reading a manga graphic novel, I think it's one of the old Robotech ones. Ooh. Retro.

Before I can get a word out, I can't help but notice the 'thing' on the floor beside the bed. No, it's not a dong... it's almost worse to me: a pink leather dog collar studded with sparkly hearts. It's connected by a relatively short chain to a set of pink furry handcuffs. Oh good grief. I can barely look at it. And it's not that I think of Ash as being too young for sexy type stuff. We're both of legal age. But, really, who *likes* thinking about their sister or brother being sexually active? Ash is as close to me as the Littles or my parents. One could almost say even closer but that wouldn't be entirely true. Best friends as tight as we are share things we could never say to our parents or younger siblings.

Honestly, the idea of Ashley being a mature woman with intimate interests is fine. It doesn't really bother me. I just don't want to see it. Same is *not* true for my parents. Don't even want to think about it. Same is also true for the Littles. One day they will be old enough to date and… yeah. No. Don't wanna know.

"Umm, Ash." I point at the thing on the floor. "Your wild side is showing."

She props herself up a bit higher on her elbows to look. "Oops. Must've fallen out of the drawer." As casually as if one of her plushies fell off the bed, she gets up, crosses the room to the dresser and picks up the collar/handcuff assembly.

"What's with the collar?"

Ashley holds it up so I can get an unwanted better look. "I'm too skinny, so I can get my hands around my butt easy. The chain's so I can't. It's not fun if I can escape whenever I want."

I facepalm. 'Things I never wanted to know about my best friend for $400, Alex.' "Not what I meant."

Grinning, she stuffs the collar/cuffs in the drawer and buries it under a stack of folded clothing. She knows exactly what I meant and decided to tease me with details to make me squirm. It's not that I'm uncomfortable with my friend having an interest in kinky type stuff. My problem is having a hard time differentiating in my mind between her playing around and someone mistreating her. Yes, it's overprotective of me, but she's so naïve and trusting it would be easy for a creep to take advantage of her.

Woe be to any who tries.

I don't understand how she gets a thrill out of surrendering control, but if she enjoys it, whatever. Maybe it's because I'm a murder victim, or a vampire with a bunch of enemies, but that's one hobby I will never have the least bit of interest in. Like I said, my best friend is a contradiction. Giant unicorn-loving cute girl one moment, sex kitten the next. In hindsight, the furry cuff thing kinda makes sense. She always has been kinda passive. She likes feeling protected and taken care of. Explains how I've always kinda ended up being the 'big sister' even though we're the same age. As much as I sometimes wonder if Aurélie 'broke' her, corrupting a true innocent into a deviant, I think she really just gave Ash the confidence to try stuff she only fantasized about. Not my thing, but, hey… if she likes it, who am I to judge?

At least she's not into the really icky side of it like pain or being humiliated. No whips, no hitting, none of that torture like stuff or being treated like she's an animal. For whatever reason, she just gets a thrill out of being tied up. I'm about as opposite to that as one can be. I *hate* it. Freaks me out. Guess it's kind of why she always deferred to me whenever we had to choose a movie, video game, or activity. I could probably write a whole paper for psychology class on what she said about how giving up control is a different kind of freedom. Anyway, not going there.

She scurries back to flop on her bed after closing the drawer.

"Got a job for you," I say while walking closer.

Ashley rolls away from the graphic novel to sit on the side of the bed, raising her arms like a zombie while droning, "Yes, master, As you command, master," in a cheesy overacted voice.

Sigh. "You know that whole thrall thing is just on paper right?"

"Yeah." She drops the act and giggles. "But, you know… if you ever wanted to really do it, I wouldn't say no to looking young forever and getting superpowers."

I chuckle into another sigh.

"Umm, why do you look so guilty?"

"No reason. This job is important."

She squints. "Why are you wearing a long-sleeved sweatshirt in August?"

"Because I can?" I smile. "Seriously, though. People at airports have zero chill when it comes to certain carry-on items."

Ashley gasps, one hand over her mouth. "Bomb? Or… did you like buy a giant dong in Chicago?"

Her comment is so random I burst out laughing, damn near cackling. "Neither."

"But you smuggled something?" Ashley raises both eyebrows. "Seriously?"

"I did." I let her thoughts run wild for a few seconds more, then pull the neck of my sweatshirt down. Four kittens poke their heads out.

Ashley squeals. "Oh-em-gee! They're *soooo* cute!"

I feel like a cow that fell into the Amazon River amid a piranha swarm. Only, rather than strip the flesh from my bones, Ashley yoinks the kittens. She places them on her bed, flops beside them, and proceeds to let them run all over her. I can just see it now. She'll be in her forties, a full-fledged veterinarian, and someone brings in a kitten for a checkup and she flops on the exam table just like this to play with it.

"You know I can't take them home or Mom would literally explode."

Between giggles, Ashley says, "So would Sophia."

I tilt one hand in a so-so gesture. "Sophia's reaction would be more of an implosion."

"True." Ash holds two of the kittens up over her face, making baby noises at them. "Where did you find these adorable fluffballs?"

Sigh. I sit on the edge of the bed and share the story.

Ashley goes from adorable to furious, spends a few minutes at 'adorably furious,' then calms. "I'll take them to the clinic for a checkup first thing tomorrow."

"Cool. Um, are you going to adopt them out or keep them?"

She blinks. "What makes you think I'd keep them?"

"Oh, I dunno..." I gesture at her. "The way you're basically 'bathing in kittens' and playing with them now."

"Darn." She fake frowns. "Busted." She pauses, mouth open, eyes almost crossed as one of the kittens climbs her hair. Once the little guy's on top of her head, she shifts her gaze back to me. "Yeah, maybe. They feel like a gift from you, so I have to keep them."

Watching her play with the kittens makes me acutely aware of the imminent march of time. Right now feels like any other random happy moment from our lives. It's going to feel like the blink of an eye before she's not a teenager anymore. Before I know it, she'll be old and I'll be wondering what happened.

"Okay." Ashley sits up, covered in kitten. "Explain the guilt. Now, woman."

I stare down. I've never been a good liar, and it's even harder to lie to Ashley. So... I take a deep breath and tell her the truth behind my somber mood—including the freaky nightmare of her showing up in my room. I'm afraid of the future. I don't want to lose my best-friend-slash-sister. I want us to stay together. We probably won't 'take on the world for eternity,' more like hang out and watch anime together for eternity.

"... but it's.... I dunno. Both choices seem wrong." I flop over backward, arms stretched out above my head. Two kittens take the opportunity to jump on my stomach. "You want to be a vet... have kids, get married."

Ashley snuggles kitten three against her face. "I wouldn't really mind becoming a vampire, too. I'd be totally thrilled if I could spend forever having fun with you, escape the world and just be stupid teenagers forever. Can we make sure I'm an Innocent, too?"

I chuckle, but it's mostly a sad noise. "I don't know how to do that. Trust me, though. If *anyone* would ever be selected by the wheel of fate as an Innocent, it would be you."

"Huh." She baby talks at kittens for a moment, then looks at me while holding one up in both arms over her face. "Is it like a desire thing?

Vampires who want to be vampires compared to someone like you who didn't ask for it?"

Another kitten curls up at the base of my neck, making sure their little tail drapes over my face. I puff the tail away from my mouth. "It might have something to do with it."

"You're thinking because I'd want to be a vampire entirely to stay with you and not for power or immortality for the sake of immortality, it might work out." Ashley sets the kitten down on her chest and smiles at me.

"Maybe, but wow. We sound like a couple of pining lovers, don't we?" I chuckle.

"Yeah." Ash fake sighs, then deadpans, "We should just get it over with already. Get those pants off right now, you sexy beast."

Her flat—and totally nonserious—tone is too much. We both end up laughing so hard we cry. I could no more think of her in a romantic context than date one of my parents. Yeah, eww. Different though. The thought of kissing Ashley makes me laugh at the ridiculousness, not want to throw up. And no, this isn't one of those 'we deny it for years then fall madly in love' type situations. We are basically twin sisters even though we look nothing alike. It's a mental wavelength thing.

Crazy thing is, she has no powers of mind reading but she's right. I really was pondering if a person's motivation for asking a vampire to give them the Transference had anything to do with bloodline. You'd think it would be a simple process like hereditary transmission. Whatever bloodline the sire is, the new vampire becomes. It isn't. Though, odds vastly favor such a direct result. Almost anyone turned by a Shadow becomes a Shadow, for example.

"I'm not going to ask you to kill me," says Ashley in a half-whispery voice.

My brain leaps straight back to the nightmare of Ashley shooting herself. I must look freaked out because she throws a plush unicorn at my head.

"Stop. I'm not gonna do anything. You had a crazy nightmare." Ashley sets the kitten on its feet beside her and sits up to hug me. "I'd never do anything like that to you. Besides…" She bites her lip. "I'm far too much of a chicken to hurt myself."

I hug her back. "So weird where all these emotions are coming from out of nowhere. Not like the monthly visitor is to blame. She lost my phone number."

Ashley snicker-giggles. "Oh, I totally would not miss that at all."

"Worth it." I pretend to lick my finger and draw a line in midair as if adding to the 'pro' column for vampire benefits.

"And it's okay." She shrugs like a little girl who's only slightly disappointed at getting a knock-off Walmart doll instead of the brand name one for her birthday. "While I don't mind the idea of becoming a vampire, I'm also okay seeing where life goes, too."

"Yay, independent thought!" I thrust a fist into the air.

She throws another plushie at me. "Hush, you."

Heh.

Her expression goes pensive. "I dunno. Becoming a vet and having kids is cool and all, but the 'having kids' part requires a boy. I haven't exactly had the best luck there."

"You seem to be into, what's her name again, Raleigh?"

"Yeah." Ashley lunges to grab a kitten before it falls off the bed. "Careful, you. That's a big drop for such a little kitty."

"They're a handful." I cuddle the nearest kitten.

"Yep. That's most of the fun." Ashley spends a moment cooing at the kitten before smiling at me. "Raleigh doesn't have a baby cannon."

I snort-laugh. "Not what I mean."

Ashley giggles again, then shrugs. "So far, so good. She's funny, and really into me, and likes a lot of the same stuff I do. Girl didn't even get jealous when I rambled about you and how close we were... and warned her."

Side eye time. "Warned her?"

"That I have a super close awesome best friend who's really protective." Ashley plucks two kittens out of plushie mountain and cradles them. "She asked about siblings and I told her about you and how close we are. Whenever I date girls, they always seem to get massively jealous toward you. Like the possessive girlfriend going into 'war mode' when her boyfriend's sister calls because they don't know who this girl is calling his phone."

I laugh.

"But yeah." Ashley kissy-faces at a kitten. "Raleigh's the first one to seem fine with it."

"There's nothing to be jealous of." I roll my eyes.

"You know that. I know that. They don't."

"Fair point." I exhale hard.

Ashley leans against me, still holding kittens. "Only problem with Raleigh is her parents. They don't know she's into girls. She's not out yet. So... I haven't seen the parents or even talked to them. Gonna be an issue if we get serious. Either way, she doesn't have the right equipment for us to spawn a bunch of red-headed demon offspring."

I laugh, then pause—frozen in dread. "Wait, two gingers reproducing?"

"Yep," chirps Ashley. "We'd summon a soul-devourer."

I fake cower. "Two redheads has to go against some cosmic law somewhere."

Another plushie bounces off my head.

"What about adopting?" I ask.

She nods. "Yeah, that would have to be the plan if I end up married to a girl. But... you know, adoption could work as a vampire, too. Going vamp doesn't mean I can't possibly have a family."

"Vampires adopting children is called 'kidnapping,' Ash."

"True..." She ponders. "Is it still kidnapping if a vampire takes an orphan who doesn't have any other family?"

I stretch out on the bed. "Deep philosophical questions."

She leans over me, staring into my eyes. Rather than swoop in for a passionate kiss, she sets a kitten on my face. "Do you want me to be a vampire?"

"Honestly?"

"Honestly." She nods.

I relocate the kitten from my face to my stomach. "I think I do—but I don't want you to die."

"That's a conundrum." She sputters.

"Yeah." I sit up, causing the kitten to spill into my lap. It mews and starts trying to climb the sweatshirt to my shoulder. "Remember years ago how you used to cry whenever it got late and you had to go home... as if we'd never see each other again?"

"Yeah." Ashley pokes me. "You did, too."

"Sometimes. Not as much as you did, though."

"Well, sure. You had a baby sister to keep you company." Ashley makes a goofy face. "And you didn't have abandonment issues thanks to a jerk father."

I look down, torn and guilty. Huh. These jean shorts are kinda short. Oh, hey, my legs don't look abnormally pale. They're pretty much the same as always. Stop distracting myself with tangents. I'm dodging the issue.

Ashley nudges me. "We better make up our minds fairly soon while we still look the same age. I don't want to spend eternity being thought of as your *older* sister... or worse, your mom."

With that, we collapse on the bed, laughing and covered in kittens and plushies. I can't think of a more 'Ashley' moment than this if ever there was one. I'm so content and happy right now I should be forgetting all my worries. But I'm not.

In fact, all I can think of is how much I don't want to lose what we have.

FROSTY BUNS

N othing like a good day's sleep to reset my overactive emotions.
Soft rustling comes from the floor beside my bed. Since this is an unusual noise for my bedroom, I peek over the side of the mattress. Klepto is playing in the empty trash bag I used to bring my original clothing back from Chicago. Swear the washing machine made a gagging noise when I stuffed them into it last night.

Okay, kitten exploring an empty plastic bag, not a crisis.

Upstairs, the thunder of multiple small boys moves across the house from living room staircase to back door. Mom yells to Sam, informing him he's not allowed to wander off to Eastern Europe again. PlayStation sound effects are a clear indication of what Sierra is doing. No surprise my ears detect zero signs of Sophia. She's probably reading, doing some kind of magic practice, or has gone to Nicole's

For a while, I reflect on the Ashley situation. Normal people might hate the idea of growing up and having to take on responsibilities, but all they can do is grumble about it. Ashley really can make a decision here. She's biologically older than me now, but not by much. She's still eighteen for two more months. She hasn't changed at all appearance wise or attitude wise. Maturation is a gradual process, supposedly. I'd say Dad is proof otherwise, but for all his geekiness and love of having fun... he really is the most dutiful, responsible person I know. Mom's seriously responsible, too... but she doesn't have his playful side, at least not to the same degree. Mom's ninety percent business.

Wonder what Sarah-at-forty would've been like? Closer to Dad or Mom? Guess it would depend on the career path I tripped down. For the moment, Ashley is still Ashley. Given enough time, though… she's probably going to become Mrs. Carter, a quiet and unassuming woman who's always so worried about everyone else, she never makes time for her own needs. She's the ultimate caregiver.

What Ash said last night is true. We don't have long to debate the issue before she's going to grow up too much and we'll no longer be a 'pair of teenagers.' This is such a tangle to figure out. Maybe I'm overly fixated on the death part. I mean, I died and I feel fine. Death only sucks when it's permanent.

Either way, this is Ashley's future we're talking about. So the decision is entirely hers. I will have to unlive with whatever she wants. This is something I'm not going to choose and impose on her—like when I insisted on watching *The Room*, because 'how bad could it be?' She's probably going to just sit there biting her lip and not making a decision until I get frustrated and tell her what we're doing. Sorry, Ash. This is too heavy. You have to do it.

For about an hour, I lay there being lazy. By the time I have enough motivation to get out of bed, my emotions have settled back to normal. Well, it's summer. No school. I'm going to spend as much time with my family as they'll tolerate. Yeah, whatever. I fail at teenager.

My family's more or less returned to normal.

Except for the whole magic and demons thing. We are still massively more tight-knit than ever before my death, but the Littles have gone back to being able to have fun without clinging to me all the time. This is healthy. They need to have friends their own age. All three of my siblings plus their respective crews spend most of the afternoon between our backyard and the cul-de-sac out front. I join in for some kickball.

Not too long after it gets dark, an unfamiliar white Toyota SUV pulls into our driveway. Out hops Ashley, Michelle, and Tilloa. Oh, it must be Till's car. Looks brand new. Since she's a presently unemployed baby vampire, I shall assume some manner of nefarious acquisition occurred. This is what I get for teaching her how to use mental influence.

Yeah, I bumped into Tilloa not too long ago when she mistook me for a mortal and tried to feed. Turns out, she hadn't been a vampire for very long at all. Her sire abandoned her sight unseen, so she didn't know much.

My unusual circumstance of living with my family inspired her to attempt reestablishing contact with her boyfriend—who had attended her funeral.

Let's just say it didn't work out well.

He once again believes her dead and gone. So what's a homeless twenty-four-year-old with no friends or family to do? She makes new ones. Tilloa and Michelle hit it off right away. Now, it's tempting to say they have some kind of black girl sisterhood going on, but really, they have highly similar personalities. Tilloa is fierce, knows what she wants, and doesn't let anything get in the way of her goals. Michelle also acts as a bridge of sorts for outside bystanders. Tilloa looks every bit in her mid-twenties. The woman's a veritable supermodel on top of that. Michelle is nineteen but gets mistaken for twenty-two all the time. Ashley... most people don't believe she's eighteen until after they see her ID. Me? No one believes I'm eighteen even after they see my ID.

The three of them coming to pick me up as a group can mean only one thing: girl's night out.

Michelle and Tilloa linger upstairs talking to the 'rents, while Ashley all but drags me downstairs to change into something nicer. None of the girls are 'dressed up,' but a T-shirt and sweatpant shorts is a bit *too* casual to go out in. While I'm staring at my closet and dresser in search of an outfit, Ashley informs me of the plans. We're going to catch a concert, then probably end up at Frosty Buns.

Once I decide on what to wear, I strip. Ash doesn't react to me flinging my top off, but the instant my sweatpants drop, she lets out an 'eep.' We've changed together often enough for the sight of my bare butt not to be worthy of such a reaction, so I peer back at her, raising the Eyebrow of Inquisition.

"You have a massive zit on your leg." She points.

I twist, trying to look, but see nothing out of the ordinary. "Umm, where?"

She hurries over and gently touches one fingertip to a hardened nodule less than an inch below my backside. "Right here. It's huuuge. How the heck did you not feel sitting on that?"

I grab the spot. Yeah, definitely a hard lump about the size of a pea. "Oh, dammit. It's not a zit. That has to be a bullet trapped under the skin. Grab a paper towel please?"

"Kay." Unfazed, Ashley rushes out.

While I wait for her to return, I slip into clean underpants and a T-shirt intact and clean enough for outside-the-house use. Real pants have to wait for obvious reasons. They'd complicate amateur surgery. Ashley returns a moment later carrying a paper towel and a knife. I give the knife another raised eyebrow since I'd been planning to use my claw, but decide to shrug, bend over my desk, and wait. Knife's probably a better idea anyway. Claws sting.

Ashley takes a knee behind me. "Never did this before, but you'll heal, right?"

I nod. "Yeah. Guess it's good practice for a future vet."

She hums. "Is this going to hurt?"

"Probably. But pain is relative. Compared to other stuff, I probably won't even notice it."

"Okay. Ready?"

"Yep."

Ashley gently grasps the nodule between her thumb and one finger and draws the knife across the top. As soon as the incision is big enough, she coaxes the bullet out, then presses the paper towel against my leg.

Didn't hurt as much as I expected it to. Slight pinch. The itching of it healing is worse than the cut. "Thanks."

"What are friends for?" She pats my butt. "Oh, wow, it's so small."

"Thanks, Dad."

She gasps. "Your father shot you?"

"No, he's why I have a small butt. Genetics."

"Hah." Ashley snickers. "I meant the bullet." She holds it out for me to see. "Tiny."

I'm not a firearms expert, but if I had to guess, I'd say it's bigger than a .22 but nowhere near a 9mm. Doesn't look like it came out of anything the biker gang in Chicago fired at us. It's as baffling as it is small. Where the hell did it come from? My knowledge of bullets and vampire healing is somewhat limited, but if I had to guess... a bullet this small might've lodged in bone and taken a while to work its way out. This could be over a week old. Hmm. I drop it in the drawer of my computer desk. Maybe I'll ask the mystics if they can somehow determine how it ended up in my backside.

"That's so cool," says Ashley while staring at me. "Do you have any other bullets in you?"

"Not that I know of."

"Don't they usually fall out?" Ash wipes blood off the area. "All clean. Oh wow, it's totally healed already."

"Yeah." I grab a pair of jeans and pull them on. "Usually, the bullets fall out the hole they made within fifteen minutes, but this one's so small, I think the wound closed up before the muscles could push it out. Or maybe it got stuck in a bone and took longer."

She whistles. "Crazy."

"Could be a stray." I scratch my head. "If someone shot me on purpose, pretty sure they wouldn't have been aiming for my butt."

"You need to stop making enemies." Ashley gives me a stern (and fake) stare.

I flail my arms. "Like I do that on purpose."

Once I'm dressed, we go upstairs. Michelle and Tilloa are in the middle of explaining our plans to the 'rents. As we gather up and start out the door, Mom forgets herself and tells me to be home by ten. Smiling, I don't bother to correct her and call back, "Okay."

Tilloa finds this hilarious.

Hey, curfew and bedtime aren't the same. I'm not too proud to humor her. After all, vampire or not, she worries about me. At least staying inside at home stops me from unintentionally making even more enemies.

We hop in Tilloa's new Toyota Highlander. On the ride to the concert, she tells us about how she walked into a dealership after dark and charmed the owner into giving her the truck. Apparently, the guy is a bit of a sleaze, and he thinks he traded the vehicle for several hookups with Tilloa. The reality, however, is much less exciting. She's making him think they had two-hour marathon lovemaking sessions by implanting false memories. Dude's actually laying catatonic in a motel room for only about ten minutes.

Michelle is shocked—more at the guy for agreeing to such a deal. Ashley can't stop blushing, and I feel as guilty as if I stole the truck since I'm the one who taught her how to do the whole mental compulsion thing. According to Tilloa, she didn't force him to give her the truck, so she doesn't think it's stealing. Even if the sex is imaginary, he can't tell the difference and the memory is 'as good as the real thing.'

Not touching that one.

"Why did you do that?" Ashley's face is still the same color as her hair.

"I wanted a vehicle," says Tilloa in a matter-of-fact tone.

"Just like *Total Recall*." Michelle taps a finger to her chin. "Pity you guys have to stay secret or you could make bank giving people all sorts of epic fake memories."

Ashley rolls her eyes. "No, I mean why the sexy type stuff. Why not just steal it?"

"Stay off the radar, invisible. No police report this way." Tilloa pats the steering wheel. "It's pretty difficult to make someone give away something this expensive and be undetected—or get some poor bastard fired or prosecuted."

"Why do you even need a truck at all?" I ask.

"Because these two can't fly." Tilloa gestures at Michelle and Ashley. "Wanted to make it easier to hang out with y'all. And they kinda stole my last car when I died. It would be a bit too obvious if I swiped it back."

"Legally, not yours anymore," says Michelle.

"Yeah." Tilloa shrugs. "It is what it is. Time for a new life."

THE CONCERT ISN'T BAD AND NEITHER IS THE FOOD.

No, the small venue doesn't have a kitchen. I'm talking about the audience. Tilloa and I take advantage of the dense crowd and dark lighting to feed. Never heard of this band, 'Savage Tenderness,' before. Yeah, they have a cringy, edgy, oxymoronic name that takes themselves way too seriously, but the music is okay. They sound like if the people from Evanescence took a whole bunch of valium and tried to cover System of a Down songs with a bit of Epica thrown in. They're doing the 'beauty and the beast' thing: an operatic female vocalist in tandem with a guy doing growly vocals. Guys, hate to tell you this, but growly vocals don't really work with slow, gothy music. Dude sounds like he's making comforting noises at his sick dog.

Not really my thing, but I don't hate it.

For ninety-ish minutes, I'm just a normal girl hanging out with my friends again. I'm able to forget about all the craziness and pretend my life is totally ordinary—except for the time I spare to go bite someone.

After the concert, we pile back into the questionably obtained SUV and drive to Woodinville. Michelle's been keen on showing Frosty Buns to Tilloa since the place is so significant to us. The three of us have spent so much time hanging out here during high school we almost count as employees. I swear we've logged more hours under the roof than everyone who *does* work there except the owner.

It's a fairly popular spot for the local high school crowd. Frosty Buns is a neat—and crazy—idea. Basically, it's an ice cream shop married to a burger joint. Not a McDonald's, either. The burgers are handmade here. It's easy to tell because they're never the same exact size or shape. The place also tries to appeal to the younger generation by offering a bunch of healthier wraps and even some vegetarian sandwiches. Neither Ashley nor I have been brave enough to try the 'milk-less ice cream' for the vegans.

We'd almost always come here after going to the movies or having a pool day, or whatever. From around age thirteen onward, if we found ourselves away from the house in the afternoon or evening, we'd end up here. Since we usually had dinner waiting for us at home, we'd more often than not split a single ice cream sundae between all three of us. However, we did get in the habit of leaving school to grab lunch here a couple times a week.

Due to it being 'girl's night out,' we order actual dinner. Michelle gets a 'New Yorker,' a burger covered in Swiss cheese and mushrooms. I have no idea what those particular condiments have to do with New York. If the burger cost $25, the name would make sense. Ash orders her usual chicken, bacon, and cheese on a bun. Michelle jokingly suggests I try the TMFD, or Tex-Mex Fireworks Display. It's a burger covered in black bean salsa and loaded with several varieties of pain in the form of different hot peppers, pepper jack cheese, and so forth.

I decline, not wanting to shoot literal flames out of a sensitive spot later on.

"Aww, come on, you're not worried about calories," says Michelle. "Looks amazing."

"You're forgetting." I hold up a finger like Socrates. "As above, so below."

Tilloa tilts her head. "Occultism? Emerald tablet?"

"No... well, maybe." I cringe. "I'm being literal. No breakdown going on. What goes in..."

Michelle, Ashley, and Tilloa all squirm in their seats.

"Ack." Michelle shakes her head. "Skip the TMFD."

I go for a much tamer barbecue burger. Alas, Tilloa abstains. Fairly sure she's either an Old Guard or a Scion. No, not the car. Scions are basically the same as Old Guard, just a newer evolution, a vampire bloodline adapting to the modern era. She can fly, which is on the rare side for Scions. What I mean by evolving to a modern world is, they by and large lost the ability to fly due to the existence of cars and airplanes. Claws are extremely rare among scions for similar reasons—guns exist. They also seem to have a knack for technology. For example: she can make her new Highlander work without having the key on her. Somehow, the computer in the engine thinks the wireless key is there.

Alas, one thing Scions cannot do is tolerate normal food. Only Innocents can. If she eats anything, she's got about twenty minutes to half an hour before uncontrollable nausea and projectile vomiting begin. Poor girl also has to concentrate on being lifelike. If she doesn't, she looks obviously dead. Not like rotting or anything, merely corpselike coloration. It's like the vampire version of getting dressed in the morning. It doesn't require continuous focus, merely a deliberate effort to activate 'lifelike mode'. Aurélie usually doesn't bother, hence her unnaturally white skin. To her, it's a time saver. When she'd been alive, it took her hours to paint her face, neck, and shoulders the same color her skin naturally is now. Something about France centuries ago. They evidently liked whiteface. Anyway, non-Innocent vampires can sometimes have trouble passing themselves off as perfectly normal. Tilloa, for example, has striking gold eyes. I'm talking shiny metallic gold irises. In the dark, they look legit unearthly.

She tells the teenage boy waiting tables she's on a strict diet and already hit her calorie cap for the day. Not hard to accept as an excuse since she is so damn pretty. The woman's nowhere near Aurélie's level of 'yeah, I could totally kiss a girl' supernatural beauty, but I can recognize she's gorgeous.

Our conversation's random as heck, straying across lanes like a drunken American tourist trying to drive in England. We eventually start sharing stories with Tilloa about how we've been coming to Frosty Buns our entire lives... or at least our whole lives since we were old enough to have the nerve to ride a bike more than a quarter mile from home. All the high school stories—from not that long ago—finally make Tilloa crack up laughing.

"Wow." She whistles. "I forget you guys are just babies."

Michelle says 'gimme a break' with her eyes while Ashley begins acting like a four-year-old upset that the table doesn't have crayons and a coloring placemat.

I smirk. "You aren't *that* much older than us."

"So, what's your Dalton like?" asks Michelle in a somewhat hushed voice.

"My what?" Tilloa blinks.

"She's asking about the one who gave you the Transference," I mumble around a mouthful of burger.

"Oh." Tilloa shrugs in a 'don't know, don't care' way. "Never saw them. Couldn't even tell you if it's a man or a woman. All I remember is being jumped from behind at night. I blacked out before I saw much of anything but a face full of dirt."

Michelle winces.

Ashley stares at Tilloa and blushes ever so slightly. "Did you wake up naked in a morgue cooler?"

"Nope." Tilloa traces her finger around the table, drawing in the condensation from our iced tea cups. "I woke up in a shallow grave. Still had all my clothes on. Muddy as hell, though."

"Eek." Ashley shivers. "I'd rather streak across Woodinville like Sarah did than be buried alive. That's horrifying."

"Not me." Michelle holds up both hands while shaking her head. "Nope. Shallow grave all the way."

I give Ashley side eye. "You would not."

She flashes this super mischievous grin. "Dare me to and I'll Lady Godiva it right here."

Giggling, I gasp, blush, and duck low to the table, mortified. "You would not! Everyone in this place knows us."

Michelle and Tilloa laugh.

"Oh, I would." Ashley holds her chin up. "But only if you dared me to."

Yeah. She totally would, but it's obvious to me she doesn't want me to dare her. That's Ash. Simultaneously shy and bold. Too shy to do something like that but also too bold to chicken out of a harmless dare. I'm not going to dare her to pull a wood nymph act because I know she'd do it to call my bluff. Since, of course, I ended up stuck outside in my birthday suit the night I became a vampire, it's something 'rule breaking and exciting' I did that she hasn't gotten to do yet. Not saying I'm a rebel who makes a habit of doing exciting stuff I'm not supposed to do. Really, the most shocking rule-breaking I do is usually writing with blue ink on forms marked 'black ink only.'

The pseudo-twin thing might be getting her. Maybe she wants to catch up.

"Sare…" Michelle leans toward me, resting her elbows on the table. "If it happened over again, what would you prefer?"

I ponder for under a second. "Streaking, absolutely."

Ashley nearly chokes on her iced tea trying to laugh at my response.

"In all seriousness, I'd prefer to be stranded outside naked." I munch on some fries. "I can make people forget seeing me. I can't make myself forget being buried alive. That would mess with me way too much. If I could change anything at all about how I woke up, I'd not be locked inside a coffin-sized morgue cooler. In the calmness of looking back on it, being stuck in such a tight space bothered me way more than having an epic wardrobe malfunction."

Michelle and Ashley both cringe.

"Yeah." Ashley shivers. "No kidding."

Tilloa shifts in the booth, mostly leaning against the wall. "Technically, I wasn't buried *alive.*"

Michelle eyes her. "How shallow a grave we talking about here?"

"It's kinda fuzzy in my mind..." Tilloa makes a 'thinking face' for a moment. "Guessing, but a bit over four feet deep."

"Uhh." Michelle gawks. "That ain't shallow. How the heck did you get out?"

Tilloa makes a clawing gesture. "Don't really remember much detail. Just darkness, heaviness pressing down on me, wet dirt in my face. No coffin. I kept clawing and clawing in the direction that felt most like up. Don't think a normal person could have gotten out. Took more strength than people have."

Ashley squeezes herself against me, shaking as if we're at the scariest part of a horror movie. The girl has a seriously vivid imagination. "That's horrible."

"I'm over it," mutters Tilloa. "Mostly like a bad dream now."

"'Chelle," says Ashley. "Would you choose being stuck in a four-foot grave or stranded outside in the buff?"

"Hmm." Michelle rubs her chin. "That's a hard choice."

"It shouldn't be," says Ashley. "Sarah used to be really shy, but it doesn't bother her now."

I grumble. "Not really by choice. Almost every time someone tries to kill me, I end up losing my clothes. And I was never 'really shy' about that. Anyone who qualifies as 'really shy' would never wear bikinis in public."

"Losing your clothes?" asks Tilloa. "You getting attacked by creeps?"

"No. Modern clothing isn't well suited to the physical demands of vampiric combat. I think it's why they wore such elaborate crap 200 years ago. Swear, some of Aurélie's dresses have so many layers my claws couldn't get through them."

Ashley snickers.

I shrug. "Embarrassment at being boobs-out seems so trivial when you've been killed, shot, stabbed, broken in half by a troll, torn up by claws, and so on."

"Wait... troll?" Tilloa gawks.

"I'll tell you about that sometime. Too long and crazy to go into now." I wave dismissively.

"You're messing with me." Tilloa squints.

"No, totally legit." Ashley un-leans from me, no longer shaking. "Stuff's cray."

I catch two guys at a booth two away from ours staring intently at me. Oops. They overheard some of what we're talking about and can't decide if we're nuts or just dorks doing some kind of vampire live-action roleplaying. Adding a tiny false memory is much easier than erasing, so I make them think they heard us talking about stats and dice rolls. We're dorks. Move along. Nothing supernatural here.

From there, the girls start talking about more mundane things like school, jobs, and romantic entanglements. Michelle and Corey are still together, but both are so busy with work and school they haven't had much time together. As far as I know, they haven't done anything more intense than kiss yet. Michelle's parents are religious enough to where they'd probably freak out if their daughter had sex before marriage. It wouldn't be as big a freakout as if they learned Ashley is bisexual or I'm undead. Still not sure which of those two would rattle them more. I think if a gay vampire walked into their house, they'd both just spontaneously burst into flames.

I'm lucky. While Mom and Dad weren't exactly thrilled when they found out I'd given away my virginity, they didn't freak. Mom took it in stride and gave me 'the talk' about being careful. For Dad, it had been a little harder accepting his little girl had become a woman... or close to one. He brushed it off and kept on keeping on as always. After a while, he got into the habit of getting his petty revenge on me for growing up by saying embarrassing things like asking me to make sure the boy has a condom or joking about hearing carpenters working on the roof the night before.

Thinking about that makes me blush for real.

I've kinda fallen out of the conversation, lost to my thoughts. Tilloa has become part of our friend group fairly fast. She and Michelle act like they've known each other for years. Ashley, as well, only she's a bit too friendly with her. I suspect a possible crush. Michelle and Tilloa go off on a long conversational thread about music. As far as I'm concerned, Till is a pretty cool person... but I also feel a little bit jealous or maybe uneasy at how rapidly she's swooped in and become part of the group.

It's nothing serious. Just me being emo. I went through the same feelings when we met Michelle. For a few weeks, I had this possessive thing going for Ashley, not wanting her and Michelle to hang out together without me. She's *my* best friend, dammit. I got over it. Now, it's like I'm scared Tilloa will replace me and steal both of my friends. She's just too perfect. Beautiful, cool, confident, athletic, smart, but also scared and vulnerable at the sudden, unexpected changes becoming a vampire dropped on her. Bleh. This isn't healthy. I'll get over this, too.

There really is no reason for me to get worked up. It makes me start questioning reality all over again. As in: is some external force—or internal vampire sense—making me hyperfocus on Ash for a particular reason? Oh, maybe that's it. I'm not jealous of Tilloa or possessive of my friends like she's trying to steal them. I'm anxious about Ashley for some unexplained reason and taking out my nerves on Tilloa.

Michelle brings the conversation back to subjects best discussed in whispers. "So the one who did it to you just buried you there and left?"

"Pretty much." Tilloa shrugs.

"Maybe he or she didn't realize they made you?" asks Ashley.

"Don't think it was an accident," says Tilloa. "After clawing my way to the surface, I found a pair of hikers handcuffed to trees nearby." She traces a finger on the left side of her neck. "Both of them had been cut on the neck to bleed a little. I don't think they even noticed that. Watching me crawl up out of the earth like a damn zombie freaked them the hell out."

"Eep," whispers Ashley.

"Dayum." Michelle shakes her head.

"I didn't know what the heck I must've looked like to them, or where I was, or even what happened to me." Tilloa swipes her hair off her face. It's a little past shoulder-length and straightened—permanently. Same way my hair will grow back to the exact same length every time I sleep if it's cut, her body is frozen at the moment of death. She likes to joke about how much money she saves not having to buy hair products now. "Didn't even process I was up to my waist in the ground. Saw some people screaming, tied to trees and wanted to help them."

"What happened?" Ashley scoots down in the seat, again leaning on me like we're watching a scary movie.

"I crawled over to them, thinking they needed help. They started screaming louder. My dumb ass thought a bear was coming up behind me. Didn't realize it was *me* they were screaming about." Tilloa gets a distant look in her eye. "Smelled pot roast... got close to them and—"

"You blacked out," I whisper.

Ashley gasps. "Oh, no... did you..."

"No clue." Tilloa twirls her hair around her finger. "Next thing I know, I woke up in a funeral home basement. Still had all my muddy clothes on, so they hadn't had a chance to do any embalming. Got my ass outta there."

Michelle nods along with the story.

"Wow." Ashley cringes. "No idea what happened to those hikers?"

"No clue." Tilloa exhales, seeming guilty but genuinely confused. "I don't think I killed anyone. By the way, that funeral place was shady as shit. After I took off, they told my family my body was too messed up for a viewing. My family buried a closed casket weighed down with sandbags."

"I'm so sorry," says Ashley.

We're all quiet for a while.

"You didn't tell them?" asks Michelle.

"Tell them what?" Tilloa stares at her. "That I'm a monster? Or send them an anonymous tip they buried an empty casket and have them go looking for my body? Why? Wasn't worth it. No bad blood with my family, but if I'm gonna be honest… we weren't exactly close. I moved out at eighteen and didn't really see or speak to my parents much since."

I lean back into the booth cushion, one arm around Ashley. "What are the odds two people were tied to trees right next to that grave?"

"Damn low if you ask me," says Michelle. "I think your sire put them there on purpose for you to, uhh, eat. Sounds like a sick freak to me."

Ashley leans into me tighter. "Eek. I hope it's not hereditary."

"Vampires aren't genetics." Michelle chuckles.

"You know what I meant." Ashley indignantly sticks out her tongue. "I guess we don't need to worry about Till going evil. Look at Sare. She didn't inherit Dalton's endearing bumbling ineptitude."

We all crack up.

I can't help but remember the time my jeans snagged on a fence while I tried to sneak into a vampire den. Where is the line between 'bumbling ineptitude,' random derps, and simple bad luck?

Good question.

13

THE BYSTANDER EFFECT

At twenty minutes to ten, we all wind up feeling like we've been at Frosty Buns long enough.

Since my mother told me to be home by ten, Ashley teasingly suggests we should hurry back before I get in trouble. I'm sure Mom brain farted or maybe even joked, but bleh. I can't think of anything else to do. Tilloa seems a bit awkward about the idea of coming over and hanging out like a kid. Michelle is not opposed to the idea, but I can tell she's not as into it as she used to be. She really is the most mature one of my friend group... or was. Michelle's in a hurry to grow up. Ashley's kinda dreading it and looking forward to it in equal parts. Me? I'm going nowhere in a hurry age wise.

Tilloa is an actual adult, though my grandparents would say otherwise. To them, twenty-four is still a kid. To me, she's 'older.' She is the age Michelle tries to act.

Funny how age works. At thirteen, I used to think high school seniors were 'all grown up.' Now I'm that age and still feel like a kid. Not a *child*, mind you, a kid. However, sudden unexpected death has a bad tendency of destroying one's life. Since Tilloa has nowhere else to go and nothing else to do with herself, so she agrees to extend 'girl's night out' to movie time at my place.

If Ashley has anything to say about it, this could easily turn into a sleepover as if we'd all gone back to being twelve. At least my room is equipped to handle vampires.

We get up as a group, leave a cash tip for the waiter, and head over to the register to pay. This isn't one of those fancy places where the table servers take your card. Ash, Michelle, and I pool our funds to cover the tab. Tilloa—since she didn't eat anything—isn't obligated to chip in.

Once outside, we all stop in a pack by the front door and do the obligatory phone thing. I send my Mom a text to let her know we're on the way back. Michelle texts her parents to update them on her whereabouts. Ashley also sends her mom a status update. Not wanting to be left out, Tilloa fiddles around with a game on her phone while she waits for us.

Ashley holds her phone out to me so I can see the giant clock display. "Ooh, cutting it close, but we should make it back before you get grounded."

Hah. I laugh.

Like a group of gunslingers in an over-stylized Western movie, we all 'holster' our cell phones at the same time. Ash and I stuff them in our bags. Tilloa and Michelle have belt holders, like adults or something.

We start walking away from the door toward where Tilloa parked. I take two steps before a flash of headlights sweeping over us damn near blinds me, reducing the world to an empty black void except for two painfully bright spots coming right at us—fast. A revving engine tells me what my eyes can't: we're about to get creamed by an idiot speeding in the parking lot.

To my left, Michelle barks like a stomped-on goose. A fast moving beige blur—Tilloa's shirt—zooms away from where I'm standing. I fly-tackle Ashley to the right. Something clips my sneakers a split second before a deafening *whud* hammers my eardrums.

Even though I'm not touching the ground in that instant, the concussion of the car smashing into the wall of Frosty Buns rattles my bones. Ashley hits the sidewalk on her back, but I'm fast enough to get one hand behind her head to stop her skull from bonking the concrete. Blaring horn and hissing comes from behind me. It takes a moment for my vision to recover from taking high-beams to the face.

I look back at a light blue sedan—Nissan or Toyota I can't tell—stopped against the building, its nose end punched into the brick wall. Loose bricks litter the exposed hood. Shattered glass from the front window of the restaurant is all over the place.

"Holy shit," whispers Ashley.

"You okay?" I stand and pull her upright.

"Yeah. You knocked the wind out of me, but I'm fine."

I twist to face the car and the haze of steam and/or smoke surrounding it. "'Chelle? Tilloa?"

"We're good," calls Michelle from the other side of the wreck.

A few guys come running out of Frosty Buns, doing the 'holy shit that almost hit you girls' routine. I don't let Ashley look at the car because the guy behind the wheel is clearly dead. The airbag didn't help him much because he missed it. The body is draped out through the windshield, head and shoulders buried under the upper part of the Frosty Buns window/roof where it collapsed on him and the car. There's nothing anyone can do for him now except maybe give him the Transference, but… too many witnesses and I don't know the guy.

Ash doesn't need to see that. I steer her around the car to the other side, rejoining Michelle and Tilloa by the corner of the building. More people come out and collect around the wreck.

Michelle eyes the parking lot, then the car, then me. "No skid marks."

"One of the rare times the lack of skid marks is a bad thing," says Tilloa in a low voice.

Ashley cringes.

It's much easier for me to examine the parking lot since nothing is dark to me except the sky at night. Michelle's spot on. No skid marks. It momentarily confuses me how this guy got up to such a speed in the relatively tiny parking lot until I notice tire gouges in the strip of grass at the far corner. The guy must have been flying down the road and, for whatever reason, veered into the Frosty Buns lot after jumping the curb.

"Yeah. The dude didn't even try to stop." I glance back down the road where he came from, shocked there isn't already a cop on the way.

Ashley gawks. "Are you saying he tried to kill us?"

"Doubtful." I fold my arms. "He might have been unconscious before the crash. If he'd had a heart attack and passed out, he wouldn't have been able to hit the brakes."

"Dude didn't have a seat belt on, either." Tilloa checks us over. "Everyone okay?"

"Yeah." Ashley nods. "I can't stop shaking, but I'm not hurt."

Michelle had the crap scared out of her. Even though she appears mostly calm, her eyes are wide as saucers. She gazes around at the scene, speechless.

"'Chelle?" I ask. "You okay?"

"Need a minute."

I fish my phone out of my bag. "Gonna call 911."

"Why?" Tilloa gestures at the maybe fifteen people all checking out the wreck. "A dozen other people already have."

"Do it." Ashley squeezes my arm. "Call."

"You don't know that." Michelle snaps out of her fog. "Ever hear of the bystander effect? Something happens and everyone who sees it assumes someone else will call for help... so no one actually ends up calling for help."

I dial and hold the phone to my ear. "Yeah. Diffusion of responsibility theory. Thank you, Professor Heath."

"911, what's your emergency?" says a youngish sounding man.

"Some guy just crashed into the Frosty Buns," I say. "He looks dead. Don't think anyone else got hurt."

As the operator starts asking me various routine questions, I glance at Ashley and send a telepathic message. *Hey, would you text Mom and let her know we're gonna be late.*

Damn. I really did intend to be home on time, too.

14

WORLD EXPLODING THINGS

A full-on sleepover never materialized.

Only Ashley spent the night. The cops didn't keep us too long, which surprised me. We gave statements of what happened, got looked over for injuries, and sent on our way after they collected our info. Nearly being smashed by a speeding car altered the mood. Rather than watching a movie, we ended up hanging out talking about heavy things like mortality and fate. It took about an hour for the shock to fully wear off Ashley and then she became mostly upset that someone died.

Tilloa hung out for a while after Ashley fell asleep on my bed. I've been coaching her on 'how to vampire,' and she's taking to it pretty fast. I'm now mostly convinced she's a Scion. Because of that, we have some serious differences. For one thing, she does not have claws. For another, she didn't get 'cute and harmless' as a superpower—she got the hotness. Don't get me wrong, she wasn't by any means ugly in her driver's license photo, but definitely closer to normal. The change in her is distinct enough to where her former friends probably wouldn't recognize her. They'd think she 'kinda resembled' someone they used to know. It's an even bigger difference than seeing a celebrity in a movie vs. bumping into them for real at the mall.

I get the same thing sometimes, only people mistake me for Sarah Wright's younger sister.

Tilloa eventually took off around three in the morning since she had the truck and needed to drive back to where she's staying before sunrise. She's really happy about being able to fly, but wanted to be nice to the group. Ashley, Michelle, and I all have fairly small cars, which makes things a little cramped on a group of four.

It's about three in the afternoon when I discover the motivation to move. Ashley got up and went home hours ago, probably around eight or nine. Mom left a Post-It on my computer desk to ask why she found bloody paper towels in my wastebasket. The wiseass in me wants to write the answer on the note and let her find it, but I won't.

This, of course reminds me of the bullet in my desk drawer. Meh. Not that important.

I grab a quick shower in the basement bathroom, then throw on a giant T-shirt long enough to be a shift dress before making my way upstairs. The boys are playing out in the backyard to my right. On the left, faint gunfire comes from the living room. Sierra must be playing *Call of Duty* and doing the sniper thing. If the shooting isn't loud, it means she's keeping her distance and hiding.

Sure enough, Sierra's sitting cross-legged on the floor in front of the living room television. This is pretty normal. What's not normal is her purple bikini. The sight of her makes me think of the time the London mystics tried to magically abduct Sophia out of her school. They didn't quite get the spell right and yoinked all inanimate objects around her. Every scrap of clothing and jewelry she had on vanished. Fortunately, they had some way to know when she'd gone somewhere no one else could see her before they released the spell. Just so happened she was in the bathroom and could hide in a stall.

I remember cracking a joke about Sierra to the effect that she can get so focused on the PlayStation, I bet she'd just sit here continuing to play without even noticing some crazy mystics zapped away her clothes. Seeing her sitting there in a swimsuit has me scratching my head and wondering what sort of magical craziness has occurred.

"Umm, Sierra?"

"Hey," she says in an 'I'm concentrating' tone.

Her character on the screen does appear to be sneaking around a trench. "What's up with the swimsuit? Botched spell?"

"No. We're going to the pool." She rounds a corner and knifes someone. "As soon as Mom gets back."

"It's not even four yet. You've got at least two hours before she gets back."

Sierra shakes her head, still not taking her eyes off the screen. "Dork. It's Saturday. Mom's not at work. She just ran to the store."

"Oh. Right." I rub my eyes. "Whoa."

My sleep schedule makes days blur. I meander back to the kitchen. Sophia, who wasn't there a moment ago when I came up from the basement, is now standing by the sink. She's got sponges in all six of her hands, which she's using to scrub the sink and counter. Yes, I said *six* hands. She's got four extra arms the same size and shape as her real ones, but they're made out of blue light. Soph's wearing a plain white dress, a pink anklet, and no shoes. From the look of her toenails, I assume the past hour or so has been spent with Priya, Megan, and Nicole doing polish.

"What are you doing?" I ask.

"Cleaning." Sophia twists around to grin at me. "Morning."

"With six arms?" I raise both eyebrows.

"Yep!" she chirps. "Why have skills if you never use them? Magic doesn't have to be great big world-exploding things all the time. Sometimes, magic is amazing for the little things."

I lean on the counter, watching the mini-Kali scrub. "Little things..."

"Yeah. Like cleaning up messes, fixing a rip in a dress, or, I dunno... trying to give people good luck."

"Riiiight." I chuckle. "The old I want to win the lottery spell."

"Nah." She shakes her head. "That's not small. It's kinda greedy, too. Magic gets weird when it's done for greed."

I gently grasp her shoulders and plant a kiss on top of her head. "Don't change, Soph. The world needs more people like you."

She flashes a weak smile. "Trying not to. Mom asked for a hand in the kitchen, so I gave her six."

"Hah." I move out of her way so she can keep cleaning on down the counter. "Are you going swimming or staying home?"

"I'm going. Just haven't changed yet. Sierra doesn't want to waste any game time."

A particularly loud guffawing laugh outside makes me look. The boys don't usually make noises like that unless something happened that a responsible adult needs to react to. These are ten-to-eleven year old boys, after all. Such uproarious laugher means someone is bleeding after doing something idiotic. Pity Mom's not here right now. They'll have to settle for me or Dad.

Sam, Ronan, Daryl, and Jordan are running around the backyard playing with toy military planes, having a mock war. It's unclear to me if they're trying to dogfight each other or all on the same side shooting at imaginary enemies. Another toy jet is flying around by itself, as if carried by a fifth invisible boy. The reason for this becomes obvious as soon as I spot Blix standing on the deck railing pointing at the phantom jet. He's sporting an oversized pair of sunglasses and purple Bermuda shorts.

The boys are all ready for the pool, wearing swim trunks. It seems Ronan has just experienced an applied demonstration of the inverse curve law of friction involving bare feet and wet grass. Sam's curled up in a ball on the ground holding his groin. Two toy planes lay in the grass near him. If I had to guess at what happened, Ronan wiped out and reflexively threw his plane as he fell. The quite pointy-nosed toy jet fighter managed to nail my brother where it hurts most. Sam appears to be paralyzed from the waist down, but he's laughing too. A flying toy jet isn't likely to cause real damage.

Still, I poke my head out and ask if everyone's okay. Other than having some green stains on his chest, Ronan's fine. Sam gives me a thumbs up.

"Are you going to come to the pool with us?" asks Sophia, after sneaking up behind me.

I jump, but not enough for her to notice. "Ehh, not sure it's a good idea. I'll either blind everyone there or catch fire."

She rolls her eyes. "You're not *that* pale. Ashley's way worse."

We both laugh. Ashley owns her paleness. It doesn't bother her. In fact, she once threatened to weaponize it on some girls who gave us a hard time at summer camp one year by turning herself into a solar death ray. Yes, we are dorks.

Dad glides into the kitchen. He squish-hugs Sophia into me, giving us a simultaneous squeeze. What can I say, he's a programmer. Always looking to be efficient. "Hey girls. Everything okay?"

"Yep." Sophia sets all six hands on her hips.

"Just woke up." I yawn out of habit.

"Good. Good." Dad either ignores or doesn't notice my sister's extra limbs on the way to the fridge.

I mean, they are bright blue and transparent so they're way less creepy than if it looked like she had six real arms.

"What's wrong?" Dad pulls an iced tea out of the fridge, shuts it, and looks at me.

Damn, he's good. "The crash."

"Oh." He nods. "What's bothering you about it? The near miss?"

Before Sophia can freak, I say, "No. I dodged it easily. Something just feels strange about it is all." Might be embellishing there with the 'easily.' After all, the side mirror clipped my sneaker.

"Indeed." Dad sips tea. "The strange part is how that guy managed to get up to however fast he'd been going without the police trying to pull him over. I swear... if it's me, I go two miles over the limit and they light me up."

This is funny for two reasons. One, his statement about the Woodinville Police is fairly accurate. They do tend to be a little aggressive with the speeding tickets. But hey, quiet town, not much crime, guess they have to kill boredom somehow. The second reason it's funny is Dad. We're lucky if he drives *at* the speed limit. I don't think he's ever been pulled over in his life and here he's talking like they stop him three times a week.

Sophia giggles even though I'm sure she missed the joke.

"It's hard to explain." I rake one hand up through my hair. "Something about the accident just doesn't feel right."

"Speaking of not right." Sophia flails her arms. "Kittens! You saved those kittens and brought them to Ashley's, but where's the momcat?"

"I don't know. Sorry." I wince. "That idiot only had the kittens with him, no older cat."

Sophia fumes... adorably. "This is a job for Klepto! We can't leave the momcat with that butthead!"

"He won't hurt her... I made sure the guy will avoid animals from now on." I try not to make eye contact. It's possible my family didn't quite get the full story of what happened. It's also possible a certain vampire may have left out some key details about how violent she got with the guy who was about to throw kittens into the water. Debatable if it counts as a lie. After my angry adrenaline wore off, I did feel bad about breaking that guy's hip. Still, served him right.

"Nice." Sophia hugs me.

"Okay, everyone," calls Mom as she comes in the front door carrying a couple of grocery bags. "We'll get going as soon as I put the perishable stuff in the fridge." Mom stops short in the kitchen upon seeing Sophia's extra glowing arms.

"Counter's done." Sophia points her three right hands at the sink.

"Umm..." Mom blinks.

Sophia claps her real hands once. All three grocery bags vanish from Mom's grip. "Stuff's all put away where it belongs." She gets this far off look like she's trying to remember something. In an instant, she goes from wearing a white dress to a pink bathing suit. "Now I'm ready. Pool time!"

Cheering about 'pool time,' Sophia runs upstairs, calling for Nicole, Megan, and Priya to get ready.

Mom and Dad exchange a glance. My father shrugs like nothing we just witnessed is in any way unusual. Mom stares into space.

"She did save us the trouble of putting stuff away," says Dad.

"Yes, I suppose." Mom exhales. "When did everything get so strange?"

"Don't think of it as strange." Dad kisses her on the cheek. "Think of it as adventure!"

That's Dad. He's not just stuck in the Eighties. He's stuck in an Eighties' movie.

A few minutes later, all three Littles plus Megan, Priya, Nicole, Ronan, Daryl, Jordan, and Blix rush after Mom outside and pile into the Yukon.

Dad sips his iced tea. "I'm starting to think the Yukon might be too small. We're going to need a regular school bus if any of your siblings make—or summon—more friends."

I laugh.

"Not going to the pool?" He asks.

"Nah. It's a bit bright today. Wouldn't be fun. I'd just stand there all twitchy and tense, clenching my jaw in a constant battle with pain like Supergirl locked in a kryptonite cage... or Uncle Hank forced to attend a gay wedding."

Dad spits tea all over the floor and wall.

Once we stop laughing, I help him clean up.

15

THE MANY FLAVORS OF LUCK

I ended up changing my mind.

For all my inexplicable maudlin grumbling about college taking time away from my family, it felt weird to skip the pool trip. Unfortunately, I wasn't wrong about the sun. My 'skill' at dealing with it has improved quite noticeably since my first day as a vampire. A day like this would have been bright enough to cause immediate smoking not even half a year ago.

Picture the stinging sensation that follows a wooden paddle across a bare butt. Not the hit, just the stinging after. That oh-so-awesome feeling is everywhere. Sunglasses, beach shawl, and bikini plus a wide hat make me look like some reclusive French actress trying to avoid media attention. At least the hot pins-and-needles feeling isn't too painful wherever I can keep the sun from making direct skin contact.

The kids do what kids do. It's a giant community pool, so they go utterly nuts. I sit in the shade of an awning by Mom. Or as close as I can get. She's sunbathing. Blix is amusing himself by causing tiny pockets of calamity here and there. A spilled drink, a loudmouthed idiot tripping into the pool, and so on. For an imp, he's really dialing it back. No one ends up bleeding or even bruised. Then again, Blix is hardly a normal imp. I wonder if, when Sam gets old enough to care about girls, if Blix is going to cause random swimsuit malfunctions like something out of a raunchy Eighties college comedy movie.

By the way, I'm past the awkward stage.

At a certain age, Dad wouldn't let me watch those movies at all. When I got a little older, he let me watch *Revenge of the Nerds* after the Littles were in bed. I think I might've been fifteen. Yeah, I pretty much wore a blush the entire time. The movie wouldn't have bothered me at all if I'd been watching it with my friends. Just... having full frontal nudity on the screen in the same room with your parents was... eek. Now, though, it doesn't bother me as much. Watching movies with content like that with my parents is still not something I'd go out of my way to do, but if a movie we have on surprises us with some swinging man bits or some girl parts, I don't feel like I want the universe to swallow me whole.

Fortunately, no one's losing their swimsuits today. Blix is behaving himself. And to be honest with myself, I can't see Sam asking him to depants any girls when he's in his teens. He's way too respectful. Him asking Blix to deliver an atomic turban wedgie to some jock douchebag harassing girls... now *that* I can see happening. What's a turban wedgie? It basically starts off like a normal wedgie, except the pants end up stretched so far they're pulled up over the unfortunate victim's head. Dad saw it in a comic strip years ago. I'm not honestly sure if such a thing is physically possible, but with Blix involved... it can happen.

Once the sun weakens a bit in the late afternoon, I hop in the water and pretend I'm fourteen again. I'm not exactly sure where the demarcation point is age wise when people are supposed to stop having fun at pools and just sunbathe or swim laps for 'fitness reasons.' Screw it. So many people mistake me for being younger than I am, it's time to exploit it. Don't think there's anyone here checking ID. *Sorry, miss, you're too old to enjoy yourself in the water. Here's a Kindle and a margarita. Go sit in one of those lounge chairs and pretend to read while complaining to your friend about your day job.*

While I don't have much command of my vampire abilities in such strong daylight, one thing remains. I still can't get tired. So, I start horsing around with the kids. This turns into me throwing Sophia, Sierra, and Sam around. Sam grumbles it would be way more fun if I was stronger and could throw him like twenty feet into the air. Poor Megan doesn't even approach me to get tossed. Right now in the day, that's probably wise. She's only eleven, but the girl's got some heft to her. Not gonna call her fat, because she isn't, merely a little chunky. Daryl, who is also a bit on the pudgy side, has no sense of self preservation. He jumps on me and... remember the time Megan flattened Sophia in dance class? Yeah. Daryl hits me like falling redwood, dragging me underwater.

We end up staring at each other near the bottom of the pool. The 'oh crap, you're not super strong right now, sorry' look in his eyes is hilarious. It's difficult to laugh while submerged. It's also not really the look I imagine it is. He doesn't remember the vampire stuff.

Anyway, I have a blast. When Mom finally calls us out of the pool to go home, I really do feel like a little kid again wanting to whine and beg for more time like everyone else—except Sierra. She's happy to go swimming, but she's also happy to hop back on the PlayStation, so the girl's not motivated enough to complain about leaving the pool. If Dad were here, he'd palm her forehead checking for a fever because a kid who gets out of the water immediately when told we're going home is clearly delirious.

Once we're home, the kids split up. Girls go upstairs to shower off the chlorine and change while the boys use the basement shower. I bide my time, since it won't really matter to me *too* much if all the hot water is gone. I'll only shriek for about a minute before the cold stops bothering me.

Sierra's right back on the PlayStation while Sophia, Megan, Priya, and Nicole get in some more sun time on the back deck with the little bit of daylight remaining. The boys hang out in Sam's room. Eventually, parents show up to reclaim their offspring and Ronan jumps in the mirror to go home. Soon, it's just us for dinner. Today feels so damn normal and awesome I don't even think about it and join them at the table.

Via a stream of texts, Ashley shares that she and Raleigh went to a day carnival… in Tacoma. Okay, weird. Heck of a drive. But okay. At least she's having fun and sounds happy.

I think I'm going to be happy tonight, too.

HAD TO EAT TWO PEOPLE ON THE WAY TO THE PARKING LOT OF MI TIERRA, BUT today was totes worth it.

Defying the sun takes a lot out of me. I get the feeling it's one of the most draining vampire abilities. Like, to put it in video game terms, if I had a 'mana pool,' it would be more expensive for me to spend a few hours outside during the day than it would be for Aurélie to charm-hammer a room of a hundred mortals and turn them into an army of mindless servitors.

No complaints. I love it. Extra feeding is a small tax to pay for the ability to feel so normal.

I'm sitting cross-legged on the hood of Hunter's old Buick, waiting for him to finish his shift. It still strikes me how different the world is to me.

Now, sitting alone at night outside somewhere is peaceful and relaxing. Pre-vampire me would've been shaking like a chihuahua after downing a whole pot of that 'extreme caffeine' coffee. Okay, I exaggerate. Live me wasn't *that* skittish, but I certainly would not have found being alone outside at night 'peaceful.'

And yeah, Hunter is still working here even after I helped his mother get a better job. She can afford to cover his tuition now, but it's still summer (meaning no school) so he's working to save up as much as possible to help out with whatever. Their family didn't win the lottery after all. They still have money issues, but Mrs. Lawrence is down to only needing one job and earning enough to survive. Even better, she's working in the field she went to college for. Unlike me, she chose a major because she loved it.

Hunter plans to keep working here even after classes start again, but only on weekends. The idea is if he does that, he won't have to find an entirely new job next summer. I mean, I've offered to guarantee the manager hires him back no matter what, but I think he likes it here. Not enough to spend the rest of his life waiting tables though. However, if he can keep the job without relying on paranormal means, he will. I think it's him trying to help me stay inconspicuous. The more often I do stuff, the greater the chances something gets noticed.

Maybe he's got a point. Seems I can't even help an old lady cross the street without pissing something off.

"Ugh!" I prop my chin up in both hands, elbows on my knees, and spend a moment feeling annoyed.

A ghost asks me to help his grandson not die, Petra wants me dead.

Help a ghost at school, an order of mystics wants my head on a plate.

A lesser nerd would crawl into her room and avoid people. Sigh. I really am too nice.

Ashley's latest text has stirred some… feelings deep down inside me. Unless she's messing with me, she and Raleigh got daring. Rather than drive home or find a room somewhere, they stayed in Tacoma and slipped into the woods 'for some fun' in the form of a nudist hike with possible other activities—to use her phrasing. The only reason I didn't freak out is she sent me the text *after* they finished and got back to the car. How many missing persons stories start out with two young lovers going off into the woods alone and no one knows where they are? Ugh. Maybe it's a good thing Ashley's usually the passive one who leaves the decision making to others.

Even though Ashley grumbled that they didn't really do much more than scamper around the woods like a pair of dryads from some sapphic Greek play—and go skinny dipping in a creek—the idea of making love in the woods is kinda tantalizing. It's not like I have to worry about creeps or even wildlife. I'm sorely tempted to suggest it to Hunter tonight. Plus side, we don't need to go as far off as Tacoma to find a suitable forest. I can only assume they drove so far because Raleigh is trying to keep her family in the dark about their relationship.

I slip into a daydream part reality, part scene from *Prince of Thieves*, where I stretch out nude on a big rock by a waterfall in a lush fantasy forest while Hunter rises like an Adonis out of the water beside me.

An instant before Hunter's, erm... 'hunter' breaches the surface, my ideal dreamworld shatters because a couple of jerkwads on the other side of the parking lot decide to start screaming at each other.

Grr. Right when the dream started to get good.

I glare over my shoulder. Two guys in dark hoodies are in each other's faces between a pair of modded-to-hell little cars. Both vehicles have so much tweaking done to them I can't tell what kind of cars they are other than small, sporty, and probably Japanese. Apparently, the two guys 'had a deal' and one of them feels like the other is trying to screw him over. The way they're hunkered down, trying to argue while being quiet, makes me assume they're conducting a shady deal of one kind or another. They're a bit too far away for me to read their minds, but they also look like they're probably going to get out of here soon since they've made an obvious scene.

Meh. Not my problem. I can't go playing superhero and constantly trying to solve every single problem I see. It's not even clear what the deal involves. Sure, they *could* be selling meth, but maybe the money they're talking about is for car parts or bets on an illegal street race.

Hunter emerges from the back door of the restaurant. Awesome. We can get away from these two idiots screaming at each other. Talk about a way to kill a romantic mood. He notices me sitting on his car and smiles.

I hop off the hood and take a step toward him, trying to act like a sexy seductress stalking her prey. Unfortunately, I'm a bit sheltered. Sarah Wright trying to do a sexy sashay is about as 'cool' as Napoleon Dynamite dancing.

A jolt of pain stabs me in the chest out of nowhere, then another. Like two seconds later, a bunch of gunshots go off from the direction of the two arguing dudes. Supersonic means an object travels faster than the speed of sound. The bullets hit me before I heard them fire. Oh, not really two seconds... just felt like it to me.

Hunter's expression hasn't even had a chance to change from adoring to horrified yet. I try to whirl or dive for cover, but my body isn't listening to me. Shit. That's a heart shot, isn't it? Son of a bitch.

There's phenomenal luck, good luck, bad luck, astonishingly bad luck... and then *my* luck.

The last trace of Hunter I see is his face twisting into an 'oh shit' expression.

Sigh. Well, I'm definitely going to get kissed tonight. Just... by pavement, not my boyfriend.

And... out I go.

16

FAST THINKING

My eyes open to a greyish-blue sheet over my face.

It's silent. Sense of touch returns next. The chilly, hard, smooth material at my back could be an autopsy slab or morgue cooler tray, but my position is all wrong for that. I'm not completely lying flat. I'm kinda-sorta sitting up a bit, almost as if I'm relaxing in a bathtub without any water. My shirt is gone, leaving me topless. Bras are evil torture devices designed by men. Since my girls are not exactly epic, I can get away with avoiding bras and not have to worry about sag or back pain later in life. Well, I mean… before the vampire stuff.

Okay, I'm definitely in a bathtub, covered by a blue plastic tarp. The washed-out greyness is an artifact of it being dark. I can still see perfectly in a totally lightless environment, but colors kinda lose their vibrance. Okay. Think. Bathtub, no water. No shirt. Tarp. Complete darkness. This is weird.

I'm still wearing my jean shorts, but my flip-flops are missing. The comforting presence of my phone is still in my pocket. So, whoever grabbed my 'corpse' isn't worried about stopping me from contacting people. Then again, they might not expect me to get back up. Who the heck steals a dead body and puts it in a bathtub?

When my nose decides to start working, all the swirling worries in my head about who kidnapped me and where I am evaporate. This is Hunter's house. I smell wood, decades of his father's cigarette smoke, a hint of whiskey, Mrs. Lawrence's Earl Grey tea, Hunter's cologne, and that strange sugary-candy-berry smell that always seems to hover around Ronan.

Know what's really strange and dark? I can tell the moment someone stops being a child and becomes an adult. They stop smelling like dessert and start smelling like normal food. No. I do not and will not bite little kids to satisfy my sweet tooth. I'm perfectly capable of eating actual candy. Okay, to be fair, I don't have a magical 'adulthood detector.' A person's flavor changes based on my perception of them. A fourteen-year-old who looked twenty-one would not smell like candy to me even though they're still a child.

Anyway, what the hell am I doing here?

I reach up and pull the tarp off my face. Towering piles of cardboard boxes, lumber, and rolled-up tarp surround me. Oh. I'm in the third-floor bathroom. Hunter's house is absolutely freakin' huge. It's literally like two normal houses cemented together with some extra space. Really, Mrs. Lawrence could rent two sections of it to other families… if the place could qualify for a certificate of occupancy. It's a wee bit run down and would never pass an inspection. They're working on it, though. But for the time being, no one lives here but Hunter, his mom, and Ronan.

Consequently, they rarely go to the third floor. This bathroom is serving as a storage closet. As far as I know, the plumbing works fine. They just don't use it. How much house does a woman with two sons really need? No one comes up here except once a month to help keep the dust from getting out of hand. Ronan is also afraid of the third flood because he thinks there's a ghost up here. I've told him multiple times there isn't—I'd know, but kids. They still believe in fantasy stories like haunted legends, Santa Claus, and trickle-down economics.

I push the tarp down past my legs. Yeah, I'm in the bathtub, boobs-out. There's no blood on me anywhere and my chest smells faintly of soap. Okay, not what I expected. No body cooler and I'm only *half* naked. Hunter must have scooped me off the parking lot and rushed home to stash me up here. Guessing my T-shirt was a bloody lost cause. I imagine him sitting on the toilet next to the tub waiting for the bullet holes to close up before gently washing me off. Aww. I choke up a little thinking about what sort of emotional state he must have been in while sponging my apparently dead body clean.

A scrap of white on the underside of the tarp catches my eye. I lift the heavy plastic to reveal a notebook page with writing on it.

Got you out of there before anyone showed up. If anyone asks why I hauled ass, it's because two guys were trying to shoot each other and I didn't want to get hit.

There's a clean shirt for you on the sink. Stay as long as you need. I told Mom you're sleeping over. Umm, had to tell your parents what happened. Sorry in advance for their freakout.

Please be okay.

-Hunter

I slouch back against the tub and let out a long sigh of relief. It's almost tempting to turn on the water and soak to relax even though I've still got my shorts on. Bigger problem than that, my phone is in my pocket. Bad idea to get it wet... if my parents haven't blown it up yet that is. Ugh. He told them someone shot me. Not looking forward to *that* conversation.

When am I?

It's too dark to tell. Even if the sun came up, the window in here is both tiny, filthy, and obscured by a wall of cardboard boxes packed with random stuff Mrs. Lawrence wants to keep but doesn't know where to put. I sit up, fishing my phone out of my pocket to look at the clock. Past a tower of boxes, the edge of the little sink comes into view. A neatly folded black T-shirt sits there waiting for me. Can't reach it while sitting in the tub. Ugh. Sorry, body. I gotta ask you to move. Come on. Get up.

I grab the tub edge and start to shift my weight forward. A dread feeling comes over me at the same instant my gaze falls on the screen of my iPhone. It's 5:55 a.m. Shit! The sun's coming up any minute. I attempt to lunge to my feet and grab the shirt but my body is not cooperating. All I manage to do is fling my arm in the general direction of the sink before collapsing back to recline in the tub... with the tarp only up to my knees.

Shit. Shit Shit.

The room races away from me as if I'm falling backward down a deep old well. Blackness surrounds me; the phantom of vampiric sleep has pounced. My final thought before losing consciousness is: please don't let Ronan walk in here and find me like this.

IT'S A FEW MINUTES AFTER FIVE IN THE AFTERNOON WHEN I SLIP THROUGH THE sliding glass door between our deck and the kitchen.

Hunter gave me a ride home on his way to the restaurant for his shift tonight. Talk about crazy. A shooting happened in the parking lot and the place is still open. We spent the time between me waking up and his having to leave just holding each other in his bed. Seeing me awake, okay, and fully intact helped him package up the trauma of watching me shot in front of him and put it away on a shelf somewhere as a bad dream.

Anyway, home now. With any luck, I can sneak downstairs and the 'rents won't notice I didn't come home last night. Wait. No they won't. Hunter told them.

"Young lady," calls Mom from the living room. "Get in here."

That tone of voice. Those words. Immediate cringe response. Damn. I'm in trouble. In flagrant disregard to being an immortal vampire with like powers and stuff, I sheepishly trudge down the hall to the living room.

My parents are on the sofa, Dad in his favorite reclining section. Sierra's on the floor by the TV, game paused, looking right up at me. She's not the type of kid to gloat when Sam, Sophia, or I get in trouble, but her expression is definitely giving off a 'better you than me' vibe. Her pantomime of eating popcorn is a bit much, though.

"Umm, hey," I say while flashing a cheesy smile. "What's up?"

Mom appears to be forcing herself to stay calm. "What's this I hear about you getting shot?"

"I..."

"We talked about this!" yells Mom.

Teenager mode activates on its own. I roll my eyes and sigh at the ceiling. "Aww, Mom. It's not a big deal. Just a nine-millimeter to the chest. It's not like I messed around with any of the dangerous calibers like .45 or .357."

Sierra shakes her head. "You are a dork."

"Just say no to bullets," mutters Dad, who appears about halfway between wanting to laugh and having a nervous breakdown. "Dear, have you, uhh, been messing with small calibers for long? You know they're a gateway that leads to harder and harder artillery."

"Jonathan!" snaps Mom. "You're not helping." She stares at me making her 'how could you do this to me again' face. "How do you think I felt when Hunter shows up at almost midnight, tells us someone shot you and can he have one of your clean shirts to bring to you?"

Sigh. I trudge around the sofa and sit next to my mother. She's trying to be angry with me for scaring her but can't resist grabbing me and clinging like I'm a giant teddy bear. "It's not my fault. I didn't even do anything."

"Someone just shot you for no reason?" asks Sierra. "Did you at least kick their ass?"

Whoa. Mom is really upset. She didn't even flinch when Sierra said 'ass.' Admittedly, it's not the worst word she could've used, and she is twelve now.

"No. They got seriously lucky. Two idiots on the other side of the parking lot tried to shoot each other and I caught a cheap stray shot from behind. First one took me out."

Dad relocates himself to sit on my other side and grabs my hand. He's worried, too, but you don't spend most of your life hiding from reality in fantasy and science fiction movies without being able to comprehend certain things. Enough of him knows me getting shot isn't a big deal anymore, but there's still enough 'normal' in him where he can't completely withstand the idea of me being shot as 'merely annoying.'

"Why are you out at all hours experimenting with bullets?" asks Mom.

Good. She's calming down enough to run with my joke. Or she's divorced herself from reality.

"Two guys erupted into a sudden argument in the parking lot. I had no idea they were going to start shooting at each other until after I caught a stray bullet. Like, legit, the first damn bullet the one guy fired missed the other dude and hit me right in the heart."

Sierra scrunches her nose. "That's crazy bad luck. Are you sure they weren't aiming for you on purpose?"

I shrug. "Umm. Can't say for sure since I had my back to them, but why would they? There's no reason for them to care about me. I don't think I've pissed anyone off lately."

"Could they have been gangbangers looking to kill some random person?" asks Dad. "Some kinda initiation thing?"

"No idea. Maybe." I scratch my head. "Gonna need a Ouija board to ask them."

"Yesssss." Sierra drags a fist downward in a gesture of victory. "Buttheads who shot you won a Darwin award."

"Who killed them?" asks Mom. "The police?"

"No. Hunter said that after I went down, they shot each other in the face at pretty much the same instant. It was over so fast he doesn't think they even noticed they hit me. There is something weird though."

Mom throws her hands up. "Oh, do point out how my daughter being shot and us talking about bullets like we caught you experimenting with marijuana is not already weird."

I hug her, chuckling. "Hunter saw a large black pickup truck lurking near the parking lot. It started following us after he threw me in the car and took off, but it only matched us for two turns before going in a different direction."

"Cops?" Sierra sits up straighter. "FBI maybe?"

"More likely the PIBs keeping tabs on me," I say. "Cops or FBI would not have let Hunter steal a dead body from a crime scene. The PIBs would be aware of what I am and let him take me away to hide and recover."

Mom shudders.

"I dunno." Dad rubs his chin. "Shady government agencies have an exclusive deal with Chevrolet for black Tahoes or Suburbans. A pickup truck seems odd. Was it a Ford or a Chevy?"

"Sare said it was driving around and not broken down," yells Sam from upstairs. "Had to be a Chevy."

I stare at Dad. "No idea, I wasn't exactly paying attention at the time."

"You're okay?" asks Mom in a vulnerable voice totally unlike her.

"Fine." I grab the bottom of my shirt. "Look, not even a scratch."

Dad turns away an instant before I lift my shirt so Mom can see there's not a mark on me... except for the faint white line Scott's knife left behind. Alas, that one's not going anywhere. Fortunately, it's hard to notice unless pointed out.

A tangible wave of relief falls off Mom. I think she might've been expecting a gore festival under my shirt. Like, gee, Mom. Relax. It's only a 9mm. The worst thing you'd have seen is a little hole. Not like that dude in *Predator* who had his entire chest cored out.

Sierra also seems comforted at the complete lack of blood, bruises, or visible damage. "How many times did they hit you?"

"At least twice." I lower the shirt. "If I got hit more than that, I didn't feel it. Safe to look again, Dad."

He gets up from the recliner and sits next to me, rubbing my back. "If you got hit more than twice by stray bullets, I'd say they weren't as stray as you're assuming." He shakes his head. "Damn glad Hunter's a fast thinker."

"Ack." I look back and forth between my parents. "Was he okay last night? Seeing me get shot didn't mess him up, did it? He seemed fine this afternoon."

"A little, I think." Dad pats my shoulder. "Knowing it won't really harm you too much only helps so much."

Mom hugs me close. "Are you all right, dear?"

"Yep. I feel fine. In fact, I—"

My breath catches in my throat. For a second, I can't breathe in or out. Despite not needing to, my body is so committed to being lifelike, panic at an obstructed airway is a reflex. I make fish out of water face while grabbing my throat. Mom goes into controlled panic mode.

"She's choking," yells Sierra.

Dad swats me between the shoulder blades—and I hock up a bullet, which lands in my mother's lap. Tears in my eyes, I gulp down a huge lungful of air I don't need… but it feels awesome.

She stares down at the bullet for a few seconds before picking it up with the same lack of disgust she applies to cleaning up our vomit or wiping snot with her bare hands when we were really small.

"Cool," whispers Sierra.

Dad plucks the bullet from Mom's palm. "Yeah, that's a 9mm all right."

As if he'd know. Given the amount of time Sierra's put into *Call of Duty*, she's probably more of a firearm expert than he is. Dad's experience with guns is strictly limited to video games and roleplaying game sourcebooks for futuristic settings, and most of that stuff is all made up.

"Honestly…" Mom face-palms. "I'm never going to get used to this."

17

SIX-INCH FANGS

As one might expect, the news of her daughter being shot soon followed by watching me spit up a bullet upset Mom.

Two glasses of wine later, guess who's driving Sophia to her dance class. Hint: it's not Mom. I don't mind. It's fun spending time with my kid sis especially when she's doing something she loves. It's nicer than taking Sam and Sierra to Taekwondo due to the lack of constant shouting. Tonight, the dance class is working on stuff for an upcoming recital. Hmm. That's an odd word. 'Dance recital' sounds all sorts of frilly and formal and high-society. They're doing some manner of performance routine set to music that's probably within the realm of heavy metal. Definitely at least hard rock.

I think it's like one of those mishmash situations like that Shakespeare-in-the-modern-world movie. Whatever it is, the kids seem to be having a blast. That arrogant piece of work Lindsey Carr is ignoring Megan and Sophia as if they don't exist. My command is holding. Good. Dance class is entirely fun, peaceful, and without conflict. One might say peaceful and without conflict are redundant, but I mean peaceful in the sense of the room not being filled with screaming children like in Sam's taekwondo class. Before becoming a vampire, that place always gave me a headache. I honestly don't know how the instructors deal with it. The loud music even spares me from having to listen to the two cougars fantasizing about their pool guy.

When class ends, Sophia and Megan hurry over to where I'm sitting among the parents.

"Can we give Meg a ride home?" asks Sophia. "Her mom had to go back into work. I, umm, maybe told her it's okay already."

I laugh. "Sure. No problem."

Megan grins. "Thank you."

She won't be home alone. Her dad might work a night shift, but they share a house with one set of grandparents, neither of whom is comfortable driving at night. Dropping her off adds about twenty minutes of drive time, but it's not like I have anywhere specific to be tonight. We exit the studio along with the rush of other dance students and parents.

"Butthead alert," says Sophia when we're about halfway across the parking lot.

I follow her stare to a pair of skinny guys with wannabe lumberjack beards, flannel shirts and hemp sandals. They're both close to thirty, one a few years shy of it, the other a few years past it. The younger of the two has dark brown hair styled short, neat, and puffy. His associate is demonstrating why certain people should not attempt dreadlocks. His hair's lighter brown and tinted green in spots. Can't tell if it's a side effect of not washing his hair in months or if it's residual THC. Both of them are vampires. It's as obvious to me as looking at them. Another obvious thing: they're clearly walking toward us. Klepto appears out of thin air on Sophia's shoulder—no purple flash of light this time—and emits the cutest little growl ever.

Hipster vamps means only one thing: Eleanor St. Ives. This is not going to end well no matter what happens in the next two minutes. Honestly, I've been waiting for her grudge to come around and manifest in some sort of badness. Here it is. I take Sophia and Megan's hands and start veering off to one side, trying to avoid the two guys. They adjust course to follow, and speed up.

The younger of the two men raises a hand in a gesture of greeting. "We just want a word."

I got a word for you. Wait, no. I'm thinking of *two* words. Grr. There's no way I'm outrunning vampires while towing Sophia and Megan. Just Sophia, I might be able to since she's so willowy. Not making a crack at Meg's weight. Even Ashley would slow me down too much to get away and we're about the same size. Vampire flight is all sports car and no truck. Good on speed, bad on weight carrying. Also, as an Innocent, I'm not the strongest flier. Don't care. Being able to do it at all is awesome. So what if I can't break 200 miles an hour or lift too much extra weight.

So, I stop short and take up a defensive posture in front of the girls. "What?"

The hipsters approach to a reasonable conversation distance.

"Might we have a word with fewer ears about?" asks the failed dreadlock experiment.

"Nope. You're not going to separate me from the girls. Sophia knows everything and Megan won't remember."

"Fair enough," says Bad Hair Day. "I'm Caleb, and this is Nathan."

Nathan lazily swipes a hand to one side in a 'sup wave.

Megan glances at me. "What do you mean I won't remember?"

"Sare means like you 'won't remember' in quotes," whispers Sophia. "Like if anyone asks."

"Ohhh..." Megan's eyes widen. "Are they doing crime?"

"No," says Sophia. "Just ignore them."

Nathan purses his lips, pausing for a moment before speaking as if he's rewriting his script to edit for children or something. "Eleanor would like your assistance with a project."

I blink. "Well, this is new. She's *asking*? Must mean she's desperate."

"The woman doesn't hate you," says Caleb, shaking his head. "That would require she had emotions."

Wow, his beard didn't move at all. It's like a rounded, ten-inch brown chin extension. Probably got more beeswax in there than in an active hive.

Nathan laughs.

"Okay, fair point." I smirk. "The woman makes Spock look like a stand-up comedian."

Both guys snicker.

"So, umm. What could she possibly need my help with? I'm kinda busy trying to be normal and stay out of everyone's way."

Caleb scratches at the side of his neck. "I don't have too many details, but if you don't help, a little girl might end up dead."

Sophia gasps. Megan conducts a test on the tensile strength of my finger bones. Damn girl, you have a grip.

In an instant, my attitude shifts from 'teenager trying to dodge a chore' to 'murderous, protective fury'. I growl.

"Not them." Nathan points at the girls behind me. "Another kid. We're not trying to make a threat here."

It takes me a few seconds to dial back the rage. I scowl. This is going to bite me in the ass with six-inch fangs, I just know it. Eleanor St. Ives probably kidnapped some random child knowing she could easily manipulate me with guilt. If I don't do what she wants, some kid dies.

Sneaky bitch. Aurélie's decree of protection applies to my family and siblings, not every child in the area. "Okay, fine. What do I need to do?"

Caleb gestures at the girls. "Take these two home or wherever you were going, then go here." He hands me a business card. "No great rush, but she'd appreciate it if you showed up at some point tonight. Sooner the better."

It's blank except for a handwritten address. South Bennett Street in the Industrial District.

"All right. I'll go. Can't promise I'll be able to help her with whatever she wants, but I'll at least talk to her."

Sophia tugs on my arm, staring desperately up at me as if to say 'don't do it.'

"Excellent. Enjoy the rest of your night." Nathan salutes me with two fingers before he and his friend walk away.

"Sare," whispers Sophia. "It's a trap."

I lead the girls over to the Sentra. "St. Ives is many things. Heartless, greedy, driven... but she's not stupid. There is no way her asking me to meet her somewhere then attacking me won't get back to Aurélie and cause her a major headache."

"Umm." Sophia grinds her toe into the parking lot. "I guess. Promise me you won't do anything too reckless?"

"I'll try."

We get in the car.

Sophia lets Megan have the passenger side since my car doesn't have the roomiest back seat. She drapes herself between the two front seats, staring at me. "Do more than try."

"Soph, if you saw that guy throw kittens in the river, you'd jump right in after them without even thinking about how dangerous it could be for you."

She exhales hard. "Not exactly. I'd scream first. But, yeah. I'd totally do it."

"Same thing here. St. Ives is about to metaphorically throw some random kid into the water. I gotta jump in and try to save her. Kids and kittens are the same."

"Yeah." Sophia laughs. "Kittens are just cat kids."

"Mew," says Klepto, holding her head up approvingly.

"So, umm, what am I not supposed to remember?" asks Megan. "You didn't talk about anything but some woman who's gonna kill a little girl."

I stare at her.

Megan blinks. "What were we talking about? I think I just had a huge brain fart."

Sophia starts chattering about the dance routines they spent the last hour or so practicing. I settle in for the ride, dreading what I'm going to walk into.

18

CHLOE

W hile it may be true that most times I get caught in a vampire fight, I end up naked, there's no reason to make it easier on fate. Showing up at St. Ives' place in a midriff-baring T-shirt, denim short-shorts, and flip-flops is like starting the race halfway to the finish line. So, after dropping Megan off at her house and bringing Sophia home, I head to my room to change.

Full-length jeans, full T-shirt, long-sleeved flannel over that, socks, and poop stompers. Yeah, I know. My mom doesn't like the phrase shit-kickers. But I have serious boots. It may be August, but this is still the Pacific Northwest. Even a mortal could wear this outfit at night now and not be too uncomfortable. People won't think I'm nuts, just one of those girls who's always cold.

Right. Okay, you crazy mad scientist vampire… what do you want from me?

I explain the situation to the 'rents, send a text to Aurélie advising her that St. Ives has requested a meeting and claims to be peaceful, then head out the door. It's so tempting to ask Sam if he can somehow get Max to follow me. A hellhound is a vampire's worst nightmare. He's like a flamethrower with legs, claws, and armor. He's also basically a dog. With Sam, he acts pretty much like a golden retriever with armored chitin and horns. The creepiest thing about him is the tail. Doesn't look like a tail as much as black exposed spinal cord tipped with a blade. Reminds me of the aliens' tails from *Aliens*. Hmm. Makes me wonder if H.R. Geiger saw real demons. Thankfully, Max's natural state in the mortal dimension is invisibility. I can't even see him unless he wants me to.

Apparently, Sam sees him all the time. Still not sure if it's a Sam thing or if Max lets the boy see him.

Yeah, my family is weird.

I fly to the Industrial District adjacent to the Duwamish Waterway. Doesn't take me too long to find South Bennett Street, and the seemingly abandoned warehouse indicated on the business card. No one appears to be anywhere in the area. The place is in better shape than the old riverside factory I used for shelter in Chicago. Probably only empty for a year or two.

Just as I'm about to start looking around for Ashton Kutcher and a camera crew, the front door opens. A tall, rail-thin woman with waist-length blonde hair and a super-expensive looking outfit steps one foot outside and waves at me in a beckoning manner. She's wearing a dark silver metal choker with an onyx square at the front bearing a Japanese character. Tiny lights flicker from an elaborate earpiece worthy of a science fiction movie. Her beige blazer over a charcoal-grey blouse and a tight black skirt makes her look like a cross between a sales rep at a Ferrari dealership and the concierge for a pleasure palace in some neo-noir cyberpunk dystopian future where clients go in to have their souls drained out of their bodies and adore every minute of it. Bit heavy on the eyeshadow, if my opinion matters.

Her expression is so emotionless, I'm momentarily stuck questioning if golems are a thing. Is this a real person or did St. Ives make an android? A hint of annoyance in her face at me still standing there proves otherwise.

I steel myself and walk over to Lurch's little sister. She's about a foot taller than me. Looks mid-twenties but carries herself mid-thirties. Probably was in her thirties when made into a vampire and the change gave her a serious Botox job.

"Hi. I'm Sarah."

"I know," says the woman. "This way."

Ooh. Not only does she look like Lurch's little sister, she has his job, too. Getting the door. Same demeanor. Not much on casual conversation, it seems. Not comparing her to Lurch because she's ugly. Far from it. Just... I dunno. Something about her face. Strong eyebrow line. Angular. Tall as hell. The straightness and perfection of her hair defies physics the same way I do whenever I fly. The dry tone and wordlessness is also kinda Lurch-y.

Her black high heels click on the floor, echoing across a cavernous room of empty steel shelves. We cross to the other side of the space and go into a hall. Three doors down on the left, we enter a room that looks to have once been a break area with multiple vending machines, tables, and a sink counter.

The tall blonde approaches a snack vending machine with a numeric keypad on it where people are supposed to type the code for whatever item they want. She taps in a nine-digit code, which causes the entire vending machine to slide backward into the wall.

Whoa. I momentarily forget entirely about fearing for my life as the coolness factor of a motorized secret door takes over. The machine retreats enough to let us into a concealed area where about twenty feet of hidden passageway leads to a platform elevator. It's essentially a ten-by-ten-foot square slab of steel with only the most basic hint of a railing around it. Go figure, a vampire mad scientist's lair isn't OSHA compliant.

I jump at the sudden start of the motors responsible for moving the vending machine, twisting to look over my shoulder at the enormous box sliding back into place. Well, guess I'm trapped now. All I can do is hope St. Ives isn't pulling a trick on me. Am I really that easy to manipulate? Just say a kid's going to die if you don't do <random task>? Yeah. Guess I am.

The woman steps onto the platform elevator, turns to face me, and clasps her hands in front of herself.

Right. On with it I suppose. I walk over to stand next to her.

"Amelia," says the woman.

Aha. The part of her brain responsible for processing social cues finally realized I introduced myself before, and the appropriate response is to tell me her name.

"Hi."

She reaches out to push a button on the wall. The elevator sinks downward without much sound or fuss. Faint squeaking, which a human couldn't hear, tells me a hydraulic piston supports the platform. Super basic. Guess they don't build evil villain lairs like they used to, huh?

The elevator lets us down into the corner of a large storage room a corridor with a double-height ceiling.

"This way." Amelia pushes the little gate in the railing open and walks off the platform.

I follow her across the storage room, down a short corridor, and through a series of crazy looking labs. Some of it feels like the interior of an ordinary hospital or whatever, but there's a lot of crazy machinery I don't recognize with strange coils, bulbs, or wires.

"Whoa. This is very *Young Frankenstein*."

Amelia glances back at me. "What does that mean?"

"Movie reference. You know… a Mel Brooks version of a mad scientist."

She frowns. Can't tell if she still doesn't understand what I mean or if she's annoyed I'm referring to St. Ives as a mad scientist. Come on, though. Look at this stuff! The only thing missing from this place is a surgical table capable of being extended out through the roof to catch lightning.

We finally enter another, smaller lab space packed with various pieces of electronic equipment. I've seen similar stuff in the science building at SCC. This room gives off a much less crazy vibe. Eight or nine vampires stand around the same sort of black-topped table they had in my high school's chemistry classroom, only this one's huge. I recognize Eleanor St. Ives among them, also Pascal Ivanov, another academic. The only other two I recognize are the hipsters who met me in the parking lot by the dance studio. Everyone else looks like a grad student from MIT.

A big grey cat carrier sits on the table. It's been modified slightly: two large padlocks stick out the side to keep the front gate from opening. Normally, portable kennels don't lock. What the heck kind of weird mad-science creature did they put in there? Oh, ugh. Please don't be doing animal experiments in here. Please? Eleanor glances at me with the faintest eyebrow raise as if she's surprised I actually showed up. The woman's kinda like a middle-aged Jodie Foster doing an impression of Sigourney Weaver playing the evil mad scientist in an *Austin Powers* movie. She's even got the lab coat and the 'I want to talk to the manager' hairdo.

Rattling from the cat carrier gets louder.

I approach the table. Yeah, I'm dreading what I'm going to see but I can't help myself. The reality is even more shocking than the skinless, demonic, half-vampire cat/dog I expect. Stuffed into this portable kennel is a pale, black-haired little girl of around seven years old. She's got her fingers through the grid of the cage door, trying as hard as she can to break out. I can't see too much of her since she's curled up, knees to shoulders without much room to move. She appears to be wearing fairly normal stuff for a kid: a peach-colored shirt and aqua tights. But I'm guessing. All I can see of her is head, shoulders, knees, and fingers. Looks reasonably clean and unhurt. Deep blue eyes like sapphires set in the porcelain face of an angelic doll widen when she notices me.

Shock lasts a few seconds, then I get pissed off and storm right over to Eleanor. "What the hell are you doing?" I shout. "Why do you have a little kid in a cat carrier?"

Pascal holds up a finger. "Actually, it's a dog transport. A *cat* carrier would have been uncomfortably small."

The kid gives him the finger.

"Beside the point." I thrust an arm at Eleanor. "Why did you put a child in a damn kennel?"

She folds her arms, talking to me in a tone like she's addressing an idiot who can't see the obvious. "She is in there so she does not run off."

"Shit yeah, I'm gonna run away," yells the child. "Bitch, you wanna kill me!"

I do a double take, mentally gasping in shock at the language coming out of this kid. What kind of damage happened here? I try to peek into her head and—can't. Oh, holy shit. My jaw drops open. This kid's a freakin' vampire. "Oh... damn."

"Ahh. Now you realize." Eleanor gives me a curt nod. "We need to address this problem."

"Fuck you, lady!" yells the kid. "I'm not Problem. My name is Chloe!"

I cringe. It's just not right hearing those words in such a high-pitched childish voice. Mom would drop dead on the spot. Though, honestly, a child in a kennel bothers me a hundred times more than an F-bomb. Words are just words. "Is she really like a grown up stuck in a kid's body or something?"

"No." Eleanor waves dismissively. "She's from New Jersey."

I blink. "What?"

"The little one has quite a mouth on her," says Eleanor in a flat voice—stating fact without opinion.

Chloe lets out an enraged scream and stomp-kicks at the back of the kennel. A pink-purple glow fills the kennel each time her foot strikes the back end. She must have lights in her sneakers. The dog carrier jolts across the table an inch or so with each kick but doesn't go far before she gives up. "Let me outta here!"

Of course, it's a dumb question to ask if she's really an adult. I asked before thinking because I'm rejecting the concept of someone turning a little kid. Barring some kind of possessed doll situation where an old ghost jumped into another body, it's not possible. I know how vampires work. I'm stuck as a teenager forever, both physically and mentally. That kid is as old as she appears to be, even if she's been a vampire for a hundred years.

"Oh, wow…" I stare mournfully at the furious child, not even fully aware that I've totally forgotten about the possibility Eleanor could be a threat to me. I'm standing next to her like we're a pair of sane adults encountering a ridiculous and tragic situation. "What happened?"

Eleanor unfolds her arms. "Some associates of mine discovered her recently and brought her here before she attracted or caused any trouble."

I blink, then look over at her. "What do you need me for?"

"Your Innocent blood is something of an enigma to us. I am hoping to study it in hopes of perhaps discovering a way to reverse the Transference for this child. I am afraid if I'm unable to do so, we will have to destroy her."

I stare at her, horrified.

"Fuck that!" yells Chloe, banging on the kennel door. "Let me outta here right now!"

The kid thrashes about so much trying to bust out of the carrier I can't help but think of that movie *Mouse Hunt* with the extremely dangerous 'Catzilla' in the box. Except for Eleanor, Pascal, and Amelia, the other vampires in the room appear afraid to get too close to the kennel. I'm wondering what the hell it's made out of if she's unable to break out of it. Looks like heavy-duty plastic and steel. It's nowhere near big enough to hold an adult pit bull, more like a beagle-sized animal. She doesn't have much room in there, but even a vampire her size should be able to summon the strength to crack plastic. Maybe the kid's so new at being a vampire she doesn't know she can make herself stronger? I didn't either at first but kinda figured it out pretty fast. Me being locked in a morgue cooler is about the same level of claustrophobic as a kennel carrier is to this kid, except the space isn't as long. She doesn't have enough room to lie down flat in there.

My brain stops finding the Catzilla comparison funny and I get all kinds of pissed off at the idea of a caged child again. But… vampire. Shit. This is the dreaded worst case scenario I'd been worrying about in regard to my siblings. And Chloe's even younger than Sam. To be fair, I'd be a ton less worried about Sam as a vampire. The boy has maturity and self-control far in excess of what any ten-year-old boy ought to have. Runs in the family. We're all kinda smart, risk-averse, and careful.

Mostly.

Part of me wants to demand they release her right away but another part is also afraid of what she might do. It's also a little strange to me that as upset as this child is, she's not screaming for Mommy or Daddy.

"Why do you think my blood could help you reverse the Transference?" I ask, barely over a whisper.

Chloe stops trying to break out and just fumes, glaring at us through the grid of bars in front of her face.

"If you can believe it..." Eleanor almost smiles. "I believe she may be an Innocent as well. Despite her mouth."

"Eat shit," mutters Chloe.

DEAL WITH THE DEVIL

There are times in life when decisions warrant long periods of careful consideration.

This is one of those times, but my heart gets the better of my brain. Giving Eleanor St. Ives samples of my blood is a scary concept. Who knows what she might do with it to gain power or influence over me in the future? I don't know for sure anything of that nature is even possible without the use of mysticism. She's no mystic, so it's probably not too dangerous.

Klepto can always get it back if need be.

And… there's a little girl in a kennel. I can't just sit here and let that continue. I definitely can't let them destroy her just because she *might* cause problems. What other choice do I have?

"Okay… I'll help." I point at Eleanor. "On one condition: if whatever you try to do fails to reverse the Transference in Chloe, she is not to be harmed."

Eleanor scoffs. "We cannot allow a vampire that age to exist. They are completely incapable of surviving on their own."

"I'm not a wimp," grumbles Chloe before raising her voice to an almost shout. "I was doing okay before your assheads grabbed me."

"You misunderstand me, girl." Eleanor leans closer to the kennel. No, she's not trying to be consoling—don't think she has it in her—she's curious. A scientist studying a rat in a box. "You appear to be a small child. You will *forever* appear to be a small child. Anyone who sees you roaming around after dark will not simply stand there. They will either call the mortal authorities or try to catch you, assuming you are lost, abandoned, in trouble, or something of that sort."

Chloe frowns. "Bet they won't put me in a cage."

Eleanor stands up. "If they realized what you are, they'd do much worse." She faces me. "My point is... while she might have the physical powers necessary to survive, it's not feasible in the modern world. We are no longer living in the age where a vampire this size will merely cause rumors of ghost children in the woods or some such thing. Even if she has the capacity to be mindful of the situation, which I doubt considering how small she is, she will invariably draw too much attention to our kind."

I fidget, feeling like a kid getting yelled at by the teacher for not doing my homework.

"This girl will require constant assistance in much the same way as any other child her age needs a parent." Eleanor folds her arms. "There isn't a vampire in the world who wants to be saddled with the responsibility of taking care of a child forever."

Yeah... vampires want to go out and have fun. Party. Make big deals. Have fancy yachts, castles, soirees, and so on. No vampire in the world could possibly be happy sitting at home most of the time... right? Just playing video games, reading, watching movies... pretending to go to college. What kind of vampire could tolerate that for eternity?

I fidget more... and make the mistake of looking at the kennel.

Chloe's hitting me with the Puss 'N Boots eyes. The stare is hard for me to resist normally. The same stare from behind double-padlocked steel bars twists my guts. Apparently, she's figured out I'm the only one in the room with functioning emotions. This kid isn't merely in a kennel... she's at a kill shelter.

Eleanor raises an eyebrow. "Or is there?"

Sigh. "If it's that or you're going to kill her, yes. I'll accept responsibility for her."

Somewhere in downtown Seattle, Stefano Bianchi just giggled in delight and doesn't know why. I've just offered him a gift-wrapped means to make my unlife a living hell. If this Chloe situation doesn't blow up to the point he demands *my* destruction, he's going to mock me for the rest of time if I fail to keep this kid from being destroyed. For the next 700 years, every time he sees me after they throw her into the sun, he'll ask me how 'my daughter' is doing.

On the other hand, Aurélie might help, too. Chloe is the *ultimate* haunted doll. While I am well aware my vampire faerie godmother can be flighty and fickle, and there's an absolute zero chance she'll want to be Chloe's 'mom' forever, she will definitely babysit. I hope.

Again, I glance at the kid. Tiny fingers clutch the steel grid beneath her chin. She's gone from furious to begging silently. Dammit. I'm so freakin' easy to manipulate. I shift my stare to Eleanor once more. "I will help if you swear she won't be destroyed 'just because.' And... can you *please* let her out of that damned kennel already?"

"What do you mean 'just because'" asks Chloe. "And yeah, open this fuckin' door."

I cringe. "Will you please stop using words like that? You're too little."

Chloe rattles the cage, snarling. "I'm stuck in a fuckin' cat carrier. I'm a little pissed off. You want polite? Let me out."

"Hmm." Eleanor ponders for a minute. Considering her academic brain, her minute or two of thinking is like me stuck on a quandary for a week. "Let me speak with the others. If they agree, be aware that you will be responsible for her."

Ugh. I know what that means. If Chloe has a fit of immaturity and throws a tantrum that exposes the existence of vampires to the mortal world, all the other vamps in Seattle are going to come after me like *I* did it. But... they're going to kill a child if I don't make this deal.

So what if it's technically killing her a second time? The first time doesn't really count. She's still here. If the elders knew who gave a little kid the Transference, they've probably already destroyed them. Then again, this isn't Europe where tradition is oppressive. Maybe they've just stopped inviting her sire to parties for having horrible manners.

"All right." I nod at Eleanor. "Do it."

Great. I've made a deal with the devil... or Eleanor St. Ives. Not sure there's much of a difference.

Her expression gives off an ever so slight trace of whimsy. "Look on the bright side, Sarah."

"Bright side?"

"Yes." She flares her eyebrows. "You will soon not be the vampire Stefano has the biggest problem with."

"Yeah, right up until he finds out who agreed to take care of her." I frown. "He's gonna *love* this."

TO GRANDMOTHER'S HOUSE

S o much for a peaceful, fun, normal summer.

Most of it was fun at least. We're in the first week of August, so there's more summer behind me than in front right now. Not a total loss. Ever have that feeling like you know you just screwed up huge but can't change it and would totally do it again? Ugh. Hopefully, I haven't bitten off more than I can chew.

Chloe clings to my back, thrilled to bits to be out of the kennel. It finally took her saying, "Bitch, I'm seven, not stupid" for Eleanor to accept the child understood the gravity of her situation and unlock the kennel. She crawled right out and practically jumped on me, clinging. Other than being a vampire, she appears to be in good health. Her clothing—a peach-colored shirt with appliqué hearts, aqua tights, purple socks, and purple sneakers with pink lights in the soles—also seemed fairly new and in okay shape. She looked as if she'd maybe spent a couple days in the same outfit, sleeping in basements or similar locations. Bit dusty, but not filthy. She doesn't even smell like wet city.

My gut tells me she's been a vampire for less than a week. Alas, my gut tells me science—even mad science—probably can't undo this. St. Ives is probably scrambling like hell to find a 'cure' assuming there's a limited window post-Transference for anything to work.

Chloe needs to stay with me or a designated babysitter who is also a vampire. She's not to run off on her own or make a spectacle of herself when mortals can see. The girl readily agreed to accept the arrangement. I don't think she preferred being on her own, it just happened to be that way. Apparently, the one who made her also took off without a trace.

That's two vampires I now know of with horrible sires.

Dalton didn't abandon me. He's just got some dodgy luck as he'd say. Authorities found my body before he could finish shredding Scott. He did come back to take me under his wing. I'm the one who chose to go home. He only left me to my own devices after I made that choice. Tilloa and Chloe both got turned and ditched. Tilloa never saw her sire. I suspect Chloe did, but she didn't say much beyond it was a man and he 'helped' her, but he's kinda scary.

Helped could mean anything. Cross the street? Chased away something scarier? For all I know, some vampire with a sweet tooth tried to feed on her, took too much, and panicked. That thing with blood tasting like mortal food? Yeah, it's not just me. Most vampires do that. Shadows don't. To them, blood tastes like blood... but they enjoy the taste. Blech. While frowned on, some vampires do occasionally nibble on kids for the proverbial sugar rush. It's quite dangerous though. Nothing gets mobs of people with torches and pitchforks as riled up as stories of some supernatural monster attacking children.

And, I'm getting all sorts of heartbroken and angry all over again thinking about it, even if the vast majority don't kill. Much like chocolate, no one eats an entire meal's worth of kid blood. Just a sip or two as a treat. Usually anyway.

Something obviously went wrong in Chloe's case.

It's so weird having her on my back, giggling in delight as we fly. She's not the least bit afraid of being up high. She can't fly and didn't even know it possible. The girl figured out she'd become a vampire pretty quick, but other than biting people, thought reading, and short mental commands, she hasn't really explored her powers yet. Maybe she can fly, maybe she can't. I don't know if there's any correlation to physical age and vampire ability. Flight came to me easy on my first night as a vampire thanks to the power of nope! I refused to fall into a puddle of nasty water and, well, stopped falling.

"What's going on with your parents?" I ask.

"I don't wanna talk about them," snaps Chloe, her mood going black enough for me to feel the fear and loathing radiating from her.

Oh, shit. This can of worms just keeps getting deeper and more rotten. Well, no need to force the issue now. It can wait.

"Okay. I'm just asking in case they might be looking for you. Are you like on any missing kid databases?"

"No. There's no one looking for me. No one at all."

Her voice is so cold and calm, I can't decide if I should feel extreme pity for her or be afraid. She's either incredibly lonely—or she murdered everyone who ever knew her. She rests her head against the back of my neck. Gonna guess lonely.

I'm quiet, unable to think of anything to say. The vast cityscape of Seattle glides on below us, people totally unaware we're up here or vampires exist. In hindsight, I think most times I used to feel like I wasn't alone somewhere, I probably had a vampire sizing me up for a bite—or encountered one of the thousands of other things that really do exist and no one believes in.

My thoughts turn to the idea of combining the volatile emotional temperament of a child with the powers of a vampire. Even though her body and mind are frozen forever as she was at the moment of the Transference, her vampire abilities will gain strength over time. She's also an Innocent, so she'll never command vast fearsome powers; however, the basic parts of being a vampire do get stronger. Two centuries from now, if she still exists, she'll be able to make herself as strong as a Terminator—but she'll still have the same emotional maturity as a seven-year-old. It's basically like giving a little kid a loaded gun and hoping nothing bad happens. Normal seven-year-olds can throw epic tantrums when they don't get their way. Imagine one capable of flipping cars. Well, small cars.

As much as the idea of destroying her permanently horrifies me to my core, I do understand the elders' worries. Really, though. It's laziness. They'd rather just destroy her than watch her. As far as I'm concerned, it makes them no better than that woman who gave her four-year-old kid sleeping pills so she could go out to party and nearly killed the boy.

Okay, fine. All I want to do as a vampire is exist and be normal. I sit at home almost every night anyway. I'll watch the kid. How bad can keeping tabs on a seven-year-old be? It's not like she's two… or an infant who can't sleep through the day. I won't have to worry about PTA meetings or soccer practice or keeping up with doctor visits, or any of the normal heart attacks and headaches that come with being responsible for a tiny human. Sigh. Of course, she's not going to have any friends her age or experience anything even close to resembling a normal life.

But I can try. It's way better than living with the guilt of her being destroyed and me knowing I might've been able to prevent it.

Given my recent possessive feelings toward Ashley, I'm not even sure having a vampire kid around is horrifying. I mean, really. Why is it so sad? Sure, she died, but… she didn't stay dead. The sad part is the notion of death. But that happened already. Now, she can't get sick. She doesn't have to be afraid of anyone. She'll forever enjoy the bliss of childhood innocence, spared from having to grow up in a mean, exploitative world that sucks all the joy out of everyone in a nine-to-five rat maze.

Whatever. No point overthinking it. It's done already.

St. Ives told Wolent about the situation and me, like a dumbass, agreed to be responsible for Chloe without regard whatsoever about consequences. Gee, committing to a huge choice without thinking about consequences. Yep. I am a teenager. Ugh. If this kid causes all hell to break loose, not only am I going to get in a shitload of trouble, they're going to force *me* to be the one who destroys her. It's like they all know this is doomed to fail and they want to drive home the object lesson in my head. If I'm forced to destroy this innocent kid for no reason other than her childish impulsiveness caused a scene that threatened to expose our existence, I'm never going to demand they spare a kid vampire ever again —or so they think.

Damn my squishy heart.

This is going to finally be what pushes me past the edge of sanity, isn't it? The single event that causes the dark vampire part of my psyche to take over and turn me into a nocturnal monster. There's no way I'm going to be able to destroy her. This whole situation is doomed. It's going to blow up and destroy everything: me, my family, my friends, any respect Wolent had for me... ugh.

I'm not going to let it get to that point. If St. Ives can't develop a way to undo this and give Chloe her mortality back, I'm going to make damn sure the kid behaves. And really, I don't get the sense she's the type of child to be disobedient or defiant or cause trouble just to do it. Sure, she got mouthy with Eleanor but I don't blame her. If someone stuffed me in a cat carrier, I'd probably drop an F-bomb or six, too. Then again, I am a bit older than her.

"Where are we going?" asks Chloe, bringing the long, moody silence to an end.

"Well, if I'm your mom now, we're basically going to meet your faerie grandmother."

"Ooh!" chirps Chloe. "Is she a real faerie?"

"No. She just looks like one. She's a vampire like us."

"Okay. Umm, do faeries exist?"

"Yep."

Chloe squeals in delight, then cringes. "Will they hate me 'cause I'm a vampire?"

"I don't think so… we're special. Different from most vampires."

"Huh?"

Over the next few minutes, I tell her about Innocents and how we're lifelike and give off feelings of harmlessness and, well, innocence. That part I'm ad-libbing. The word Innocent is just the name of the bloodline. We're neither required nor compelled to be naïve, nice, or sweet. I think some ancient vampire coined the name for the bloodline as sarcastic and condescending. Don't care. However, if we are actually squishy, good, and nice, our power radiates more strongly into the world. Like, if Sophia ever became an Innocent vampire, she could probably walk straight through the middle of a raging vampire war and no one would notice her presence or attack her.

And I'm going to stop thinking about my kid sister becoming a vampire. Besides, she could walk through a vampire war right now and not be noticed or touched. She'd turn herself invisible with magic.

My unlife… sigh.

By the time we land on the patio deck on the fifty-whateverth floor of Aurélie's building, Chloe has a reasonably good understanding of what she is, who Aurélie is, why it's important for her to be nice to Aurélie, and generally why the best thing for her to do is try to act as normal as she possibly can.

Right as my boots touch the deck, she asks a question that cracks my heart wide open.

"What are normal kids like?"

"Umm. What do you mean?"

She slides down my back to her feet and scoots out to stand next to me. "I wasn't normal. Not like the other kids. I had bad parents." She stops herself, then squints up at me. "Still don't wanna talk about them."

"Okay. I'll help you figure out normal."

Chloe's mood evaporates to a smile. "Okay."

We step inside. Aurélie, having sensed my approach, is already on the way over to the sliding glass door.

"Ooh," whispers Chloe. "Is she a princess?"

"Yeah." I wink. "As close as anyone can get these days."

"Her dress is *soooo* pretty." Chloe bounces on her toes.

Upon noticing the child, Aurélie stops short. She stares, her 'aww how cute' expression shifting to alarmed horror. She gasps, presses a hand to her forehead and starts rambling in rapid French. All I can pick out are several repetitions of *mon dieu*. I'm guessing she's stunned and appalled at a seven-year-old vampire. She soon blurs over to us and starts pawing at the kid like we just found her pinned under the wheel of a car after an accident on the highway and she's checking for injuries.

Seeing nothing wrong with the girl, Aurélie, crouched down to eye level with the kid, just gives her this sorrowful stare of 'why'.

"I'm okay." Chloe reaches out and touches the frilly dress. "It's awesome having super powers. No one can ever hurt me again."

Aurélie's attitude shifts from sorrow to complete delight as if she'd discovered another old haunted doll. I update her on the situation and the agreement I made to take responsibility. Chloe sighs in annoyance when I start telling Aurélie about St. Ives working to find a cure.

"What's wrong?" I ask.

"I don't want them to take my powers away." Chloe stomps, making a pink flash come from her sneaker. "I don't gotta be scared now."

Eek. I cringe mentally. This kid didn't have the best parents. In fact, she probably had some seriously horrible ones. We escort Chloe down the hall to the second doll room, the one containing the less old, less expensive, and less haunted ones. After making Chloe promise to be gentle with them, Aurélie gives her permission to play with the dolls.

I should be alarmed at the child's complete non-reaction to Aurélie talking about the dolls as if they were alive and actual people. Then again, kids that age pretend dolls are real and talk to them, so who knows what she's thinking.

Aurélie and I sit on the cushioned divan in the middle of the room while Chloe runs back and forth checking out the dolls.

"Think it might work?" I ask.

"*J'en doute*," says Aurélie. "If such a thing *is* even possible, it would not be through any means Eleanor St. Ives has at her disposal. I have never once heard of such a thing as *inverser le transfert*."

Part of me is almost happy to hear she's likely to stay a vampire. Sentencing her to growing up, growing old, getting a job, and all the crappy parts of life seems cruel. Maybe it's my vampire side selectively ignoring all the good things that can happen in life, but... I can't bring myself to care. Hope this doesn't mean I'm changing too much. I've only been a vampire for a year. I shouldn't be thinking of mortal life as a bad thing this soon, right?

"If it were even possible," says Aurélie, "It would certainly require mysticism, not science."

"Since when does what St. Ives do count as science?" I mumble.

Aurélie giggles.

Yes. It's cute. Yes. It's unnerving. But she's awesome. So difficult to contemplate her age. She looks like she's barely past twenty. Even though she's my 'vampire mom,' appearance wise, she's closer to my 'slightly older sister.' A giggle like that coming out of a woman who I've witnessed rip the heart straight out of a vampire's chest is never not going to be unsettling no matter how much you like them.

Hmm. Mysticism, huh. Wonder if I should involve Sophia or Darren Anderson and his people? I mean, if it comes down to a choice between making her mortal again or she is going to be destroyed, the obvious answer there is mortality. Dare I mix Chloe with Sophia? Cue the nightmares of vampire Littles having a tea party with their new friend. 'But, mommy, I wanted to keep them forever' pleads my imaginary Chloe while justifying why she turned all three of my siblings into undead.

Ugh. Easy Sarah. Don't panic yet.

Chloe, much like any ordinary kid, plays with the dolls. Aurélie and I sit there watching her going back and forth between aww and worry. The strangest, creepiest thing about the kid is I can't tell if she's pretending or really talking to the dolls. To be fair, the creepiness there is all on the dolls, not the child. Some of these dolls might really be able to talk back.

Wolent is a very reasonable man. He'll probably let me handle this situation as long as I can actually handle it. Aurélie randomly suggests letting Chloe stay here for a while.

Yay. Bonus. Don't have to beg her to babysit. And, it's probably better for Chloe to have a 'real' vampire teach her the basics. Also, unlike me, Aurélie *can* read the kid's mind. She's much better equipped to deal with problems before they start up. I'm sure she's doing it to help me out since it's my ass in a sling if this goes pear-shaped. What does the geometric proportion of pears have to do with calamity? Not sure. Ask Dalton. It's his phrase. The British are odd. Anyway, Chloe is happy to spend a couple nights at 'grandma's place.' Also, I'm pretty confident Aurélie is going to oppose arbitrary destruction.

It really is great to have a vampire faerie godmother.

21

FULL CONTACT

Home again, staring at my ceiling.

How anxious am I? Anxious enough to where it's unclear if I'm about to fall asleep or just woke up. The last conversation I had with Aurélie replays in my mind. We will need to be extremely careful regarding Chloe. If anyone sees her here at the house, they will need to be made to forget. Having a seven-year-old around might lead people to ask questions about why she isn't going to school, going outside to play, or growing up.

Haven't told any of the family about her yet. It has to happen eventually, but I'm going to chicken out for as long as possible. Now that I've had time to actually think about what I've agreed to, it's slapping me in the face with the painful possibility the future might force me to make an impossible choice. Keeping Chloe around could demand I take her and go away from my family. If it's leave home or this poor kid gets destroyed, I...

Ugh.

Really don't know how I'd handle that. Obviously, destruction is permanent and me leaving my family to take the kid into hiding won't kill them. Honestly, in another eight years, there's a good chance the Littles will no longer live here. Eight years from now, Sam will be eighteen. Okay. He will still live here unless something super crazy happens and he joins the military straight out of high school. Don't see that happening. He might go to college out of state. But, yeah. When the Littles are adults and not living here, it wouldn't tear my heart out so much to have to distance myself from home and family.

On the other hand, we could keep Chloe in the basement like some super disturbing horror movie plot. Or hell, maybe Eleanor will find a way to undo the Transference. As awesome as being a vampire is, it's really complicated to manage an eternal seven-year-old. I mean, if the world knew about vampires and we didn't have to keep everything so secret, it wouldn't be a big deal.

I'll find a way. There's got to be *something* we can do.

After a while of stewing over unpleasant what-ifs, I finally get the urge to move. Sure enough, it's 3:18 p.m. I've already slept and woken up. Talk about the epic suck of Mondays. I've never woken up under such a heavy cloud of dread before. Oh, crap. Chloe's an Innocent. She's probably awake now, too. Aurélie won't open her eyes until sunset. How is she going to... oh, right. She has 'people.' At least we don't need to keep Chloe's existence a secret from vampire society—or the humans who work for it. That takes a huge weight off.

I randomly text Ashley to ask what's up.

She's at the vet clinic now—and busy—so we can't talk. Over the course of the next several minutes, we have an intermittent conversation in colorful message bubbles. She's planning to go on a date with Raleigh and says tonight's going to be 'the night.'

‹What do you mean by 'the night',› I text.

Her response pops up a minute or so later. ‹You know… full contact.›

Aha. Wait… ‹Thought you guys did that in the forest in Tacoma?›

‹Argh. No, just walking holding hands. Skinny dip and a kiss.›

I'm not sure where the line is that separates messing around from 'going all the way' when it's two girls. There's gotta be a line, but damn if I know where to call it. Pretty easy to say when it's boy and girl or even boy and boy. As soon as the tiny warrior goes spelunking somewhere, that pretty much counts as all the way. You know what? I don't really need to know. As long as Ashley is happy and having fun, who cares about semantics. And hey, she's got an idea there.

‹Cool! Have fun and be safe.›

I let my arm fall over limp to the mattress beside me. The light from the phone screen turns my rumpled bed sheets into a tiny scale model of a snow-covered mountain range. There it is again. Jealousy. Raleigh is hanging out with Ashley, taking her away from me. Life doesn't feel right without her. I know how it sounds but it isn't like that. We're just best friends who should always be together.

It's immature and childish of me.

And kinda strange. Ever since I formally declared her my thrall, she's been on my mind more often. It could simply be that we aren't spending as much time together these days due to school, work, and my nocturnal-ish schedule. Maybe I'm finally adjusted to unlife enough to slip back into my old attitude when all I wanted to do was hang with Ash and have fun.

Okay, Sarah. Grow up. We're not tweens anymore. I can't be jealous of Ashley wanting a romantic partner. What kind of awful friend would I be to deny her that? And yeah, she does have a good idea there. I smile to myself, thinking of Hunter. I wouldn't mind some 'full contact' either... considering the last time I had such activities in mind, I got shot.

Speaking of that, Hunter's okay. I would've mentioned it before, but who wants to hear about a two-hour long cute-mushy-emo phone conversation? He said it was pretty much over before he could snap out of the shock of watching me crumple to the ground. Both punks shot each other dead. Whoever they were, and the reasons behind their argument, will forever be a mystery.

My phone chirps.

I lift my arm back up to read the screen.

‹We don't have to 'be safe.' Ral doesn't have a baby cannon.› A whole string of silly face emotes follows.

I laugh. ‹Dork. You know what I mean. The other kind of safe. Btw. Good idea. Full contact sounds fun. Gonna see if Hunter is busy tonight.›

‹Cool!›

I stare at the little blue speech bubble containing Ashley's response. Out of nowhere, I think of Chloe. Ashley really wants to be a mom someday. Well, vampire-Ashley could adopt a vampire little girl and no one would call that kidnapping. The three of us could be some oddball eternal family.

Ugh.

I bonk myself with the phone. Bad Sarah! I am not killing my best friend.

22

SURREAL

How bad does something have to smell to make a minor demon gag?

I am so glad I don't *need* to breathe. It's almost six, still Monday, and I'm in the Sentra driving Sam and Ronan back home from taekwondo class. Ro and Sam are about as tight as Ashley and me. Since Sam's into the class, Ronan decided to enroll as well... now that his mom can afford it. One of them has reduced their pants to a smoking ruin. Neither one is claiming the fart. Blix is overacting choking to death. Naturally, both boys find this utterly hilarious.

Wait.

Neither boy is claiming ownership. Boys are proud of their gas. The smellier, the better. However, Sam has honor. So does Ronan. It must have come from Blix. Certainly isn't mine. I can't do that anymore. Not that I ever did such a thing. Girls don't do that, after all. Okay, we do, but we don't brag. Well, most of us don't. Sierra has been known to claim triumph on occasion when she drives the boys out of a room.

Anyway... I open some windows.

"Hey, Sare," says Sam. "You're really getting better about the whole sun thing."

"What do you mean?" I look around, caught by a sudden worry something's on fire.

"I mean exactly what I said." He grins. "You're like all normal and stuff during the day now."

With him mentioning it, it does occur to me going outside today doesn't feel uncomfortable at all beyond the unpleasant nerfing of my superhuman senses. "Yeah, wow. I guess I'm levelling up my sunscreen power or whatever."

The boys laugh.

Blix abruptly stops overacting being the victim of a poison gas strike. He jumps up into the space under the back window, staring out at the traffic behind us. This isn't a huge highway or anything, just a fairly rural two-lane road connecting Woodinville to Cottage Lake. The imp chatters rapidly in an incomprehensible series of babbles.

"Oh, crap, Sare." Sam also twists to look out the rear window. "Blix said that guy's gonna hit us."

I tense up. For an instant, I'm stuck, unable to choose between stomping on the brakes, speeding up, or pulling over. "Uhh, which guy?"

Blix babbles.

"Pickup truck," says Sam.

"Is it black?" I stare at the side mirror.

"No," says Sam.

Five or six car-lengths behind us, an old green pickup truck has strayed into the oncoming lane. Fortunately, there's not much traffic here at the moment, but enough to where the sight of this dude crossing the line makes me yell, "Ack!" Being offline, I don't have the benefit of zoom-in vision, but I can still tell there's something not right with the driver. He's drunk, or high, or half-awake, or having a stroke. Other cars right in front of and behind this guy start beeping.

"Sam?" I say, my voice shaking from nerves.

"Yeah?"

"Is Blix saying 'he's gonna hit us' based on a demonic bit of precognition about him literally crashing into us, or is he saying it as a general statement because the guy's driving like an idiot?"

Blix chatters something that sounds like 'norbelz neem gaa-boo.'

When Sam looks back at me, his face is pale. "Demonic precognition. Ro... seat belts!"

Shit.

Ronan scrambles to secure his seat belt, as does my brother.

"Uhh..." I look around at two lanes of road, trees on both sides, guardrail on our side. Nowhere to go. "Is it unavoidable or can I do something?"

Blix emits a warbling noise.

"He said it's avoidable. Would have happened if he didn't say anything." Sam peers back at the old pickup which has veered into our lane again. "Isn't sure what you need to do. And, umm... telling you about it might cause you to do something that makes the crash happen anyway. He can't say."

Blix mutters.

"Precognition isn't an exact science." Sam shrugs. "He wants to know if he should kill the guy before he can hit us."

I bite my lip. Wow. Talk about a moral dilemma. Do I kill a total stranger to save Sam and Ronan's life? Absolutely. No question. Do I kill a total stranger to prevent the boys from being rattled around and having the hell scared out of them? Probably not. I gotta do something in the middle. That's me. Every time I'm faced with two crappy choices, I try to squeeze between them and find an option three. Worked so far, right? Mostly.

A box truck rumbles by in the oncoming lane, missing the pickup by mere inches as he swerves back and forth. Not sure if it's the wind effect of a big truck or whatever is wrong with the guy, but the instant the truck is past him, the pickup swerves hard left into the oncoming lane to get around a tiny neon-green car that's right behind us. The small car isn't riding my bumper, merely the closest vehicle going in the same direction. The pickup idiot has to be doing seventy miles an hour to our fifty-five.

If he's going to hit us, I have about two seconds before impact. He's in the other lane. Best idea I have is to hammer the brakes. Gonna scare the hell out of the woman behind us but... oh well.

"Hold on!" I stomp on the brake pedal, making our tires chirp as the anti-lock system engages.

Blix screams and goes sailing from the platform under the rear window into the front. He smacks into the windshield with a wet *splat* like dropping a raw steak on the kitchen floor—and sticks to the glass, his arms and legs out in an X like a scene straight out of a Wile E. Coyote cartoon. Sam and Ronan lurch forward, but their seat belts hold.

"Ow," mutters Blix.

The little green car veers left across the yellow line to dodge my rapid deceleration while the pickup whooshes past us, swerving back into my lane. Our side mirrors would've slapped into each other if his wasn't so high off the ground. I swear it's almost like the son of a bitch deliberately tried to hit us but couldn't manage a lane change fast enough. Smoke peels from his tires as the truck spins sideways on the road, totally out of control. Little green car nimbly avoids the spinning truck and takes off down the road. Good thing I'm offline right now or I would have stomped the brake pedal straight through the floor.

Time seems to stop as I lock stares with the driver. His truck's presently in my lane maybe fifteen feet ahead of us facing toward me, still in a sideways slide. His expression is rage… but it jumps to absolute confusion an instant before his driver side tires smack into the guardrail. Time returns to normal.

With a tremendous metallic *whump*, the pickup flips longways over the guardrail and flies out of view, falling into the ditch paralleling the road. Even though I'm pushing on the brakes with all my strength, we keep going past the spot he went over, coming to a hard stop about thirty feet from the mangled section of guardrail.

I sit there in the middle of the lane trying to swallow my heart back into my chest. Blix peels away from the windshield, bounces off the dashboard, and lands in the empty passenger seat. I'm floating in a timeless fog, removed from reality until the whump of the Sentra's doors slamming snaps me out of it. In the rearview mirror, I spot Sam and Ronan sprinting back down the shoulder toward where the truck went over. Before some random person can come zooming along and plow into me from behind, I pull off the road onto the shoulder, then hop out and run after the boys.

As soon as they start climbing over the guardrail, I yell at them to stay put. I'm so lucky these kids are obedient. They stop, both with one leg over the rail, pointing emphatically down. I rush up behind them, one arm around each kid to hold them back. The ditch is deeper than it looked from driving by it. At least twenty feet below the road surface, the truck's come to rest upside down in an enormous muddy puddle deep enough to cover all the windows. Between us and the truck is a fairly steep incline covered in weeds, roots, and jutting rocks.

"Okay. You two stay up here. Call 911." I pull my iPhone out of my pocket, hand it to my brother, then step out of my flip-flops and jump the guardrail.

"On it." Sam pulls out his phone.

I turn my back to the ditch and monkey-climb to the water. The truck doesn't appear to be floating and in danger of sinking, but if the crash knocked him out, he could have his head trapped underwater. Since the upside-down truck is pointing in the opposite direction this side of the road is supposed to be going, the driver's side door is already facing me. I scramble into shin-deep muck and fumble around under the waterline for the handle.

The door handle's only a few inches under the surface. Cool. Good sign. I grab the handle and pull. Door doesn't move. Desperate to get this guy out of here before he drowns, I grab on with both hands and pull so hard my feet begin to plunge deeper in the mud. A flash of burning pain scorches all over me—and the door handle pops off in my grasp, sending me flying over backward. I land half in water, half in weeds, and completely covered in smoke.

Oops. Subconsciously overrode my daylight shield. The sun snuck in and slapped me.

Grr. How the hell did the stupid handle break off before the door opened?

I fling myself at the truck again, grabbing metal, pulling in random spots. Reaching under the water to break the window doesn't work. I can't find the damn window, only crumpled metal. Huh? One instant I'm futilely clawing at the side of the truck, the next thing I know, a guy grabs me from behind and pulls me away.

Another two men—firefighters—move past me to the side of the truck and start attacking it with a strange prybar type tool. The fireman who grabbed me effortlessly pivots to scoop me up in his arms like I'm the child who needs saving. The road above and behind me is awash with all these flashing lights. Multiple police cars, one fire truck, an ambulance. Wow. I must have been freaking out. It seems like I'd only been trying to get the poor guy out of the wreck for a few seconds but it had to have been minutes. Reality doesn't even feel real right now.

"I wasn't in the truck. I… he almost hit us," I rasp.

"Okay. Are you hurt?" asks the guy.

"No. Just trying to help the other driver." I stare at the wreck. "Couldn't get the door open."

The fireman holding me makes this face like there's something he really doesn't want to say. At that point, it finally occurs to me the puddle is only like two inches over my ankles. The truck shouldn't be submerged as deep as it appears to be in water this shallow. Oh, holy shit. The top of the cab must have been crushed flat. Eek. Still not a death sentence, right? Maybe the dude threw himself sideways across the seats and he's okay but pinned… under water.

Dammit.

Realizing the man probably died right in front of me leaves me stunned.

Crazy since I've shredded people. Well, vampires. We're still people, but shredding vampires isn't permanent, merely painful. Why is this accident messing with me so much? Is it because I couldn't save him? Or am I having a nervous breakdown over the thought it might have been Ronan and Sam trapped and drowning in an upside-down Sentra instead of this guy?

The fireman hands me up to a big bodybuilder of a cop who lifts me as easily as my Dad used to when I was four. Outwardly, I must be way more composed than I feel. He sets me on my feet, looks me over, and then guides me to an older cop wearing sergeant stripes.

Numb, I answer the sergeant's questions about what happened, being completely honest except for Blix warning us. The version he gets is me seeing the guy swerving all over the place and speeding. When I hit the brakes, he shot past us, went into a spin, and landed in the ditch. I don't mention it seemed like he swerved at me on purpose. I also don't say a word about how the guy appeared to be furious at me, then bewildered. It would be too difficult to explain how I noticed such detail in the middle of an accident.

I'm still kinda curious about that, myself. Probably just vampire stuff. Moments of extreme stress making me tap my power at a subconscious level.

Sounds fairly cut-and-dried. The boys likely gave the cop a similar story to mine. They wouldn't talk about Blix. Another cop escorts me back to the Sentra, where the boys are sitting on the road by the guardrail under the watchful eye of another cop who's been engaging them in a conversation about the police dog he usually works with. Sam hands me my flip-flops.

"Wait here a bit, okay?" The cop gives my license the same doubting squint they all do, but decides it's legit and I really am eighteen before handing my paperwork back over.

"Sure." I sit and put the flops on.

"He didn't make it," whispers Sam. "I was gonna ask Olmaz for help flipping the truck over, but Blix said the guy died right away."

I watch a small red car glide by, rubbernecking us. "Just as well you didn't ask Olmaz for help. Someone going by might have seen something unexplainable."

"Yeah." Ronan exhales. "Thanks for keeping us safe. You drive really good."

"Heh." I ruffle his hair. He's got a long blonde mane almost rivalling Sophia's. Hers is much longer though. "I can't let you guys get hurt."

We sit there in silence. I can't help but think about the near miss at

Frosty Buns. What are the odds I'm involved in two car accidents and a shooting in under a week? I know my luck can be bad, but this defies simple bad luck. Either I've pissed off a leprechaun, faerie, or other critter like that... or—I dunno. Maybe the accidents are unrelated.

But... what if they're not?

23

ORPHANS, GIRLFRIENDS, AND VAMPIRE WARS

I'm staring at the rug in the middle of our living room, mesmerized by the distant chugging of the washing machine chewing on my muddy shorts. The scent of mango shampoo clings to my hair. My long T-shirt is big enough to entirely cover my crossed legs as I sit on the sofa, gradually compacting myself into a shape like a giant mochi ice cream bun.

Mom's had some wine.

Sam is obligingly close to Mom, leaning against her while playing his PSP. Ronan left with his mother only a few minutes ago, one of the rare times he takes a conventional method home instead of going through the mirror. Sierra is, as usual, monopolizing the living room TV with the PlayStation, but she's switched gears to a fantasy dungeon exploration game. It's relatively quiet since, you know, guns and missiles don't exist in that genre. Sophia cling-hugs a big pillow at the end of the couch, roughly equidistant between Mom and Dad. Her facial expression is a mixture of an attempt to project positivity, worry, and nervous relief as if the pickup truck almost hit her instead of us.

No one's really saying much.

Can't explain why it feels like I'm bracing for the yelling to start. I didn't do anything wrong. While I credit blind luck for the most part, I handled that situation about as well as any other person my age could have. There isn't a single scratch on the boys, me, or my car. Good thing the Sentra has anti-lock brakes, though. Dad needed to point out to me that stomping on the brakes would've been really bad if I happened to be driving a car without anti-lock. He probably just said it because he needed to say something dad-like and cautionary to distract himself from thinking about what might have happened.

I've been replaying the last twelve seconds of the accident on a loop in my thoughts for the past hour. Things you don't see in the moment, but you remember later. In the chaos of a highly emotional event like an accident, the brain seizes on only the most major things. Speed, where the road is, where the other car is, and so on. The color of the flowers in the weeds on the side of the road isn't even registering on a conscious level. Sometimes, I see them in the replay when I'm staring left out the door window at the truck gliding past us. They're whitish-green.

And the guy was glaring at me, the sort of glare that tells me if we both managed to stop intact, he'd have jumped out of his truck, run over to my car, and tried to drag me out the window so he could kick my ass. He looked so furious I doubt he could've processed the reality of me being a teenage girl and would have gone to town on me as if I was some grown man who cut him off on purpose and said something inappropriate about his mother.

For the unlife of me, I can't recognize him. Never saw the guy before. I've come up with a bunch of explanations for how a total stranger could be so angry with me. Drunk people are irrational. Maybe he sincerely thought I cut him off. To someone like that, simply driving the speed limit when they want to do seventy or eighty—or faster—is as infuriating as if I'd thrown a brick at his windshield. He'd certainly been weaving between lanes like a drunk person. Might have been drugs, too. Maybe the guy had been legit crazy, one of those tinfoil-hat guys who thinks everyone's out to get them. To him, I might have been an alien overlord disguised as an ordinary person. An E.T. trying to abduct two boys and he wanted to save them from me.

Only, his attempt to swerve over and cut me off didn't work out so well. Cutting the wheel as hard as he did at however fast he'd been going is not smart. Now I'm wondering if the split second look of confusion he gave me right before his wheels slammed into the guardrail came from him not understanding why his attempt to get in front of me and force me to stop had gone so spectacularly wrong... or something else.

That 'what the hell am I doing here, what's going on' stare was a bit too intense for a drunk guy realizing he'd committed a serious error of physics. Or am I overthinking? Anything could've been messed up in his head. Maybe he hallucinated seeing me in my 'true alien form' with tentacles and everything.

Ugh.

So, I had to play normal and pretend to be ordinary to the cops. Hey, pretending to be ordinary is my bloodline's specialty. Go me. Since the guy hadn't made contact with my car, the police considered me a witness to the accident and not a participant. Basically, they back-patted me for trying to help the guy, then made sure I wasn't too rattled to drive before sending us on our way.

Mom's a little woozy but she never hits the wine so hard she gets drunk. She thinks it calms her down, and maybe it does. Honestly, Sam leaning against her is doing more to ease her nerves than two glasses of red wine. Dad keeps giving me this look like he thinks there's some greater scheme going on than simple bad luck. Maybe this is why I'm reading too much into the guy's confused expression right before he flipped over the guardrail.

We just kinda exist more or less communal silence, no one really doing much, until about ten. Neither Mom nor Dad makes a big deal about bedtime. The Littles are officially supposed to be in bed by 10:00 p.m. now. Unofficially, they kinda want Sam to crash closer to nine since he's younger and they let Sierra push it to 10:30 without too much of a fuss. It's tempting to help my mom relax but, dammit. I promised not to tweak her mind. As soon as Sierra shuts down the PlayStation, it's as if she broke the spell over us. The 'rents both snap out of the 'holy shit our son almost died' trance like they're waking up from a coma.

Everyone except me stands up at roughly the same time.

"Mom?" asks Sam in a low voice. "Is it bothering you I'm not upset? Would you feel better if I acted scared?"

She hugs him. "You're so brave, Sam. It's okay."

"It's not really brave." He grins. "We had Sarah with us."

The boy conveniently forgets I'm offline during the day sometimes, but still acts like he's hanging out with Supergirl. Who'd be afraid of anything when their big sister is an immortal? Somehow I doubt Sam would be too affected by a near miss even if I'd been normal. Still don't know how he does it. Ten-year-old boys shouldn't be so analytical and brave. Maybe Sophia scooped up all the 'fear and worry' genes inside Mom and didn't leave any 'on the shelf' for him.

Silly thoughts like that help me deal.

A mild explosion of chaos erupts as the Littles all scramble to get ready for bed in a house with only two bathrooms. Technically, three, but the ground floor one is only a toilet closet. The sink is tiny, has no toothbrush holder, and Mom loves putting useless decorative soap seashells all over it. The fragrance in there is kinda strong. No one wants to brush their teeth in there anyway because the taste of soap in the air fouls the toothpaste.

I spend a few minutes holding onto Mom in the living room, having the surreal experience of feeling like I'm the parent comforting her.

"Keep your eyes open, hon," says Dad. "I've watched enough vampire movies to realize someone is probably up to something."

Though it's tempting, I don't roll my eyes at him. "It's more likely I've offended a voodoo witch doctor. Feels like I've been hexed."

"Have you talked to Darren Anderson yet?" asks Dad. "Maybe they could do something, or we could ask Sophia to gaze into her water bucket again."

That gets me chuckling. Ancient seers and fortune-tellers once used bowls of water as scrying devices, hoping to peer through the surface into another world or time. These bowls were typically wood, but sometimes made of more exotic materials like bone, gold, or whatever. Sophia... she uses a Barbie pink beach pail with little yellow flower bits stuck to the outside.

"I dunno." I let out a heavy breath. "If I can avoid dragging her into whatever this is, I will. Not fair to any of the Littles that my craziness keeps landing on them."

Mom squeezes me tighter in an 'I appreciate that' gesture.

"Fair." Dad nods. "Well, if anything else happens, I hope you'll start to believe me that it's more than just bad luck and maybe give Darren a call."

"Sure. I can do that." I smirk at nothing in particular. The mystics have proven to be trustworthy now. But they did initially steal Sophia's body for a little while to use as a possessed spy. Possibly exposing them to harm from whatever is messing with me wouldn't bother me at all. They're adults—skilled adults—and ought to be able to handle it.

We talk for a little while more without the Littles in the room. Of course, I am totally honest with my parents and tell them about Blix's warning, my insecurities about the nature of precognition—meaning the worry that being warned of an event is what makes me cause it—and so on. Eventually, Mom is satisfied Sam and Ronan weren't in as much danger as she assumed. Once they head up to bed around midnight, I make my way to my room downstairs in the basement.

I flop heavily into my computer chair and stare at the blank screen. Should I go to Aurélie's and visit Chloe? Am I merely a babysitter or legally 'mom' now? Call me cautious, but it might not be the best idea to get the kid used to thinking of me as mom. If we're ever out in public and she calls me mom, people are going to give us weird looks, the 'did that girl get pregnant at ten' kind of weird looks. Big sis is definitely the approach to take here inasmuch as any effort at having anything close to a normal 'family relationship' with her is concerned.

She doesn't look like me at all. No one in our family has jet black hair or is as pale as Chloe. Granted, she isn't ghoulish nor even as white as Ashley. The kid's got these large blue eyes and a pixie-like face. Prosthetic elf ears and faerie wings wouldn't seem out of place on her. What gets me is the tragic look to her. Some girls have 'resting bitch face.' Chloe seems to have resting 'why is everyone mean to me' face. Honestly, the more I think about it, the more her expression strikes me as not so much feeling sorry for herself but wariness. The kid looks like some underfed little mouse trying to sneak through a world of cats without being noticed. Question is, did that come from being a child vampire in a world that thinks she deserves to be destroyed for simply existing or is it from her mortal life?

I need to distract myself from this train of thought or I'm going to drive myself over the edge with sadness and anger. Aurélie offering to watch her 'for a bit' might mean a century. She's not at all confident Eleanor will have success in developing a 'cure.' Hmm. Is it right to do so? As much as I've come to adore being a vampire, it's hard for me to think of the word 'cure' as appropriate for reversing the Transference. It would be like a supervillain force-feeding Supergirl a kryptonite smoothie and permanently turning her human, stealing all her powers.

Is it right to do it to her if she doesn't want it?

Where do Chloe's wants and needs end when they interfere with the needs of vampire society? How volatile is a child vampire? I guess it would depend on temperament. A spoiled brat would definitely be a problem. Someone like Sam? He'd totally handle it perfectly. But he's also ten, not seven... and really mature for his age.

I don't know Chloe. She acted shy and quiet the whole time—after they let her out of the kennel. Poor kid basically clung to my side, hiding behind me for the remainder of the time we spent at Eleanor's mad science lab. My part hadn't been too demanding, just giving some blood samples. Not sure why they wanted it. Chloe's an Innocent, too. Maybe St. Ives wants to do some manner of comparison. It's almost tempting to think she got wind of Chloe's existence, sent her people all the way to New Jersey to capture this kid, and bring her back here specifically to use her as bait to lure me in to get a blood sample. But, nah. I'm not significant enough for that, am I? If Eleanor was only interested in studying the Innocent bloodline, she wouldn't need me. She had the kid already.

An argument rages in my head between if it would be better for Chloe to be made mortal again or not. For all I know, it might be a completely pointless argument. If it's impossible to reverse, no sense worrying about the ethical question. I remember being little and thinking how I couldn't wait to grow up. I wanted to drive, have freedom, stop being treated like a little kid. Chloe doesn't seem to care at all about growing up. Maybe she thinks vampire 'super powers' are better than being an adult. Maybe she's never seen anything that made her jealous about older people the way I used to want so bad to be able to drive like Mom and Dad. Or stay up late. Though, as best I can remember, my desperation to grow up didn't really start until I was around twelve or so. Can't really desire what you don't understand.

Hah. Stay up late. What bedtime do you give a seven-year-old vampire? Three hours before sunset? I laugh at the silliness. Doesn't matter how old she looks, vampires can't sleep until the sun's poking over the horizon.

My iPhone rings.

Good. I need a distraction from this sad philosophy.

It's Ashley. Seeing her name on the caller ID reminds me I never got the chance to have 'full contact' with Hunter tonight thanks to the stupid accident. Totally forgot about anything but family stuff. Wonder how her date went?

I answer. "Hey, Ash. What's up?"

She babbles and cries.

Crap. Not again. Ashley's luck with romance is about as good as my recent luck with automobiles. I wouldn't be terribly surprised if I almost get hit by a car while *flying* to Seattle to feed later.

"Ash, slow down. I can't understand you. What happened? Whose ass am I going to go kick for you?"

She takes a few deep breaths, sniffles, exhales hard, then coughs once. "Ugh. Nothing really but my nerves."

"Spill!" I say, leaning forward. "Speak all the words."

Ashley chuckles. "It's Raleigh. We did it tonight… or tried to anyway."

"Fuzzy cuffs freak her out?"

"No." Ashley laughs. "She didn't want to do that yet. Strictly vanilla. But, I dunno. It was just so weird. One minute, she seemed super into me. The next, it's like she couldn't wait to get away and wanted to stop touching me. Then she'd get into it again and… shy away and come back and… ugh. We barely did anything at all past kissing. I mean, she went down there to… you know, and made this face. Stared for a bit then came back up and kissed me. We get into it again. I try to, umm, 'dive' and she scoots away. Like do you want to have sex or not? So frustrating, but now I'm feeling like an ugly, undesirable creature."

"Aww, Ash. You are far from ugly and undesirable. The problem is a hundred percent with Raleigh. I bet she's just terrified her parents are going to find out before she's ready to be honest with them."

"Ya think so?" Ashley sniffles. "She didn't seem to have a problem using the toys on me, but actually touching me herself… she got all weird."

Of all the things I adore talking to Ash about, her date and artificial dongs is not even in the top ten thousand topics. However, she needs me, so I push through the awkwardness.

"Okay, that's odd. Maybe she's afraid you're going too fast from first date to full contact?"

"Maybe. I'm afraid she's decided we aren't working and she's just going through the motions because she's too nice to hurt my feelings. Or too chicken to have a confrontation." She huffs. "Two redheads breaking up could be explosive."

I lean back, stretch one leg out to rest my heel on the computer desk, and flick my big toe at the purple-and-blue tassel from my high school graduation, which is hanging from the little bookshelf above my monitor. "Can I say something at risk of sounding like an immature jealous best friend?"

She snickers. "Go for it."

"Something about Raleigh has been bugging me, too."

"Uhh, how? You haven't even met her face to face yet. How could she possibly bug you?"

"No, you're right. I haven't met her yet." I flick the tassel again. "Just from talking to you about her. Honestly, it's probably just me being overprotective and jealous."

Ashley sniffle-giggles. "I'd say yeah but umm… I dunno anymore. Seems every time I think I'm in love, something bad happens. Hey, will you 'Corey' her?"

"What?" I lean back a little more, gazing up at the ceiling. "What's he have to do with this?"

"You know, Corey? Michelle's boyfriend?"

"Yeah, I know Michelle's boyfriend." My computer chair decides I've leaned back too far and tries to dump me over backward. Fortunately, I can fly.

"Ack, what the hell was that crash?"

"Chair fell over."

Ashley emits a faint squeak. "You okay?"

"Yep. The chair fell. I didn't. I'm still floating here as if there's a chair under me."

She laughs.

I levitate higher, swing my legs down, and land on my feet. After righting the chair, I flop on the bed. "So, what about Corey?"

"Remember how 'Chelle got nervous about him being too perfect and wanted you to read his mind to see if he was really interested in her or just trying to get laid?"

"Oh." I laugh. "Yeah, sure. Totally. I will absolutely brain scan anyone you are going to get involved with if you want me to."

"You're the best."

I close my eyes and let the wave of premature sorrow pass. Ashley is still my best friend. She's still the same age as me. It's not too late to keep her forever. I'm mourning her death to old age before it happens. What's wrong with me? People my age aren't supposed to care what's going to happen an hour into the future, much less seventy years. I'm as upset as a twelve-year-old who's best friend-slash-twin-sister is about to move across the country and we'll never see each other again.

The mood passes in the span of a few breaths. "When do you want to do it?"

"Well, I did it tonight already. Or at least tried to." She sighs into a chuckle. "But if you're talking about the Corey-ing, umm, soon. I'll set something up. Maybe a double date? Or would a girl's night work better?"

"Is it technically a girl's night out if one of the girls is dating you?" I scratch my head.

We debate. Ashley completely believes a romantic interest in a girl doesn't prevent them from joining in on a girl's night. To her, it's not exclusively for friends. I don't really care either way but I argue the other side just for laughs. She knows I'm only doing it to keep the conversation going, so we have a non-serious 'argument' with plenty of laughing. When that runs out, we get into a meandering chat about random crap the same way we used to do when we were tweens, except for the discussion about the ethics involved in mind reading Ashley's girlfriend to see what her true intentions are. Sure, it's an invasion of privacy, but this is Ash we're talking about. I will invade the hell out of anyone's privacy to keep her safe.

Around 1:45 a.m., Ashley finally notices the time and eeps out of our phone conversation to go to sleep.

I sprawl there on my bed having all the emotions at once. Happy, content, freaked out, sad, pissed off, dread, lonely, restless, lazy, and anxiety like a soldier or astronaut who just volunteered for a dangerous mission they might not come back from.

Ugh. Chloe and Raleigh. Two heavy moral dilemmas.

Can I please just go back to getting caught up in vampire wars or fighting hydra-tarantulas as big as trucks?

24

THE PROPER FEEDING OF HELLHOUNDS

I t's a pretty good clue I'm in a strange headspace when a few days going by without a catastrophe happening nearby feels odd.

Once again, I'm lying in my bed searching for answers on the ceiling. One of these days, I'm going to install a conference room projector so I can have Wikipedia on my ceiling. Then there might actually be some answers up there. I've visited Chloe the last three nights in a row, spending the time between my family going to bed and sunrise with her. Aside from being up all night, she seems pretty much like a normal kid except for the casual use of the F-bomb when she isn't even upset. For example, she'll see one of the more elaborate dolls and blurt 'that's effing cool!' only without censoring it like I just did. The first two nights, she was a little standoffish and nervous around us. By night three, she started sitting in arms reach. Since the kid only had the clothes on her back to her name, Aurélie's been dressing her in these super cute but elaborate gowns like something royalty might've put their kids in back in 1704.

Not sure if it's knowing she's a vampire, sensing the energy in her, or what... but a small, pale kid in elaborate gowns drifting around the darkened corridors of Aurélie's apartment kinda creeped me out. She legit looks like the eerie, forlorn spirit of some poor child who died to a now-eradicated disease 300 years ago.

There's definitely something not right, though. The girl is hiding something. Aurélie told me not to worry too much and once Chloe feels safe enough around us she'll share. This, of course, on top of her strong reaction when I mentioned her parents, has me worrying what sort of horrible crap happened. Fairly sure this kid either witnessed her parents brutally murdered right in front of her or the parents abused her somehow. Ugh. I'm inclined to think it's abuse. She hasn't once expressed any sense of missing her parents, caring about them, or wanting to see them. In fact, she almost sounds happy she's not with them. The kid is a little flinchy, which makes me think someone used to hit her frequently.

Grr.

Tilloa called me on Wednesday to ask about vampire stuff. Specifically, she wanted to know if it was normal for a pair of vampires she'd never seen before to come out of nowhere and try to kick her ass. Apparently, in Chicago, that's a yes. Where we live? Not so much. We met deep inside Banner Forest, which sits across Elliot Bay from Seattle on the other side of Vashon Island to talk. We try to keep conversations about supernatural stuff off the airwaves. Middle of nowhere forest is a great place to not be eavesdropped upon, unless you believe in Bigfoot.

She told me two guys dressed in black 'techno ninja' suits jumped her —or tried to. After a brief scuffle, she decided to bail out and flew away. The men didn't have the ability to fly, so they couldn't chase her. When I asked what she meant by 'techno ninja,' she described them as wearing black all over with a bunch of stuff hanging off their belts and maybe a vest like cops. Pouches, possibly grenades, devices she didn't get enough of a look at to recognize, and so on.

As far as I know, vampires don't have a police force or a special operations team. I briefly considered they might be connected to the Persons in Black who made contact with me soon after I came home, it doesn't feel right. They don't actually employ vampires. You know, trust issues and everything.

Tilloa ended up thinking it's just a pair of jerks who have a problem with a black person being a vampire. Maybe. No way to know. According to her, they came out of nowhere, said nothing, and just pounced on her. She held them off rather well for a while until they appeared to get frustrated at not being able to take her down, so they decided to soften her up with guns. As soon as she saw the hardware come out, she jumped into the air.

So, yeah. *My* life has been calm the past three days. Hers, not so much.

My 'third sister' is also a nervous wreck. Apparently, Raleigh has been oddly busy ever since their awkward attempt to have some 'full contact' time. Ashley is worried the girl's avoiding her on purpose because she wants to break up but doesn't have the balls to say it to her face. She hasn't quite gone into complete alarm mode yet. It's only been three days of 'can't tonight, busy' delaying a date. If this keeps up for too much longer, I'm going to get another phone call from Ash asking me to let her out after she handcuffed herself to the bed again to avoid eating a whole box of rocky road ice cream.

Oh wait, no. She won't. I fixed that already at her request. Instead of grief eating, she'll grief-cuddle plushies. Ashley's biggest problem is her need to make people around her happy. If someone doesn't like her, she internalizes it as if she did something wrong. Pretty sure this all ties back to her abandonment issues thanks to her father leaving. Even though the man specifically told her to her face it wasn't her fault and she had nothing to do with it, claiming he's just not cut out for a nuclear family and so on… that's not something an eight-year-old can logically process.

I mean, she figured her parents lied about Santa Claus, so when Mr. Carter said that, she took the exact opposite to be truth, that she absolutely did something wrong to make him leave. Major ugh. If another two days pass without Raleigh showing up for a date, I may escalate the situation and go track her down. Ashley wanted to be present for the brain scan, but if the girl doesn't show up, I'm going to act before serious emotional damage occurs.

An imminent sense of doom falls over me like my whole house is about to blast apart into toothpicks thanks to a gas leak. I know it won't. We don't have natural gas. However, the dread is the same.

Someone's coming toward my room.

One thing about Ashley, she loves to sleep naked. I totally get why. Sometimes, I do it. It's really comfortable. Gonna go out on a limb here and say the supposed health benefits no longer matter to me. Guess what I did last night? Figures the one time this week I decide to sleep in the pajamas I was born with, I have a Little situation.

Sam barges into my room without knocking. He doesn't appear upset or hurt. His orange Marvel Comics T-shirt and camo shorts are in immaculate shape—no mud, blood, or damage. His legs have the usual amount of small bruises and cuts common to any boy his age who loves running around the woods, playing hard. Nothing new or recent. Some grass stains on his toes tell me he's recently been outside. Just looking at him offers me zero clue as to what might be serious enough for him to come running into my room so urgently.

At least he's alone. No friends trailing after him. I'm also lucky. While I *am* sans clothing at the moment, the sheets are covering everything critical. Ashley often jokes that she's not sleeping naked, rather, she's 'wearing the bed.' Not sure that counts, but whatever. He can't see anything he shouldn't… not that he hasn't already barged into the bathroom while I'm in the tub. It's one of the annoyances of having six people living in a house that doesn't have six bathrooms.

"Sare," says Sam, skidding to a halt at the foot of my bed. "Max ate someone last night."

I gather the covers to my chest and sit up. "What?"

"Max. The hellhound."

Sigh. "Yes, I know Max the hellhound."

"He ate someone," says the boy as casually as if he told me Klepto stole his homework.

"Sam…" I stare at him. "When I said 'what,' I meant why did Max eat someone and who did he eat."

"Oh." Sam takes a breath. "Since he's a hellhound, he can't really talk much. I'm kinda guessing based on body language and just feels."

"Out with it, kiddo."

Sam walks over to my computer desk, grabs the oversized T-shirt draped on the back of the chair, tosses it to me, then turns his back. "The guy wanted to hurt one of us. I guess he came after you."

I trust my li'l bro not to look, so hurriedly get out of bed and pull the shirt on. "Okay. Safe. What makes you think he came after me?"

Sam faces me and hands over a soft case about the size of a college textbook. "He had this."

The case is black nylon, thin padding over a hard backing. A zipper runs around three edges, so I pull it all the way around then open it like a book. Inside, multiple elastic loops hold four stakes, a small mallet, a bottle of water with a crucifix on it, a flask of kerosene, a lighter, and a huge knife.

"It's a vampire slaying kit," says Sam. "Probably bought it online."

I facepalm.

"I know, right?" Sam rolls his eyes. "Such an idiot. You tick anyone off lately?"

"Not that I know of." I open the bottle of supposed holy water and sniff. Smells stale, but like water. Out of morbid curiosity, I dribble a bit into my hand. It sits there behaving just like water should. Heh. Some guy in a robe muttering in Latin over a bowl of water doesn't do anything. It's still only water.

Sam makes an 'I didn't think so' face. "It's probably nothing to worry about."

"More concerned how he found me here. It's not like I'm being obvious."

"Umm. I could ask Olmaz or Mel to find his ghost and drag it back here for interrogation if you want."

I cringe. I'll sometimes comment on a three-year-old Facebook post, but internet necromancy is the extent of my interest in raising the dead. "Nah. Not worth it. Messing with that stuff is too dangerous."

"Good call. So, anyway, I just thought you should know an idiot showed up this morning." Sam starts to walk out, but stops at the door to peer back at me. "Don't worry. No one will find the body."

Stunned, I stare at the doorway as he leaves. In no world should a ten-year-old say the phrase 'no one will find the body' in a completely serious reference to an actual dead person, and have so little emotional response. Wow, my life is weird. Then again, this is Sam. He's probably thinking about it in abstract terms. A video game bad guy tried to hurt his sister and his pet video game monster ate the bad guy. My little brother takes Pokémon Go a bit too far.

"Uhh, Sam," I call, worried and confused as to what he means. My brain runs away with a Stephen King-like scene of him and his friends dragging chunks of gore out into the woods and burying them.

He returns to my doorway in a moment, his expression curious. "Yeah?"

"*Why* won't anyone find the body?"

"Oh." Sam shrugs. "Because there isn't one. Max ate him, bones and all."

"Right. Ate him." I biff myself in the forehead.

Sam nods, then walks away again.

"Wait..." I reach toward my doorway.

He leans back into view, peering at me. "What?"

"Didn't you say Max consumes like negative emotions and stuff? Remember Dad's joke about him going to a call center full of telemarketers as an all-you-can-eat buffet?"

Sam grins. "Yeah. He mostly eats that. But... people can eat ice cream even though we don't need it to survive. Same thing. Max *can* eat solid meat. He just doesn't have to."

My brain is a little scrambled at this news. How scrambled? I say, "Okay, just make sure if your dog's going to eat anyone else, they're really a threat to us."

"No problem." Sam grins and darts off.

Thunder rolls over the house. I swear. How can such a skinny, barefoot boy his age make so much damn noise going up stairs? It's not like he's wearing heavy boots, or fat, or the size of an adult. Guess it's one of the great mysteries of the universe no one will ever understand right up there with why the Kardashians are famous.

I'm too busy being disturbed at his causal attitude toward a man being killed—eaten alive—in our backyard. At least he didn't see it happen. I'm sure his anger at some jerk coming to hurt me is overpowering any sense of horror he might feel toward a random stranger meeting such a gruesome end. Heh. I smile. He's so small but he's being protective of me. Note to any wanna-be vampire hunters: do not get your vampire killing kit from Walmart.

Seriously?

I flip the thing closed and zip it. The stakes aren't even real wood. They're like that weird plastic-permeated whatever they make outdoor furniture from. This kit has to be for a Halloween costume.

What am I, the vampire hunter initiate's first challenge? Baby vampire gets the baby hunters?

My unlife. Sheesh.

25

DALTONED

ate doesn't give me much time to ponder what sort of mental damage sent an idiot into our backyard with a cheesy vampire slayer kit.

My phone rings. It's an unfamiliar number. Normally, I don't answer calls when they aren't in my contacts list. Spam phone calls are seriously getting out of control lately. I've never purchased a car through normal channels, nor do I even *have* a credit rating, but I still get calls from people telling me my vehicle's extended warranty is about to expire. Yeah, like it expired eight years ago.

Total scam.

A strange feeling makes me decide to answer this one.

"Hello?" I ask, fully expecting to hear the long silence that happens when a computer dialer scrambles to patch me through to a live scammer —err, operator.

"Hey," says Chloe.

Oh. It's the kid. It's not even four in the afternoon yet. Definitely an Innocent like me if she's awake now. "Hey, squirt. What's up?"

"Why do windows hurt?"

It takes me a few seconds to translate 'child' into a reasonable question. I sit on the edge of my bed. "It's light sensitivity. We both have the same condition. It'll get better as you practice."

"Grandma Aurélie is really nice and I love the fancy dresses, but I wanna play with you today. You made those buttheads not wanna kill me, and you said you'd watch me. You're not trying to dump me, are you?"

Wow, master of guilt-fu and she's only seven. "No. No way. I swear. I'm just, well… kind of a kid, too, and trying to do the best thing for you."

"Okay. Can I come over? Grandma won't wake up."

Normally, that phrase coming out of a little kid is disturbing. And yeah, there are certain undeniable changes that come with being a vampire. One of which is Chloe having the ability to see Aurélie 'sleeping' (when she looks like a corpse) and not freaking out. Or seeing Shadows. Any ordinary kid her age seeing a Shadow would scream. Chloe would be like 'oh, it's one of those guys.' She may or may not find them unpleasant to look at, but she won't lose her mind like a child seeing a literal monster.

Hoo boy. I bite my lip. Yeah, I've been trying to avoid it as much as possible but the moment of truth is at hand. "Sure. Be there in a little bit. Gotta drive."

"Awesome!" chirps Chloe.

We hang up. I let out a long breath. Mom's going to love this.

When I stand up from the bed to change, I bump the 'slaying kit' to the floor. Dammit. I stoop to pick it up and notice one of the plasti-wood stakes has bounced out and rolled onto the rug. This would normally only be a slightly deeper layer of annoyance at making it take more effort to pick up. But… the bottom has popped off.

Curious, I pick up the stray 'stake' and the square beige endcap. Weird. This fake vampire killing implement is hollow. It appears to be packed full of pale grey clay. Something that looks like a big microchip from a circuit board is stuck in the end of the clay. It's got a few teeny buttons on it like an old 1980s calculator watch as well as a LCD time display.

I stare at it in confusion for all of eight seconds before my brain kicks in.

This is a stick of C-4 about the size of a whole stick of butter. Staking a vampire doesn't do much but hurt. However, a stake stuffed with semtex *would* be the end. We can regenerate from a lot of damage but if the biggest piece left of us is smaller than a pebble—or an insurance adjuster's soul— we're done.

So, I didn't get the attention of an idiot vampire hunter. This dude meant business. How the hell did he find me? Another question: where can I find a Milk Bone treat the size of my arm? I need to do something nice for Max to thank him for saving my ass.

A bomb stake. Probably three if they're all the same thing. I hastily yank the other two from their loops in the 'toolkit.' Sure enough, their bottoms pop off to reveal the exact same interior. The 'microchip' has to be a combination timer/trigger/detonator. C-4 is pretty stable. Takes a bit of doing to make it go off. There's probably a blasting cap embedded inside the clay wad. Yes, I know this. I've already delivered bombs for Wolent and spent a few minutes talking to the vampire who prepared the device.

Three C-4 loaded pointy sticks.

Our 'stupid noob of a vampire hunter' takes on a sudden, far more sinister tone. I can't tell if this thing is not armed yet, ticking down already, or set to go off at a specific time. The only thing I *do* know is that this shit needs to get the hell out of my house now.

Dammit! It's daytime. I can't fly. I'm terrified it's going to go off before I can even get pants on.

"Blix!" I yell.

The imp pops into being on my bed, head tilted to one side in curiosity. *"Eebu?"*

I hold the case out toward him in both hands. "This is a bomb. Can you put it somewhere it can't possibly hurt anyone?"

He makes a strangled warbling noise while nodding so emphatically his big leathery ears flop around. The little guy pounces, clings to the case, then disappears, taking it with him.

Whew… I owe him another video game.

Sometimes, I complain about the weird stuff in my unlife—but every now and then, I'm *really* happy it's here. It takes me a minute or two to stop shaking. Eventually, I realize the guy who tried to kill me probably wouldn't have set the timers on the bombs until after he stuck it into my chest. Or… at least planted it in my room. I don't need to have a nervous breakdown thinking about Sam carrying a bomb around without realizing it.

For the unlife of me, I can't think of how a vampire hunter found me or what I did to draw the attention of—oh wait. A running shootout through the streets of Chicago. Yeah, that might get noticed.

Grr.

I WALK IN THE FRONT DOOR, KICK MY SNEAKERS OFF IN THE DESIGNATED SPOT, then remove my sunglasses. My mother hates it when we use our feet to shut the door behind us, so I take the time to turn and close it like a civilized human.

Mom's relaxing on the couch. She got home from work early tonight.

For her, 'early' means she left the office at the time she's scheduled to without being stuck late for one reason or another. Dad's in the kitchen prepping food. Smells like we're grilling out on the back deck tonight. Sierra's on the PlayStation—shocking, I know.

My mother looks up from her Kindle and stares at me, one eyebrow up. It's not that I'm entering the house after having been outside during the day that's getting the Eyebrow of Inquisition. Pretty sure she's fixated on the big black hockey bag slung over my shoulder. It's unusual. I never played organized sports in school. Up until about an hour ago, I did not own a big black hockey bag. In fact, the store tag is still dangling off the strap.

I know better than to just casually walk by and act like the bag doesn't exist. Me trying to leave the room as fast as possible would only succeed in getting my mother to go into interrogation mode.

She pulls her reading glasses down. "What's with the bag? Moving a body?"

"Uhh..." I grind my toes into the rug. "Kinda."

My mother sighs. "Not funny, Sarah."

Chloe's voice emanates from the bag. "She's not joking."

"Young lady, do you have a child in that bag?" asks Mom, aghast.

The PlayStation instantly goes on pause. Sierra whips around to gawk at me.

What else can I say? I shrug. "Yeah." Hey, don't look at me like that. The bag has more room than the kennel did... and it's not locked. She's too new to cope with sunlight at all yet.

Sierra gives me a 'what the hell is wrong with you' squint.

Mom sets her Kindle down on the sofa and scoots to the edge of the cushion as if she's about to stand. "Do I need to be upset?"

I look at my mother. "Possibly, but not with me."

"What's this about a child in a bag?" Dad walks in, drying his hands on a dishtowel. "What happened to Sophia?"

"Nothing happened to Soph as far as I'm aware." I gently set the bag down on the rug and scurry over to the living room's front window to pull the curtains closed.

Sierra gasps, going wide eyed. "Holy shit."

"Sierra Renee Wright!" snaps Mom. "Language!"

My sister points at the bag. "It's gotta be a vampire kid. Sare's shutting the curtains."

Dad makes a face like he just watched someone shoot a puppy.

With the curtains secure and the room suitably dim, I crouch and unzip the hockey bag. Chloe's curled up in the middle of it wearing a super frilly doll dress, surrounded by cute animal plushies. She pushes herself up to stand inside the bag, stretches, then steps one bare foot over the side onto the carpet.

Mom emits this muffled squee almost like the noise Sophia made when she saw the kittens I dropped off at Ashley's, only about $1/50^{th}$ the volume. "Oh, my."

Sierra can't help but cringe a little. It's not the idea of a vampire kid bothering her. It's the extreme girliness of that dress. The hair ribbons aren't helping. Aurélie has her done up like a porcelain doll. At least three paintings have happened.

My mother proceeds to melt into a puddle of aww.

Dad's giving me this 'who the hell could do this to someone so little' glare. He's simultaneously furious and heartbroken. I'm pretty sure I've changed somehow. Chloe's condition doesn't break my heart. She's been given an awesome gift. Yeah, maybe it's a gift she's too little for, but it's hardly anything to be sad over… or I'm rationalizing so I don't have to think about the price of admission.

"Do *not* let Sophia see her," says Sierra. "The squeesplosion will flatten every house within five miles."

Chloe gives her a flat look. "I'm not a doll. She just dresses me like one."

Mom glances at me. "Why?"

"Not me, Aurélie."

"Oh," says Mom, Dad, and Sierra at the same time, like they all totally understand.

"What happened?" Mom stands and walks over to Chloe.

The girl squeezes her hands into fists. For a second, I think she's going to bolt and run away but she stands her ground. Mom sits on the floor next to her, and begins doing the 'mom thing' and fussing over her.

"I… umm." I shrug. "Not really sure. She won't tell me."

Chloe hangs her head.

The 'rents proceed to try talking to her, asking if she's okay, if she needs anything, while intermittently telling her how sweet and adorable she is. For the first ten or so minutes of this, the kid stands there in a barely suppressed flinch, like she's waiting to get slapped at any second. Finally, after listening to my parents get emotional at the idea someone hurt her, she looks up. After a long, piercing stare at Mom, then an equally probing stare at Dad, she relaxes and gives this little irritated huff. "My parents were assholes."

Mom gasps while Dad whirls away, undoubtedly so Mom doesn't see him trying not to laugh.

"Not fair." Sierra gestures at Chloe. "How come she gets to swear and I get in trouble?"

"She's from New Jersey," I deadpan.

This is too much for Dad. He bursts into laughter.

"Why is that funny?" I ask.

"It is not." Mom scowls.

A moment later, Dad wipes tears from his eyes and collects himself. "It is funny. Things are... umm, different there. The East Coast has a totally different energy to it and all the impatience, irritation, anger, and negative energy kinda concentrates in New Jersey."

Sierra raises both eyebrows. "You've been watching *Ghostbusters II* again, haven't you?"

"It's been about five months." Dad taps a finger to his chin. "Sounds like an idea for later tonight."

This is an opportunity I've been waiting for. I kneel, sitting back on my heels next to Chloe and put an arm around her. "My parents are not assholes. You can trust them. I promise."

Mom gives me the look of death, but stays quiet. She knows what I'm trying to do.

"You keep asking about them." Chloe looks down and away from me. "Why?"

"Because I care about you."

Chloe scrunches up her nose. "You don't even know me. How can you care about me?"

I gently cup her cheek and pull her head around so she's looking me in the eye. "I agreed to be your caretaker knowing if anything goes wrong, it's going to be me facing destruction."

The kid bites her lower lip, staring at me with an 'oh... yeah' sort of expression.

"Wait what?" Mom gawks. "Destruction? What did you do, Sarah?"

Dad stops smiling.

Chloe sighs. "My parents used to hit me a lot. Even if I didn't do anything bad. Daddy would grab me out of bed sometimes at night and just hit me until his arm got tired. Sometimes, I'd be awake and hear him coming, so I tried to hide under the bed. It only made him hit me more. I think he hit me too hard one night, so I didn't wake up until the vampire fixed me."

Sierra cling-hugs the 'rents, sniffling.

My parents both stand there with their hands over their mouths, crying silently. All I can do is squeeze Chloe tight and mutter about how no one will ever treat her like that again.

"Oh." Sierra sneakily wipes a tear, then grins at Chloe. "You got Daltoned."

THE EXACT OPPOSITE OF
NORMAL

C hloe's willingness to talk about her former life is short-lived.

My parents dote over her for a bit before Dad goes back to getting ready to cook. Despite being pretty sure the kid read their minds, wary of them being a possible threat, she still seems unsure how to handle being around 'parents' who aren't mean to her. Mom's all about taking Chloe to the store to get her some modern clothing. I subtly sneak in a few words of warning that we need to be extremely careful with letting people see her. Unless we have a solid cover story to explain who she is and why she might not always be here, it's a risk letting anyone outside the 'circle of trust' see her.

By circle of trust, I mean those who know about the vampire stuff.

Hunter, Ronan, Ashley, Mrs. Carter, and Michelle are okay to meet Chloe. Nicole and Priya both know about Sophia's magic but not the vampire stuff. If either of them meet Chloe, memory surgery of some form will need to happen. We can only get so much mileage about an 'out of state cousin' story. Ugh, maybe it *is* kinda cruel to make a child vampire. She's going to live like a character from a creepy British movie where they keep some sickly little girl hidden away in the bowels of a massive manor house and never let her go outside or see anyone.

I'm being melodramatic. She can be part of vampire society. We don't have to keep her hidden away all the time. But... maybe bringing her to the soirees is a bad idea. The more they are reminded of her existence, the more the older vamps might call for her destruction simply as a precaution or a 'mercy killing.' Some of them regard it as cruel to deprive someone the ability to grow up. But they're thinking about it from the point of view of people who have grown up. Can a little kid really miss things she never imagined? How can they say it's cruel she'll never have a lover when she has absolutely no concept of what it even means? It's not like the movies where she will develop an adult mind with adult desires but still be trapped in a child body. *That* would be horrid.

Even if she 'can't wait to grow up,' it won't seem real to her. Like her seventh year of life is stuck on repeat. Kids don't really have a detailed sense of time anyway. I mean, at that age, waiting three months for Christmas felt like an eternity. To me, a year feels like a long wait. To my parents? A year goes by in a blink. My grandparents think 'twenty years ago' wasn't too far back. Happens with age. Must be comparative to lifespan. Except for vampires. When I'm 200, I'll still think of a year as long, because it's how my mind works at the age I turned. Same with Chloe. For her, 'a couple of months' will always feel like a really long time.

EVENTUALLY, MOM GOT HERSELF UNDER CONTROL... ABOUT AN HOUR AFTER I brought the kid here. Chloe's upstairs with Sierra and Sophia. Yes, the squeesplosion was epic. It fell short of setting off all the car alarms in our cul-de-sac though. I'm in the kitchen with the 'rents having a whispered conversation about their worries. Primarily, they are concerned Chloe could be unintentionally dangerous because she can't control her impulses. If she gets hungry, she might bite one of the Littles or their friends. As she starts to discover how to use her mental powers, she'll become impossible for a mortal to parent. If Mom or Dad tells her to do something (or not do something) and she is defiant, she could mind control them to go away.

Their concerns are valid.

I sigh, rubbing my forehead. "Yeah. It's something to worry about. She should be reasonably okay unless she gets emotional. Kids can't control themselves when they get emotional... like Uncle Hank."

Mom tries to keep a serious face but she almost laughs. Dad chuckles.

"Should we brace ourselves for the entire family turning undead?" asks Mom. "Maybe it wouldn't be so bad. Hardest part is going to be Fowler demanding I be in the office at seven in the morning."

I know she's not serious, so I let myself laugh. It's so weird. As cool as I am about Chloe being a vampire, the notion of it happening to the Littles still freaks me out. At least we don't have to wonder what kind of fiend turned her anymore. Somehow, a vampire happened to be there when the girl's father beat her to death and did the same thing for her Dalton did for me.

The universe works in weird ways sometimes. I wonder if our paths crossed because of those similar circumstances. Another thing to ponder: does a mercy Transference affect the odds of someone becoming an Innocent? Honestly, there couldn't be a better result in her case. Imagine a child Fury? Or Beast? Eek. Kids can be volatile enough without having a bloodline prone to random, unprovoked fits of violent anger. Like, someone shuts off *Little Mermaid* before the movie ends and the next thing you know there's a car flying through the window of the house next door.

"I don't think it will come to that point," says Dad. "What's the plan here?"

I lean on the counter. "St. Ives is trying to find a way to reverse it, but no one really thinks it will work. She's a scientist and vampires aren't science."

Dad tilts his head. "Sophia? She did whatever she did to Sierra. Maybe she could help."

"Heh." I overact a wince. "If you ask me, Sophia got super lucky her enchantment on Sierra worked. If she tries to do something to Chloe, she might turn the poor kid into a bunny rabbit unicorn."

Mom barks out a cackle at my unexpected remark, then sighs. "Well, you know, Sarah, it's a really big responsibility."

Don't I know it. Most parents don't have to worry about being immolated into a pile of ash if they screw up raising their kid. And really, how do you 'raise' a vampire kid? They'll never change. It's not so much 'raising' as being permanently on 'damage control detail.' This is exactly why I'm going to take the 'big sister' route rather than try to act like her mother.

"Hmm." Dad sniffs the air. "Steaks are almost ready." He reaches for the patio door, but pauses to smile at me. "I always assumed you'd give us our first grandkid. Hadn't quite expected you to do it at nineteen, though."

I roll my eyes. "Guys… what do I do here?"

Dad heads out onto the deck toward the grill. I trail after him with Mom behind me.

"I mean." I sigh. "It feels like the harder I try to keep everything normal, the crazier everything gets. Looking after a little vampire kid is going to be a full-time job. It's so easy for her to do something that might blow up and expose us all."

"Not as bad as having a two-year-old," says Mom. "At least you can reason with Chloe."

I snicker.

Dad lifts the lid on the grill, examines the steaks, and seeming satisfied, begins tonging them over to a serving platter. "I'm proud of you, Sarah. Ask yourself one thing. Could you destroy her if you had to?"

I shudder. "No, Dad. How could you even ask that?"

He pauses, one steak dangling from the tongs, to grin at me. "I'm not asking you because I think you'll need to do it. Your reaction to the question tells me you know you did the right thing. You aren't doubting whether or not you made the right choice; you're worried you won't be good enough to follow through. Don't be."

I hug him. "If I got pregnant as a teenager, you'd have helped me take care of the baby, right?"

Mom twitches. "Sarah, you can't take care of a baby by yourself at your age. Of course we'd help."

"Good." I wink at her.

Dad glances at Mom. "Allie, I think we just volunteered to babysit."

It's 10:00 p.m., do you know where your undead children are?

I'm in my bedroom sitting on the floor watching Chloe play with a bunch of dolls and toys we brought down from the attic. It's mostly Sophia's old stuff. Sierra wasn't as into the girly stuff and she totally hated the concept of pink play kitchens. She liked puzzle toys, robotics, builder kits, and so on. Watching Chloe now, it's easy to believe she's normal. The only sign anything is possibly unusual is her habit of whispering. Like a veteran from a warzone, the poor kid's used to making as little noise as possible. If she made noise, it might attract the attention of her parents.

While her psyche is forever frozen as a seven-year-old, I'm hoping she eventually overcomes being frightened of adults or feeling like she constantly needs to hide to avoid random beatings. Ugh. I really need to think of something more cheerful… like leukemia.

The elaborate old-timey dress seriously adds to her eeriness. While she might be perfectly innocent as well as Innocent (with a capital I), she's still a vampire and that comes with a certain radiant energy. Kids, animals, and some adults will be able to feel something off about her. It's situational though. In a dress like this, alone, at the end of a hallway in an abandoned old house, standing there in silence, she'd scare the ever loving hell out of someone. Here, in my room? They wouldn't really notice.

It's why I scared those two urban explorers so bad. My energy is *not* normal. If I'm frightened or angry, it kicks up a notch. When I tried to act all creepy and stuff to make them run away, they not only saw a chilling sight, they *felt* me. In hindsight, it's kinda funny. Maybe a few years from now if I'm super bored, I'll take Chloe with me to some random city at night, find a hotel, and get her to stand silently in the middle of a dark corridor wearing a white nightgown with her hair over her face... and video people's reactions to her.

Nah. I'm not that mean.

I watch her playing with the old Barbie stuff and fall into this bottomless mental pit trying to debate the nature of eternal childhood. Is it happy and free from all the anxiety, responsibility, and worries that come with adulthood or is it tragic? A child being killed is absolutely tragic, but she's right here. To paraphrase one of the TV shows my Dad liked as a kid, they built her better, stronger, faster. She's the six-million-dollar rugrat, only she doesn't make that weird noise whenever she runs.

A blood curdling scream comes from upstairs in Mom's voice.

Chloe looks up, a doll in each hand. "Uh oh. Something scared the shit out of grandma."

"I haven't heard Mom scream like that since Daryl walked into the house without taking his sneakers off." I float up to my feet. "Gonna check on her."

The kid nods and resumes playing with her dolls.

One thing about minding a vampire kid? I don't have to worry so much about her having accidents. If she sticks her finger in an electrical outlet, drinks poison, runs with scissors... no lasting damage.

I rush upstairs to find the 'rents on the back deck. Dad's standing there with his hands on his hips, attention focused on something in the yard. He looks impressed and horrified. Mom's pacing around in a figure-eight pattern, trying to talk and or scream in between retching and gagging.

Okay, this is weird.

A second later, the smell hits me. It stinks so bad my mind blanks out and I forget my own name for a few seconds. Imagine rotting eggs, rotting meat, shit, mold, and the liquid from the bottom of a garbage truck all thrown into a pot and boiled. I'm legit astonished my father's keeping a straight face.

Shudder. I clamp a hand over my mouth and nose, then step out onto the deck. Curiosity pulls me to the railing, trying to get a peek at what

Dad's staring at. Near the middle of our yard sits the most epic of epic turds I've ever seen. The damn thing is about the size of a fireplace log, maybe a little bigger. However, it's unmistakably a number two. The intensity of the stink is so severe I can almost *see* waves of odor in the air. I swear, if any birds try to fly over our yard right now, they'd have a heart attack at the smell and drop dead out of the sky.

I gurgle.

Dad glances over at the sound, realizes I'm here, and goes back to admiring the turd from hell. "I think it's from the dog."

Mom gags. "We don't have a—oh. Good grief, Jonathan, what did it eat?"

"A vampire hunter," I deadpan.

Mom's expression tells me she thinks I'm kidding. Probably for the best I leave that alone. She looks at me, then Dad. "How is it we've had a hellhound this long and we've never had to, umm… scoop after it?"

"I think we're going to need more than a pooper scooper and a Ziplock bag for this." Dad wags his eyebrows. "More like a snow shovel and outdoor trashcan… maybe a backhoe."

"They don't usually eat meat," I say. "He chewed in defense of the home."

"Wait, you're serious?" asks Mom. "He killed and ate someone?"

"Seems that way. Some guy was trying to break into the house and attack me." I grimace. "He chewed in defense of the home."

I don't know how to process my parents seeming to brush this off as an 'oh, okay' moment. Maybe having an actual hellhound in the yard is already so far beyond reality to them it's no big deal if it eats someone, especially a man intending to break in and cause harm. Someone coming after me could easily have hurt one of the Littles on the way. If anything can be said about my parents, they are extremely protective of us.

"Should we wake Sam up and make him clean this since it's his dog?" asks Mom.

Dad gestures at the yard. "That turd is bigger than our son."

Mom gags again, then coughs, then mutters, "I haven't seen a load of poop this big or stinky since that opening argument from Tyler Lawson in '14."

Sigh. "I got it. I'm the only one here who can stop breathing for an hour."

"Not technically true," says Dad.

"Yeah, but she's seven. She couldn't even lift that monster log."

Dad laughs like the ten-year-old he misses being.

"I'm going inside." Mom throws her hands up. "I'm going to be smelling this in my dreams."

An odd sort of low rumbling growl comes from the corner of the yard. Sounds like a huge dog moaning in apology.

"It's okay, Max," I call. "Natural process. You're okay. And thank you for stopping that idiot."

A hellhound making a happy noise is a truly odd thing. The sound is canine enough to be recognizable, but demonic enough to make all the little hairs on my arms stand up.

Dad pats me on the shoulder like a sergeant wishing the new recruit good luck before sending them off on a suicide mission. "Let me know if you need a hand with that."

"I should be okay."

"What are you going to do with it?"

I glance to the right. "Contemplating putting it in Niedermeyer's yard."

He cackles.

"Kidding. I'll get rid of it… probably fly it out to sea or something."

"Uhh…" Dad cringes. "Are you prepared to be responsible for wiping out a few thousand fish?"

"Are you serious?"

He pats me on the shoulder, then heads for the door. "Nope. If you're feeling adventurous, you could always put it in Stefano's coffin."

"Hah!" I giggle-snort. "Funny, but I'm not going to escalate things. Besides, as much of a prig as he is, no one really sleeps in a coffin. That's Hollywood."

Dad gives me this 'I know, just teasing' face, then runs inside, overacting taking a huge gulp of 'clean' air.

I stare at mega-turd and sigh. Talk about a shitty way to spend my night.

THE DIRE WHIMS OF GREATER POWERS

hloe stayed with us for a few days, sleeping in my bed. I made a disturbing discovery that's kept me in a somber mood ever since.

Know how I have this little white line scar on my chest where Scott stabbed me? When she's asleep, Chloe is *covered* in bruises. There's a recognizable hand mark on her left calf that makes me picture her father reaching under her bed, grabbing her, and dragging her out to be hit. Thankfully, except for being grey—just like me while sleeping—she doesn't look as though someone beat her to death. If the fatal blow hit her in the head and cracked her skull, that part isn't lingering behind as an immortal scar.

I swear, if the bastard wasn't already dead, I'd totally go hunt him down and I'd make it take a while. I'd let him see my claws and fangs and chase his ass into the woods for hours, trying to push him into dying of sheer terror and only killing him physically if he wouldn't drop dead.

She's so new she isn't waking up until around five. It took me awhile to get up earlier and earlier, too. About ten minutes before she opens her eyes, her body goes lifelike and all the bruises and stuff heal. I don't think she even knows she looks so battered at night. It makes me wonder if that little scar of mine appears to be an open wound when I'm out.

I've been a complete mess the past two days. Seeing her little battered body before she wakes up is beyond my heart's ability to tolerate. Her being a vampire is not tragic. What happened to her before that is. Even if no one can 'cure' her Transference, I have to find a way to fix that 'death mark.' I'm not going to be able to handle having my heart broken every damn afternoon.

Thankfully, as an Innocent, Chloe does have the ability to go outside during times when no one would find it strange to see a kid her age awake. If I'm walking around with her at like three in the morning, someone's going to call the police on us. We've got a few hours though, any time between five and eight or nine is reasonable enough. It's probably going to take her a while to develop her sun tolerance.

She's back with Aurélie now, having the time of her unlife. The kid's got a vampire faerie godmother, two grandparents she's starting to trust (my parents), and me. I seem to have successfully slipped into her psyche as a mix of big sister and mom. Feels like I'm in a Lifetime movie where the parents die and the teenage girl is stuck raising their younger sibling.

It's a little after midnight and I'm in downtown Seattle with Tilloa. Despite me being buried under some serious responsibilities, I'm still a teenager. Slacking is going to happen. Today was a friend day. Spent most of the afternoon with Michelle and Ashley, primarily focused on keeping Ash's spirits up. Raleigh did resurface, having popped over to Ashley's house unannounced yesterday. I'd been home alone with Chloe at the time, so didn't get a chance to go 'Corey' the girl. Ashley didn't seem overly concerned as Raleigh wasn't giving off the uncertain, hesitant vibes she did when they fumbled through an attempt to have sex. Whether or not they *had* sex or merely attempted to is a matter of opinion, I suppose. Depends on what one's definition of where 'bedroom play' ends and intercourse begins.

Maybe it had been Raleigh's first time and nerves got the better of her? Dunno. I *will* know eventually, however. A promise is a promise.

Tilloa joined us once the sun went down. We had a spontaneous mini 'girls night out' again, going to this place in Woodinville that couldn't decide if it wanted to be a bar, a night club, or a comedy house. The guy doing the stand-up routine tonight wasn't too bad, but his humor seemed aimed at the thirty-or-older crowd. I didn't get most of his jokes.

Ash and Michelle went home after due to it being midnight. Tilloa and I decided to keep hanging out and flew to Seattle for a bite. After feeding, we wandered around looking for something to do to amuse ourselves. This mostly took the form of people-watching or climbing around roofs and skyscrapers up high where no one is usually allowed to go. Simple curiosity at what the heck is up there. We're not like the Portland Lost Ones. No casual vandalism because it's funny.

We joke about being basically superheroes. Tilloa suggests—

THE DIRE WHIMS OF GREATER POWERS | 169

sarcastically—that we fly around looking for crime to stop. While I don't necessarily object to the idea, it's the opposite of trying to stay under the radar.

Around three, she decides to show me her new place.

Tilloa has relocated her 'lair' to a night club in downtown Seattle called Starlight. Arthur Wolent sorta owns it. I say sorta because his name isn't on any paperwork. He owns a corporation or an investment account that owns another company that owns this night club—plus a whole bunch of other stuff. Via some byzantine network of command hierarchy, he's technically in control of the place but he doesn't manage it directly.

I've never been there. Tilloa tells me there is a secret door to a basement level where mortals aren't allowed unless they're thralls or snacks. It's not shown on any building plans or whatever. The mortal authorities have no idea it exists. Down there, it's basically vampire apartments. Sounds kinda neat.

The only real problem with the location is it's in the heart of downtown among all the high rises. Flying there is tricky due to this thing called windows. When people are living or working fifty stories up, it gets much easier for them to notice us flying. A one-off sighting in an emergency isn't such a big deal. Who would believe them? Generally, we move too fast for anyone to get a cell phone on us in time to take a picture before we're around a corner. Still, we play it safe by landing and walking a few blocks. Not like we get tired.

A strange twangy fluttering comes from behind and above us.

"Till," I whisper. "Do you hear—?"

Air whooshes against my back like someone swung a baseball bat at me and missed by an inch.

Wham!

A massive object slams into the sidewalk behind us with a bang as loud as ground zero of a nuclear bomb. The pavement shakes under my feet from the force of the impact. Pure indescribable loudness morphs into the jangling of metal and crystalline shattering. An explosion of glass bits washes over us, the tiny fragments like an ocean wave of white snow. Metal scraps clatter and bang about, pipes bouncing on pavement. A steel cable slaps down to my right, scuffing the sidewalk and caving in the side of a bus stop shelter like a stepped-on soda can. More cables slap into the sidewalk behind and to our left. Somehow, nothing deadlier than a rain of un-sharp safety glass bits strikes us directly.

It's not really as loud as a nuke. My ears are hypersensitive.

Tilloa stands there rigid as a corpse, eyes so wide her eyeballs seem about to fall straight out of her skull. Swear she looks like the cat from *Tom and Jerry* right after the mouse popped a paper bag behind his head. If not for the eek factor of what just happened, I'd probably laugh at the face she's making.

I twist to look behind us.

A mangled metal frame sits on the ground in a twisted heap. For a second, I'm confused because skyscrapers don't have fire escapes. Then it hits me: it's a window washing rig, and it's crashed to the earth less than a hand's width behind us. The man who'd been operating it is now a mostly liquid mess in the middle of the road oozing out from the sleeves of a white jumpsuit.

"I ain't eaten no solid food in three months," rasps Tilloa, "and I damn near just shit myself."

All I can do is cover my mouth and gawk. More cables sway back and forth in the air, sixty stories up. The armature that used to raise and lower this platform extends out over the roof, four broken cables dangling from it. I squint, zooming my vision in as much as I can manage. The ends are frayed apart, burst out into 'dandelions' of individual thin steel cords.

"You okay?" whispers Tilloa, still not having moved.

"I think so."

Two security guards from an office tower across the street, one from the building attached to the fallen rig, and a random cop who happened to be close enough to witness the drop all come running over to us. One of the security guards gets stuck in a loop of saying, "holy shit," over and over again. The cop gives us a quick look as if he can't believe neither one of us is a bloody mess.

A tall, black security guard grabs me in this overly protective 'big brother' sort of way. "Don't look, hon."

I mildly resent being treated like a kid, but no sense complaining. The guy means well. I still sneak a backward glance as he escorts me away. The worker who fell is pancaked to the street. Can't see too much detail from this distance or angle, but it's abundantly clear he's dead. The real world is not a *Tom and Jerry* cartoon. When someone is *that* flat, they don't re-inflate and stumble around in a daze for a few seconds before shaking it off. Another somewhat nauseating revelation: people falling forty stories onto pavement burst open like a dropped Stromboli.

A spirit manifests right next to the lump. Looks like a middle-aged Hispanic man. He shoots me this glare like I'm the one who killed him before fading away.

Okay, dude. Seriously? I had nothing to do with this. Why are you pissed at me?

Am I paranoid? I guess he could've just been pissed off in general at dying and since I'm the only one here who can see him, I got the glare of doom. Great. Wonderful.

"Let's get out of here," I whisper.

"Good plan." Tilloa shakes off the shock of a near splat.

We hastily delete ourselves from the cop and security guard's minds, then run around the nearest corner.

THE STARLIGHT CLUB IS A SLEEK, BLACK-AND-SILVER AFFAIR WITH A MODERNIST design.

We make our way inside. Despite it being so late, there's a fair amount of people here, many of whom are mortal. I follow Tilloa across the room. Purple lights and periwinkle blue carpeting is kinda weird on the eyes. EDM fills the air but it's not turned up too loud. No one's dancing. Most people are hanging out in clusters among round seating booths against the wall. The crowd gives off a professional or business vibe. No punks or anyone overly young here. I do get a few 'what's a kid doing here' looks, but no one cares enough to do more than raise eyebrows.

At the back of the room, a black curtain separates the main area from a corridor to the bathrooms and some employee-only offices. Tilloa goes around a corner at the end and approaches a door marked 'storage closet.'

Inside is, shockingly enough, a storage room. Bit big to call it a 'closet.' Multiple shelves hold various things like toilet paper, napkins, paper towels, light bulbs, and other ordinary supplies a place like this would want to keep on hand.

I follow her inside and pull the door closed. "Are we slipping into a closet to make out or is this where it is?"

She laughs, then gestures at the back right corner. "Over here."

Three narrow pipes run down the wall, probably for water. One has a red valve with a tag marked 'Emergency Use Only.' I can't say I'm surprised when Tilloa grabs the valve and pulls on it. The cover plate opens to one side, exposing a keyhole. She fishes a key from her purse, sticks it in the lock, and gives a turn.

A soft *click* comes from the door behind us, and a second later a door-sized panel of cinder block wall slides away to reveal a stairwell going down.

"Neat." I whistle. "All high tech and stuff."

She chuckles, puts the key away, and goes down.

The switchback stairs take us about two stories below the surface—probably skipping past the building's official basement—to a hallway full of doors. It's super minimalist and very modern. The walls are white, the doors black, and not the slightest sign of any lights exist. To be fair, it's a little claustrophobic, but everything except the doors appears to be concrete, so it's not like fire could do much here.

"Reminds me of that one scene in *The Matrix* with all the doors," I say.

"Basically, yeah." She goes left. "Except this is real, not a simulation."

I follow her to a plain black door with a silver '53' on it. She unlocks it with another physical key and goes inside.

"Wow, no fancy electronic access card thing?" I ask.

"Nope. Physical locks. Guess it's so we can get in or out if there's a power interruption or something." Tilloa does a little spin, holding her arms out to either side as if indicating the room. "This is the place. What do you think?"

It's really easy to give a tour. Her apartment is one big room with a small sofa, entertainment center in the near left corner, black faux wood table with four chairs, a little kitchen area in the right corner closest to the door, a bed in the innermost right corner, and a small bathroom in the inner left corner. The bathroom is the closest thing this place has to a separate room. No door, but a partition offers privacy to a little six-foot-square area containing a shower and toilet.

"What's with the bathroom?" I ask.

"Haven't thought about it much. What do you mean?" Tilloa sets her purse on a little partition counter separating the 'kitchen' from the 'dining room.'

"If this place is for vampires, why even put toilets in?" I scratch my head. "Innocents are supposed to be rare, right? No other vampires have any need of a toilet."

"You do?" She blinks.

"Umm." Blush time. "Thought I already covered this. The fireworks burger?"

"Oh! Right." She laughs, squirming. "Eww. That has to feel nasty."

"You asked." I sit beside her on the sofa and decide to get my revenge at the embarrassing topic by over-sharing details of what happened when I ate spicy chicken nuggets.

Once we're done laughing, she gestures at the bathroom. "Guess they put toilets in case someone has a mortal over. Thralls or whatever. A snack."

"Oh, true. Gotta have a litterbox for the pets." I smirk, hoping my sarcasm is obvious. I might be a vampire, but I will never understand the older ones who legit look down on mortals as lesser beings.

"Man…" She sighs. "I thought this shit would stop after death."

"Which shit?" I raise both eyebrows.

"Feelin' exhausted."

"Umm, yeah." I tilt my head. "That is odd. We're not supposed to feel tired unless we overdo it with supernatural stuff. Flying too fast, getting our asses kicked. Healing… that sort of thing."

"I've had a wild damn week." She exhales. "That stupid window washing rig is like the cherry on top of the sundae."

"Wow. That bad?" I kick my sneakers off and pull my legs up on the cushion.

Tilloa groans like an old woman as she leans forward to remove her boots. "Yeah. Some crazy son of a bitch tried to car-bomb my favorite Starbucks, for starters."

I gasp. "Tried? How does one 'try' to car-bomb?"

She reclines, stretching and yawning. "Yep. Tried. The damn thing didn't explode. Guy drives right through the front door. Broken glass goes everywhere. People scream, jump away. This dude's sitting there in his little wind-up car pushing a button and making faces."

"Button?"

"Yeah, like one of them hospital call things." She pantomimes holding a small cylindrical object and pushing a button on the end with her thumb. "He's mashing this thing over and over again. Looks terrified and annoyed at once. Pretty damn obvious he was trying to set off a bomb and it wasn't working."

"Holy shit." I gasp into my hands. "What did you do?"

"The hell you think I did?" She laughs. "I got my ass out of there pronto is what I did."

I whistle. "So what happened?"

"Don't know except that the bomb didn't go off. Police probably got him. Or he ran away." She shrugs. "That Starbucks is already open again. They replaced the door and window. Good thing he had such a tiny car."

"That's crazy." I cringe at the thought of being close to a car bomb since I'm almost positive a vampire wouldn't come back from being liquefied by a concussion wave. We're hard to kill but it's not impossible. Certain things *can* kill us permanently, like acid, being cremated, thrown in lava, or being subject to more than ten continuous minutes of political talk radio.

Tilloa grumbles. "Day after the idiot with the car bomb, I got caught in between two more idiots having a shootout. Couple days ago, a broken power line nearly fell on me and lit my ass on fire. And to top it all off, the place I was stayin' before this burned last week."

I stare at her. We seem to be having awfully similar streaks of crazy bad luck. "Any chance this stuff isn't random? How'd the place burn?"

"Couple of mortals decided to squat there. One of them gets the bright idea to make a damned campfire *inside*. I mean, ain't like it was *my* place, just some abandoned old apartment. How damn dumb does a person gotta be to think making a campfire *inside a building* is a good idea?"

Whoa. I whistle in awe. "Damn, are you all right?"

"Yeah. I don't know how the hell you do it."

Blink. "Do what?"

"Stay up when the sun's out." She shakes her head. "That fire woke me right up. Don't even know what time it was other than the damned sun had me in its sights. I left a smoke trail out the door. I can't remember much more than seeing fire, then being outside and it's so god awful bright it's like I'm in the heart of a nuclear reactor. Next thing I know, I'm in a basement, half burned and naked. I felt like a damn French fry that fell out the basket and sat in the deep fryer all day."

"Ack. You read that article too, huh?"

"Article?" She raises an eyebrow at me.

I explain the thing we found about the health benefits of sleeping naked.

"Oh, nah. I had a sexy little nightie on. Bitch of a sun lit me on fire so bad it burned the thing to ashes."

"Ouch." I cringe. The only thing that causes vampires more pain than claw wounds is fire… or listening to Justin Bieber music.

Tilloa tells me about spending a whole night hiding in an industrial basement—possibly a hotel—and feeding on a couple of maintenance workers. Unfortunately, she was so burned and messed up, the first poor bastard she found didn't survive the feeding. We talk for a while about how guilty she is over it. She didn't want to kill anyone, but the feeding frenzy just took her over. I cringe sitting there listening to her describe how that first meal caused her crisp-i-fied skin to break up and heal. What scares me the most, though, is she doesn't mention anything about feeling a rush or surge of energy when she drank the guy to death. With no real context to base it on, I assume she didn't get the 'high' kill-feeders crave because she'd been so badly hurt. All the power-slash-energy that would've gone into giving her the rush went to regeneration. It's tragic she killed someone, but at least she won't become addicted to it. Also, not like she had a choice. A blackout... just like me when the drug dealer whipped open that hotel room.

"Felt like I went for a swim in that deep fryer all over again." She shudders. "All I could do was curl up in a ball and try not to scream. Sounded like a bunch of people munching on overcooked bacon."

"Ack. And I thought I had it rough cleaning up a forty-pound turd."

She gives me side-eye. "Are you being metaphorical?"

"I wish."

Now, I like Tilloa. I'm inclined to trust her. But this is my family. It's not her I'm wary of, it's her sire. Dalton can read my mind even from afar. Pretty sure he can't go deep and root around for any thoughts, only see what's at the tip of my brain if he's far away. I don't know what kind of jackass can make someone a vampire and just leave them behind, much less bury them and chain a couple of hikers nearby as a snack. Really a sick bastard. Whoever they are, I don't trust them at all. Maybe her sire is an Academic like Eleanor St. Ives doing an experiment. Make a vampire, leave food nearby, then sit back out of sight, and see what happens.

In the interest of not wanting people I don't trust to become aware of my family's details, I don't yet tell her about Max the Hellhound, so I talk about it as if it's a mystery turd from nowhere.

"A literal forty-pound poop?" She blinks.

"Yeah. We're kind of feuding with a neighbor. I think he left a mound of crap in our yard as a middle finger."

"Ugh. Hate people like that." Tilloa gestures around. "So, anyway. After the last place burned, I heard about the Starlight club. I knew it existed before, but didn't realize it had apartments, thought it was a vampire hangout. Came here to ask for suggestions on a safe place to sleep. Figured I could do with a place a bit nicer than a rat-eaten condemned house."

"This is really kinda nice... in a 'stuck on a long-distance colony spaceship' sort of way."

She laughs. "What's that supposed to mean?"

"Oh, right. You're not a geek." I wink. "It feels like we're inside personnel quarters on a big starship. Maximum efficiency of available space."

"That's true, except for the outer space part."

"Seriously though," I say. "It's nice. Lush even. Did it come with the big TV and Xbox or did you bring those?"

"Pre-furnished." Tilloa smiles.

"Nice. Sorry you lost all your stuff."

"I didn't have much stuff. Lost most of it when I died. Snuck into my old place before my parents showed up and sold all my crap. Kept a few sentimental things. Got unbelievably lucky. Box I kept 'em in survived that fire somehow.

I frown, fixated on thoughts of her family believing she's dead. Hope she didn't have to watch her family selling off all her stuff. "Sorry."

"Ehh. It happens. I got eternity to collect new crap. Really, though. How much do I need? We can take whatever we need whenever we need it. Can't really have a proper house to fill up with junk. What's the point of endlessly collecting stuff?"

"You're going all *Fight Club* on me now."

"Something like that." She stretches and yawns again. "Thanks to that damn fire, all I had was my bare ass and my box of sentimental stuff." Tilloa tells me about her adventurous trip. Two days after the fire, once she'd fully healed back to normal, she stopped living like a troll in the underground hotel parking garage and went streak-flying across the city to break into a high-end department store via a skylight at three in the morning. She's since acquired a new wardrobe and doesn't seem the least bit guilty about stealing thousands of dollars' worth of clothing and handbags.

Tilloa yawns. "Damn, I'm tired. For once, it's kind of annoying I can't sleep until it's time to."

"Crazy week for both of us."

"Oh?" She glances at me. "What happened to you?"

I tell her about the two car accidents, the vampire hunter with C-4 packed stakes, as well as getting shot in the parking lot of the restaurant where my boyfriend works.

Tilloa rubs both hands down her face, then whistles. "Damn, girl. What gods did we piss off?"

"Heh. Not too long ago, I'd think you were kidding. Now, I'm not so sure."

She quirks an eyebrow. "Didn't think you believed in that religious stuff."

"I don't. I mean... like demons are real. But that doesn't immediately convince me all the religious stuff people have been conditioned to believe is real, too. Think about it. A sufficiently powerful thing can be considered a god by a weak mortal. If you take a primitive person from like 2,000 years ago and show them Aurélie or Arthur Wolent going full vampire, they'd consider them a god, right?"

Tilloa mulls for a bit, then nods. "Yeah, I suppose."

"To a mouse, humans are gods." I shrug. "Maybe there *are* entities out there who are to vampires as we are to humans, comparatively more powerful. To us, they'd be gods. Not saying I think there are. But there could be. If they do exist, no damn idea what I did to get on their bad side."

She reaches over and lightly pinches my cheek. "Maybe they simply hate your adorable altruism. Who did you help lately?"

"Ugh." I sigh at the ceiling. "Right? Every time I help someone, it proves the 'no good deed goes unpunished' thing." Yes, I've told Tilloa stories about Petra, helping Coralie, and so on. "Umm, the only one I can think of who I've helped recently is Chloe. And this crazy bad luck started before I knew about her. It might've even started before she got her Transference."

"Hmm." Tilloa leans forward, rubbing her chin. "Well, whatever's doing it must blame me, too. I haven't done shit except try to survive and get used to this whole vampire business."

I think about what we might have possibly both been involved in capable of pissing off anything from an ancient god, to a demon, to a ghost, to the universe itself. "I'm stumped."

"Yeah. Same." She shifts sideways on the sofa to sit cross-legged facing me. "So, where were we?"

And so I proceed to spend the next few hours playing sire-slash-mentor, helping her adjust to unlife. There's only so much I can help her with being an Innocent while she's a Scion. She has some options in her toolkit I don't even know exist much less how to help her use them. But, I can give her the basics that her asshole sire didn't bother with. At least Dalton found me as soon as he could. He didn't mentor me full time because *I* made the choice to go home.

If not for me, Tilloa wouldn't have had anyone to help teach her how to vampire.

EARLY REGISTRATION

In the past, I've sometimes teased Ashley for her ability to ignore bad things and pretend everything's just fine.

Like if the news said nuclear missiles had been launched and would obliterate civilization in forty-five minutes, Ashley would be like, 'hey, let's watch a movie.' Thankfully, the worst apocalyptic event we've yet faced has been school projects being due with only a few days left. Ashley could go on with everything else—trips to the mall, hanging out, watching movies, etc.—as if we didn't have this major piece of homework hanging over us for school. It's her defense mechanism. Anything past her ability to cope with, she pretends isn't happening.

Today, I'm feeling a bit like her.

As if agreeing to be responsible for a child vampire didn't inexorably alter the course of my future to an apocalyptic degree already, some ancient god of luck has it in for me. Far less dangerous, but still important is the Raleigh situation. I still need to get together with Ashley and set up a proper ambush. It doesn't have to be elaborate. Just her telling me where and when to be in the same place with both of them. I'm not going to change anything about Raleigh at all. I merely need to know what her feelings for Ashley are and if she's feeling trapped in a relationship she wants out of but is too chicken to admit it.

Ash has made it clear she wants the truth no matter how painful. She fully expects Raleigh to dump her soon. It's been that way for her ever since she started dating. One thing or another always goes wrong and her relationships never last. The longest relationship she ever had was this guy Austin Herrera who she dated during sophomore year. They lasted almost six months. He seemed like a really sweet guy, right up until he got caught making out with Kimberly Cowan in the gym teacher's office while supposedly being Ashley's boyfriend. He'd evidently bet one of his friends he could—quote unquote—nail every redhead in school before they graduated. Ashley wanted a real relationship. It took her too long to take her pants off for him. Hint: she didn't. He'd hooked up with at least two other girls before Kimberly while still pretending to date Ashley, hoping she'd 'come around' eventually. And of course, the instant she relented and had sex with him, he'd have dumped her. So glad she didn't.

Ugh. Boys.

Ashley and I both suffer the problem of respecting our parents—and ourselves—too much. Neither one of us did more than kiss a boy until we were eighteen. Mostly. What's a few weeks? Scott was a bit pushy and I caved in.

And yeah. My first time did not go well.

Anyway, enough bad romance. I'm too busy pulling an Ashley and ignoring reality.

How? I've gone to Seattle Central College to register for fall classes. Might seem crazy for a vampire to go to school at all. Crazier with a kid to look after. But, I have parents and Aurélie. Attending classes won't run any later than eleven at night and I can try to avoid taking anything in the latest time slot. I'll have most of the night hours free from school to look after Chloe, do whatever jobs Wolent throws my way, exist in vampire society, fulfill any requests or favors Aurélie asks of me, find time to be with my friends, and… good grief.

I really am in denial.

No. I have to do this. Going to college is a dose of normal and it makes my parents happy. To some degree, I think Mom is pretending nothing's really wrong with me and I'm still the same daughter she's had for the past nineteen years. I don't think anything is 'wrong' with me per se, I mean that in the sense she thinks I'm still mortal and going to have an ordinary life. Nah, she knows exactly what's going on and appreciates the effort I put into giving her an illusion.

So here I am in the office filling out paperwork. I'm debating switching to a psychology major. Even though I can't use it professionally, having some knowledge might come in handy for reading vampires since telepathy doesn't work on them without a massive age gap. It's going to be a really long time before any vampires exist sufficiently younger than me for their minds to be open to my powers. I wouldn't need to be an actual psychologist or psychiatrist to deal with mortals. Easy enough to read their mind, see what's messing with them, then use mental commands to deal with problems. I think. Coping with phobias or past trauma is one thing, but I'm not sure it's possible to command a person to stop being schizophrenic for example. Then again, if a traumatic memory is bad enough to generate a phobia, it might pop loose from a mental command.

Blergh.

There's always a generic liberal arts degree, just to make the 'rents happy. It doesn't matter whatsoever the subject I get a degree in, it's not going to make a difference in my 'career.' I could even major in English or Anthropology and not feel like I wasted four years because I've ended up a waitress with an expensive wall hanging. I could even major in Art History and... no, wait. I'd still feel like I wasted four years.

Though, working in the bowels of an art museum might be a good career choice for a vampire with any interest in getting a real job. Like Professor Heath, it could work for a decade or two in an area before I'd have to move. The more people a vampire interacts with on a regular basis, the less time they can spend in a place. Heath can get away with remaining in the same area longer because he's got this indiscernible age thing going. Depending on how the light hits him, he could seem anywhere from late thirties to early sixties. Me? Even ten years in one job would be pushing it. People would notice I still look too young to buy liquor.

While I am in the sweet spot to embrace the perfect balance of acting like a child or a responsible young adult as whim or need strikes, it's crap for being out in public on a regular basis. Good thing teenagers are expected to be slackers.

Hmm. I could major in history. That's another one that's fairly useless in terms of getting a job. Short of teaching or working as a tour guide somewhere, I can't think of where majoring in history would lend itself to a career. It would at least give me something to talk about at the vampire soirees while mingling with people who happened to be around when all the famous stuff went down.

Nah.

I could keep going with programming. It's not over my head or too complicated. I'm just kinda lazy and unmotivated. You know what, yeah. Hell with it. Call it a tribute to Dad. I will stick with computer science as a major. It makes him proud I'm carrying on the geek tradition and maybe

I'll be able to help him out with work projects at some point. Nothing like having an assistant who doesn't sleep at night and can type a thousand words a minute.

It took me longer to make this decision than fill out the schedule request for next semester's classes. Oh, what kind of sadistic son of a bitch made public speaking a mandatory class for the computer science path? Know who mostly majors in comp-sci? Introverted basement-dwelling nerds, the exact opposite sort of people with any interest in public speaking. I'm going to visit a school administrator in the middle of the night and give him a compulsion to hack the system and mark me as having completed that class.

So what if I fought a multi-headed spider-scorpion-nope monster. I'm not a fan of speaking in front of crowds, especially crowds of strangers. I have the power to avoid it, so dammit, I'm going to.

After turning in my paperwork to the clerk—a fiftyish woman with a pewter-colored bob hairdo and giant eyeglasses so thick they could serve as the lenses for Archimedes' death ray—I head out. The woman kept calling me 'sweetie' and giving me strange looks. Can't read minds during the day, but I suspect she's a little confused as to why a 'kid' is taking night classes.

Ever find yourself walking along and not knowing what the heck to do with your hands? It's warm out so I'm not wearing a sweatshirt with pockets. My jeans are a little bit too tight for it to be comfortable stuffing my hands in those pockets. Letting my arms swing at my sides all of a sudden feels overwhelmingly gangly and awkward. I don't have any backpack to carry. Half a block from the parking garage, I stop to rub my face and try to think about anything else other than being overly aware of what I'm doing with my hands.

"Excuse me, miss?" calls a late-twenties guy with a white ball cap. "Do you have a minute?"

I lower my hands from my face to take a longer look at this guy walking toward me. He's kinda average. Short brown hair, blue button down shirt, khaki shorts and Docker shoes with no socks. He's got a small blue backpack over one shoulder like ninety percent of the students here and a clipboard in his hand. His stare is a bit creepily intense, but maybe I'm the only person who's bothered to make eye contact with him in the past two hours. This dude is either a Mormon or some manner of salesman.

Ugh.

"Thanks for stopping," he says past a huge smile. "I'm Evan. We're doing a survey. Do you have a few minutes to answer some questions? I promise I'm not going to try to sell you anything."

A loud mental sigh of annoyance echoes in my brain, but I'm too nice to crush this guy's dreams of getting someone to participate. He looks so excited to be talking to someone who doesn't scurry away while conspicuously avoiding looking directly at him.

"Sure, why not? What kind of survey is it?"

"Coffee." He smiles, readying his clipboard of papers. "Have you consumed coffee in the past three months?"

This is Seattle. Any answer other than 'yes' would probably result in him calling the police or the men in white coats. Fortunately, I don't have to lie.

"Yep."

He marks a box on the clipboard. "Do you primarily buy coffee grinds and brew at home or buy prepared coffee?"

"Umm. About fifty-fifty."

Evan makes another mark. "What brand do you drink at home?"

"Starbucks or flavored coffee from some place my Dad orders from on the internet."

He nods, then marks another box. "Do you tend to buy prepared coffee drinks at a particular establishment or wherever you happen to be?"

"Starbucks again. I mean, they're everywhere. It's not like I'm a fanatic." I chuckle.

"Right?" Evan laughs while marking a box. "Relax. I don't work for Starbucks. We're an independent consumer research agency."

"Cool."

He proceeds to ask me a bunch of questions about what kind of coffee drinks I buy most often—latte vs. espresso, and so on. After that, he moves into questions like 'if a new coffee company were to open stores here, what flavors or types of offerings would you be most interested in?' I've never really thought about coffee to this level before. I'm of the opinion that as long as it doesn't suck, I'll pick something from the list of whatever is available. But hey, market research is market research, right? Any product people can buy likely has guys like Evan putting entirely too much effort into thinking about them. Somewhere, there's probably some poor bastard walking up to people asking them questions about their preferences for artificial dongs.

Thank you, random brain. I do my best to keep a straight face while coming up with some believable sounding answers.

After about five minutes of this, he looks over the clipboard, smiling.

"One last question. Are you willing to associate your name and email address with these survey responses? It's not obligatory, but you can register and be contacted by the company sponsoring this survey for some follow-up questions and sample offers, freebies, and even gift cards."

Shrug. "Sarah."

He absentmindedly scratches above his left ear, then sticks his left hand in the pocket of his khaki shorts. "Sarah Wright?"

Whoa. Does this guy know me? I stare at his face, annoyed to death at the sun for existing. Can't read his mind. How does this dude know me? What are the odds he'd correctly guess my last name right away? Is he an old teacher I had in grade school? Dude doesn't look *that* old. Twenty-six maybe? No way he taught me in grade school unless he was a teenage intern.

"I'm sorry… have we met before?" I ask.

Evan fidgets with something in his pocket. For a few seconds, he appears to forget who he is or what we've been talking about. "Oh, right. The coffee survey."

"Are you okay?" I take a half-step back.

"Fine. I, umm…" He again fidgets, seeming annoyed like someone trying to place a phone call and getting a 'no-signal' message. "Just a few more que… oh, all the boxes are filled in. There aren't any more questions to ask."

He says this in a tone like he's disappointed our conversation is ending. Getting mild creep vibes off him now. But, he's not like leering at me or giving off any sense he's stalking me. So, so, strange. Almost like he's about to have a psychotic break or something.

"Cool. Happy to help," I say, trying not to sound as uneasy as I feel. Dude might be high or having a seizure. My gut tells me to get away from him before he does something weird.

Evan stares at me like he forgot how to talk. Again he fidgets, scowling in annoyance, his pocketed hand twitching. I'd say 'eww', but it doesn't look like he's trying to touch himself through his pants. He's definitely fighting with something in his pocket, though.

"Right, well. Have a nice day." I slip around him and fast-walk the last twenty feet to the corner of the parking deck.

Within half a second of me going around the big concrete column at the corner of the parking deck, an explosion goes off with a meaty *whud*. Next thing I know, I'm lying on my chest surrounded by smoke and dust. Everything is sore. Feels like I'm a human ping pong ball that just got slapped by a giant paddle. Can't see a freakin' thing. The world is absolutely silent. That doesn't seem right. No screaming? No car alarms? No one shouting? Not even the soft clatter of debris falling out of the air?

Holy shit. A damned bomb just went off.

I push myself up off the sidewalk. A pattern of debris on the ground traces out in a line from the corner of the building. The concrete cracked, but the massive, square column at the corner of the parking garage appears to have shielded me from the worst part of the blast. It's like the bomb picked the exact perfect nanosecond to go off. Even one second later, I would have been past the column and exposed through a gap in the side of the parking deck.

It hits me that the source of the explosion had to have been Evan. It felt *that* close.

A sinking, sick feeling churns in my stomach. I stumble to the corner and peek around. The sidewalk and street are littered with papers, clipboard bits, and a pair of smoking Dockers. The biggest piece of him left is about the size of a potato. Wait, that's a hand, rather fist... clutching a button clicker thing like to unlock a car. A left hand. The one that had been in his pocket.

People emerge from the various side streets and buildings in front of me, gawking at the blast site. Their mouths are open like they're all shouting but I still don't hear anything at all. The world is utterly silent. It occurs to me a warm trickling sensation is dripping out of my ears.

Oh, shit. I'm deaf. The blast ruptured my eardrums. Before I can freak out too much at this, a flash of white draws my attention downward. A slightly charred—but surprisingly intact—paper has fluttered to the ground right at my feet. It's a coffee survey with the name Sarah Wright written at the top.

I crouch to pick it up. I'm gonna take this. Don't need written evidence of my presence at a blast site. The people coming to investigate the explosion don't appear to have noticed me amid the swirling dust/smoke cloud. A bunch of windows in the SCC buildings across the street are peppered with tiny holes, likely from nails or metal balls in the bomb. Eek.

While I'm still unnoticed, I back around the corner of the parking deck and run down the steps.

Normally, Follows Rules Girl wouldn't take off from such a scene, but... this has vampire weirdness written all over it. At the bottom of the stairs, I duck into an alcove far enough removed from sunlight to come online. A wicked itching sensation floods my ears. I clench my jaw and weather it, though I really want to scream. It doesn't hurt, but it's *so, so, so* damn unpleasant. Like having 500 ants crawling around inside both ears.

After about two hours—kidding, it's really like two minutes—sound floods back into my brain with a whooshing rush and a crackling like someone crumpling parchment. I think I just heard my eardrums growing back.

Whew. Well that answers one question I've had since I've become a vampire. Injuries I take while offline *will* heal. At least non-fatal ones.

Once the panic of potentially losing my hearing for good wears off, I narrow my eyes.

Okay, Evan... who the hell were you and why do you know me?

Umm, I mean why *did* you know me?

And okay, this is going beyond bad luck now. 'Bad luck' would have been ill timing putting me in a place at the same time some crazy domestic terrorist sets off (or tries to set off) an explosive device. This Evan dude got all fidgety and twitchy when he heard my name. Either I'm paranoid, or the guy had some manner of delayed-action mental compulsion that triggered as soon as he realized who I was. His hand fidgeting in his pocket... holy shit. He was pushing the button! The annoyance had to come from the bomb not going off... until I wound up standing in the exactly perfect place to survive it at such close range.

I stare up at the bottom of the concrete stairs I'm hiding under. Holy shit. I got it all wrong. My luck isn't bad.

It's phenomenal.

A BIT MORE RELAXED

There are precious few times in my life where I've truly wanted to lie to my parents.

They've all been kinda trivial. The most significant lie I ever failed to get over on my mother was trying to tell her 'nothing happened' the night Scott and I attempted to have sex the first time. In hindsight, there's no possible way even a blind person could have believed me. I was a mess. Suppose I got lucky there. Mom didn't take it as me trying to lie but merely being upset and not wanting to talk about it right then and there. Still, she pushed. I caved. We cried. Mom wanted to rip his balls off. Ice cream happened.

Ooh. I'm getting mad just thinking about him again. What kind of asshole starts making love to his girlfriend who he knows is a virgin, sees bleeding, and nopes out of there after two minutes, leaving me alone, curled up in pain, and not knowing if I'm about to bleed to death or if it's normal for the first time.

Grr.

I should have left him right there. Never spoken to him again. It would have made my life a whole lot less complicated. Might've still been at that party, but I wouldn't have gone into the woods with Scott and been spotted by Dalton. And who cares if he fed from mortal me? People don't remember it. Considering the number of people I've bitten since then, it would be really hypocritical of me to freak out at the idea of being a vampire's meal. For all I know, it happened a hundred times to me before that night. Ever feel randomly tired for no reason? Might be due to a vampire feeding you don't remember.

Anyway...

How lame was I? Trying to tell my mom nothing happened with Scott wasn't the lie I stressed out over the most. No, the stressful one, I actually got away with until guilt caught up to me and I confessed. But yeah, lame. Ashley and I snuck into an empty classroom our freshman year of high school and doodled on the dry-erase marker board. Nothing rude or obscene. Just kinda made fun of the teacher for having an unfortunate name and being an insufferable wench. Come on though... if your name is Carol Crotchfelt (I swear, it's a real name) you should not be a teacher, especially at a high school. And if you *do* take that job knowing full well how kids can be, you damn sure better not be one of those super strict, pedantic 'smiling shall not exist in my classroom' type teachers everyone hates.

So yeah, Ash and I covered the dry erase board with little 'cootie critters' because you know, 'crotch.' We got caught because we couldn't stop giggling. No damage, I mean... dry erase markers on a whiteboard. The teacher who caught us—not Mrs. Crotchfelt by the way—made us clean the board and promise not to do it again. Honestly, I think the only reason we didn't get sent to the principal's office for it is because Mrs. Weems disliked her too.

I mean, how horrible does a teacher have to be for Ashley and me to 'vandalize' their room?

Anyway...

I'm tempted to lie to my parents again, but via omission. I don't want to tell them how close I came to being blown up. But, argh! It's going to blurt out of my stupid mouth at some point and then there'll be the 'how could you not tell us something like that' guilt heaped on top of it. Starting a conversation with the 'rents using the phrase 'don't freak out but...' is going to make them freak out.

Suppose I could try downplaying it. How was your day? Oh, fine. Almost got pasted by a backpack bomb. Yeah, that'll go over well. Ugh. No good way to have that conversation. Mom's going to want to yell at me for being reckless or doing whatever I did to annoy someone to the point they're sending assassins after me.

Problem is, I have no damn idea what I did this time.

It's impossible for me to avoid telling my parents, but it's totally possible for me to delay doing so. I hide in my bedroom for the remainder of the day. If I don't see them face to face, I won't blurt. All I can do is sit here stewing on emotions and confusion. It now feels as if someone deliberately tried to take me out. Because of that, Chloe is going to stay with Aurélie until this is sorted. Can't risk her getting hurt.

The only possible idea to make any sense is one of the other elders is pissed off at me for demanding the vampire child not be destroyed. Stefano Bianchi and Paolo Cabrini aren't my biggest fans. They're both butthurt over my decision to remain with my mortal family. However, Paolo's kind of mellowing out a bit now that I've demonstrated some aptitude and loyalty to vampire kind. Stefano, on the other hand, is like an over-forty mafia version of the bratty entitled prep school douchebag from an Eighties college comedy movie. The better I do, the angrier he gets. Dude simply cannot stand losing to a girl. And it's not like we're even in competition. By 'losing,' I mean he's failing in his bid to get me cast out or ordered to abandon my family and make them forget I exist. That a reasonable portion of Seattle's vampire society is now accepting of me living at home has got to be frying his bacon.

He can't come after me directly due to Aurélie's decree of protection. So, he's using mind-controlled humans as living guided missiles. The more I think about it, the more it makes sense. The car accidents, why the guy looked so angry with me, then confused. Pickup Truck Man probably had a mental compulsion to kill me. And in that last second when we stared at each other, the abject terror from knowing he was about to die broke him out of it—and he didn't understand how he got into the situation he found himself in.

But... hang on. Maybe the Chloe thing pushed Stefano over the edge, but it still seems a bit much for him. He doesn't like me, but his contempt is just that: contempt. The man looks down his nose at me like I'm some punk teenager who refuses to dress up nicely to go to the fancy restaurant. Wanting to blow me up—permanent death—seems a bit excessive for him.

And it doesn't explain Tilloa's narrow escape of a car bomb in Starbucks.

Or the window washing rig almost pancaking us.

Or that this stuff started before I met Chloe.

Hmm. Could Evan have been a crazy stalker who became obsessed with me and wanted to kill me because he couldn't have me? It's kinda laughable, honestly. I'm not famous. Never saw the guy before. How could he know me? Nah. Too much about that encounter feels like he'd been sent by a vampire to take me out. Hooray for glitchy electronics. If that thing went off when I'd been standing right next to him, I would have been splattered all over the pavement just like him.

Ashley and Michelle are busy with work. Hunter calls a little after 4:30 p.m. to ask if I'm awake and want to come over. He's painting a room on the third floor today and invites me to help. Sure, why not? If I'm away from home, I can't be tempted to talk about the bomb.

It really is kinda cool how much my body has adjusted to sunlight. Much like becoming a vampire, the rapid development of that power had a high admission cost. No way would I have volunteered to be chained to a tree and roasted. To be fair, the jackasses who did it to me weren't trying to help me. They wanted me gone. But... what's that phrase? She persisted? Yeah. I persist. Might've developed a little phobia of trees. No, it's chains. Probably why Ashley's bedroom hobbies bother me so much. I've never been a big fan of handcuffs or other things of that nature. A boyfriend or two of mine in the past wanted to try it. Not for me. And the whole 'meet the sunrise while chained to a tree unable to move' thing made it worse.

Anyway... Hunter and I spend the afternoon painting. One small oops dribbles paint on my shirt, so I take it off. One thing leads to another, and we both end up naked, making love on the floor in the middle of an empty room, high on paint fumes.

Ahh, at last. Glorious 'full contact'.

Don't worry. Ronan's at my house and his mom's still at work.

WHEN IT GOT DARK, I TOOK A QUICK SHOWER AT HUNTER'S, THEN FLEW OUT to Wolent's giant mansion.

Why am I going there? Simple. Another idea hit me in the shower. Initially, I'd considered telling him about the bomb and asking for his advice. As soon as the ideas of Wolent and 'someone tried to blow me up' existed in my thoughts at the same time, it occurred to me I'm one of 'his people.'

Sure, it's a 'well duh' fact, but... it made me think. These attacks might not be related to anything I did personally. Someone who wants to metaphorically 'pee in Wolent's Cheerios' might be targeting me because I'm the lowest newbie on the totem pole of his organization. Kill the expendable new girl to send him a message type thing.

So, he needs to know about it.

One of the scariest things for a girl is being around a man who's taken by uncontrollable rage to the point they start smashing up their environment. It's not any less scary when the girl happens to be a vampire, mostly because the man is also a vampire and much older. However, I do know Arthur Wolent is not coming unglued, shouting, screaming, and breaking stuff to intimidate me or even because he lacks the capacity to maturely deal with emotions. It's not some kind of theatrical performance or because he gets violent with women.

He's a Fury.

They have a short fuse and legitimately can't help themselves sometimes. Often, it doesn't take much at all to set a Fury off. Like, hand him a Post-It note that's green instead of yellow and it might throw him into a blind rage for being the 'wrong color.' It has nothing to do with the actual item or scenario. Like a narcoleptic person, when their brain wants to go to sleep, it goes to sleep. The 'trigger' is merely a convenient excuse. In the case of Furies, they randomly rage. It's in their brains. They can't help it.

Now, when something actually pisses them off, they also rage. And it's epic.

Standing here watching Wolent smash things in his office, I can't help but think of Chloe terrified and hiding somewhere while her father goes off on a drunken rampage. The level of terror that poor child endured is indescribable. No kid should ever have to go through that. I'm glad the bastard is dead. Hope it was painful. Yeah, me, Sarah Wright, takes glee in a man's death. Sue me.

But, the reason Wolent is raging is that someone tried to hurt me.

This is the exact opposite of Chloe's piece of shit father. Wolent is breaking stuff in his office because he doesn't know whose neck to snap. I'm not afraid of being hurt here because he's raging out of protectiveness. I'm sure there's a little bit of him angry someone disrespected him by attacking one of his people in there, too. But the feeling I get from him is almost like... umm. I'm the daughter of the local Mafia don and someone just tried to kill me.

The comparison is more apt than I'd like to admit.

His usual hangers-on keep their distance. No one judges him for being a hothead because... Fury. Vampires know it just happens. This isn't a Kylo Ren rage tantrum. One good difference between Furies and Beasts is a Fury's random raging only lasts a minute or two and they usually retain enough mental faculties not to attack people nearby— except when the person is the reason they're angry. Beasts flip out randomly, too, but they are worse. The rage lasts much longer and they lose all rationality. A Beast *will* attack anyone and everything nearby... except animals. There's some sort of weird connection between Beasts and actual beasts. But, yeah, if one of those guys flips out, everyone should run.

When Wolent calms down, he fixes his suit back in place, sits at his lavish desk like he didn't just trash the place, then talks. Within seconds, a group of employees rush out and start cleaning up in the background... reminding me of those guys at Wimbledon who zip out to grab stray tennis balls while everyone sorta ignores they exist. He can't think of anyone who's messing with us, but promises me whoever it was is going to regret it. His people will be investigating.

Cool.

Oh, he also gives me a quick job. Yay. At least it's routine and nothing I haven't done before. I do the 'yes, sir. Right away, sir' thing and head out. Modern me still feels a bit awkward talking like that and being so servile, but the dude's an old-as-hell vampire. I always found it laughable how people could bow and scrape to kings in antiquity. Like, why are they afraid of some old man in a crown? These beefy knights and soldiers behaved as if the king's mere word could kill them. If any of those soldiers wanted to kill the king and take over, it's not like the king had any chance of surviving.

A vampire like Wolent has real power. And, well, he's not a dick about it. So I respect him. He likes being called sir by people younger than him, so... whatever. I'm not so full of myself I can't swallow a little bit of pride now and then. No way would I have 'yes sir, right away sirred' a manager at some place I waited tables, but again... elder vampire.

My job tonight is basically what's come to be my regular task. I fly around the city, stopping by various places in his network. It's mostly a bunch of restaurants, bars, night clubs, a hotel, two office buildings, a limo company, and a few other miscellaneous businesses. I pop in, talk to the vampire in charge, and collect any messages they might have to send around. Remember that thing about *old* people being technology averse? Yeah. Vampires apparently don't know what email is. I pick up these fancy wax-sealed envelopes and deliver them as needed. If I worked for Wolent Inc. as a corporation, I'd be the mail room girl.

Hey, it's simple. It's easy. It gets me seen by other vampires and accepted. Risk is low. My kind of job. It reminds me of the early quests in some fantasy video games to run messages around. As long as no bartenders ask me to go into their wine cellar to deal with a giant rat problem, I'm good.

The work is a pleasant distraction from my present worries except for some of the various vampires I talk to asking me about Chloe. Mostly 'is it true? Did someone really turn a little girl?' You would think vampires who enjoy being vampires wouldn't talk about making someone a vampire as if some unspeakable, horrible thing happened to them. To be fair, they're not cringing at the idea of the Transference in general. They're shocked at her being denied the chance to grow up. Most sane vampires are quite happy being adults and think it's awful to be stuck as a child forever with no freedom, no adult urges, no ability to enjoy the 'finer things in life' like fancy cars, yachts, parties, and so on.

Whatever. Chloe is as happy playing with dolls and watching cartoon movies as those vampires are playing with their expensive boats, cars, and priceless art objects. What difference does it really make? Besides, Disney cartoons are *way* cheaper than yachts, diamond necklaces, Armani gowns, or Lambos. If you ask me, Chloe is way ahead. She gets the same—or more—happiness for a tiny fraction of the cost.

I don't really get into arguments over it. The vampires I'm dealing with are all part of Wolent's, uhh, team I guess. It's kinda surprising none of them tell me I messed up or say she should be put down. Almost all of them are like 'it really happened? Oh wow. Okay' and we move on to business. Guess since the big man is tolerating her existence, they have no opinion yet.

Running messages around is not prestigious or terribly exciting, but I don't mind. The work is easy, it earns points with the boss, and feels appropriate for 'the new girl.' Can't say I'm being treated like a kid or given such a job because no one trusts me with any serious responsibility. I've already been tapped once to deliver an incendiary bomb to a lair of hostile vampires. No, Wolent trusts me. He knows Follow Rules Girl lives rent free in my head. He's been in there to visit her. Doesn't matter the set of rules she adheres to has changed.

Really, I'm kinda happy being the low girl on the totem pole. I don't want power or responsibility. The less of both I have, the less danger I'm in. Also, with the Chloe situation, keeping Wolent as happy as possible is important. I'm dreading the idea he and the other elders might eventually decide the girl needs to be destroyed. Good chance they don't really think it's somehow cruel for her to exist as a vampire. Being eternally free to experience the joys of childhood without ever knowing the craptitude of adulting is hardly the worst thing that can happen to someone. They'd be worried her existence poses a threat to secrecy. However, as long as she's got a vampire willing to take care of her, it shouldn't be a problem. The actual problem is, no vampire in their right mind wants to get saddled looking after a child for the rest of time. Kids get in the way of fancy parties and whatever else it is they love to do.

Guess I am not in my right mind.

Here I am flying across Seattle with a briefcase of old letters—they're not old; they just look it. Is the artificially aged parchment really necessary? Sometimes, it feels like I'm playing a vampire LARP where everyone except for me is taking themselves far too seriously. My thoughts wander amid worries of what might happen to Chloe. I daydream about running off with her to the middle of nowhere, far away from any other vampires who might care she exists.

Sounds romantic in a tragic fairy tale way, but it would probably turn into us eventually going feral and becoming talked about like a pair of pale-skinned cryptids skulking about the woods like some 'legend of the hills' thing in West Virginia. Nah. Running away never helps. Besides, I can't abandon my family.

So who might have tried to blow me up? Have the LA vampires reconstituted under a new leader and decided revenge is in order? Could it be the Oblivare? Nah, I doubt that. They don't really carry grudges. As twisted as they are, if you kill one of them, they congratulate you for the victory. Survival of the fittest is like their thing. Ladonna would be angrier at me for talking about her running away to save herself than if I'd killed her best friend. Good thing I haven't said a word—nor did I kill her best friend.

Hmm. Stefano. Again, I doubt it. While he definitely is not one of my fans, it's a stretch to think he hates me enough to want me gone. Although, if he did, using a bunch of enthralled people to kill me in ways that look like accidents is a potential way to avoid having Aurélie come down on him. Here's the crazy thing about her. For as petite, polite, and sweet as she is, part of her adores the release of extreme violence. Hate to say it, but when I attacked that guy about to dump kittens in the river, I totally understood. She doesn't particularly like or want violence, but when the opportunity presents itself, it's a cathartic release. Sort of like a stressed out college student randomly screaming in the middle of the library as a tension breaker. If Chloe's dad wasn't already dead, I'd use him for a damn scratching post and love every minute of it. Yes, that's way out of character for me, but you didn't see the bruises on that poor kid. Similarly, if Stefano tried to kill me and got caught, Aurélie would be free from the chains of society and consequences to get medieval on him.

I can't accuse Stefano openly of trying to kill me without some evidence or it would blow up in my face... kinda like the coffee survey dude did.

By the time I finish running messages and have my night back to myself again, my brain is looping around the notion it might be related to Chloe somehow. That, too, seems weak. If all the bad luck and crazy near misses are related to each other, it started before she became a vampire.

No. Can't be her.

Ooh. Idea. Times like these, it's great to have weird friends. I have two such weird friends who are a massive help. Coralie is a ghost, and an oracle. While she's awesome, her thing is the future. She's not so tuned into the past or present. If someone is about to kill me and succeed at it, she'd probably pop in and warn me before it happened. That she didn't show up before Evan turned himself into hamburger tracks proves something. I survived, after all. Nothing to warn me about.

Glim, on the other hand, is a Shadow. I don't really understand it too much, and it gets confusing to talk about. But, they—meaning Shadows, the vampires—have an entity or something they call 'The Shadows.' Real original, right? It's often difficult to know if they're talking about their vampire bloodline or the mysterious entity-slash-force. I'm fuzzy on the explanation here. It might not be like a living spirit as much as it's similar to the Force from *Star Wars*... without the telekinesis bit or lightsabers.

It's kind of like the vampire version of an internet. Shadows (the vampires) in one area share information and knowledge across the world in minutes by essentially whispering to the darkness. Their information network not only communicates among vampires, it involves ghosts, other creatures, and even—according to Glim—literal shadows (not vampires). Apparently, a shadow is not merely the absence of light. Sometimes, it's a coalescence of substantive sentient darkness. Say that three times fast while drunk.

Anyway, Glim drinks blood and knows things.

Who better to ask when I have such a damn strange problem?

Most times, he spends the hours between sunset and midnight sitting on the roof of an apartment building watching his ex-wife and two sons. He still loves her. The only reason she's an ex is he died. Unlike me, he hasn't had any contact with his family post-Transference. To be fair, it's much more difficult for Shadows to do that given their ghoulish appearance. His kids probably wouldn't even recognize him. They'd scream and faint if they saw him. So, he lets the three of them believe the fabrication he died in Iraq during the war. Technically, he's MIA presumed dead. The Army never found his body because it's here.

It's a bit late—almost four in the morning now—for him to be on the roof. I take a chance and whisper into the night, "Glim, can we talk? If you're not busy, please meet me on your roof."

Over the next few minutes while flying, I repeat the request a couple times. It's not too surprising the roof is empty. Knowing how he is, I decide to sit there and wait for a while. The apartment complex is still and quiet for the most part. A handful of residents are awake. I can hear at least two different video games, one movie, and an alarm clock beeping. Ugh, what poor bastard has to set their alarm for 4:30 a.m.? Does the 'time to make the donuts' guy live here?

A whorl of inky blackness spirals up from the roof beside me, rising into a shadowy column seven feet high. I jump at the sudden manifestation... but I'd jump if Sophia snuck up on me, too. Glim steps out of the vapor 'tornado,' which promptly collapses into nothingness. His long, black trench coat billows in a breeze that doesn't exist. He stands there for a moment being epic. Like a grey-faced, pointy-eared version of Batman. Gotta give it to him. Dude is theatrical. Having illusion powers helps, too.

"Nice entrance," I say.

Glim flashes a fangy grin. Making me jump amuses him. He's like the big brother who takes delight in scaring me with innocent pranks, but if anyone gave me trouble, he'd kick their ass. "Thanks. I try. You are concerned about the little one and your spate of near misses." He sits beside me on the roof.

"Yeah." Guess he got the 411 from the shadows before he left home. See, this is how I know he's the real deal. If you call a psychic hotline and they ask you what your problem is, they're obviously fake. Wouldn't a real psychic already know what you're going to ask them?

He gazes off at the glimmering landscape of Seattle at night. It's such an odd spectacle. Except for the sky overhead, nothing is dark to us, yet all the lights of the city still glow as bright to me as they would to a mortal. It's pretty in a retina-searing sort of way.

"Glim?" I ask. "Is it bad?"

"Somber." He sighs. "The one who gave her the Transference endured a brutal childhood in the 1930s somewhat similar in circumstance to hers. By chance, he happened to be close enough to hear the shouting the night Chloe's father beat her to death. It most likely reawakened some long forgotten memories of his past. I believe he punished that girl's parents as if lashing out at the man who tormented him as a boy. The shadows say he turned her without thinking of the consequences. Unsure what to do and afraid of reprisal, he disappeared, leaving her to fend for herself."

"Ugh." I grab my head in both hands, staring down at the spot of roof inside my crossed legs. "The guy killed her parents? Both of them?"

"Eventually," says Glim. "Not right away."

"I'm lost." I flip my hair back off my face and glance at him. "Not right away?"

"Specific details are blurry." Glim examines his dagger-like fingernails. "I do know he initially tried to let Chloe take her revenge on them a few days after she awoke as a vampire."

I gasp in horror. "What kind of sick bastard tries to encourage a little kid to kill anyone, much less her own parents?"

"I can't answer that." He scowls, seemingly agreeing with me. "She refused."

"Innocent. Truly," I whisper.

"That may have something to do with it. But, she is still a seven-year-old. If you ask me, trying to get her to kill her parents—abusive as they were—is almost as bad as anything they did to the girl in life."

I cringe. "Bad, yeah, but it's not like he *forced* her to do it, right? You said he tried to get her to do it and she said no way."

Glim nods.

"Guessing he killed them?"

"He did."

"What did the mother do? Did she abuse Chloe, too?" I bite my lip.

"I cannot say. Perhaps nothing worse than simply ignoring the abuse her husband visited upon the child. Perhaps she is a victim in all of this, too."

"Hang on. Didn't you say the sire abandoned her because he was afraid of getting caught?"

"He did." Glim nods. "I believe once the initial panic at what he'd done subsided, he found her and tried to encourage her to get her revenge. Honestly, I believe the man wanted to exact revenge on his parents more than anything... and so when the child refused, he killed them both."

I cringe. "Did he make her watch?"

"This, I cannot say. The shadows do not speak of it."

"Wonder if her mother was also a victim here?" I grumble. Something tells me not quite. Chloe sounded like she resented both parents. When she initially met Mom, she shied away as if expecting to be slapped. Ugh. Guess that means they both hit her. Maybe I'll be happier not knowing the details. "Kid seemed mad at her, too. Not at all upset she'll never see her mother again."

Glim shakes his head, seeming sad. "That suggests some level of abuse. They were neither poor nor wealthy. The house was in a nice area. Chloe didn't want for anything."

"Except love," I mutter. "And safety."

Sensing my crashing mood, Glim puts an arm around me. I lean against him and rant for a while about how can people be so damned awful to treat a child like that? Having him listening to me vent is a huge help. Finally, I calm down and growl. "Ugh, so where did he go?"

"The shadows are unaware why the two parted ways, only that they did so the night the man killed the parents."

I glance at him. "Do you know how she got here? Did St. Ives send people to grab her all the way from Jersey?"

"No." Glim picks at his bladed fingernails. "The child was placed in a cargo container by a sympathetic vampire who feared elders in the area would destroy her for being so small. She gave some warehouse workers in Portland quite a scare. Eleanor's people found her the next night and brought her here."

"Wow… they mailed her?" I gawk.

"Not exactly. More like smuggled." He flicks a bit of lint to one side. "To evade an order of destruction."

"Order?" I raise an eyebrow.

"Not exactly. I misspoke thinking of Europe." Glim chuckles. "It isn't so formalized here. Many traditionalists would destroy one so small without a second thought. The West Coast is more laid back than the east. Here, they will watch her for a while to decide if she should continue to exist or not. Some may regard her with curiosity and intrigue."

I frown. "Not gonna let anyone treat her like a circus freak."

He shifts his yellow eyes toward me. For a second, it seems as if he's about to offer to help me take care of her, but doesn't… probably afraid of how she'd react to him, or maybe he simply doesn't want to traumatize her with his appearance. Sigh. He's not *that* scary.

"I am sure you will manage. Happy to help if I can."

I smile at him. "Someone's gotta dress up like Santa Claus."

He throws his head back and laughs so loud it startles a stray cat rummaging around the trash dumpster beside the building.

"Thanks. Umm, now for the big question if you don't mind?"

"You worry someone is trying to kill you."

"Yep. Pretty much." I flop over backward on the roof, gazing up at the stars. The sky has taken on a 'you best get your ass home soonish' quality. We maybe have twenty minutes before sunrise. Plenty of time for me to fly to Cottage Lake from here. "What god or gods did Tilloa and I piss off? Think it might be Stefano? Or Chloe's sire?"

He lets out a long, resigned sigh. "The shadows did not have much to speak of this matter yet. Too little time has passed for a matter of such minor consequence."

I give him side eye, being playful. I know Glim isn't saying my life is of no consequence. I'm also not so arrogant as to think someone trying to kill me is as 'consequential' as global events or strife between vampire kingdoms. Sometimes, it takes the shadows (not the vampires) a while to get around to gossiping about the small stuff. The trials and tribulations of one individual—newish—vampire are definitely small stuff to them.

"Drat," I mutter.

He pats me on the shoulder. "I will keep my ears open when next I am at the Sanctuary." He twitches one of his tall, pointed ears. "Should hear something soon. These things are so damn big I can hear a mouse fart on the moon."

I laugh.

"It's almost sunrise." Glim turns up the melodrama in his voice. "You should seek the safety of your lair."

"Yes, my dark prince. I shall retreat anon." That's my best attempt at delivering Shakespeare with a bad British accent.

It will have to do.

THE GIRLFRIEND

My parents reacted to the news of the bomb about as well as could be expected.

I knew it was serious when Dad didn't crack a joke. I'm not sure if it counts as a lie, but I modified the truth for them. Letting them know I only survived by the freak randomness of a malfunctioning button would not help. They'd probably demand I stay in the house for the next twenty years. Just my luck to get grounded for being a victim again. Not my fault. Anyway, the story they heard is I sensed something wrong with the guy—which is true—and ran for cover—also true. Letting them think I survived by guile and not blind luck reassures them. Honestly, my actions had nothing to do with surviving. The bomb picked the perfect instant to detonate when the corner column of the parking deck happened to be in the way. But hey, a massive square obelisk of reinforced concrete is one hell of a shield.

Clinginess happened. I'm a little too old to truly like being held like a little kid who had a nightmare. But, of all the annoying things parents do, letting them cope by using me as a human version of a squeezy stress ball is mild.

TWO DAYS LATER. IT'S FRIDAY AGAIN. UNLIFE HAS BEEN CALM RIGHT UP UNTIL it decided not to be.

It's a few minutes to six in the evening and I'm at the hospital visiting Grandpa Sheridan. Mom, Dad, the Littles, and Grandma Sheridan are here as well. Grandpa fell off a ladder and broke his hip while trying to clean crud out of the rain gutters on their house. I think grandma has told us over twenty times in the past hour about how she insisted he call a service to do it but he wanted to save the money. I'd say this explains much about Dad, but the Sheridans are Mom's parents. I don't think it's a genetics thing as much as it's a dad thing.

"Nonsense, honey, I can do it," are my father's proverbial 'famous last words.'

They have poor Grandpa hopped up on painkillers and Sierra is taking advantage of him being high by getting him to say silly things and recording video for later blackmail use. Jokes on her though. He would laugh if she posted a video of him being goofy on Facebook. Sophia's sitting on the bed next to him making a whole bunch of suspicious facial expressions. I think she's weighing the risk vs result of attempting to use magic to help him.

As far as any of us know, healing injuries is not something that falls within the realm of her abilities. She's basically a wizard, not a cleric. Gotta admit, my life is super strange when references to roleplaying games actually apply.

Despite being ten, Sam insists that grandpa call him over to help next time the gutters need to be cleaned. He's more than happy to scramble up a ladder and run around on the roof. Predictably, Mom is *far* less enthusiastic about this idea even though she knows the boy can conjure wings. Though, to be fair, a single-story fall might not be enough time for him to use them before he smacked into the ground. He'd be much safer falling from the fortieth story, odd as that sounds. Both parents give me the 'you can do it for him after dark' glance, to which I nod.

There's a career I never even considered. Vampire gutter cleaning. No ladders, no fuss.

On the positive side, Grandpa Sheridan is really healthy for a sixty-four year old and the doctors expect he'll be just fine in a few weeks. Won't be walking much for a bit, though. Ugh. I can't help but wonder if my recent spate of horrible luck is somehow to blame for him falling from the ladder. As much as I've started to suspect someone or something a whole lot more tangible and earthly than an ancient offended god is responsible, it's still not possible for me to rule anything out. My thoughts return to the bullet in my desk drawer. Maybe I could ask Sophia to scry it and see what her Barbie beach bucket tells her, but I dunno. If someone shot me on purpose, she's going to see, hear, and / or feel someone trying to kill me. That would upset her too much. Can't do it to her.

Everyone I can possibly think of who has a grudge against me either isn't angry enough to go this far or wouldn't be indirect about it. So damn infuriating.

My phone vibrates. The sudden buzz and sensation of motion in my pocket in a more or less quiet room makes me jump and let out a reasonable 'Gah!' This, in turn, causes Sophia to startle-scream, which makes both Mom and Grandma jump-shriek, too. Mom and Grandma yelping re-startles Sophia into screaming. It's like escalating high-strung dominoes.

Sam cuts Dad a 'what the heck is wrong with them?' glance.

Ten seconds later, Grandpa's eyes widen in reaction to all the noise. "What happened?"

Bzzzt.

"Sorry. My phone startled me." I pull it out intending to silence the call —but it's Ashley. "Sec. This could be important. It's Ash. Be right back."

Mom rolls her eyes at me. Dad nods once. Grandpa doesn't even know what a phone is right now. Sophia's staring at me with this 'why did you do that to me' pouty face. Her usual reaction to being jump scared is to cry, but she's holding firm this time. Not too bad a scare. Sierra's got both hands clamped over her mouth to hold in laughter.

As I slip out into the hall to answer the phone, Grandma starts talking. Apparently, the room being quiet enough for a phone on silent to startle me is a problem. They need to be a little louder and a little happier to help Grandpa feel better.

I ease the door shut. Swipe. Phone to ear. "Hey, Ash. What's up?"

"Hey," whispers Ashley. "Raleigh's over. We're about to go on a date. Can you meet us and do the Corey thing?"

"Ugh. Bad timing. I really can't go anywhere for a non-emergency right now."

"V stuff?"

"No… Grandpa S fell and broke his hip. We're all at the hospital now, visiting him."

She gasps. "Oh, no. Is he okay?"

"He's high as hell." I grin, not quite able to laugh. "The doctor said he'll be fine but he's in pain."

"Aww." Ashley makes a consoling noise. "Crap. We'll be right there."

"Be right here?"

"Of course! It's grandpa! How could I not come see him?" She sighs. "Which hospital are you at?"

"Virginia Mason," I say. "Room 904."

"Okay. See you soon."

I slip back into the room and let everyone know Ashley's going to stop by. For most people, the best friend probably wouldn't rush over to visit like it had been *her* grandfather in here, but in Ashley's case, he's pretty much like her grandfather, too. I don't get how people can be so spiteful. Her actual grandparents on her father's side haven't seen much of her since she was eight. After the divorce, they refused to have anything to do with Mrs. Carter, believing the divorce was all her fault somehow. Ashley told them if they wanted to see her, they had to be nice to her mom. They chose no contact.

Ugh.

People.

ABOUT HALF AN HOUR LATER, GRANDPA IS STILL HIGH.

The door opens. Ashley walks in. She's wearing a fairly tight shift dress in super pale pink, almost white, along with bangle bracelets, a necklace of metal discs, pink heels, and a little pink handbag barely large enough to hold her phone. Looks like she's dressed up to go somewhere nice-ish.

"Hey," whispers Ashley. "Grandpa, you okay?"

"Oh, hi there, Ainsley," mumbles Grandpa.

No one bothers to correct him. It's the painkillers.

Ashley walks into the room, waving at someone to follow her.

A girl I assume to be Raleigh follows somewhat reluctantly. She's also wearing a dress, but it's not as form-hugging. It's black and on the slinky side, the sort of thing a woman might wear to a nice restaurant at night— in an episode of *Miami Vice*. It's a back-baring gown, but her hair is long enough to mostly cover the exposed part. She's wearing high heels, too. Hers are more extreme. Ashley's are kitten heels. She's not a big fan of crazy shoes. Not only does she regard herself as too clumsy for them— she's not—she read somewhere online about how high heels cause all sorts of problems later in life. She's as afraid of wearing them as I used to be wary of NutraSweet. I say used to be because I'm undead now.

Raleigh clutches a somewhat larger shiny black purse in front of herself, edging into the room while making this face. She looks like a pirate is standing behind her with a sword at her back, prodding her out on a plank above shark-infested seas. The girl's as visibly uncomfortable as if she'd been on stage giving a presentation to a massive crowd and all her clothing vanished. I get the awkwardness of showing up at a hospital to visit someone you don't know while surrounded by people you have no connection to. It's not like Grandpa is legit related to Ashley. However, this girl's either taking shyness to the next level or... oh wait.

Her family doesn't know she's gay. She's gotta be terrified being seen with Ashley is going to get back to her parents somehow. That explains it. Alas, it's too daylightey for me to read her mind.

"Ack. Hide!" Sierra flails her arms. "Ashley's duplicating. The gingers are gonna take over!"

Ashley snort-laughs. Raleigh manages a brittle smile.

Mom and Dad give the girl the same sort of intense head-to-toe glance they always hit any of my new boyfriends with. Dad radiates an 'okay, well if this is what you want to do' air. Mom's body language is stronger. She's definitely decided this girl is not a good fit for Ashley. It's my initial feeling too. She seems a bit too... I dunno. Upper class? No. That's not the right phrase. It has nothing to do with having money or seeming aloof. This girl just doesn't vibe like she enjoys being around Ashley. Unfortunately, my protective-slash-jealous self is biased. I can't take my inexplicable sense of something not being right seriously since I'm a child. I'm a pre-interested-in-boys little kid fuming because this girl is stealing my best friend from me, so of course, I'm not going to like her. I have to forcibly make myself concentrate on the idea we're not kids anymore and need romantic relationships to set that aside.

Whatever it is about her presence that doesn't click right with me, I can't trust it. Mom might simply be picking up on my jealousy and using that to inform her reaction. Strange thing is Dad doesn't seem on board, either. If his expression had a title, it would be 'that'll end in divorce within two years.' I'll need to get into this girl's head and do some digging before I trust my opinions.

After a few minutes and Ashley introducing her as 'my friend Raleigh' rather than girlfriend, the girl calms down. With the anxiety of being exposed out of the way, she chills out totally. Not a trace of being awkward around us remains. Raleigh goes from acting like she'd been reluctantly thrust into the most embarrassing moment of her life to a total extrovert who keeps happily chattering about random stuff. She even manages to get Sierra laughing.

Mom doesn't seem sold. In fact, the abrupt change has her guard up. Dad's not giving Raleigh any odd looks now. Ashley grins, standing near her date with a 'she's awesome and she's all mine' attitude. Hanging out with everyone here becomes a fairly nice social moment, as nice as is likely possible for a hospital room. Even Grandpa seems in good spirits.

Alas, the 'rents decide to call the visit short before the sun goes down.

I feel like a cat sitting there staring at a bird cage waiting for the human to leave the house so I can feast. Only, I'm not intending to bite Raleigh, merely read her mind. On the walk down the hallway to the elevator, I sidle up on Ashley's right side. As much as she wants to, she's not holding hands or locking arms with Raleigh.

"Yeah. I'm aware," says Ashley. "Too bright."

"Idea." I grin at her. "Let me call Hunter and see if he's up for a double date."

Ashley makes 'ooh, yeah' face at me.

In a couple hours, I will know exactly what this girl's deal is. If she's into Ashley and only on edge due to having crappy parents, great. If she's hanging on by a thread, too chicken to break up with her, ugh.

Tonight is either going to be a lot of fun—or super crappy.

THE SUCKITUDE OF RESPONSIBILITY

shley and Raleigh go off to their car while I stay with my family and pile into the Yukon.

As soon as we get home, I zoom downstairs and rummage my closet for something comparable in 'niceness' to the dresses Ashley and Raleigh had on. I'm assuming they had plans to go for dinner at a place where they don't let people in the door wearing T-shirts and jeans. While sifting among my vast collection of plain and ordinary garments, I call Hunter.

Barely three minutes into me explaining as much of the situation as I feel safe talking about on a cell phone, a call waiting beep startles me so bad I drop the phone. No, I'm not overly jumpy. I had the phone pinned between my head and one shoulder. Super easy to drop.

I fully intend to ignore the call waiting until I notice the name of the caller: King Kamehameha Beeotch.

Thank you, Eric Cartman.

Ugh. It's Eleanor St. Ives.

I damn near scream an F-bomb. The only reason I don't is not wanting Mom to come storming down here to yell at me while I'm in my underwear mid-changing.

"Babe, it's important V stuff. I really have to take this call."

"Understand. Call me back as soon as you can."

"Absolutely."

I flip over to the other line. "Hello?"

"Sarah," says Eleanor. "Bring Chloe here tonight for a test."

"Umm. Any chance we could do this tomorrow? Or at least after midnight?"

"The longer we wait, the more difficult it may be to correct." Eleanor pauses a second. "Remember, Wolent is watching how you handle this."

Follows Rules Girl takes this to mean 'do as you're told or you get in trouble'.

I hang my head. "Okay. I'll be there as soon as I can."

Eleanor hangs up without saying anything else. Maximum efficiency. Minimum social grace.

I call Hunter back. "Gotta postpone. Important V stuff. Got yoinked."

"Threatened?" he asks, worried.

"No, guilted. Rugrat needs a doctor visit."

"Ahh. Okay. How long will you be? If not a double date, do you want to do something after?"

"Yes… if it isn't too late." I re-hang the nice-ish dress and grab the most convenient plain T-shirt in reach from my closet. It's plain grey with *Fifth Element* font spelling out: 'negative, I am a meat popsicle' across the chest. "Gotta get on this fast. I'll call you again as soon as I can."

"Okay. Stay safe, babe. I love you."

"I love you, too." I listen to the sound of him breathing until he hangs up. It's only a second and a half, but it's a wonderful second and a half.

My phone beeps. It's Ashley calling.

I answer with a frustrated groan.

"Hey, we good?" she asks. "Or not?"

"Alas." I grumble. "You know who called about you know what and I have to take a certain someone to the doctor."

A few seconds of silence makes me picture Ashley blinking in confusion. "You're taking Sierra to get her rabies shots?"

I cackle. Oh, I needed that laugh. "No, the Zerg Queen demands my presence."

"Oh, *that* 'you know who.'"

In my imagination, Ashley's thoughts coalescing around my meaning sound like glass Tetris pieces falling into place. She knows I refer to Eleanor St. Ives as either The Kerrigan, the Zerg Queen, or King Kamehameha Beeyotch. I told her in person about the Chloe situation. Now, I'm only being careful on the phone. The NSA guy listening to us doesn't need to know about vampires. Whether or not it's tinfoil hat paranoia, enough vampires are wary of talking by technological channels that I've inherited the habit. Better to suffer the inconvenience of not saying certain things where they can be overheard than wiping out everything I love.

"Aww, okay. I understand. Hope she's okay." Ashley sighs.

"I could tell her something came up and be an hour late."

"Nah," says Ashley. "Raleigh isn't worrying me now. She seems okay tonight. I'm simply insecure about if she loves me or not. Definitely not worth a kid's life. I'll try to get her to stay late so you guys can get to know each other a little better."

"Sounds good. This shouldn't take all night."

"Stay safe!" chirps Ashley.

We hang up. Damn. Why did I say that? Telling her it won't take all night guarantees it *will* take all night. Grr. Sarah! You're old enough to know better than to jinx yourself like that. Oh, well. Too late.

I think I may have obligated myself in two directions once the St. Ives thing is done. Spending time with Hunter doesn't only mean sex. He would totally be cool going to Ashley's with me and hanging out. That is the best course of action. No one gets left out that way.

Good. Decision made.

I throw on some jeans then run upstairs and zoom straight out the back door. I'm two minutes into the flight to Seattle before I realize my brain is spinning so bad I forgot to put on shoes. Dammit! I swing around and power-fly back to my house. It would be just my luck to go in barefoot when I need to boot some ass. Poop-stompers it is.

32

EXPERIMENT ONE

After picking Chloe up from 'grandma's,' I fly her toward the Industrial District.

"I don't wanna go back there," says Chloe. "Hate that bitch."

I pat her hands where she's clinging around my neck. "Same. I don't really like her either. But, you don't need to be scared. I'm not going to let them hurt you."

For a moment, the only sound is the fluttering of her elaborate doll dress.

"What's she want? Can't she just leave me alone?"

"In her strange way, she's trying to help you."

Chloe squeezes a little tighter. "What's gonna happen to me if it works?"

"Well, most likely... you know how we can make people forget things and also make people remember things that aren't real?"

"Yeah," she whispers in a nervous voice.

"I'm going to find some super nice people who will be your new mom and dad, and make them think you're their kid. I'll also take all the nightmares out of your head."

"Sarah," says Chloe. "I'd much rather *be* a nightmare than have them."

"You're not a nightmare. Not at all. You're adorable."

She giggles. "Not to nice people. But I'm a nightmare to bad daddies."

Uh oh. Alarm bells. "What would you do to bad daddies?"

"I'd show them my teeth and growl and make my eyes light up so they run away and cry."

Whew. Okay. Kid appropriate. But... also not awesome for secrecy. However, it's not like she's going to get stuck living as a vampire with some random guy who might want to smack her around. If she is stuck as a vampire, she's staying with me—or Aurélie. She won't find herself in a situation where she needs to vamp out in self-defense. I'm comforted hearing her say the worst thing she wants to do to someone is make them cry.

"You won't have a bad daddy. I promise."

"Are you gonna make me forget you an' Aur-lee?" Chloe sniffles. "Please don't."

Sigh. Okay. What harm could it do? She's seven. No one would believe her stories about a vampire teen and a creepy goth faerie godmother as real. "All right. I won't. Promise."

Amelia is waiting for us outside the same abandoned warehouse. She takes one look at Chloe's dress and gives me a 'really?' eyebrow lift. The garment is exactly what one might expect the eerie ghost of a little girl who died in 1825 to be wearing as she floats down the corridor of an old Southern manor house. How a kid can be so adorable yet creepy at the same time is beyond me. The woman's looking at me like I'm one of those strange people who put little costumes on their underarm dogs, as if I've dressed Chloe like this on purpose to be melodramatic or extra.

Did you know that getting period shoes in child sizes is difficult? More so than the dresses? I'd never have imagined. Yes, that's sarcasm. Chloe didn't want to wear her light-up sneakers because they don't match the dress. I'm sure Aurélie would've fainted if she saw the combination. I may only be eighteen, but I'm not stupid. This kid is smarter than she looks. Being outside barefoot is a convenient pretext for her demanding to be held the whole time we're here.

Honestly, it's not like walking on broken glass will do permanent damage to a vampire's feet. It'll heal in a minute or four. But, it still hurts. And she's little. And I don't get tired. Sarah, you are so easy to manipulate.

I perch the girl on my hip and follow Amelia inside. Chloe is, as expected, perfectly content being carried. She's a bit clingy, too. Vampire or not, she's afraid of Eleanor. I am also sure she's doing this on purpose to get me attached to her.

Eleanor, Pascal, and a handful of other vampires in lab coats meet us in one of the more mad-sciency labs. At the center is a surgical table with straps. Chloe starts to panic until she—and I—realize the straps are way too big for her. They're too big for me as well. This is basically where they made Frankenstein's Monster. Thankfully, the table is empty.

"Thank you for being punctual," says Eleanor.

Chloe stares at her, shying away. The instant St. Ives takes a step toward us, Chloe hisses like a cat, fangs out. Again, cute but oh so creepy.

"Calm yourself, child." Eleanor pauses. "You will not be harmed."

Her saying that is about as reassuring as anyone from the government saying 'trust me.'

"What do you intend to do?" I eye the table. "That's not happening."

"Oh, no. Of course not." Eleanor waves dismissively at the surgical slab. "This is the bio lab. The secure specimen table happens to be here. Its presence is unrelated to the matter at hand."

A late-twenties guy with short, spiky blond hair and a whole mess of neck tattoos approaches us. He's wearing a lab coat and carrying himself with the demeanor of a scientist even though he looks like a minor character from *Street Fighter* or the lead singer of an underground punk band. The four eyebrow rings totally sell the Oxford education.

The guy nods at me once, then hands Eleanor a small, silver thermos-like container. She takes it, opens it, and pours a viscous red liquid into a paper cup. It's somewhere between blood and cough syrup.

"You may wish to set her down before she drinks this." Eleanor holds the paper cup out. "There is a possibility it may cause some violent convulsions if it works."

"What does that mean?" asks Chloe. "Is it gonna hurt?"

"No." Eleanor shakes her head. "She might flail around hard enough to make you drop her, and bang her head on something."

I fix the woman with a stare. "I won't drop her."

"Even if your arm snaps?" asks Eleanor.

"Yes." I narrow my eyes. "Even if my arm snaps."

"May I suggest at least you sit?" Eleanor gestures at a small divan against the back wall. Looks like a psychiatrist's couch.

"Fine." I walk over there and sit, pulling Chloe around into my lap.

The child clutches her hands together under chin, shying away from Eleanor and shivering. I can't tell if she's hamming it up in hopes I get pissed and take her out of here or if she's genuinely frightened.

I squeeze her. "Shh. It's okay. We don't have to do this."

Eleanor isn't having it. "There is no need for such theatrics, child. This is not going to hurt you. It will either work or do nothing."

Chloe stares at the cup the woman's holding in front of her. Finally, she huffs a sigh and takes it. After a sniff, she takes a single sip. "Eww. This tastes like ass."

"Medicine usually does, sweetie." Eleanor folds her arms. "Go on. Finish it."

The kid knocks the rest of it back like an old alcoholic slamming a triple vodka. She squirms, shuddering, then gags. In case she starts having convulsions, I hold her in a firm grip that would likely be painfully uncomfortable for a mortal kid. Chloe doesn't protest. She continues grimacing and making faces for a minute or two.

Five minutes after drinking it, all she's done is grumble about how bad it tasted.

Eleanor seems disappointed.

"What was that?" I ask.

"A tonic created from her sire's blood, modified with components developed from your blood."

I raise both eyebrows. "Her sire? You found him? Is he, umm... dead?"

"Of course." Eleanor frowns.

I cringe.

"Don't be melodramatic, girl." She rolls her eyes at me. "Of course he is dead. He's a vampire."

Ugh, semantic bitch. "You know what I meant."

"No. He is not destroyed. We merely impressed upon him our displeasure at the situation."

I rub my forehead. "He didn't kill her. He tried to save her... kinda like Dalton and me."

"Yes." Eleanor's frown deepens. "You, however, are at least old enough to go outside after dark without a parent."

Grr. How to call someone a child without calling them a child.

Chloe fidgets.

"Vampires are not science," I say. "If there's any chance of fixing her, it's going to need a mystic... or something like that. No lab is going to manage it."

"Umm." Chloe looks at me. Her expression is a little foggy, which makes me worry the 'tonic' might be doing something to her Eleanor didn't plan on. "Stealing superpowers is not fixing. It's breaking."

"Would you rather be stuck as a little kid forev—?"

"A little kid with *superpowers*!" blurts Chloe.

"Fine." Eleanor sighs. "Would you rather be a little kid with superpowers, or not remember any of the bad things that happened to you, have *good* parents, friends, grow up, experience a normal life?"

Chloe fidgets again, making faces. She appears to be having trouble choosing. But, is the question fair? It's asking a little kid to have an opinion on being an adult. How can she comment on things she can't even begin to comprehend yet? She shrugs. "If these guys are gonna kill me anyway, it's not much of a fuckin' choice, is it?"

Eleanor's right eye twitches. Pascal frowns. The others all laugh at an F-bomb flying from such a little kid.

"They're not going to hurt you if you behave." I kiss her on the head. "Vampires have to stay hidden. If people who aren't vampires find out about us, they'll all gang up and wanna hurt us. The other vampires are afraid you can't keep secrets."

She looks down. "I can keep secrets good. I never told no one at school about how daddy hit me alla time. He said I'd get in big trouble for being such a bad girl I made him hit me so much, so I never told on him. Even when I hadda wear the cast. Just fell off the swing 'cause I'm stupid and clumsy."

Eleanor's knuckles creak. Holy shit. Is that a single tear in her eye? Can't really tell. There's like four hundred of them in mine right now.

"I'll keep a secret," says Chloe, still looking down. "Children are s'posed ta be threatened with grounded. Not bein' burned to ashes."

Eleanor clears her throat. "The world would be a much different place if cremation was an acceptable punishment for misbehavior."

I'm honestly not sure if she tried to make a joke or she's being serious. Her tone is flatter than six-month-old Pepsi left open.

Chloe suddenly convulses. I grab on, expecting a violent seizure while heartbroken at the idea I'm going to have to give her up once she's mortal again. Only... she twitched once. No seizure.

"Are you okay?" I ask.

She shakes her head to the negative.

I squeeze her, gripped with the sudden fear the blood tonic is doing something dangerous and unplanned. "What's wrong?"

Eleanor crouches down to take a closer look at her.

Chloe faces her, convulses again—then lurches, projectile vomiting the red, syrupy stuff all over Eleanor. The child convulses once more after the puking stops, then coughs. A thin red trickle runs out of her left nostril. I wipe it with my finger. Oh, ack. Touched bloody snoz without hesitation. Crap. Does that mean I really have become mom?

"Shit, that hurt," whimpers Chloe, grabbing her stomach.

Stunned, Eleanor blinks and sits there with the stuff dripping off her face.

"I'm not a scientist, but I'm pretty sure it didn't work," I say.

Pascal and the others cover their mouths, stifling chuckles.

The weird fogginess in Chloe's eyes is gone. Must have been simple nausea and not the effect of a crazy mad science potion. Now, she's wearing a sour face like any other little kid after getting sick. She reacted to the tonic the same way any non-Innocent vampire would react to food. Considering she *is* an Innocent and ought to be able to eat standard food, I'm not going to ask how nasty the stuff had to be in order to erupt out of her like that.

Yeah. Pretty sure it didn't work.

33

ACHERON

Interesting fact I never knew I didn't want to know: everyone tastes like candy to Chloe.

In a rather normal way for a kid her age, she requested food with the standard 'I'm hungry' plea as we left Eleanor's lab. Even though she's been a vampire for less than two weeks now, she's got a handle on how feeding works. So weird. The girl doesn't really comprehend death or what happened to her beyond her father hitting her so hard she went to sleep, and the 'nice vampire' helping her wake up.

She's never going to understand death.

I try telling her she'll 'get in a lot of trouble' if she takes too much blood from someone. This makes her cry. Why? Because to her, 'getting in trouble' means her arm or leg is going to end up in a cast again. Trouble is a *severe* beating versus just being hit on for a while. Ooh. I really want necromancy to be a thing so I can raise that guy from the dead and kill him over again.

It takes me a few minutes to put out that fire and explain that kids get in trouble all the time when they do things they shouldn't, and what her father did to her is absolutely evil and awful. Chloe seems to accept this. The closest I can get her to understanding death right now is if she drinks too much from one person, they'll go to sleep and never wake up. She doesn't want that to happen because she thinks it's as bad as what her father did to her.

Ack. Maybe the kid understands more than I think she does.

Anyway, it's way too late for a seven-year-old to be outside. So, I park her on a rooftop out of sight and go hunting. Not going to let her feed off drunk people coming out of a bar; she's underage. Hell, I'm underage for drinking, too, but willing to bend that rule in an emergency. Security guard or random night owl it is. Once suitable prey is located—a guy staffing a gate booth at a truck yard—I move Chloe to the bushes near the guardhouse, then walk over acting like I'm lost and need directions. As soon as the guard opens the little window to talk to me, I hammer his brain into Derptown, and lead him over to the bushes.

It's simultaneously alarming and cute that she already knows exactly how to feed. She goes right for his neck like a tiny shark. Well, a tiny shark with polite manners. Given how small she is, she's more like a remora fish clinging to a shark. Thankfully, at her size, I don't think it's *possible* she could drink enough blood to kill an adult. Her stomach probably can't hold that much.

She detaches from his neck long enough to hastily whisper, "Ooh. Chocolate cherries," before resuming feeding.

While carrying her home after we get the obliging guard back to rights, she tells me everyone tastes like candy. I guess it makes sense. Adult vampires biting kids taste candy. Why wouldn't a kid vampire biting adults taste candy, too? Or ice cream, or cookies. The more likely explanation is the flavor we experience is coming from our imagination. She's going to taste what she wants to taste. Most of the flavors I get are foods I'm fond of unless there's something significant about the person I'm feeding from that forces a particular flavor into my subconscious.

Well, that's one worry out of my brain. She's not going to bite Sam, Sophia, or Sierra because they're kids, taste sweet, and she wants candy. No, she'd bite them because she's hungry and they happen to be right there. Speaking of... I spend the rest of the time flying home explaining why they—and the 'rents—are off limits for food. Chloe doesn't seem to have any problem with the idea. I'm new at this whole 'being responsible for a kid' thing. Is it a bad sign if a child does not ask 'why' a hundred times when you tell them not to do something? If they simply accept a thing without question, does that mean they plan to ignore me?

I land on the deck behind my house.

Tilloa's there, peering in through the sliding glass door. At the soft thud of my boots on wood, she turns to look at us. "Hack!"

I think she tried to say 'Hey, Sarah' and 'ack' at the same time.

"Nope. I have not attempted to gain unauthorized access to a computer recently." I smile.

She points. "What are you doing with a kid at his hour? How is she awake?"

Chloe promptly flashes a fanged smile.

"Oh, no..." Tilloa covers her mouth. "How could anyone?"

"Long story." I glance at Chloe. "Careful."

"I know." She retracts her fangs. "I could tell she's like us."

Tilloa walks closer, studying the girl. "She's creepdorable. The dress is a bit extra."

"I love it." Chloe hugs herself. "Ooh. You have pretty eyes."

"Thanks, kiddo." Tilloa pats her on the cheek.

"Tilloa, this is Chloe. Chloe, Tilloa."

"Hi." The girl waves, then looks at me. "Wow. There's lots of us around here."

"Yeah kid. My house is a ley line nexus of weird." I pull the patio door open. "Better get inside."

We make our way into the house and down to my room. Chloe promptly sets about playing with Sophia's old Barbies and such. Tilloa gives me a 'not for kid ears' nod and drifts out into the basement. Of course, being a vampire, Chloe is going to hear us talking even if we're upstairs. Kinda pointless, but I humor the woman and step out of my room to the larger basement area. Mom's left a couple baskets of laundry near the machines.

"What's up?" I head over to get the laundry started. Wonder if the neighbors think we're weird for running the machines this late all the time.

Tilloa rakes her hands through her hair. "I almost got shredded by some jackass robbing a liquor store downtown."

"Shredded? I'll assume he wasn't running around with lethal office equipment."

She frowns. "Are you for real?"

"I'm not sure. I could just be a figment of someone's imagination." I dump in the requisite amount of detergent.

"Girl..." Tilloa chuckles. "You're too much. So, some guy is robbing a liquor store. I was just walking by outside. Dude comes running out the door, sees me, and decides I need bullets."

"Ack." She's not giving off a scent of blood. Her top and jeans don't have any obvious holes in them. "Did he miss or did you clean up?"

"Cleaned up. Came over here as soon as my ear regenerated."

I grab the side of my head and cringe. Hearing about someone having their ear shot off—or split in half—by a bullet is the vampire equivalent of watching someone else ram their little toe into a bed post.

"Any more crazy shit happen to you?"

"Just a backpack bomber. Though I have managed to go a few days without an automotive related fatality." I shut the lid on the washing machine and start the cycle.

"The heck did we do to deserve this?" Tilloa paces. "All I can hear in my head right now is my great grandmother rambling about voodoo curses." She stops to stare at me. "Backpack bomber?"

I lean against the wall by my door and relay the story. "That didn't feel like an accident. I think there's someone out there a lot more tangible than 'ancient gods' trying to get rid of me."

"Get rid of us." She scowls. "What the hell did we do?"

"Maybe nothing. Mortals have serial killers. Could be the same thing." I pull my phone out. "Hang on."

She nods.

I call Glim.

His phone picks up to silence. This is normal for him.

"Hey, it's me. You there?"

"Hello, Sarah. How are you?"

"Still in one piece. Curious if you had any luck figuring out what god or gods I've offended."

He gives a contemplative hum. "Acheron is all I've gotten so far."

"Eek. That sounds bad. Isn't he like a god of death or something?"

Tilloa tilts her head. "No, I think it's a river."

"Oh, right. The Greek mythology. River Styx with that boatman."

Grinning, Tilloa makes a goofy face and whisper-yells like Ozzy Osborne shouting Sharon.

"I think it's Charon. The 'c-h' is pronounced like a k."

"Acheron," says Glim from the phone, "Is the river of Woe in Hades. I believe it's also a real river in Greece."

I smirk. "I'm going to assume a river is not trying to blow me up."

Glim chuckles. "My guess is some pretentious bastard is using it as a nickname."

"Heh." I start to laugh, but stall, wide-eyed. "Wait, so that means there *is* someone after me?"

"After *us*," adds Tilloa.

"After us," I say into the phone.

"So it would seem," replies Glim. "Whoever it is, they are taking great pains to distance themselves from direct involvement. The Shadows are far reaching and wise, but they do not hear everything."

I let my head loll back against the wall, staring up. He's talking about the strange, enigmatic entity, not his bloodline vampires. So damn confusing. You'd think they'd come up with a different name for it like, oh, the 'Whispering Dark' or something. "Thanks. Please let me know if you hear anything else."

"Of course."

We hang up. Tilloa and I stand there in silence for a few minutes before randomly migrating back into my room and watching Chloe play. I'm sure she heard everything we said, but thus far hasn't reacted to it. I already told her the other day she needed to stay with Aurélie for a bit because some idiot was trying to hurt me and I didn't want her to get caught up in it. So, overhearing us wouldn't have been any new, shocking information.

Tilloa whistles. "Wow. Anyone ever tell you that you've got a kid's bedroom."

"Nope." I shrug. "Probably because I am a kid, so it's normal. You mean kid as in teenager, right? Not like *child*."

"Yeah." Tilloa grins. "Sixteen is still a kid to me."

I know she said that on purpose to tease me, so I ignore it.

"Uh huh. Teenager." Tilloa gestures at the rug. "'Cept for all them Barbies on the floor, this looks like a teen's room."

"Those are for Chloe and bingo. I *am* a teenager. Keep forgetting you're an old maid of what, twenty-four?" I examine my fingernails. "Fill out that AARP application yet?"

She laughs while flopping to sit on the edge of my bed. "So weird you're kinda older than me in a way."

"I'm not though. If I hadn't been turned, I'd only be nineteen."

Tilloa waves dismissively. "I mean you've been a vampire longer than me. You're all experienced with it and stuff."

"Fair. But I hardly consider myself experienced. I don't even know how much stuff there is I don't know about how to vampire."

She laughs.

Chloe giggles.

"So." Tilloa leans forward. "What do vampires do for fun when everyone else is asleep?"

"Play with dolls," says Chloe in complete seriousness.

"Or video games." I point at the computer desk. "Or read."

"Girl, you need a life." Tilloa shakes her head.

"Too late." I flap my arms.

She groans. "Seriously. What else can we do to relax?"

I flip my computer chair around to face the room and sit, spending the next few minutes telling her about the Portland Lost Ones and their habit of running around most nights doing random mischief.

"Sounds fun. Wanna?" She raises an eyebrow.

"It's kinda mean," says Chloe, not looking up from her dolls.

"I dunno. Messing with people isn't really my thing."

"We don't have to mess with normal people." She pretends to be drawing in midair. "We could paint some goofy stuff on billboards or stick it to 'the man.'"

I grimace. "Kinda sounds like asking for trouble. We're already catching hell and don't know why."

"True." She ponders. "Hungry?"

"Yeah, that I could do." Taking Chloe to feed before did make me a little peckish.

Tilloa stands. "Great. Let's go grab a bite."

Hmm. Tempting. It's irresponsible of me to bring Chloe back outside after midnight. If anyone sees her, they're either going to give me crap or call the police. I can't leave her alone. Vampire or not, she is still seven. Good thing I'm mostly a homebody and not a party girl. Wanting to go out and not be stuck watching a child is unlikely to be a common issue. It's more likely I'll get ordered to go out and do stuff (by Wolent) and will need to find someone appropriate to watch Chloe. Aurélie will help. Maybe Wolent, too. There's always the 'if you want me to do this, you have to watch her until I'm back' angle.

My parents, too, will help up to a certain hour. I can't ask them to stay awake all damn night. Right now, though, I might just be stuck at home. Shit! I was supposed to hang out with Ashley and Hunter and mind-read Raleigh. Son of a… I got so emotionally tangled up with Chloe I forgot.

I pull out my phone and send apology texts to both Ashley and Hunter. Ashley responds instantly with an away message ‹Busy. Date night. Will respond asap.› Hunter sends back an ‹Are you okay?›

Either I woke him up, or he hadn't quite fallen asleep yet. We trade text messages for a few minutes as I explain getting caught up in 'v stuff' and sidetracked by heavy emotional crap. He's obviously disappointed we don't really have time to do anything, but understanding.

"Coming?" asks Tilloa.

I gesture at Chloe.

Tilloa momentarily has this 'why is she not in bed yet' face, then a dawning look of realization takes over. "Oh, wow. Uhh… bring her with us?"

"You want to take a seven-year-old outside at midnight?" I stare at her, both eyebrows up.

"I don't want to be in-cim-a-rated," says Chloe. "I gotta stay inside."

Tilloa's look of confusion is epic. As if the girl confused bright sunlight with night time. Really, she's afraid of getting in trouble with the elders. "Incinerated? At night?"

"Explain later." I look up at the ceiling. "Umm. Possible idea. Hey, Blix?"

The imp appears hovering in front of me at eye level. *"Ooba?"*

Tilloa jumps, startled by his sudden appearance. Chloe merely waves hello.

"Till and I need to go grab a bite to eat. Would you mind keeping her company until we get back? Won't be long."

He nods, making his leathery ears flap up and down.

"Is that wise?" asks Tilloa.

"Should be fine. Blix is smart. Chloe is a good girl... and there aren't too many places in the area safer than this house." Again, a hunch keeps me from going into details since I have no idea who might have access to her mind. "If something happens, he can wake my parents up."

Chloe looks up from the dolls. "I don't want to get in trouble. I promise I won't do anything bad. You can go eat. I'll stay right here."

Blix flops on the rug and starts playing dolls with her.

"Okay." I glance at Tilloa. "Let's go grab some food."

"You feel like Chinese, Italian, or Indian?" asks Tilloa.

I groan. "Okay, another lesson about vampires." I hold a finger up as we cross the basement to the stairs. "That joke is so old no one uses it anymore."

DRAGON BREATH

Maturity is weird.

So, I'm mature enough to think leaving Chloe alone—mostly—with only Blix to keep an eye on her is probably not the wisest thing to do. I'm also teenager enough to do it anyway. Why do people think leaving kids alone for a few hours is a bad thing? Let's analyze. Kids might get into poisons. That's not going to bother Chloe. They might play with an electrical outlet and zap themselves. That'll hurt, but she'll regenerate. An unsupervised child could do something like cover the entire kitchen in flour and/or peanut butter. Okay, problem, but not a horrible one. I can clean that up, and she's too old for mischief like that.

Kids might play with fire and burn the house down. There we go. Good reason not to leave her alone. Fire sucks, even to vampires. Blix might be an imp, but he's immune to fire. And… he can almost assuredly stop her from starting one. I also don't think she's going to play with matches. Vampires have an instinctual aversion to fire. So, if any pyromaniacal tendencies ever existed in the kid's mind, they'd be gone now.

Other reasons people don't leave kids alone are mostly stuff like what if something happened? It's not so much what they're afraid the kid's going to do to themselves, but outside forces. Burglars, kidnappers, acts of nature, and so on. Thanks to Max, it's fairly unlikely anyone with ill intent is going to survive long enough to get *to* the house much less into it—as long as they try to go in through the backyard.

Between Sam's demonic friends, Sophia's magic, and Sierra being essentially as strong and fast as a vampire thanks to magic—*plus a vampiric child*—in the house, I'd almost feel sorry for anyone who broke in. Even if they survived the gauntlet of supernatural weirdness, they'd have to deal with the horror of Dad making a pun.

It's also not like Tilloa and I are ditching the kid to go out to a club and have fun. We're making a food run. I expect we'll eat, then go back to my house and spend the rest of the night watching a movie or playing a board game with the kid. Real nerdy rebels we are.

About eight minutes after liftoff, we arrive in a secluded alley in downtown Seattle. There are good places to land and not so good places to land. By now, I've learned what to look for in order to minimize the odds of being filmed in flight. It can be annoying sometimes because, unlike the vampires of years gone by, it's kind of difficult to easily swoop down on top of someone, feed, and zoom back into the air.

That sort of thing came much more easily to rural communities where a vampire could find someone wandering the woods or fields at night alone. Cities are a whole other ball game. Way more people to choose from, so it's easier on us in the sense we don't have to worry about overfeeding and killing anyone. However, more people being clumped together in a city also makes it trickier to get a single person alone somewhere in a dark place.

I've also decided to kill two birds, so to speak. Since we're going to Seattle for feeding, I decided to bring the bullet Ashley cut out of my posterior. It's too late to catch Darren Anderson or any of the other mystics at The Brass Tap, but the place is still open now. They close the doors a little after two. I don't bother explaining anything to Tilloa beyond saying I need to run a quick errand for someone. Not technically a lie even if the 'someone' in question is me.

"Just need to stop for a moment at The Brass Tap."

"What's that?" she asks.

"Umm, it's either a bar pretending to be a steampunk-inspired restaurant, or a steampunk-inspired restaurant pretending to be a bar." I point at the place. "Here we are."

It looks fairly unassuming and normal from the outside... but as soon as we go in, Tilloa gawks around at the extreme amount of brass décor. There is a reason they call it The *Brass* Tap. Swear the owner has a serious love of the Steampunk aesthetic. I've been in and out of this place often enough that none of the staff give me weird looks, mistaking me for a kid out too late. I don't know how much of an awareness the employees have regarding mystics, but they seem to be aware my presence is nothing to consider strange.

Ignoring a few patrons giving me the usual 'hey, what's a fifteen-year-old doing in a bar at this hour' stares, I approach Toby, the bartender. He's about six foot, little potbellied, bald, fuzzy black goatee. Dude kinda looks like the stereotypical town blacksmith from a fantasy game only with something of a pirate-steampunk air about him. Gotta be the fluffy white shirt.

"Hey there, Sarah," says the guy, his accent slightly British. He's a Seattle native, merely playing a character. "The guys aren't in."

"Figured." I hand him a metal Altoids mint tin. It contains a plastic baggie holding the bullet plus a handwritten request for scrying. "Can you give this to them when you see them again, please?"

"Course, love." He winks, takes the box, and stashes it under the bar. "You got it."

"Thanks." I smile at him and head out, not bothering to point out he said 'love' rather than 'luv.' Wherever Dalton is, if he's able to see my thoughts, he's probably cringing or laughing.

Tilloa follows me out the door, not saying much.

"Okay." I stop about a block from the place, looking around. "Now to find some food."

"Easy," says Tilloa. "Just find a fairly quiet spot. Take your shirt off and stumble around like you're drunk. When some guy starts following you, go into an alley. He'll think he's found the perfect victim."

"Ehh…" I grimace. "Not my style, and I don't have a bra on."

"Even better." She wags her eyebrows. "Besides, I feel less guilty about feeding on the sort of creep who'd stalk me into a dark alley."

"What if they're a nice guy?" I ask.

"You don't feed from nice guys?"

I shrug. "Not what I mean."

"A decent guy will call out and ask me if I'm okay or need help. Not quietly follow me where no one can see what goes on."

"Fair point." I fold my arms over my chest. "Still not comfortable."

"Thought you said you got desensitized."

"Yeah, I am. Ending up with my clothes shredded off me by chance is way different than waving the girls around on purpose as bait. That just feels… wrong."

"Forgot you're a good girl."

I smirk at her. "It's called dignity and self-respect."

"Says the girl wearing a GoBots T-shirt."

"It's Optimus Prime. *Transformers*. Not *GoBots*." I overact scoffing. "GoBots are like the cheap knock-offs."

"Girl…" She shakes her head. "No idea what to say back to that."

"Most people would call me a nerd or a dork." I shrug. "I'm not really. At least not off the deep end with it. I'm a geek who's really good at pretending to be, well… not one of the 'cool kids,' but I can fake not being 'uncool.'"

Tilloa laughs.

We wander past a few large groups leaving bars. Too many people in one place to try luring anyone away for a snack. Tilloa seems to enjoy being out in the city at night. Becoming a vampire has definitely opened up an entirely new world for us. No need to be afraid of the dark. She does kind of have an idea there. Turning ourselves into bait to prey on creeps *is* an idea. Feeding is much easier when the prey does us the favor of moving themselves to a secluded area. I still can't bring myself to act slutty. Just feels too icky. Of course, as young as I look, I don't have to resort to tactics like that. A seemingly scared, lost teenage girl alone in the city at night will attract creeps just as easily as a peep show.

Tilloa's smile and general good mood at having fun walking around fades. She doesn't start walking faster as she'd usually do if sensing danger. However, she does seem to be trying to look behind us without being obvious about it. Window reflections are a big help.

"What's up?" I whisper, too low for most humans to hear.

"Think we're being followed."

"Creep or another 'accident.'"

"Can't tell." She turns left at the next cross street. "Let's see if he really is following us."

I scurry around the corner to catch up, once again falling in step beside her. "Did I tell you about the 'vampire hunter' yet?"

"Yeah. The one with the, uhh, bangin' stakes?"

"Ugh." I roll my eyes. "Think it could be some kind of paramilitary version of a vampire hunting group who found us?" My ears tell me someone is definitely tailing us, getting closer.

She glances over at me. "How would they arrange random car accidents?"

"True." I exhale. "I don't think they were accidents."

"I thought we figured that out when your friend said Acheron." She grumbles. "That backpack bomb wasn't an accident."

"Yeah, well… a name doesn't really prove anything." I flap my arms. "But, way too much has happened to blame bad luck." I glance down at my boots. "Wore my poop-stompers tonight. Seems I'm going to get some use out of them."

Tilloa almost laughs. "Poop stompers? You can't possibly be that sweet and innocent."

"Hah. No. I'm not. It's my mom. She's funny about swear words. Doesn't like the phrase shit-kickers."

"What is it with moms?" asks Tilloa. "Mine's the same way. She'll watch a movie with twelve murders, a rape scene, and a little twelve-year-old boy snorting cocaine and the only thing she complains about is someone said the f-word once."

I sigh at the stars. "I have no idea. Maybe because language is easy to pick on. It's meaningless. They don't have to think about anything deeper than being offended at a word."

"True." Tilloa glances at me, then side eyes the reflection in the store we're passing. "We definitely got a tail."

Can't help but think he's been following us for a while. "He's been behind us since we left the Tap. Let's keep going a bit. Might as well bite the guy following us, but… not here."

She raises an eyebrow. "Why?"

"I have some associates at the Tap. Probably best if we go a couple blocks away from it before snacking. Wouldn't want to attract the wrong kind of attention to a place I might have to come back to often."

"Makes sense, but… we got the wrong kind of attention already."

"Let's look for an airport."

"Okay."

She knows I mean a dark, secluded space from which we can fly without being seen. The man following us continues to shadow us over another few blocks, then heads right into the alley behind us. Hmm. Surprising. Wasn't expecting the guy to be this stupid. Tilloa and I stop, exchange a 'time to kick someone's ass' glance, then spin to face the source of the none-too-quiet footsteps that have trailed us for the past five minutes.

The guy is probably late thirties, sporting short black hair and a goatee. He's quite tanned, muscles sorta-bulging under a rather tight white polo shirt. Dude is no bodybuilder, but he definitely works out. The intense, angry stare is a big clue he's looking to do more than ask us what time it is. But, honestly, the shotgun he's pointing at us is a bigger clue we have a problem.

I don't feel like spending the next hour picking pellets out of my chest, so I fly-dodge to the left the instant I see the gun. Tilloa goes full *Karate Kid* crane stance. If I wasn't experiencing the world in seemingly slowed down time thanks to my boosted reflexes, I'd have yelled 'what the hell are you doing?' She looks ridiculous, even more so when she snaps her right leg in a stupid little kick at nothing. Her right shoe flies off her foot, zooming like a shuriken straight into the dude's nose.

Sure, it's only a flat, but with the amount of strength she put into that kick, it hits him with a *slap* loud enough to echo off the concrete walls. His head tilts back from the force of impact. The shotgun angles up, then spits out a fourteen-foot-long stream of bright orange nope.

I'm in mid-Supergirl pose, rolling onto my left side while cruising toward the ground when a wave of light and heat blasts all down my front. I feel like a teriyaki chicken skewer being thrust into the broiler oven at a Chinese restaurant. Fortunately, the fire doesn't touch me—it's merely close—and only lasts an instant. Hang on. Am I a character in a video game? Did something glitch? Honestly, do game companies actually test their software before release day anymore? This guy's holding a shotgun, not a flamethrower.

The conical blast of fire collapses in on itself, leaving only a few hundred tiny glimmering sparklers in the air, all pyrotechnics over with before I hit the ground beside him. His head starts to come forward again, Tilloa's shoe bouncing off his nose and wobbling away. I lurch upward, grabbing the shotgun in both hands and forcing it upward so he's pointing it at the sky. Tilloa comes in with a spinning kick, slapping him across the face with her now-bare foot. Well, more like she rammed her foot into the side of his head like a club.

Dude flies into the building beside us, bounces off, and collapses on a row of trashcans. He's babbling and delirious. Unlike what you see in movies, it's *really* damn hard to knock a person out with a blunt impact to the head. If one shot to the skull renders someone unconscious, they're more than likely actually suffering from death. If not killed instantly, they've sustained a concussion and serious brain damage and will still probably die.

Sure, you might say boxers knock each other out all the time. That's a cumulative effect of many repeated blows to the skull over a short span of time. Still a concussion, and still far from harmless. The James Bond chop to the neck and the enemy spy is unconscious for hours is total fiction.

This guy isn't unconscious, but he's stunned. I'm also holding the shotgun which he obligingly lost his grip on when she hoofed him in the ear.

"That was easier than I expected," said Tilloa.

I crouch to pick up her shoe and hand it back to her. "Nice trick."

"Thanks." She lifts her foot up and sticks the shoe back on.

"He's human."

"I see that now." Tilloa pounces on the guy, drags him up to his feet, and swings him around to pin his back against the wall. "All right. This ain't no accident. You said you come around here all the time?"

I walk closer, holding the shotgun sideways. "Not *all the time*. Twice a month." Again, for certain reasons of not trusting her sire, I don't tell her about bringing Sophia here for meetings with Darren and the other mystics.

We both dive into Shotgun Boy's head at the same time.

He's been given a mental compulsion to lurk around here looking for me... and shoot me with this shotgun, which magically appeared in his home. No, not literal magic. I feel this needs to be clarified since Sophia exists. As far as this guy knows, the shotgun appeared one day without explanation. I see a box of ammunition next to it with the word 'dragon breath' on it.

"Wow," I mutter. "What thought process goes into some guy thinking 'I have a shotgun. How can I turn it into a flamethrower?'"

"For real," says Tilloa. "Dude was sent to kill you."

"Yeah. I'm still reading." I burrow deeper into his memories.

This guy is aware I have some kind of association with The Brass Tap, but not the exact nature of my business there. More digging for any sign of who gave this guy the compulsion comes up utterly blank. Whoever sent him erased the guy's memory of being programmed well enough I'm unable to find it. This doesn't scare me too much yet. After all, I am still relatively new, and an Innocent. Some vampires have advanced abilities at memory alteration.

So, yeah. I now definitely know a vampire out there wants me dead.

"Grr. Damn."

"What?" asks Tilloa.

"I have another freakin' nemesis, but I have no idea why." I look up at the stars. "This is so not fair."

"Totally," mutters Tilloa.

"Freeze, kid," calls a man.

I glance left. Two cops are at the mouth of the alley, pointing guns at me.

"Did you order take out?" whispers Tilloa.

"No, but I'm not going to turn down free food." I hold still, raise my voice and try to sound frightened. "Please don't shoot. This guy just tried to kill us. Can I drop this gun?"

"You do scared kid well," whispers Tilloa.

"Thanks," I whisper. "Had a lot of practice."

"Okay kid. Put it down and back away from it. No sudden moves," calls the other cop.

I smile as I oblige. Good timing, guys. I'm hungry.

IT'S ONLY FOLKLORE UNTIL
IT'S REAL

Sometimes, the universe can really be obliging.

My luck isn't that good... usually. Those two cops ended up being a massively convenient thing. Tilloa and I both ate. I made the assassin forget as much as possible. Both cops now think they responded to a report of gunfire, but found two young women trying to help a guy who appeared to have passed out. The shotgun—which I had no interest in keeping—happened to be lying there in the alley and we didn't notice it.

The cops confiscated the weapon and gave the man a ride home. Tilloa's shoe left a weird purplish almost-bruise across his face. Her kick left a real bruise. In fact, his entire right ear is purple. Easy enough to make the cops think whoever belongs to the shotgun tried to mug this guy and somehow ran off leaving the weapon behind. Don't want him to get in trouble for the gun, right? It's not his fault a vampire used him as a pawn.

Tilloa and I hurry away from the area to the nearest dark spot safe enough to fly from. I momentarily want to slap myself for not grabbing some hair off the dude. Maybe Sophia could use magic to scry and figure out who charmed him. But... ugh. Involving the Littles in my supernatural messes when fate is being nice enough to leave them out of it is a bad idea. I'm a big girl. I don't need to ask my little sister for help and I really don't want to traumatize her.

For no particular reason, I reach out to hold Tilloa's hand, but stop myself before touching her.

Yeah. I'm a big girl all right. What are we, tweens in the mall? Ugh.

"The heck was that?" asks Tilloa.

"What?" I blush.

"The hand flick thing. Is there a bug on my arm?"

"Not anymore," I say, which might not be a lie.

I'm about to leap into the air when a shiver jolts through me, powerful enough to make me drop to a knee, feeling sick to my stomach.

"You okay?" Tilloa crouches and pats me on the back. "Didn't think you'd freak out over some guy trying to shoot us."

"Not that." I swallow saliva. The emotion is so strong and sudden it's unfocused for a few seconds. But it rapidly evolves into a specific sense of worry about Ashley. "Something's wrong with Ash."

"What?"

"I dunno." I force myself to stand. "Out of nowhere, I just got this horrible feeling like she's in deep shit. You know how they say twins just kinda know if something bad happens to their other half? Like that, I guess."

"You guess?"

"We're not actually twins," I deadpan.

"Oh." She biffs herself in the forehead.

I pull out my phone and try to call her. Ringing... ringing... "It's too significant to be me having a random thought. I do randomly worry about her, but this definitely felt like something from the outside slapping me upside the head. What do you think it could be?"

"How should I know? You're the expert at this stuff."

I squirm. "Hardly. I'm new at this, too. Just, less new than you are." No answer. I redial. "I mean, she's technically my thrall, but I haven't like *done* anything to her. It's just metaphorical paperwork to keep other vampires off her."

Tilloa stands there radiating moral support as my phone rings into voicemail for a second time. "Think you might'a done something mentally to her? You guys close?"

I exhale hard, rapidly becoming too upset and worried to think clearly. "It absolutely ruined her when she thought I died, almost more than even my mom. I truly believe that if I'd run off into vampire obscurity and allowed everyone to think I'd died for good, Ashley would have been dead in six months."

"Whoa... suicide?"

"Either that or a broken heart. Lost the will to live." I grab Tilloa—because she happens to be there—and sniffle on her arm. "We... like, wow.

From age four or so up, the only times we weren't together, we were either sleeping at home in our own beds at night, off on some family trip, or we had different classes in high school. Mrs. Carter worked super long hours, so Ashley basically lived with us."

"Wow. That explains why you two are like the way you are."

"Yeah." I wipe my eyes, hands shaking. Come on, Sarah. Keep it together. That hammer of dread doesn't mean something irreversible has happened to Ashley. It's just worry. Gotta stay focused.

"They say some twins and super close friends have a connection."

I exhale a shuddering breath. "That's folklore."

"So are vampires." She raises both eyebrows.

"Good point. No time to waste. Let's go."

Not giving a rat's ass who might see what, I fling myself into the sky.

My gut knots up the instant Ashley's house is in view.

From the sky, I can see the front door is half open. Both Ashley's Jetta and her mom's car are there. I swoop down to land directly on the porch and rush inside. Mrs. Carter's sprawled on the floor, unconscious. The coffee table is out of position, the stuff usually on it is on the floor closer to the TV. Her clothes are slightly disheveled as if someone grabbed her and a brief struggle ensued. It does *not* look like she's been assaulted or hurt.

An odd chemical smell in the air, strongest around her, says chloroform —or something like it.

I crouch to check on her. Heartbeat sounds strong.

Tilloa glances around at the room. "I think we can safely say something messed up has happened."

AN EXTRA HELPING OF WTF

T oo worried about Ashley to bother diving into Mrs. Carter's head just yet, I lift her up and reposition her on the sofa, then bolt for the stairs.

There's no one in Ashley's bedroom. Clothes are all over the super plush pink rug. The bed is disturbed but still made, her massive pink bedspread comforter in place but heavily rumpled. Another girl's scent is in here, too. Strong. I suspect it's Raleigh. I didn't get a good 'sniff' of her at the hospital since I hadn't been online at the time. Really don't want to think about it, but I can guess what particular activity disheveled the bed. Looks fairly energetic, too.

"Hmm," says Tilloa in the doorway behind me. "Smells like sex in here but not getting much of a dude scent."

"Ash is bi. She's dating a girl right now."

"Ah. That explains it."

I'm too upset to really take note of Tilloa's 'no big deal' tone, but it does register in my brain. Some of the clothing bits on the floor are definitely not the type of thing Ashley wears. She's not really into expensive clothes… and definitely not a Victoria's Secret kinda girl. Gotta be Raleigh's stuff.

"Here." Tilloa crouches, pointing at the rug. "This carpet is epic."

"Yeah. Ash adores it. So lush." I squat near her. Yeah, there does appear to be a man's boot print in the rug. For an instant, I almost turn Fury. The idea of someone kidnapping Ash is as baffling as it is rage inducing.

All the information flooding into my head from my various senses tells me Ashley and Raleigh must have been in the middle of having sex when some guys stormed into the house and abducted them—after chloroforming Mrs. Carter. It's a bit strange her room doesn't show any signs at all of a struggle. Ashley's phone is still on the nightstand. Dammit! Dammit! Dammit!

I run past Tilloa out of the room and Supergirl dive over the railing above the stairs, flying into the living room to hover over Mrs. Carter. The woman is *out*. I peel her eyelids open and stare into her eyes. Her memory is a swirl of chemically-twisted blur. She's sitting on the sofa watching *Supernatural* with the volume up a bit higher than normal to mask the sound of Ashley squeaking. While she knows her daughter is grown up now and is about as cool as a parent can be about their kid having sex in the house… she doesn't want to hear it. Other than a few giggles, she couldn't hear anything going on upstairs over the television for about an hour until someone grabbed her.

She didn't hear the door open nor did she realize someone broke into the house until a guy grabbed her from behind and held a wet cloth over her face. Out of the corner of her eye, she spots two other men in black tactical gear like straight out of *Call of Duty* going up the steps. There's still sunlight showing in the doorway behind them outside. This happened hours ago. Shit! They must have given Mrs. Carter an injection of some other drug to keep her unconscious. I don't think chloroform alone lasts as long as it appears she's been out.

Both men carry Mp5 type guns, but slung on their chests. Mrs. C is freaking out, but to me, it's clear they aren't going upstairs expecting trouble—or they'd be holding their guns at the ready. Their black vests have FBI on the back in yellow letters. Mrs. C passes out at that point, overcome by the fumes she's breathing. Since her memory has 'stopped recording,' I break the link to her.

My head spins. Do I call the Persons in Black and ask them WTF happened? It makes no sense whatsoever for the FBI to grab Ashley and Raleigh. Wait… Raleigh's parents are like important bigwigs at Amazon or Microsoft or something like that. Could they have done this to scare the hell out of Ash and chase her away from their daughter? Did my best friend get SWAT-ted?

Umm. Should Mrs. Carter remember this or not? Ehh, no. She's kinda brittle. If she remembers guys dressed like that storming into her house, she's never going to feel secure in here ever again. Might even move. Gotta erase it.

Mrs. Carter lost consciousness before hearing anything happen upstairs. Maybe the knockout agent did something to her memory. Her heart rate and breathing feel normal. As far as my vampire senses can tell me, she's fine—merely sleeping. I pivot upright and land on my feet beside Tilloa, who's come downstairs.

"Someone kidnapped Ashley," I mutter. "They had FBI on their vests."

"FBI doesn't usually kidnap people." Tilloa tilts her head. "Your friend isn't into some crazy international espionage stuff you don't know about, is she?"

"Get real." I grumble. "Ashley is the sweetest, most benign… harmless…" Don't cry. Don't give up yet. I clench my jaw. "They can't be real FBI. That's gotta just be to stop neighbors from calling the police."

"Maybe." Tilloa walks to the front door. "No sign of a break in. Cops would have kicked it in."

"Or knocked."

"Yeah, they tend to knock with a giant concrete battering ram. Door's undamaged. Either they had a key or it wasn't locked." Tilloa nudges the door closed. "Why would someone take Ashley?"

I growl. "Unless the market for hiring cage cleaners at vet offices has suddenly gone super competitive, it's probably that damned Acheron douchebag. If he knows I sometimes go to the Brass Tap, he obviously knows how close I am with Ashley. I bet he took her to use as bait to lure me into a deathtrap."

Tilloa grabs me by the arms as I start to swoon to my knees and cry from pure anger. "Sarah, stop that. There's no crying in vampire abductions."

I shudder, consumed by directionless rage. "This isn't baseball. They have Ashley. How can I be a damned vampire and still feel so freakin' helpless?"

"Try that feelings thing."

"Now is not the goddamned time to get in touch with my inner self."

Tilloa shakes her head. "No. Not what I mean. I used to do meditation."

"Not helpful." I want to storm off somewhere, but have no idea where to go, so I just stand there with her holding me by the arms.

"Try to push everything out of your thoughts except for Ashley. You felt something when it happened, right?" Tilloa leans in, staring into my eyes. She's so close, my face is kinda reflecting on her gold irises. "You have a connection to her. Some kinda link. Try to use it. Clear your head of everything else. Set emotion aside."

"Yeah, sure. You expect me not to be emotional?"

"I expect you to care enough about Ashley to put that shit on pause for a minute." Tilloa pulls me down to sit on the floor. "Just a minute. Try it. Freak out later if it don't work."

"I dunno."

She pushes my arms and legs into a meditation pose. I don't do the weird little thumb-to-pinky thing, just grab my knees.

"You told me you can talk to that Dalton guy, right?" She pats me on the head. "Try the same thing, but think of Ashley instead. Open your head. Listen to whatever is being broadcast."

Okay. She's got a point there. I *can* communicate with Dalton. But… he's my sire. I haven't done any bitey-bloody stuff with Ashley at all. Desire, huh? The Transference requires desire plus blood. Can desire without blood do anything?

I close my eyes.

Time to find out.

37

MEDITATION... OR SOMETHING

T rying to think about nothing is a lot more difficult than it sounds. I've only managed to completely blank out my brain twice in my life: once when Michelle's mother decided I needed to hear all about her church, and for the couple days or whatever that passed between when Dalton gave me the Transference and I woke up in the morgue.

Even in a moment of complete happy normal, it would be a task for me to do the Zen thing. With Ashley in danger, this is a request about as impossible as taking a weekend trip with a vegan and a crossfitter and asking both of them not to talk about their lifestyle at all until Monday.

However, I have a chance. I don't have to completely *blank* out. I have to think about only Ashley. Right now, it's pretty damn easy. There's also the added benefit of me knowing how it feels to make a brain call to Dalton. He can be halfway around the world and given sufficient quiet, I can telepathically talk to him. Of course, the mind link between a vampire and their sire is seriously deep.

Can't argue the feeling of dread I felt earlier had been imaginary. *Some* manner of connection must exist between me and Ashley beyond the simple rules of normal reality. It could take hours before Glim's shadow whisper stuff is able to tell where she is. Ashley might not have that much time left. She might not have *any* time left.

A spike of dread sorrow at the idea this guy already killed her sets off a bomb of grief in my chest that echoes in my head. It's like crazy scientists just used a nuclear blast to power the world's biggest radio antenna.

Out of nowhere, I'm totally convinced Ashley is still alive. She's furious.

I mentally reach out for more... and a rapid-fire slideshow of Ashley streams across the back of my eyelids. I see her standing shyly at the edge of a room on our first day of preschool. I'd felt bad for her being all alone there while other kids played in groups. They hadn't shunned her or anything. She'd just been too shy to initiate. Once someone else starts a conversation, she'll chatter their ears off. Her little face lights up as soon as I walk up to her and say hello.

"Hi, my name is Ashley," chirps a little kid voice in my head. "What's your name?"

Again and again, I see images of her throughout our lives. There's no order to it. She's a tiny kid in one glimpse, the next is from last week. Back and forth from high school to grade school to summer vacations and all points in between.

A long pause of blackness contains only the feeling she's in a serious amount of trouble.

Yeah, no shit, psychic vision. Thanks. I knew that already.

She appears again. We're sharing a bed having a sleepover. Maybe eleven years old. Wow, her hair was epic then. Fluffy and long. It's gotten tamer over the years, straighter. Scenes shift. Mall. School. Amusement park. Swimming pool. School again. Ashley laughing at me when I got stuck in a locker on a dare. Yes, I was skinny enough to fit inside the lockers during seventh grade. Now I'm seeing Ashley curled up in her bed sobbing uncontrollably. I can't possibly know or see this, but it's got to be the night she thought I died.

I don't want to see her like this.

Ashley! Where are you right now? Can you hear me? Say something!

A snug sensation encircles my throat. Is that her astral projection grabbing me?

Ash! I shout mentally. *Where are you?*

The slideshow stops, freeze framed on Ashley in a pink bathing suit flying at me in a cannonball pose. Her grin is so damn big. She's so happy. Above and behind her, the summer sky is as blue as her eyes. Deep, endless, pure. As pure as the joy in her face in that moment. We had so much fun that summer. First year of high school behind us, the whole world to go... not a care in the world.

She fades away once more to blackness.

I get frustrated. Then… something. An urge, pulling me almost straight back. I want to go in that direction. Bingo. I've either gone completely insane or we really do have a connection.

"Got something. Let's go." I spring to my feet and run out the door, not really caring too much one way or the other if Tilloa follows.

She dashes out, jumping into the sky right behind me.

The pull leads me south.

Tilloa flies up alongside me. "Where are you going?"

"No idea." I point. "I just feel a direction. Don't have a map link, just whatever weird mental thing vampires used to navigate before iPhones and GPS existed."

She nods. "Any idea what happened?"

"No… not really. Uhh, you ever see one of those Arnold Schwarzenegger action movies from the Eighties?"

"The heck does that have to do with… probably. Why?"

"Remember the generic soldiery bad guys he always shoots hundreds of?"

"Yeah."

"Dudes dressed like that have her, and probably Raleigh, too."

Tilloa shakes her head.

"What?" I yell.

"You told me that already. Fake FBI, remember?"

"Ugh. Sorry. I'm a mess right now."

She glides closer and takes my hand. "It's all good. I got you, boo."

38

THE MILL

The mental pull leads me quite a distance south of Seattle into the woods.

My emotions are too out of whack for me to have much of a sense of time. Suburbia gives way to less developed areas, then forest. Not too long after I find myself zooming along above a vast expanse of trees, light draws my attention to a huge, rectangular metal buildings set in a distant clearing. The instant I look at the place, the pull guiding me evaporates. This must be where Ashley is.

I veer toward it. As we get closer, it becomes obvious we're approaching not just one big building but a fenced-in compound. The second biggest building isn't even half the size of the first one. Only the huge one has any lights on inside. Seems bright to me but it's probably only one or two bulbs in an otherwise abandoned industrial facility. If I had to guess, I'd say it's an old lumber mill or mine. Can't be a factory. No one would put a factory out here in the middle of complete nowhere. Except for some roads—and possibly a sasquatch or two—there's nothing within at least fifty miles in any direction other than trees.

I dive down into the forest, aiming for a spot close enough to see the compound without being too obvious. To mortals, it's super freakin' dark out this far. The area outside the large building is lit up via some freestanding contractor lamps, the double-headed ones they sell at like Home Depot and stuff. They must be on batteries. I don't hear any generators running, and this place is so damn remote, it's unlikely to have actual electrical connections.

Only one road leads to the facility. Like pretty much every other road around here, it's a narrow two-lane strip of blacktop without a shoulder, flanked on both sides by a wall of trees. If someone veers even a few inches away from the pavement, they're smacking into a tree trunk if they're lucky. If they're unlucky, they're going tumbling down a steep tree-studded hill. These are the kinds of roads you always see in those creepy haunting stories where the supposed ghost of an accident victim wanders the lonely country road where they lost their life.

Unsurprisingly, I have such a weak cellular signal, the navigation app can't figure out where I am. Washington State has some really beautiful natural country. It's great for hiking and unwinding. Not so great for getting lost in or kidnapped to. Vast swaths of land have zero cell signal. Go figure, Verizon or whoever doesn't want to invest in the necessary infrastructure for bears and squirrels to go online. It's as expected as it is annoying the Forces of Evil have taken Ashley to one such dead zone.

It's now about 1:18 a.m. Based on the time, I figure it took us roughly an hour to get here, so we're at least 120 miles from Cottage Lake, quite possibly more if my emotional state affected my flight speed. I can worry about figuring out where 'here' is later. Ashley first.

I float up off the ground again while staying mostly hidden behind a tree. Less effort than climbing, and a high vantage point helps me see. Eight huge black pickup trucks—just like the one Hunter saw following us when he took my body home from Mi Tierra—sit in a row about thirty yards away from the biggest building inside the fence. A windowless, black cargo van is parked at the far end of the truck row. About a dozen armed men in all black are arranged around the largest building. Some stand still, others patrol on sentry duty. Two guys are on the roof. None of them have FBI on their tactical vests. They're all wearing black military BDUs, or something really similar with a whole crapton of various gear like freakin' paramilitary commandos or something.

This is getting really damn bizarre. What the hell is going on? Has my father's fascination with Eighties movies collided with Sophia's magic to bend reality and make my life literally into a 1980s action film? There better not be a damn invisible predator around here.

My phone emits a voicemail reminder chirp.

Did I mention it's insanely quiet here? Some of the men look around at the chirp, which seemingly carried all the way across the mill property. I manage not to curse out loud. Fortunately, they seem to be wondering which one of *their* phones did it. Whew. I drop to ground level, turn my phone volume all the way down and go to stuff it in my pocket... except, a weird feeling comes over me that I ought to listen to the message.

Okay. Strange, but I'm not going to question it.

I hold the phone up, give it one button click of volume, and open the voicemail screen. Looks like a message came in forty-six minutes ago. Grr. Didn't notice it while focusing so damn hard on finding this place. Also, it is kinda hard to hear a ringing phone in my pocket with the wind ripping past my ears.

And, shit. The voicemail is from Ash. This can't be good. I tap the button to play. Tilloa leans her head closer to the phone so she can listen in.

"Ooh, you are so lucky," yells Ashley. "If I could move, I'd *totally* kick your butt!"

"Read it," says a self-important sounding man, seeming annoyed, bored, or both.

Twenty seconds of silence.

"*Out loud*, you overly literal whelp. Read it out loud," says the man.

"No way, creep," snaps Ashley. "I'm not saying that." She sucks in a breath, then yells, "Sarah! Don't do it."

"Read. The. Message," says the man in a stern tone.

Five seconds of silence.

"Sarah," says Ashley, her voice lifeless and robotic. "I have been kidnapped by powerful forces beyond your comprehension. If you do not destroy Tilloa and.... And..." She gasps. "Argh! Go to hell!"

"Read the *entire* message," says the man, close to shouting.

Ashley's shuddering breath comes from the little speaker on my phone. "You... must... destroy." She gasps, fighting to stop speaking, but unable to. "Tilloa and then... yourself. I will be killed. You have forty-eight hours." She gives a strangled cry that mutates into a growl of rage. "Don't do it, Sare! This creep—"

The voicemail ends.

Tilloa's giving me an 'oh hell no' glance.

Not that I'm even considering it, but I could probably take her, if only because I have claws and she doesn't. One year a vampire vs. a single month isn't too much difference. But, no way. I'm not going to attack my new friend because some overstuffed asshole thinks he gets to threaten Ashley. I'm a hundred percent convinced that no matter what I do, he's going to kill her. Even if I *did* kill Tilloa and then flung myself into a volcano, Ashley's going to die.

Besides, she told me not to do it.

"I don't think this bastard realized his voice came over the phone," I whisper.

"Heh." She exhales out her nose. "Sounds like a real charmer."

"Literally." Wow… Ashley almost fought it off. She did break out… briefly. The thought of it chokes me up. As far as I know, it's really damn difficult for a mortal to resist a vampire's control. It would be one thing if we tried to command a mortal to murder their family. But just reading text out loud? That's a simple request. That she fought it off—twice—because of what he said… about me. I'm… ooh. Easy Sarah. Don't lose your head. Think.

"We have an advantage," says Tilloa.

"Really?" I bow my head, trying not to surrender to feeling way out of my depth here. "Doesn't feel like it."

She gestures at the compound. "They don't know we found her. We have forty-eight hours to get her out of there and the hard part's already done. Don't gotta waste two days trying to locate her."

I nod. "True."

We both freeze statue still at the soft crunching of approaching footsteps. Seconds later, a man in black—not to be confused with the Persons In Black—approaches our position. This is just a guy wearing black clothing. He's not part of a shadowy government agency responsible for keeping tabs on vampires.

I turn sideways to hopefully hide behind a tree. Tilloa takes a slightly different approach. She blurs around in a tight circle and lunges at him from behind left, driving a spinning kick into his head that throws him off his feet. Dude sails about four feet to smooch a tree, bounces off it, and staggers around to face her—right as she kicks him in the chest, knocking all the air out of his lungs. Guy wheezes, struggling to raise his M4. Yes, I know what an M4 is. Sierra plays an *epic* amount of *Call of Duty*.

She grabs the barrel and yanks the weapon out of his hands before he can fire it. Her gold eyes glow like those of a succubus—and he's done. Just stands there gobsmacked. Two seconds later, he faints.

I edge closer, mouth agape.

Tilloa drags the guy deeper into the woods away from the facility.

"Whoa. Did you scare him into passing out?"

"No. Just a sleep compulsion."

"What's the glowing eye thing?"

"Wanted to scare him first." She smiles and her eyes light up again. "As far as I know, it's just cool, creepy, and cosmetic."

"Metallic gold irises are already cool, creepy, and cosmetic. Making them glow is a factor of ten type stuff."

She crouches over the sleeping guy and searches him for like keys and stuff.

"By the way," I whisper. "That was impressive."

"Used to be an amateur kickboxer before the thing happened."

I blink. She never mentioned that before. "Any other surprises? Like, is there anything in your past that might explain why a paramilitary force wants us dead?"

"Nothing I can think of." She grins. "Unless you count being the only girl on my high school baseball team for two years. Even got a varsity letter. I had a wicked fastball." She poked herself in the arm. "Probably be ridiculous now with vampire strength."

"Neat." I take a knee and stare into the unconscious man's eyes.

What are we dealing with here?

Hmm. He's not charmed. This guy isn't under a vampire's compulsion to become a bodyguard. He—and I imagine everyone else in black—is a hired mercenary. He's also aware of vampires. This dude and all the others here know they're working for one. In fact, the vampire owns the mercenary corp. Ugh. Lovely. It's the sort of thing untrained teen girls do all the time: infiltrate a remote compound guarded by professional soldiers of fortune.

That'll work. Right?

Since I'm not in an anime movie, I do somewhat doubt our odds of success. Though, to be fair, I'm not exactly a normal teenager. Maybe my life *is* an anime movie after all. Okay, creep. Where's Ashley?

I burrow deeper in his head.

This man saw Ashley inside the big building. Giant rotary saw blades and steel roller pathways tell me it's definitely an old lumber mill. No, they didn't tie her to a moving conveyor in perilous danger of being split in half by a huge saw. We're in an anime, not a horror movie or a whimsical spy film. Ashley is kneeling on the concrete floor by a massive steel roller conveyor assembly. Two pairs of pink furry handcuffs and her hot pink dog collar are the only things she has on.

Oh, good grief. They really did barge in on them in the middle of sex and cart her out the door as she was. I could make a joke here about my friend being so sweet and obliging she'd even tie herself up for kidnappers, but... no. I'm too pissed off.

As far as this guy's memory tells me, there are at least another fifteen mercenaries inside the big building in addition to all the ones outside.

Ashley is in that building and these sons of bitches haven't even covered her with a blanket, just leashed her to a giant metal trackway like a stray dog they aren't sure what to do with.

Murderous rage fills me. I snarl, launch myself into the air—and eat dirt.

It takes me a second to realize Tilloa grabbed me by the ankle. My attempt to fly toward the millhouse dragged her a few feet, her boots digging shallow trenches before they went deep enough to yank me to a halt. I stop trying to pull myself forward and growl at her.

"Calm your ass down." Tilloa pulls me back. "They might just shoot her if they see us coming."

"I'm going to kill every last one of these bastards if they've touched her."

She releases her grip on my boot and pats me on the shoulder. "I'm on board with that. But, we gotta be smart about it. This is a trap to lure you here."

I push up onto all fours, then sit back on my heels. "No, it isn't. You heard the message he made her read. They're gonna hold her here for two days waiting to see if I try to destroy you, then myself. They aren't trying to lure me here."

"Then what's with all the security?" She gestures at the lumber mill.

Rage fades to determination. Tilloa is right. If I go charging in there like a maniac, they could easily shoot Ashley as soon as they realize their threat isn't working. We're not in a Schwarzenegger movie. We're in a Jason Bourne film. Stealth time.

"Umm, probably because he's worried I might find him." I scowl. "Doesn't mean he wants to lure me here. He's just prepared in case I show up. Bet he's thinking I wouldn't be stupid enough to come alone and would bring twenty of Wolent's people."

She points a thumb backward over her shoulder. "Should we run to the city and get help?"

I shake my head. "I don't want to leave her in there like that any longer. And… we're already here. And, like you said, a big frontal assault will probably only make them kill her."

Tilloa nods. "Okay. We got this. We're vampires. Sneaking around at night is what we do."

"Who the hell is this Acheron guy?" I rasp.

"I have no damn idea. Don't matter. I got your back."

On one level, it sounds really stupid for me to go in there right now. But I can't shake the notion Ashley doesn't have the time for me to do anything else. Even if this Acheron douche won't kill her until his deadline expires—so he can hold her life over me—it doesn't mean he won't torture her. I can't take the chance he's going to do irreversible damage to Ash before I return with the cavalry. Also, Wolent's people aren't exactly the most subtle. They're door kickers and leg breakers. Bringing them here is bad news for everyone involved.

"All right. Let's not mess this up." I start crawling toward the fence.

39

TIME FOR CARNAGE

T he only experience I have even remotely close to sneaking past a bunch of mercenaries is playing *Call of Duty.*

Silly as the idea is, Sierra might actually be better at this than me. No damn way in hell am I going to bring her anywhere near this place. Just saying, she's logged so many hours playing that game, she could probably get to the building unnoticed. Can't even say she'd be clueless because real soldiers don't behave like AI idiots. *Call of Duty* is against real players. But, yeah. Pretty sure stealth mechanics in combat video games aren't exactly the best representations of reality.

I'm on a hair trigger. This is not a video game. If I screw up and get spotted out of 'stealth,' failing the mission because the bad guy killed the hostage, there's no 'oh dammit' and reloading the game to try again. I have to be perfect. Of course, this is me we're talking about, so something is going to go wrong at some point. Okay, Universe. If you're listening to me now, *when* this screws up, please let all the shit hitting the fan spray on me. Not Ashley.

I'm ready for the fail. As soon as all hell breaks loose, I am ignoring everything and flying as fast as I can into the lumber mill building. If I can get to Ashley, it's possible I can protect her, buy time, get out of here maybe. I'm not thinking about killing Acheron… at least, not now. Not with Ash in harm's way. Fortunately, that one guy's memory of her showed her furious, not terrified. I'd have a much more difficult time keeping myself under control if Ashley was freaking out and sobbing.

Tilloa and I fly so low we're almost belly-crawling over the ground. There isn't enough space between my body and the dirt for my hand to fit in. We're hover snakes at the moment. While we look stupid, moving like this has the advantage of making no noise. We're also keeping our arms and legs still, which eliminates the 'humanness' of our presence. If someone catches sight of us drifting by, we'd look like a strange object in the wind. If we notice anyone glancing in our direction, we just stop moving. Maybe they'll mistake us for logs.

These guys crossed a line. They attacked Ashley. You know that joke about a party of D&D characters who need to interrogate a guy to save someone but the paladin in the party can't tolerate even mild torture like slapping someone around? Follows Rules Girl is currently the person playing the paladin being a good sport and wandering off to 'admire the rustic architecture' so they aren't paying attention to what the rest of the party does to the bad guy.

Yeah, the proverbial safety is off. If I kill any of these guys, it's not gonna bother me. I might feel bad if they'd been simple mercenaries, but these guys know about vampires. They work for one. A vampire owns their company. They are absolutely aware they've kidnapped an innocent, mortal eighteen-year-old girl to serve the ends of a crazy vampire named Acheron. They didn't even have the humanity to give her a blanket. So, no. Not much pity from me. I'd kill them… but.

I'm like Dad playing *World of Warcraft* and running a dungeon. We're trying to skip as much 'trash' as we can and go straight to the boss. Well, straight to Ashley. I don't want a boss fight now. Once I get her somewhere safe, I'm absolutely going to be the little girl who goes running to tell Daddy what just happened. Only, I'm thinking Wolent, not my actual Dad. Let the boss deal with this moron.

So far so good. We're halfway to the building without anyone noticing us. The sentry walking at the fence line didn't hear us glide over him and sink to the ground. It had been tempting to ambush him but… I stopped myself. For one thing, I'm too impatient to spend the time on him instead of getting to Ash. For another, we already took out one guy. If they have radio comms, one of their people going silent isn't necessarily going to kick the hornet's nest. Two guys going offline would. There's also the problem that it's much more difficult to disable someone than a single bonk to the head. We might be seen during the time it takes us to apply a mental derp hammer. So, we ignored him and kept weaving around old piles of moldy lumber stacked up near the back of the property. Two more guys walking from the mill building to the fence also went straight past us about twenty feet away without seeing us.

We make it to the row of pickups and slide under one. The trucks are great cover from the two dudes on the roof. Our biggest problem now is the roughly thirty yards of open ground between our hiding place and the building. Having a giant truck over us affords us some sense of security enough to take a break here and survey our situation.

Tilloa's flat on her stomach by the left front tire, watching to that side. I crawl to the front right tire and watch our other flank. The smell of fast-food burgers lands on my tongue. Someone probably grabbed a Big Mac and ate it in the truck we're hiding under. From here, I spot a large black sedan parked on the other side of the van. It looks like an unmarked police car, even has that little spotlight above the driver's side mirror. Nothing else stands out as odd about it—except for two bare footprints on the rear quarter panel, close together. Either Ashley or Raleigh must have been carried past the car and put up as much of a fight as they could. I picture one of the girls planting her feet against the car and trying to push off.

Probably Ashley. She doesn't think too far ahead when she's furious. What would she do if she got out of the man's arms? Kinda hard to run away with fuzzy handcuffs on your ankles. I really don't know how she finds that exciting.

Right. Focus, Sarah.

Tilloa and I lay there under the truck for a couple minutes watching the mercenaries patrol or stand around. It seems the real world is a bit different than a video game—who'd have guessed. The men are not walking around in clock-perfect patrol paths. Most of them are kinda loafing to be honest. Just hanging out. Replace the abandoned lumber mill with a lakeside cabin, and their tactical gear with flannel, and this is a bunch of guys having a relaxing vacation weekend, camping, drinking beer, and fishing.

Wow. Maybe I do have a chance to get in. Spetsnaz, they are not.

It's fairly quiet... except for the soft thumps of boots on dirt, scuffs of boots on concrete inside the building, the rattle of steel rollers in the wind and crumbling metal walls, someone's stomach protesting—probably the guy who ate the Big Mac—a tinny radio type voice muttering something about politics, and intermittent feminine grunts like Ashley trying to brute-force her way out of handcuffs. None of the mercenaries are talking about significant things. Sports stuff, mostly. A few kinda grumble about having to be out in the sticks for two days. Nothing they're saying gives any clue they are aware of our presence.

One guy says, "Why don't *they* take the damn night shift? I'm getting too old for this five-in-the-morning shit."

Crap. That's bad. I can only assume the 'they' he's talking about are vampires. Duh. Of course. If a vampire owns a mercenary company, at least some of the mercs working for him are going to be vampires. Night operations much?

Tilloa pats me on the arm, then points. I follow her finger's path to a big, square hole in the side of the mill building near the roof. It kinda resembles a hay loft door, but it's a fair bet no one used it for hay. It's probably for whole tree logs moving along the series of elevated conveyors connecting the mill to the second largest building, which has the look of a warehouse. Guessing it's where they stored incoming timber before sending it to the mill for processing. The skyway looks super rickety, but possibly climbable. It would make a ton of noise if even a squirrel scampered across it.

Fortunately, we don't need to climb. Follows Rules Girl obeys the law for the most part, but there's one she doesn't mind ignoring: the law of gravity. The hole is perfect.

I nod once.

A mercenary on the roof right above the opening is a problem. As soon as we crawl forward out from under this truck, he's going to see us. No amount of 'stealth skill' is going to keep a person hidden while crossing thirty yards of open dirt. Annoyingly enough, I don't have a silenced gun to effortlessly neutralize the dude looking at us.

So, I do the best thing I can think of: focus my gaze on him and attempt to implant the strong urge to go use the bathroom. Mind control type stuff is difficult to use at a distance. If I'm nose-to-nose with someone, staring into their eyes, I can create entire full memories of stuff that never happened. This dude is like thirty yards away and three stories up. A short command like 'look at me' or 'go away' is probably doable. But 'away' isn't specific enough. He might walk ten steps before turning around and coming right back. I need him to be away from his post for at least a minute.

I keep focusing, trying to give him the feeling he's in urgent need of taking a number two, since that'll keep him occupied for a while.

The stillness of the lumber mill is broken by a high-pitched squeaker of a fart that kinda sounds like the 'doing something sneaky' trumpet in the background of a *Looney Tunes* cartoon. Somehow, his standing on the roof of a cavernous metal-walled building acts like a resonance chamber. As quiet as it is here, he may as well have tooted into a microphone connected to a PA system. For the entire nine second duration of his warbling butt-trumpet solo, the whole camp stops moving. Even the birds in the nearby trees freeze at the unearthly, echoing noise. It ends with a sharp, upward pitch shift, almost as if he farted a question.

"Talk about a tight ass," mutters Tilloa.

"What the hell was that?" yells a guy across the yard.

The guy I attempted to charm gets an urgent look on his face and hurries away from the edge of the roof. Other mercenaries lose it and start laughing. Even Tilloa cracks up. Got rid of the sentry watching our path plus distracted every mercenary in the mill yard. Win-win.

I swat her on the arm and zip forward.

We fly low, fast, and silent over the dirt to the wall, then pull a ninety-degree vertical, skimming the corrugated steel. As soon as we reach the big, square opening near the roof, we slip through it to perch on a massive conveyor path. There's no rubber belt, only big metal rollers like four-inches thick. Seriously heavy-duty stuff. It's made to carry whole tree logs. The spaces between them are kinda scary. Hands and feet could get trapped in there and twisted.

This massive building is one big room inside, not a separate three stories. The opposite wall from us has platforms of small rooms connected via metal stairs, offices technically at the second and third story level, but they aren't very big compared to the size of the whole place. Machinery takes up most of the space in here, the centerpiece of which is a massive rotary saw. The blade is all rusty and corroded. Doesn't look like it's moved in about twenty years. But it's gotta be ten feet in diameter, capable of splitting a whole tree in half lengthwise in under a second. Other, smaller machines around the room had likely been used to turn big logs into smaller logs, two-by-fours, planks, or whatever. None of it is operational.

This place has no connection to electricity. Some of the smaller buildings out in the compound must be enormous diesel generators.

Six battery-powered contractor lights arranged around in a rough circle illuminate a smallish area fairly close to the back wall by the offices. Where Tilloa and I are hiding at the moment is completely dark. I'm not wholly secure in the darkness this time. Lack of light works great on mortals, but since some of these mercenaries are vampires, it won't conceal us.

Ashley is pretty hard to miss. She's so pale her skin basically glows in the glare from the halogen lights. She's kneeling on the concrete beside a much smaller steel-roller conveyor track than the one we're on. Her hands are locked up behind her back, hidden under her hair. Pink furry handcuffs link her ankles together. An ordinary dog leash tethers her collar to the frame of the conveyor track via a padlock through the hot pink leather loop at the end of the chain. Dirt from the floor is smudged all over her legs, butt, back, and arms, proof she's been seriously fighting to escape but having zero luck at it. She still seems more pissed off than anything, grunting, squirming, and attempting to break the leash.

She doesn't appear to be hurt, at least not that I can see from this angle. Then again, I can't see her face because she's got her back to us. Grr. I seriously want to tear someone apart for this. Couldn't they at least have covered her with a T-shirt? At least it's summer, so she won't get hypothermia.

It's kind of surprising none of the mercenaries—who all appear to be guys—aren't sitting around watching her, taking pictures, or touching her. They appear completely ambivalent to her presence. I can't help but think of Petra keeping a harem of naked men chained up in her lair. Is this sort of thing no big deal to most vampires? Humans as animals? I mean, don't get me wrong. It's awesome they aren't assaulting her. I love that. Just kinda unsettling they're not even staring at her.

Me? I'm staring at Ashley. Seeing her so helpless and in such danger is seriously pissing me off. I can't even move right now or I'm going to go all Tasmanian devil on these bastards… and that's going to get her killed.

Tilloa gestures for me to follow, then slides off the massive conveyor track.

We glide straight down to the floor in what's probably the darkest corner of the building.

"She looks okay," whispers Tilloa.

"Yeah. Can't believe they didn't wrap her in a sheet or something."

"Some of these dudes are vampires." Tilloa crawls forward and takes a position hiding behind a truck-sized lumber-processing machine. "To them, she's just a food animal. People don't put clothes on pigs or cows."

I glare at her. "Did you just call Ash a pig or cow?"

"No." She shoots me side eye over her shoulder. "I meant it as a metaphor. Calm down."

Calm down? Is she serious? I crawl up next to her, barely managing not to grab her by the shirt collar. "Considering Ashley's life is in danger *again* because of me, this *is* me being calm."

Tilloa makes a 'shh, you're getting a bit loud' gesture. "How is this your fault?"

I snarl. "I have no freakin' idea and that's making it ten times worse."

Ashley sighs. "Drat. Why did I have to buy the extra heavy-duty leash? This sucks." Handcuff chains rattle.

I peek out around the machinery.

She's trying to twist her back toward the conveyor track and grab the padlock, but can't reach it.

"Drat!" She sits back on her heels, bounces a few times in impatience, then yells, "Will one of you jerks at least give me a blanket or something and stop ignoring me?"

Overprotective 'sister' mode kicks in. Ashley looks surprisingly calm given her situation. But her voice carries an ever so slight but noticeable note of despondence. Part of her believes she's not getting out of this alive, and as much as she's trying to conceal her fear with anger, I can still sense it. My claws come out subconsciously. Pretty sure the fangs did, too.

I narrow my eyes. As Sierra would say right before starting a match in *Call of Duty*, it's time for carnage.

40

WHEN SAFEWORDS FAIL

Tilloa grabs my wrist like she's trying to keep her kid sister from running off in the mall.

I'm so furious at what these shitheads have done to Ashley it's a miracle I don't swipe my claws at her. Guess there's enough reason beneath my anger to appreciate she's trying to help. All the mercenaries inside the building are concentrated in the rear third, in the area around the lights. None are particularly close to Ashley, anywhere from thirty to seventy feet, often behind industrial machinery or conveyor paths. I study the layout of the equipment like I'm analyzing a level in a video game.

Who says being a geek is useless in the real world? After a moment, a 'stealth route' from us to Ash looks fairly doable. There are too many mercenaries in here. I can't allow a fight to start. This is going to end in one of two ways. Either we get out of here unnoticed with Ashley safe, or she dies and I leave ribbons of flesh strewn across the woods not caring at all if I make it out. If they hurt her, I will absolutely kill every last one of these bastards... or die trying to.

Ashley rolls around to sit on the concrete floor. She braces her feet against the conveyor frame and leans back, trying to snap the leather handle at the end of the leash. She's not thinking. Even if she pops the leash off, does she expect to inchworm out of here without being noticed? Every second she is stuck like that is grating on my soul as badly as if I'm the one who put the cuffs on her. There's also no sign of Raleigh. Acheron or whoever's in charge here must have 'started' with her, taking her into 'the back room' for who knows what. Ashley's turn is no doubt coming up next once they finished with Raleigh.

I can't keep waiting.

"Okay. Plan," I whisper, too low for a human to pick up.

Whispering is kind of not the right word. It's this weird sort of thing where I just move my mouth around like I'm talking but no air is coming out of my lungs. At close range, vampire hearing is enough to kinda understand the words. I'm hoping none of the mercenary vampires hear us. C'mon Ash. Make more noise. Struggle, rattle that conveyor.

Almost as if she heard me, she starts fighting again. Nice.

"Plan?" Tilloa glances at me.

"I see a way for us to sneak over to Ash. We go there, snap the cuffs off her, then the three of us sneak back here."

Tilloa blinks. "You can break cuffs?"

"Yeah. I've snapped them before."

"Didn't think you were into that."

I frown. "I'm not. Got kidnapped once by some vampires who kept mortals snacks in a dungeon under a nightclub. They mistook me for a mortal. Got caught trying to sneak in."

"Wow. That's damn strong." She smiles. "Cool, though. Can I do it?"

"Yeah. It's not difficult, but they don't exactly break like cheap plastic toys. Gotta build up strength and pull on them until the metal gives out. Takes a minute or two... and it's kinda tiring. Also, easy to break bones. Not a big deal to me, but Ashley doesn't regenerate as fast as we do. I want to be careful."

She peeks out for a moment, then ducks back. "I don't think you got that kinda time. She's right out in the open. Literally in the spotlight."

Sigh. True. If even one merc sees me next to Ashley straining to break her loose, they're going to just hose us with machine gun fire. "Okay. New plan." I hold up my index claw. "Slice the leather end of the leash so I can carry her out of here. We try to sneak back the way we came in. If anyone sees us, I'm going to fly for that opening in the wall as fast as possible."

Tilloa pats my arm. "Right. If we get seen, I'll try to buy you a few seconds to get outta the building."

"Don't get yourself killed."

"Not planning to."

Both of us peer around the edge of the machinery. Ashley's out of breath, slouched forward. Her hair's draped in her lap, exposing the fuzzy cuffs on her wrists and the chain connecting them to the collar. There's also a little pink heart-shaped padlock through the buckle. The 'sex kitten' collar is not coming off without a key—or a claw. Easy enough to slice leather, but it's a bit tight on her. Not something I can do in a hurry without slicing her open.

Ashley is oddly calm. I wonder if she somehow knows I'm here.

Tilloa and I observe the mercenaries. Some of their eyes are too bright, reflecting the glow from the contractor lamps like highway signs catching headlights. Vampires. Ack. More than I thought. Maybe a third of them are vamps. It's way too dangerous to risk starting a fight in here. I'm still kinda young as a vampire. If they overwhelm me or shoot me in the head for lights out, Ashley's as good as dead and I probably won't wake up again.

Being scared out of my mind and this pissed off at the same time is definitely a new experience.

Maybe I should've gone to get help. Too late now. I can't leave Ashley like this any longer. As soon as it looks clear, I fly low and slow out of my hiding place. The path that appears most likely to keep me from being seen generally follows the route of the roller tracks formerly used to transport wood around the building. I stay under them and glide along at a walking pace, my chest maybe three feet off the floor. The old metal framework blocks the light and casts shadows in the same spots my shadow is drifting. If any mercs are up in the second or third-story offices, they'll have a really hard time seeing me looking down on the conveyor tracks.

Tilloa follows, her face only a few inches behind my boot soles. The two of us move like logs channeled by the equipment, only under the conveyor. Ashley starts low key complaining to no one in particular that her nose itches. She sniffles and snorfles for a bit before repositioning herself to sit and rubbing her face against one knee. My 'third sister' still isn't crying. If anything, she looks annoyed. Gotta be denial. That's Ashley, all right. She's really good at pretending situations aren't as bad as they are. I really wish she never again has to use that ability for anything more dangerous than an approaching homework deadline.

We glide right past a small folding table where five mercenaries play cards. No, not poker. *Magic: The Gathering*. Unreal. Guess it's one way to kill time on a forty-eight-hour kidnapping assignment.

"Such an overreaction from the boss," says one. "This is overkill for one girl."

"You saw how damn angry he was?" Another man whistles in awe. "That project he's been working on is not going well. Thought his damn head was going to explode from sheer rage when the backpack bomb failed."

Three guys at the card table laugh.

"No shit," whispers a third guy. "He tells us to go black bag a young girl, we go black bag a young girl. I ain't about to ask one damn question and get him pissed off at *me*."

"Right?" The second guy hums and taps the table a few times. "Attack Ed with these three, and plainswalk."

Guy three, likely Ed, grumbles while moving dead creature cards to his graveyard. "Suck my ass. At least he had the package gift-wrapped for us and we only had to go pick it up."

I stop. He just called Ashley 'a package.' Tilloa grabs me and stops me from zooming over there and beating his face into the table a few times. I calm down, give her an 'I'm okay now' nod, then continue gliding forward, leaving the guys to grumble about how unnecessary they think it is to have this many people here to 'babysit one mortal teenager.'

We follow the maze-like route of the track for a few minutes, slip across an open aisle between two different pathways, squeeze between some sawdust-vacuum hoses sticking out of the top of a huge boxy machine, and finally land again under another roller track only about six feet away from where Ashley is. The curved section of track she's tethered to is not connected to the one we followed here. An open aisle the width of a car separates us. Worse, the area's well lit by those stupid freestanding contractor lights. By the way, those things throw off a surprising amount of heat. With three of them almost pointed right at her, Ashley basically knows how cafeteria food feels sitting in the case under a heat lamp. Considering she's surrounded by vampires, comparing her to food waiting to be eaten is probably too apt.

Our hiding place puts a metal box as big as Mom's Yukon between me and most of the mercenaries. Every breath tastes like dirt, wet wood, and rusty metal. The fragrance of Ashley's sweat mixes with a fruity strawberry-sweet aroma. It's either her shampoo or her heart is racing so much the smell of her blood is detectable even though she's not bleeding. She's usually about as white as chalk. At the moment, she's a bit pink in the face and chest, so yeah. Racing heart.

I stare at the side of her head. *Ashley. Look at me.*

A few seconds later, she glances in my direction. The instant she spots me—and Tilloa's gold eyes hovering in the dark behind me—she stops fighting the leash and grins. Her 'oh, hey guys!' expression is as if we just randomly happened to walk into the same restaurant where she'd already gone to eat. She seems to be oblivious to the reality she's been kidnapped with only furry handcuffs to wear and is presently chained to a decaying lumber mill's inner workings. I think she even tries to wave hello.

Can't get any closer without being in the open and spotted, I say telepathically.

Is Mom okay?

I nod. *Yeah. She's fine.*

Ashley slouches in relief. *Get me outta here!*

That's the plan. Where's Raleigh?

She leans toward me as much as she can. *I dunno. Not here. They took her somewhere else. Oh, I think something's wrong with her.*

I blink and mouth 'what?'

She ignored the safe word and wouldn't let me out.

Don't have time to worry about that at the moment. I shake my head. *What's going on?*

She rolls her eyes, attempting to point toward the office on the third floor. *Some vampire jerk has a serious bug up his butt and wants to kill both of you.* She tosses her head to whip her hair around behind her back, off her face, then gets this stupid little grin. *Remember how I said the mortal best friend in all the vampire stories always ends up being a plot device?*

"Yeah," I whisper.

"Hi," whispers Ashley, bopping her head side to side. "My name is plot device. Sorry he's using me to get to you."

"Not your fault."

Tilloa nudges me from behind.

"Hurry up," whispers Ashley. "They're gonna see you."

I peek around as much as I can while hidden behind this bulky machine. Feeling like this is about as good a chance as I'm going to get, I rapid-crawl to Ashley, reaching out one hand, one finger, one claw toward the eight-inch-long hot pink leather leash handle studded in tiny hearts. All I need to do is slice, grab her, and drag her back to our hiding spot before any of the mercenaries see me. Easy.

Right as my claw touches the leather, a man appears standing at the end of the aisle between machinery, facing us. "Ahh, there you two are."

His voice carries over the building in standard supervillain volume, even echoes a little.

Like a kid caught with their hand in the cookie jar, I freeze. Claw's still touching the leather. Haven't sliced yet. Not sure why. It's probably because I feel 'elderness' radiating from this guy. He's no Aurélie, nor even Arthur Wolent in terms of age, but he's powerful enough for me to sense age. The odds of me beating this guy in a fight are slightly worse than the chances Sierra will decide to play a video game involving fluffy bunnies jumping around in a rainbow candy land.

I'm a bit preoccupied having the metaphorical shit scared out of me by his sudden appearance to notice whether he teleported or flew.

The man walks toward us in a causal, unhurried gait. If not for the air of power he's giving off, he'd seem kinda unassuming. White guy. Older, maybe fifty, super-short salt-and-pepper hair. Thin, not even close to muscular. Kinda looks like the sort of wealthy middle-aged douche who owns a grey Porsche 911 but still goes to McDonalds. His aura of age and power is strong enough to where I'm sure any attempt to cut the leash and run will result in him going blurry fast and tearing my head off. Things have changed. The only chance Ashley and I have of getting out of here in one piece is me coming up with some way to *talk* us out of this mess. Problem being, I still don't know what the hell this mess even is.

"I'd hoped to avoid such direct unpleasantness," says the man I assume to be Acheron. "Alas, you have both proven to be gifted with obnoxiously frustrating luck. I'd ask how you found this place so quickly, but… honestly." He claps his hands in front of himself and comes to a stop two paces from us. "I don't really care how you did it."

"Uh oh," says Ashley at normal volume, no longer trying to be quiet. "Guess he heard us."

"Ya think?" I mutter.

41

NOT EVEN GOING TO
MONOLOGUE

E verything grinds to a stop.
No, I do not possess Sophia's magical power to halt time. This is entirely in my brain. I'm having such an extreme oh shit moment, my thought processes are racing like the engine of a Corvette in neutral with the gas pedal stomped. I'm not in the most advantageous position crawling on all fours, one arm extended, claw still touching pink leather. It's too close to either kissing this guy's boots or waiting for a beheading strike from a swordsman who—thankfully—doesn't exist.

What really pisses me off is having Ashley between him and me. It should be the reverse. I need to shield her from him.

Mercenaries have appeared around us. All in black BDUs, tactical vests, and various headgear from dark wool caps to baseball hats to Kevlar helmets. I stare at M4 rifles, magazine pouches, flashbangs, zip tie handcuffs, knives, and other pouches/gear I don't recognize. These guys are taking the soldier cosplay to the next level. Damn. Oh, there's one other minor detail that's just become obvious to me: more than half of the mercs are vampires.

As some people in my high school would say: shiz just got complicated.

I never really did that whole 'putting z's where they don't belong to sound edgy' thing. I'm far too goody, too suburban, too geeky... too lame. It just doesn't sound right coming from me. Ashley's tensed her arms like she's trying to snap the chain on the handcuffs—so she can kick this guy's ass. For the first time ever, I'm actually kinda relieved she's contained. She's the nerd who roared. We didn't get into many physical fights at school, but the one or two times we did, the 'mean girls' teased quiet, geeky Ashley until she snapped and pounced. Same thing would happen here if she could move. Only, this guy is going to put up a bit more of a fight than Susan Cooper and her entourage did. The perfect, popular girl in seventh grade folded like a house of cards as soon as Ashley's fist said hello to her nose once.

Not all girls fight by pulling hair. Ashley and I have watched way too many anime martial arts movies. Nope. Ash opened with a right hook Susan never expected.

But yeah. Vampires. At least fifteen of them. This is not good. Only the one guy feels scary old. On an individual basis, I wouldn't necessarily be too worried about picking a fight with any of the others, but fifteen-on-two is bad odds. The only possible chance we have—if I can't talk us out of here—is some kind of distract-and-run maneuver. If the look of 'aww shit' on Tilloa's face is any indication, she's on the same page. We have to run.

In a paradoxical sort of way, my fear reaches a point where I become completely calm and casual.

"Hang on a second." I push up to kneel rather than stay on all fours. "I don't know who the hell you are. What did I do to make you want to kill me?"

The man flashes this tiny smirk of annoyance. "You interfered with a most sacred ritual passed down among us for thousands of years. In doing so, you destroyed the purity of my apprentice."

Oh boy. This guy's nuts. I doubt it's going to be possible to reason with him. He also seems to take himself *way* too seriously. That appears to be a common theme among vampires of a certain age. Anyway, it gives me an idea. Probably a crazy, stupid, and reckless one... but if I can throw him off balance, it might give us an opening to get out of here. If he's too angry to even speak, he might not react fast enough to stop me from grabbing Ash and running. I figure we're pretty screwed either way so a super risky plan beats no plan.

Ashley twists to glare up at him. "She hasn't touched anyone's purity lately except for Hunter's."

Acheron sighs in annoyance, ignoring her remark. "Before I rid myself of your existence, I have just one question for you."

"Wait." I shrug with a cheesy smile. "No monologue?"

He furrows his eyebrows. "What do you mean?"

"Well..." I tap one clawed finger to my lip. "In situations like this, the bad guy always rattles on for a while about their plans, or how foolish we are before getting on with the 'trying to kill us' part."

The guy frowns.

"Come on, man." I thrust my arms out to both sides. "You call yourself Acheron for crying out loud. No one is douchey enough to name themselves something like that and *not* want to monologue."

Ashley gawks at me for a second before giggling.

Noises like pigeons farting come from the lips of several vampires surrounding us. It's like they *really* want to laugh but don't dare.

Tilloa glares at me, her expression—and glowing gold eyes—asking me what the hell I'm doing taunting this guy.

Acheron's eyes flare with rage. He jams a finger at me. "You are not fit to address me using my high name. To you, I am Malcolm."

I blink, waving both hands. "Whoa. Whoa. Hold on here. That sounds so backward. Shouldn't the ego-tripping jackass be like"—I try to mimic his imperious tone—"lowly peasant, you shall know me as Acheron.' Telling me to call you 'Malcolm' is like so mundane... *Malcolm*."

At least two vampire mercs muffle snickers.

"Enough of this foolishness," bellows Malcolm. "There is no monologue!"

Another vampire merc starts twitching, red faced, fighting to control laughter.

"I simply intend to destroy you both, right here. Right now." He closes his eyes, seething to himself, trying to calm down.

"Riiiight here.... Riiight now," sings Ashley, bopping her head side to side while going into full Jesus Jones mode.

Tilloa gawks at us both like we've cracked.

Malcolm pinches the bridge of his nose, seeming an awful lot like the asshole high school principal from *Breakfast Club* having a stress headache at the idiot kids.

Ashley stops singing and peers up at him again. "Let me guess, you're gonna force me to be your new apprentice?"

He sneers at her like a rich guy expecting filet mignon and getting a gas station frozen cheeseburger. "No. You already know far too much for the process to be untainted."

"Why Ashley?" I yell. "What did she do to deserve this?"

"Yeah!" shouts Ashley. She twists to look at me for a second before whipping her gaze back to him. "I'm kinda wondering that, too."

When elders get angry, every vampire around them can feel it. If my senses are to be believed, a few more wiseass comments might make this guy simply explode and die from sheer fury. I will give him some credit, though. He looks calm.

"Several efforts to utilize your immediate family as... well, bait, failed for reasons I have yet to determine." Malcolm adjusts his tie. "Getting things done during daylight hours is most cumbersome. Especially when attempting to be subtle. This mortal proved the most readily available given the resources at my disposal. Your devotion to each other made the choice obvious."

What? He tried to grab my family? I snarl. Wait, he's gotta be lying. The Littles—especially Sophia—would absolutely have told me if someone tried to kidnap them. Unless, whatever he tried failed so badly the kids never even noticed.

"Oh stop, child." Malcolm waves dismissively. "Had my agents succeeded in obtaining one of your siblings, I would not have harmed mere children. I may be a vampire, but I am no monster."

I shift my gaze to Ashley, helpless and totally exposed in the middle of a disused lumber mill. You lying sack of shit. Anyone who could do this to her is absolutely a monster.

"What's your damn question?" asks Tilloa.

A mortal mercenary sidles up to her, aiming his M4 at her head. Dumb of him. He's in arm's reach. She seems to take note of his presence but doesn't show much of a reaction beyond a quick flick of her eyes in his direction.

Malcolm lets out a long, forceful exhale of relief as though a bothersome headache finally cleared. "Would you prefer I kill this mortal first so she does not suffer the sight of your destruction? Or would you rather I save her for last to spare *you* having to watch her die."

"Stupid fuzzy cuffs," whispers Ashley to herself. "I kinda wanna run now."

"Just let her go." I scoot on my knees closer to Ash and wrap her in a hug. "There's no reason for her to die now. You have me."

"I am afraid the intensity of this experience has imprinted it upon her psyche deeply enough for certain parties to find even if she is made to forget." Malcolm examines his fingernails. "I simply cannot afford the risk."

I squeeze Ash protectively and narrow my eyes at him. 'Certain parties' has to mean Wolent. Or maybe he's aware of Aurélie's protection. The idea of this dick knowing about my mentor would certainly explain why he's been attempting to get rid of me using such indirect means. If I disappeared, it's reasonable to hope that Aurélie would look into what happened, eventually discover Ash, and mine the memory out of her deep subconscious. All this dancing around trying to kill me and make it look accidental has to have been him trying to avoid retaliation.

"It's too late," I say. "Wolent or Aurélie will figure out what happened. Your only chance to survive is to let all three of us go and forget we exist. I'll pretend nothing happened. I have no damn idea what ritual you're talking about, but I didn't do it on purpose. Look, I'm sorry. Let's just call this a misunderstanding and go on with the rest of our immortality, okay?"

He stares at me for a few seconds. Makes a fist. Shudders. For an instant, it almost looks like he might actually do it but then he goes red in the face and shouts, "You tainted the ritual! The sanctity of the ancient rites must be preserved. I cannot allow a transgression to go unpunished or others may do as you have done. This must be punished with destruction. Now choose! Does your simpering little *friend* here watch you die, or would you prefer to hear her scream her last breath?"

"Oh go to hell!" shouts Ashley. "You... you... mean person!"

Yeah... Ashley is clearly not from New Jersey.

42

WHAT'S WORSE THAN MERCENARIES? UNDEAD MERCENARIES

I t's painfully obvious there's no chance we're going to fight our way out of here.

Starting to look like I'm not talking my way out of this either. I can't even see a way for me to sacrifice myself to give Ashley a chance to run. There's only a one-inch chain between her ankles. When vampire mercenaries are chasing you, hopping along like a rabbit isn't going to cut it. No matter what I do, Ashley cannot get herself out of here. Had I been a Fury, I could've snapped those cuffs off her in an instant... and probably ripped one of the steel conveyor rollers out of the track and beat Malcolm into spaghetti sauce with it. Alas, my strength takes a bit more effort—and time—to build up to supernatural levels, and even then, tearing one of those rollers out is a bit beyond me.

The guy standing close to Tilloa gives me an idea. Specifically, the flashbang grenades on his belt. It's kinda dark in here and vampire eyes are extremely sensitive to light. Car headlights blinded me for like two minutes. I've never seen a real flashbang go off, but it's gotta be at least as bright as a passing car. It should buy us a moment. Tilloa said something about having a wicked fastball. It's a desperation move and probably going to get us all killed. But... we're all going to die anyway. Not like I need to worry anymore about being nice. A low chance of success is still higher than zero.

I turn my head to glance at her. Malcolm probably thinks I'm breaking down in tears. Tilloa locks stares with me. I mouth, 'flashbang, asshole, face.' She nods.

"Well, about your question..." I lift my head and glare up at him. Being on my knees in front of an elder is demeaning even if I'm not intentionally showing subservience to him. The bastard probably takes it as such anyway. "You want me to decide if you kill Ashley while I watch or make her watch you destroy me. I've made my choice."

"Admirable," says Malcolm. "What have you decided?"

"My choice is..." I throw composure to the wind and scream, "*Kobayashi Maru!*"

Vampire combat reflexes kick in. All the mortal mercenaries become department store mannequins, insofar as they're not moving anymore. As I thrust my arm out and swipe a claw at the leather handle at the end of the leash, Tilloa yoinks one flashbang off the mercenary next to her, springs up to her feet, and fastballs it straight into Malcolm's face. The guy is so damned furious with me I don't think he even noticed Tilloa moving. The grenade whizzes over me and Ashley at visually the speed of a normal baseball pitch despite my weird time perception. My claw slices the leather at the same instant the 'bang smushes into Malcolm's nose—and detonates on impact.

The mortal mercs would not have even seen us start moving yet. Some of the vampire mercs are turning their heads away because they know what's coming. Flashbangs suck when you have mortal eyes. They must be effing awful to vampires, especially in a room this dark.

I'm faced away and shielding Ashley as much as I can when the thing explodes. Tilloa's got her left arm crossed over her face, hiding her eyes in the crook of her elbow. The concussion wave is highly unpleasant to me, but it doesn't stun me. Ashley barks like a kicked goose in slow motion. I'd honestly expected just to blind Malcolm and the other vampires, but when I look back up after the flash subsides—I can't believe the sight waiting for me.

Dude is standing there in a haze of white smoke literally without a face. All the skin is gone, reduced to a blackened patch of exposed muscle. Strips of flesh ring the blast area like the droopy petals of a daisy. He no longer has eyelids, or lips, or a nose. The blast left him with a cartoonish big-eyed, toothy grimacing expression of utter surprise.

He's probably blind right now thanks to the flash but seems to stare at me for a second before emitting a throaty gurgle and collapsing over backward, stiff as a board as if knocked clean out. If I wasn't in a room full of jerks with guns—and Ashley—I'd probably have collapsed laughing at the sight. His skull appeared mostly intact, but an explosive device—even one as 'tame' as a flashbang going off right up against his face had to have caused significant brain damage. Hopefully, he'll be out for a few hours.

Tilloa's in mid ass-kicking, pummeling the crap out of the guy she swiped the flashbang from. I scoop Ashley up in my arms in a twisting leap to my feet and start hauling ass for the giant machine I hid behind while talking to her. Gotta put a solid object between Ashley and bullets. Tilloa grabs two more flashbangs from the guy's belt and tosses them at the group of vampire mercenaries. It's really easy to tell who's mortal right now. All the non-vamps are slow-mo crumpling in place, grabbing at their eyes from the first 'bang.

The shooting starts. Vampires farthest from the detonation try to tag me before I'm in cover. Sparks fly from metal components above and to either side. Luck is with me. Not a single burrowing drill of hot pain hits me before I zip around the corner. The other two flashbangs go off one after the next. Behind me, it's daylight for eight hundredths of a second. Feels like a second and a half to me.

Coppery glimmer draws my gaze to a bullet going by, six inches from my head, its back end lit in the glow from the detonating stun grenade. Eep!

Metallic banging ahead and behind me is a clue Tilloa is taking the high ground, jumping from conveyor track to crane to catwalk. Time accelerates to a more normal speed. I can't push my reflexes up to eleven for too long at once. Not being surrounded anymore or within arm's reach of an elder has allowed my adrenaline to relax.

"Sorry," I rasp while running. "I'll get you out of those cuffs as soon as I can."

A bullet hits a saw machine inches to our left. Sparks land in her hair.

"Eep!" she yells. "Alive now! Free later!"

I jump a conveyor track, sprint down an aisle, and swerve behind another garbage-truck-sized machine right as a flashbang clacks into the floor at my heels. Wait. Flashbangs don't 'clack.' They're not metal. That's a real damn grenade.

"Shiiiiiit!" I yell, scrambling to keep my footing while running on sawdust-covered concrete.

I get around the massive metal behemoth an instant before the grenade goes off. Every bone in my body rattles from the blast wave. It's nowhere near as bad as the backpack bomb, though. Ashley appears stunned but unhurt. Fortunately, no shrapnel made it through the machinery to us. We have zero time to think. I keep running and weaving around machinery for a few more seconds until I'm sure we're near the damn corner.

We take refuge behind a concrete column as I try to get my bearings and find the big opening in the wall near the ceiling. I'm having trouble spotting it thanks to the multiple flashbangs. My eyes are protesting the bright light, even though I hadn't been facing any of the detonations.

"It's fine," wheezes Ashley, breathless. "I've had the fuzzies on for hours now. A few more minutes won't matter."

"It's kinda disturbing how calm you are."

She holds her chin high. "I don't look it right now, but I am a seething pit of boundless rage."

I finally spot the huge hole in the wall above us and dart for cover behind another machine closer to it.

Ashley squirms. "I really am furious. I understand what they mean by the saying 'fit to be tied.' The fuzzies are the only thing keeping me from surrendering to my irrational level of rage and getting myself killed."

"Half of them are vampires. Malcolm's an elder. You can't kick their asses."

She sighs. "I know that. Doesn't mean it would stop me. Hence, *irrational* level of rage, and me saying 'get myself killed' and not 'kick their butts.'"

"You need help."

"Yes. I do." She fidgets her feet back and forth, clicking the furry cuffs. "Thanks for the assist with the embarrassing situation."

Sigh. An 'embarrassing situation' is Ashley accidentally getting herself stuck in cuffs in her bedroom and calling me to help her get out of a compromising position before her mom comes home. Right. Denial.

"Now!" shouts Tilloa.

Her voice isn't even done echoing in the room before another flashbang —or three—go off in a huge booming explosion. Startled and pained wails come from all directions.

"Hold on," I say. "Going airborne."

"I can't hold on."

I jump into the air. Ashley's sideways in my arms, but that's a big opening in the wall. We should fit okay. "Metaphorically hold on."

"That, I can do." She curls into me. "Metaphorically holding on."

We sail through the square hole and out into the night sky. Bullets nip at the corrugated steel walls on either side. I pull upward to put the roof between us and mercenaries, then aim for the forest on the far side of the property fence. Tilloa zooms out behind me. Within a second, we start catching fire from multiple mercenaries, some on the ground outside, one on the roof, a few from other windows in the mill. A meaty slap comes from Tilloa's direction in time with a spurt of blood at her lower abdomen. She gasps in pain. Another bullet decides to have an aggressive conversation with my right knee, but I barely feel it.

The only thought on my mind is Ashley. We're not going to make it to the forest without becoming Swiss cheese. Being up in the air makes us sitting freakin' ducks for vampire mercenaries who can see in the dark and have automatic weapons. I do the only thing I can and dive hard for cover, zooming down behind the row of giant black pickup trucks. Chattering rapid gunfire fills the night air, petering out as soon as we're down.

Guess they don't want to shoot their own vehicles.

Tilloa crashes to the ground about ten feet to my left, a hand clamped over her lower back. "Ow, son of a bitch."

"How bad?" I yell.

"Not too bad. Missed the spine."

I look down at Ashley, who's presently draped over my lap. She's not bleeding, but has become noticeably dirtier. Flashbangs and grenades kicked up a bunch of dust. Her ribs are pretty prominent, and she's breathing so fast it verges on panic, but her facial expression is serene, almost like we're only on a ride at Universal Studios and those bullets flying at us aren't real.

Shock. Has to be.

She notices me staring down at her. "If you tickle me right now, I will kick your butt."

"As tempting as your defenseless belly is," I say, completely kidding, "we don't have time."

"I'm okay," says Ashley, though it's unclear if she's talking to me or herself.

A rip of bullets tears up the dirt nearby. Multiple clanks and pings come from the truck. So much for them not wanting to shoot their vehicles.

"We gotta do something!" yells Tilloa. "It's all wide open. I don't think we'll make it to the woods."

"Take one of their cars," says Ashley. "Just please don't put me in the trunk again."

"They put you in the trunk?" I gasp, then snarl.

She nods.

"Change of plan. I'm going back in there to kill them all," I mutter.

Ashley raises both eyebrows. "You're not serious."

"No... I'm not. We need to get out of here. Cars?"

"Yeah." She nods. "Umm, well… one car. Rest are trucks. All the keys are in them."

Tilloa and I exchange a 'we got no better ideas' look.

We stand at the same time, but she's faster to get upright due to not lifting Ashley. A mercenary rushes into view between us, having sprinted through the gap between two trucks. She catches him by the arm and judo-flips him into the ground so hard his neck—and a few other bones—break on impact. If he's a vampire, he'll be in that face down, ass in the air ostrich pose for a few hours. If he's mortal, he's dead.

Tilloa swipes his M4 and starts shooting back toward the lumber mill. "Get in!"

I run past the tailgate of the truck she landed behind, swing around into the narrow space between it and the next identical truck, and yank open the passenger side door. The thing's fairly high up off the ground. It's huge, but not a monster truck. The wheels aren't ridiculous. Sorry Ash. I'm in a hurry. I toss her headfirst into the back seat as gently as possible. She lands on her front with a, "Mrrph" noise as her face mushes into the cushion.

The scene out the windshield is the exact opposite of comforting. This lumber mill looks like a scene out of an Oliver Stone war movie. Like twenty guys are advancing on us, shooting, darting between covered positions. Smoke grenades fizz around, some flying, some bouncing on the ground. One of the mortals has set off a couple bright magnesium flares so they can see. I think this is why we aren't dead. The sudden change from darkness to almost daylight has blinded all the vampire mercs. I can see well enough to maneuver, but shooting at people more than five feet away is not gonna happen. Everything's a blur.

We got maybe thirty seconds tops before their—and my—eyes adjust.

I'm about to climb in on top of Ashley when I become aware of something flying at my face. Instinctively, I catch it.

It's an M4. Tilloa must have thrown it to me over the roof.

"Cover us!" shouts Tilloa as she hops in behind the wheel.

Grr. I want to break Ash loose but there's no time. Too many mercs shooting at us. I hop up to stand on the running board and grip the searchlight rack. One-handing the M4, I pop off shots randomly at the moving blurry spots. The truck starts, then reverses hard. I've never touched a rifle like this before, but it's already loaded and the safety's off, so shooting it isn't exactly difficult to figure out, especially when I'm not really trying to aim at people.

Acceleration makes Ashley log-roll off the seat. She flops on the floor with a squeak of an, "Oof."

I keep wasting bullets in hopes the mere act of shooting in their general direction will keep them ducking behind cover. Tilloa throws the truck into a sliding spin, rams it into drive, and peels out in a spray of dirt and weed bits. Wow. Slick move.

"Nice driving, Vinola Diesel," I yell.

"This thing ain't too fast, but I'm definitely furious," says Tilloa.

Incoming fire rakes over the truck like a brief pelting of hailstones. I get nipped in the arm and grazed on the right hip.

Ashley, still on the floor, jumps at the sound of bullets hitting the truck, but the girl's still eerily calm. Crap. Did Malcolm do something to her? Maybe I should dive into her brain to look for tampering before I take the cuffs off? He's been sending mind-controlled people after me for over a week. He's had Ashley for hours. I wouldn't put it past him to embed a failsafe kill command in my best friend.

Or try to. She might've resisted it.

Remembering how she actually did fight off a compulsion to read his 'kill yourself' message to me chokes me up briefly. They say a real best friend will help you hide the bodies. I'd totally kill someone for her.

In fact, I think I'm going to have to do just that tonight.

We blast through the chain link gate in the fence surrounding the mill yard, tires chirping as they go from dirt to rain-soaked blacktop. Incoming fire peters out. My eyes are adjusting... enough to make out the shapes of over a dozen mercenaries scrambling to get in pickup trucks and come after us. I take aim and empty the remaining seven bullets out of the M4, concentrating them on the driver of the first truck to turn on headlights. The gunsights do look an awful lot like in *Call of Duty* when you hit the aim button. He slumps over. Oh wow, I hit something.

I slip inside to the passenger seat and slam the door, tossing the empty rifle to the floor at my feet. This damn truck is so big I feel like I'm eleven again in Dad's Sentra.

Ashley's managed to get herself up off the floor. She's sitting in the center of the back seat, half her face hidden behind her hair. Her expression is too surreal, as though we're just on our way to the mall or something.

Tilloa speeds along a narrow, isolated road in the woods. A blurry wall of trees rushing by on both sides makes it feel more like we're rocketing down a tunnel. Headlights flicker into view behind us. As fast as we're going—maybe sixty-five, which is too fast for this road—they're gaining on us.

Ashley twists to peer out the back window over the truck bed. She takes in the sight for a few seconds, then faces forward again. "This is like that dream I have of being arrested, except for the army of vampires chasing us."

"They're not *all* vampires," I say, blurting the first idiotic thing to squeeze out of my brain sponge.

"A lot of them are." Ashley peers down at the leash draped in her lap.

Tilloa peers up at the rearview mirror, looking at Ashley. "Don't you mean it's like your dream of being arrested except for being naked?"

"Nah." Ashley shakes her head, making her hair swish side to side. "I'm not naked. I'm, umm, wearing the truck."

How many times have I heard her refer to sleeping in the buff as 'wearing the bed?' The moment is too surreal. I laugh. Wearing the truck. Wow. That's the kind of reality-rejecting mental gymnastics I'd expect from someone trying to defend flat-Earth idiocy or YouTube science... or anyone who thinks the Alien franchise has more than two movies in it. Sorry. I agree with Dad there. They stopped after the second—and best—movie. Anything anyone tries to say about further movies in the franchise is unsubstantiated rumor. They don't exist.

"Wearin' the damn truck." Tilloa chuckles. "Okay then."

Ashley giggles. "The dream's the same. I don't have clothes on there, either. It's a sexy dream. I'm not *really* getting arrested. The cop is hot."

I grab my head in both hands. "Dammit. Someone broke Ashley."

"Aww stop." She laughs. "I'm kidding. I don't really have a dream like that. If I don't find a way to laugh at what's going on right now, I'm going to freak the hell out."

Grr. I want so badly to break those things off her, but what did Malcolm do to her brain? Screw it. I can't leave her in cuffs any longer. I grab my seat, brace another hand on Tilloa's seat, and start to pull myself into the back seat with Ashley—but stop short, staring past her out the rear window.

Muzzle flashes go off all over a literal convoy of trucks chasing us. No sooner does my brain process the meaning of the orange flashes than I notice an equally—or maybe even more scary—problem. A bunch of vampires are flying up on us. They're catching up *much* faster than the trucks.

"Uhh... we got problems," I mutter.

43

HOW TO MAKE TEN MINUTES FEEL LIKE TEN HOURS

A vampire mercenary lands standing in the bed of our pickup truck.

You'd think the hard turn we skid into would send him careening to one side, but he catches himself using his flight power—or so I assume based on his absolute defiance of physics.

"Grab a gun from the glove box and shoot back!" yells Tilloa, as a bullet clanks into the truck somewhere.

I whip my head around to stare at her. "How do you know there's guns in there?"

"A mercenary company owns this thing. There's gotta be."

Ashley points with her nose at the back of Tilloa's seat. "There's a shotgun here. If I could reach it, I'd show these buttheads the true meaning of naked aggression."

Tilloa cackles.

The vamp in the truck bed punts the back window, sending bits of safety glass exploding all over the back seat.

"We got company," says Ashley, shaking her head to throw glass bits out of her hair.

I rip open the glove compartment. Sure enough, it contains a bunch of handguns and magazines.

The guy kicks out the other half of the window.

Ashley cringes from the fall of not-snow. "Oh, awesome. Broken glass bits all over the seat when I'm naked. This just keeps getting better."

"Thought you said you're wearing the truck." Tilloa grunts as she tries to keep us from skidding off the road on a turn.

"Yeah, well. I am." Ashley sighs in exasperation. "All this broken glass back here is like getting sand in your bathing suit."

I jam my hand into the glove compartment and grab the first gun in reach, swinging it up and aiming right as the vamp-merc ducks to come in the window headfirst. We lock stares for a tenth of a second before I open his third eye for him. A good portion of his brains spatter across the truck bed, soon followed by his limp body. The empty brass from my shot zings into the air, bounces off the roof, and bee-lines for Ashley's unprotected lap. I snag it out of the air before Ash even sees it coming—yay for vampire reflexes—then yelp in pain at the hot metal on my palm. Better me than her. I drop it and wave my hand rapidly to cool it.

Tilloa hits the brakes a bit hard to negotiate another turn. Ashley slides forward, but manages to get her knees up in time to catch herself against the back of my seat, stopping herself from eating floor again.

"Eep!" yelps Ashley. "There's glass *everywhere* back here."

"It's safety glass. Not gonna shred you," yells Tilloa.

I'm kneeling in the passenger seat, facing to the rear, gun aimed at the now-missing back window area, waiting for the next mercenary target.

"Sarah?" asks Tilloa.

"What?" I keep aiming at the trucks following us, waiting for the next vampire to try playing boarding party.

"You shouted some Japanese shit at Malcolm. What did that mean?"

Ashley gawks at her. "Oh em gee. You've never heard of the *Kobayashi Maru*?"

"Uhh, no," says Tilloa, accelerating into another left curve. "Is that a sushi restaurant?"

"Sare, slap me in the forehead." Ashley stares at me.

"What? Why?" I blurt.

"Because I can't facepalm myself right now." She bounces in annoyance. "Till doesn't know *Kobayashi Maru*. We have to get her to watch it."

"Is that like some Pokémon type cartoon?" Tilloa hammers the brakes as we go skidding into another curve, tree branches thwapping at the passenger door mirror.

"Augh!" screams Ashley, horrified. "Are you serious?"

I facepalm. "It's a *Star Trek thing*. Unwinnable scenario. Two choices and they both suck, so… Kirk chooses a third option."

"You guys are serious dorks," mutters Tilloa.

"Yep!" chirps Ashley, right before a bullet blows a puff of white foam out of the top edge of the back seat two feet to her left. She cuts her gaze sideways to stare at the crater. "And we should drive faster."

"Working on it," yells Tilloa. "Road's wet and this thing ain't the most nimble. It's jacked up so high it's easy to roll over."

Another vampire lands rather clumsily in the truck bed thanks to our constantly shifting speed and skidding around. As soon as it's clear he's not going to fall out, I snap off a few shots as fast as I can, hitting him in the chest and thigh. A second later, his buddy comes down on the hood, gun already out and pointed at Tilloa. Crap! She throws herself to the side as he fires. The headrest on her seat spits out a puff of foam bits. She sits up again and starts swerving back and forth between both lanes. Vampire or not, he has to work too hard to avoid being thrown off the hood to keep shooting at her. I toss my gun to Tilloa and reach behind me into the glove compartment, grabbing for another weapon. Hood guy shoots Tilloa in the stomach before she gets a bead on him. The instant my fingers touch a gun, I whip it up and pump three bullets into the vampire squeezing in the back window. Ignoring my shots, he keeps reaching and stretching into the cab until he gets one hand on the headrest of my seat.

Tilloa fires at the guy on the hood.

The vampire merc coming for me bares fangs and hisses in pain as my ninth shot goes uselessly into his clavicle. He draws a gun with his left hand. I put the barrel of my handgun right against his forehead. Ashley picks that moment to lunge at him, biting at his gut. To my horror, she lurches away with a hand grenade pin in her teeth.

The spoon pops off a grenade on his belt.

Shit! Ash! That's not a flashbang! Flashbangs don't have spoons!

No time to shoot this guy in the brain. I let my gun fall onto my seat, grab the merc with both hands, and shove him out the window in my door. No, the window wasn't open. It is now thanks to his skull. Well, the window is *gone* now. Vampire dude's body tumbles in the road behind us for about two seconds before it vanishes with a loud *boom*, turning into a smoke cloud. A hail of shrapnel bits rattles metal around me. The truck he happened to be underneath at the time the grenade went off catches about six feet of air before crashing down, then careening off the road into the trees, all four of its tires blasted to tatters.

One down. Thumping and clattering come from the roof above us. I hastily grab the gun from the seat by my knee and fire wildly straight up through the roof. Tilloa starts screaming at the rain of hot brass falling on her. The merc above us loses his grip and tumbles off to the woods on my side. Pretty sure that loud *crack* when he hit the tree came from his spine, not the trunk.

Yet another vampire attempts a hood landing. This time, Tilloa fires twice before he can put a bullet into her. First shot kneecaps him, second gets him in the nose. He's down.

Ashley fake cries while struggling to pull her hands apart. "Dammit! I can't plug my ears. Shooting is soooo loud."

Since my side window is obligingly gone, I lean out the window up to my waist and start firing at the driver of the nearest chase vehicle. My first shot gets him in the collarbone. Second one misses entirely as he starts swerving lane to lane. Shot three probably went into the grill. Fourth one's the charm. Right in the head.

Another one down. Truck in the trees, rolling.

"Good grief!" I shout. "Who the hell is this guy that he's got so many minions?"

Ashley puffs in a futile attempt to blow her hair out of her eyes. "Obviously, he's the main bad guy of the movie our life has turned into."

"Umm." I duck back inside the cabin to reload. The mercs were nice enough to pack the glove box with spare magazines. "Isn't that Stefano?"

She again puffs at her hair, this time exposing her eye. "He's the series villain. This jerk is just one episode. Maybe we're living a TV series instead of a movie."

I pop out the window and fire at the next truck in line. Yeah, it's stupid considering I could just shoot out the missing rear window. Hanging off the side of the truck, I might end up smooching a tree at sixty miles an hour. But... out here, my brass isn't going to land on Ash... and it's not as loud for her.

"Darn." Ashley sighs. "I should have known something was wrong when Raleigh suggested we get kinky. She hadn't been into it at all before. I hope they didn't hurt her."

A vampire leaps out of the third truck in line and comes flying at us. I fire seven or eight shots at him as he cruises in, unsure if I'm missing or hitting. He keeps coming. As he gets closer, he pulls a round, black—live— hand grenade off his belt like he's intending to toss a little gift in the window and haul ass instead of barge inside. I empty the rest of my magazine, trying to put a bullet in his head for the knockout... but I'm too rattled. I miss four times.

An instant before he crashes down in the truck bed, Tilloa stomps on the brakes. I whip backward, about to go flying entirely out the truck, but manage to catch myself with my legs. Grenade Boy's foot scuffs the bed liner for only a second before he tumbles over the roof and ends up lying on the hood. Ashley faceplants the back of my seat.

All the trucks chasing us also slam on the brakes, swerving side to side, a few bumping into each other. We didn't stop, merely went from doing seventy to doing like forty. For a second or so, I'm leaning so far out the window bent backward, my head is above the hood. Gives me a great view of Tilloa shooting Grenade Boy in the top of the head. We don't linger at turtle pace for long; as soon as the mad bomber is out, Tilloa stomps on the gas. Grenade Boy slides off the truck to the left, blood spraying out of his forehead. I yell, "Whoooooaaaah!" as acceleration flings me in the other direction; my face slaps into the side window for the back seat. Ashley peers up at me from the floor, making a 'what are you doing out there?' face. Tilloa tosses her gun in the center console cup holder, grabs me by the belt, and pulls me inside. Somewhat freaked out at nearly being flung from a speeding truck, I cling to my seat, facing to the rear.

Ashley slithers up to the seat and wriggles around to sit upright. Hey at least all her hair is off her face now.

"What happened with Raleigh?" I ask.

"Not much," says Ashley. "She's all sexy and wound up. Suggests we break out the fuzzies. She puts them on me. We start kissing and she's running her hands all over me. But before we really go anywhere, she just stops. Gets up, and stands there."

"Your bed was all kinds of roughed up," says Tilloa. "Looked like something hot and heavy happened."

Ashley rolls her eyes in an 'I wish' manner. "That was me trying to get loose while she just stood there like a derp. Thought she was like playing some kinda kinky game, you know. Making me wait."

A vampire thuds against the passenger side of our truck, clinging, his face right in my window. I casually raise my gun, pointing it to the side and pump a bullet up his nose. He falls away into the woods.

Ignoring this, Ashley keeps talking. "She acted really weird, just staring into space. Eventually, I got freaked, so I used our safe word. She didn't do anything except send a text message. She wouldn't unlock the fuzzies or even talk. Just stood there for like an hour."

"Your mom didn't hear you yelling over her TV?" I ask.

Ashley's cheeks pink a little. "I didn't yell. Too embarrassed. Had some toys just sitting out in the open, and you know... Mom doesn't really want to see this sort of thing."

Odd. I was in her room. I don't remember seeing anything laying around except for discarded clothes and her army of plushies. Who put the 'toys' away out of sight?

"Yeah... I would've been too embarrassed to call for my parents, too." I squirm. Not that I'm ever going to allow Hunter to use handcuffs on me. He's not into that stuff either.

Another wave of gunfire clanks all over our truck. A few bullets whizz through the cabin, hitting nothing.

"And then..." Ashley shivers. "These guys just showed up and grabbed me while Raleigh just stood there. I saw Mom on the floor when they carried me out and stuffed me in the trunk of a cop car. Are you sure she's okay?"

"Yes. She's okay. Just sleeping."

"Grr." Ashley bites her lip. "You were right. Something's weird about her. I shouldn't have trusted her enough to play with the fuzzies. I swear. From now on, I won't do it with anyone you haven't brain scanned."

"Happy to brain scan anyone you need, Ash." I pop out the window and feed eleven bullets to the driver of the nearest truck. He veers into the trees. Wow, Mom would totally ground me for a month if she finds out I'm shooting guns. "You know I'm there for you anytime. You need a ride to work, help cleaning your room, lost your car keys, get abducted by a crazy evil vampire again..."

She laughs nervously. "Gah. I am such a gullible, trusting idiot. I knew something wasn't right."

"Stop blaming yourself." I stare at her while reloading. "You are sweet, and kind, and adorable. Don't change because of some asshole vampire."

"Okay." She exhales. "Don't be upset. I know you'll get the fuzzies off me as soon as you can. No rush."

Hissing overhead makes me lurch out the window again. A vampire merc is flying in high, firing his M4 at us from above. I think he's trying to take out our engine. One thing about vampire reflexes, as fast as I can move my finger, it makes a handgun go off like full auto. He tumbles forward, his aim veering away from our hood, stitching holes across the entire length of the truck. A few bullets thump into the seat, likely missing Ashley by inches. I take another one in the leg. Tilloa's shouted F-bomb tells me she absorbed a round or two as well.

I burn all seventeen bullets in the mag. Pretty sure the last eight hit him in the face. He goes from flying to falling in an instant, smacks face-first on the road... then gets run over by the four remaining trucks chasing us, one after the next. And yes, my vampire hearing lets me enjoy his bones breaking more with each successive impact.

"Sarah Wright wins. Brutality," I mutter in an attempt to do the deep *Mortal Kombat* voice.

Ashley doesn't react whatsoever to little geysers of cushion material spurting out of the seat so close to her. She's staring at the leash dangling in front of her, making it sway side to side like she's in a waiting room somewhere bored and totally not in the back seat of a truck during a deadly rolling gunfight.

"Ash?"

"Hmm?" She looks up.

"Please tell me you're not like… enjoying this?" I wince.

"No. In a safe environment, the fuzzies are fun."

"This ain't a safe environment," grumbles Tilloa.

"I know. Just saying." Ashley shrugs. "I really have to trust who I'm with. I'm not freaking out right now because I trust you."

I slide back into the passenger seat, grab another—and the last—magazine for this Glock, and load it. "This conversation is making me kinda uncomfortable."

Tilloa gurgles. An unexpected, hard curve forces us to negotiate a turn going about twenty miles an hour too fast for it, especially when the road's wet. The maneuver rams me against the door and throws Ashley off the back seat. She lands wedged in the space where rear passengers' feet should be, on her back. By some miracle, despite us sliding sideways for several seconds, Tilloa regains control of the truck and straightens us out. The next truck right behind us isn't so lucky managing the surprise turn. They go sailing off the end of the curve into the woods, tumbling down a fairly steep hill out of sight. Headlights flash against the trees four times before they stop, making it look like the truck tumbled nose over tail.

Ouch. That had to sting.

Ashley grunts, squirming, but can't seem to get herself unwedged. "Uhh, *you're* uncomfortable?"

"Sorry," I mutter. "Different kind of uncomfortable."

"Yeah, I know. Just being silly." Ashley growls and struggles, but still can't get up. "Right now? No, this isn't fun. I *really* want to take the fuzzies off. They're starting to hurt and I'm not having fun at all."

Tilloa speeds up to about eighty since the road is pin straight for a good long stretch. "Don't those sex shop cuffs have like an emergency release button?"

I hate that I know this but, I say, "She got real ones. It's more of a thrill for her if she can't take them off whenever she wants. Not gonna claim to understand it."

"Yeah. I'm really scared," says Ashley in a completely not-scared tone. She grunts again, trying to get up. "If you want to break them, I won't be upset. They weren't cheap, but I don't care."

"Scared?" asks Tilloa. "You're acting so damn calm, it's eerie."

Ashley smiles. "I am selectively ignoring the reality of my present situation and pretending this is just an ordinary late-night road trip with friends."

Her 'professor' tone punches a pinhole in my anxiety enough for me to chuckle.

Tilloa cracks up.

"I'm just gonna stay on the floor for a while," says Ashley. "I'm kinda stuck. It's hard to un-wedge myself without hands. Ow. These little glass rocks are super annoying to lay on."

"Sorry!" I yell, staring out the missing back window at the three remaining trucks still chasing us. Dammit. Why are they so freakin' determined? What did I ever do to them?

"Stop apologizing," yells Ashley. "This isn't your fault. It's mine if anyone's for ignoring my gut and trusting Raleigh too much too fast."

Loud, booming, rapid gunfire comes from behind us.

Tilloa swerves into the oncoming lane, then back, then again into the oncoming lane, slaloming around a stream of orange tracers. Bits of branches tumble down onto the hood as the heavy caliber weapon shreds trees ahead and above us. Despite her efforts, multiple clonks jar the frame of our truck. A few bullets rip through the rear seatback, ripping out huge foam craters. So damn lucky Ashley's on the floor.

"Dammit," says Tilloa. "They have a machine gun."

"*Why* do they have a machine gun?" yells Ashley.

I pop out the side window. Huge muzzle flash draws my attention to the third truck in the convoy, the last one. A dude's standing in the back manning a .50 cal. Are you freakin' serious? It's a bit far for a handgun to reach him, but I have no other choice. Shooting the dude won't help much. Another merc can hop on the gun. I focus on the driver instead, taking as much time to aim as I can force myself to while staring down a stream of incoming tracer bullets. In a rapid, but relatively controlled series of shots, I empty the rest of my magazine. Somewhere in the barrage, I get lucky. The driver's forehead explodes. Truck three drifts off the road. The vampire on the .50 realizes they're about to crash and abandons ship—or abandons truck—flying straight up as the vehicle smooches a pair of trees, going from seventy miles an hour to zero in an instant. A mercenary in the passenger seat launches out the windshield like a meat missile. I lose track of him in the forest before he hits anything.

Problem: I'm out of ammo.

Stunned at having an actual machine gun used on us, I slide back into my seat and just kinda stare into space. "They, uhh, no longer have a machine gun."

Mercs on the two remaining trucks pop out of their windows and rip bursts at us from M4s as well as handguns. Bullets zing by, clank on the roof, and strike the tailgate. A few hit the road and bounce up into the cab. Clanks tell me quite a few seem to be hitting the wall below the rear window and somehow not making it through into the cab. Not gonna argue. I've lost track of the number of times I've been hit. Just getting super lucky none of the bullets found my heart or head yet. Tilloa's a bloody mess as well. Not questioning our fortune, but somehow Ashley hasn't taken a bullet. She's bleeding from multiple superficial scratches thanks to the safety glass, but she's gotten worse from cats at work.

Ashley squeals in fear at the incoming fire.

"Ash! You okay?"

"You're asking me if I'm hit. No. I'm not hit. But I'm not okay either." She takes a deep breath. "I'm really pissed off."

I close my eyes to weather a wave of fury. "Elder or not, I'm going to kill that bastard for what he did to you."

"Hate to break it to you," says Tilloa, "but he's already dead."

"I mean kill him *again*."

"Sare," says Ashley. "He's an elder. He didn't do anything but embarrass the heck out of me and make me read that stupid thing. Forget him. I don't want you to get hurt."

Grr. I lean into the back seat and peer down at her. "Ash, he was going to *kill* you. And he's not going to just give up and disappear because we got away. When he wakes up, he's going to be furious."

Tilloa bursts out laughing in flagrant disregard of the bullets intermittently hitting the truck around us.

I push myself back far enough to stare at her. The blur of passing trees in her window makes my stomach twist over. We are going *way* too damn fast for this road. "What the hell is so funny?"

"Did you see his face when that 'bang went off?" Tilloa cracks up.

Ashley giggles. "Yeah, he looked so surprised. Like one of those aliens from *Mars Attacks*. The flashbang hit him and he's like... *ack. Ack ack!*"

My life will never get weirder than being in a speeding truck trading gunfire with vampire mercenaries while my best-friend-slash-sister is tied up in the back seat making nasal alien noises. This is almost beyond a glowing, flying, teleporting kitten for sheer absurdity.

The headrest of my passenger seat explodes into foam bits.

Ashley stops making *Mars Attacks* alien noises because she's screaming now.

A sharp pain stabs me in the left upper arm, right shoulder, right thigh, and hand. I raise my arm and peer through a hole in my palm big enough to stick my thumb in. Tilloa gasps and swears as she absorbs a few bullets, too. I don't feel it for long. Ashley's terrified scream—her *finally* acting like her life is in danger—pushes my button. I grab the bigger gun Tilloa left in the center console cup holder and take aim at the sons of bitches behind us.

"Sare," calls Ashley, for the first time tonight sounding worried. "Promise me… if they kill me. I want to come back. I absolutely want you to turn me if I die."

I narrow my eyes, taking aim on the driver behind us. "I promise."

44

PLOT DEVICE

I shoot.

The mercenaries shoot back.

A whole bunch of bullets go flying around but nothing overly noticeable happens beyond sparks and shouting. If I'm hitting them, it's as annoyingly superficial as the bullets hitting me. I say 'superficial,' but that's in vampire terms. Had I been mortal, I'd be dead already to blood loss. So glad vampires don't bleed much.

Some manner of beeping alarm starts going off from the dashboard.

Oh, that's not good. They probably hit something vital. Or maybe the damage the flying guy did to the engine has finally worsened to a critical point.

"Stay down, Ash." I hastily reload this huge gun. I think it's a Desert Eagle, but not a .50. The bullets are too small. .44 maybe? A .357? I dunno.

"Yeah. No problem," she says in a soft voice. "These are kinda warm."

"What are?" Oh, please don't be shot.

"The empty bullets on my tummy." She grunts. "It's fine. The glass under me hurts more."

Seriously. I am going to rip Malcolm apart for this.

I pop out the side window again to spare Ashley more brass falling on her. An incoming bullet scores a slash of pain across my left hip. Ow! Son of a bitch! Jaw clenched, I fire at the driver of the nearest truck. My second shot nicks the steering wheel and somehow detonates the airbag mechanism. Shots three and four hit him in the face while he's in mid-flinch. They veer so hard to the side, the truck rolls and goes slide-spinning upside down on the pavement before skidding into the woods.

One truck left.

I'm too distracted by the spectacle of the crash to notice a flying vampire merc with a shotgun before he's in our truck bed. Dude ducks in through the window, raising his shotgun at my wide-open stomach while I'm leaning out the passenger door window. Time seems to freeze for me. I have two choices. One: throw myself out of the truck and hope I'm faster than his trigger finger, or I'm going to be blown in half at the waist. Even if I make it, I'm going into the trees at seventy miles an hour. That's gonna sting. Two: try to duck back inside and eat the shotgun blast in the face.

Decision paralysis sucks.

Ashley screams, "No!"

In my present state of altered time perception, she sounds truly demonic.

Two dirt-smeared bare legs thrust up from the floor of the back seat. Ashley plants a double kick into the vampire merc's groin. The guy lets out an 'oof,' his point of aim diverting down and left. He fires a dragon breath round into the middle of the dashboard console. The cab fills with smoke and burning chemical flakes. Feels like a hundred fire ants just started going to town on half my body. Tilloa and I both shriek in pain and reflexively swat at ourselves.

Ashley pulls her legs in and double-stomp-kicks him in the balls again, snarling and growling. Groaning, the guy doubles over. With a war shriek worthy of Red Sonja, she flies up into a seated position, then mashes her forehead into his nose, breaking it and spraying blood all over her face. I'm still swatting burning flecks off my arm, consumed by the deep inner nature of vampirism that *fire is bad*. I can't do anything but swat at myself and watch as she headbutts him twice more, then makes a feeble attempt to grab the shotgun on the back of Tilloa's seat. She's not even close to being capable of reaching it with her hands cuffed to her collar. Even more furious at her failure to grab the weapon, she lets out an even louder war cry and mashes her forehead into his face a fourth time.

I did not think it possible for a mortal to knock a vampire out. However, it seems she managed it—or came close.

There is something to be said for having a truck with half a windshield and no back window left. The smoke is already gone. More smoke is peeling from the smoldering melt hole in the console, but it's streaming right out the back window, not choking us.

Two more vampire mercs leap into the air from the bed of the last truck chasing us. Are you serious? It's like a damn clown car act. How many of them are there? I start firing at them.

"Hold the wheel," yells Tilloa.

I'm still hanging out the door, shooting at flying vampires. No idea what makes me think this, but I believe they are both planning to lob hand grenades at us. I can't let them get close enough. Without thinking about it, I raise my right leg and brace a boot against the steering wheel, holding it steady—yay for superhuman vampire agility—while still shooting at the bombers coming in. Since I'm facing backward, I really hope the damn road stays straight for a while. Might be a wise idea to at least watch where we're going.

Tilloa grabs the semiconscious vampire out of the back seat, hauls him up front by two fistfuls of his collar, pulling him nose to nose. "You just got your ass kicked by a mortal girl with her hands tied behind her back. Pretty sad." Without waiting for a response, she throws him out the windshield.

He bounces off our hood, spills over the front end… and we run him over.

The truck still chasing us also runs him over.

Tilloa takes the wheel again. I twist around and resume shooting at the incoming vamps, managing to nail one of them in the mouth. Attempting dentistry with a .357 has predictable results. He's unconscious in an instant. The bastard drops like a stone and also gets run over by the truck chasing us.

Ashley pops up and sits in the middle of the back seat again. "I am *not* a helpless plot device! And he was going to kill Sarah!"

"They're *all* trying to kill me," I yell in between shots at the final flying vampire.

"Well, I could reach that guy. I can't reach the rest of them. I'm a little tied up right now."

The second vampire eludes the rest of my magazine and swoops in for a landing in our truck bed. He's halfway in the window when Ashley lunges upward, ramming her shoulder into him and knocking the dude back out into the bed. I drop back inside to kneel in the passenger seat. Tilloa chucks another gun at me. This one's kinda small, but the Desert Eagle is empty.

Growling, the dude in the bed sits up—and I shoot him in the face. Brass flying out of my gun zips past Tilloa's nose and goes out her window. The vampire manages to glare at me for about a second before he flops over backward, unconscious in the truck bed.

Ashley sits again, whips her hair out of her face, and huffs. "Not so helpless after all, am I?"

I stare at her in disbelief. Bits of safety glass from the broken back window are all over her like she's wearing body glitter. She kinda looks like one of those silly sparkling vampires. I am suddenly overwhelmed by the complete inability to tolerate her being stuck in handcuffs for another instant. There's only one truck left chasing us and for some reason, we're enjoying a lull in gunfire. Maybe they're finally out of ammo. I jump into the back seat, shove Ashley over, and grab the chain between her hands.

Careful to be aware of her delicate—and very breakable wrists—I pull on the cuffs with increasingly supernatural strength, concentrating on the weakest part: the chain. Tilloa's swerving around again. The road's gone curvy. Aha. That explains why they aren't shooting right now. Ash lays still, waiting. I'm tired. Shot to hell. Low on blood, and shaking. Takes a bit over a minute of straining, but finally, the cuffs snap apart. Her hands are free. They're not handcuffs anymore. She's merely got a pair of furry bracelets.

Ash whips her arms around in front and hugs me.

It's brief. I'm still worried about her getting hit, so I push her down toward the floor. Within half a second of me doing that, I catch a bullet in the left shoulder that throws me against the passenger seat.

Ashley roars. She yanks the shotgun from the mount on the back of Tilloa's seat, spins up to point it out the rear window, and fires. A gout of dragon breath fire covers the back end of our truck but doesn't go too much farther than the tailgate, falling far short of the last vehicle chasing us. The recoil flings her backward into the driver's seat.

I clutch the bullet hole in my left shoulder, waiting for the burning tingle to stop.

"Whoa," whispers Ashley, blinking in awe at the weapon in her hands. "Shotgun flamethrower. Awesome."

"These guys expect to fight vampires," says Tilloa.

"You okay, Sare?" Ashley peers up at me.

"It's like whacking your funny bone on a chair. Stunned for a bit, then I'm okay." I struggle to push myself upright with one arm. Damn this hurts.

Thud.

Another goddamned vampire has landed in our truck's bed. Where are they coming from? It's like we're in a video game and bad guys are spawning endlessly.

Ashley raises the shotgun and melts his face off. That time, she's ready for the recoil so it doesn't rock her too much. She fires again, incinerating a little more than half of his head. The exposed portion of brain chars black and spews smoke. Ack. I'm pretty sure he's gone for good. No idea if vampires can regenerate two thirds of their brain after it's been turned to charcoal.

Not finished yet, Ashley pumps the shotgun, pushes herself up enough to aim out the back window, and shoots the corpse in the balls—since he's flat on his back with his legs a bit parted.

"Stop trying to kill Sarah! You stupid meanies!" shouts Ashley.

Yeah… she is definitely not from New Jersey.

45

HOT FLASHES... TO THE FACE

"Okay, now this is getting damned silly," says Tilloa in a tone like she's scolding kids. "How the hell many of them are there?"

Ashley moves to sit/kneel on the backseat against the driver side wall, aiming the shotgun out the back window hole. She'd probably smell like a strawberry ice cream sundae due to a bunch of tiny cuts—if I could smell anything more than the reek of burning plastic and whatever chemicals are inside Dragon Breath rounds. The final truck is still chasing us but they're far enough behind us that a flamey shotgun can't do more than possibly blind the driver.

"I don't see any more in the air," grumbles Ashley, sounding disappointed.

Girl wants payback.

"What's that smell?" Tilloa sniffs.

I glance at the smoldering vampire corpse in the back, open fire eating away at the crotch of his pants. "Ash is roasting some nuts back here."

"Hah. No. Not scorched meat. This is like chemical or something."

"Melted plastic from the dashboard?" Ashley peers back.

A man leans out of the passenger window of the truck behind us, Mp5 in hand, and rips a few bursts of automatic fire at us. Bullets clank, thump, thud, and ping everywhere. Some zip in the back window. The center mirror explodes into a shower of silvery glass and plastic bits.

Tilloa cries out in pain as another bullet punches through the back of her seat into her.

"Fuck this. Let me have that." I reach toward Ashley.

She holds the shotgun out to me. "All you, but it won't reach."

"Yeah. I know." I roll my left shoulder, gritting my teeth at the grinding itchy pain of splintered bone trying to reconstitute. It hurts but there doesn't seem to be serious structural damage. Bullet hit the bone and cracked it, but not a dead-on shattering of my shoulder joint. "Got it handled."

I wait another few seconds for Mp5 guy to run out of ammo and pull his hand in to reload.

Ashley emits a yelp of alarm as I dive out the back window, flying. There's no need for me to accelerate much since they're driving at me doing over seventy. Seconds before they slam into me, I throw myself into backward flight. My timing is good—or lucky—enough for me to land on the hood of the other truck with only a slight wobble. I point-blank the driver in the face, turning him briefly into Ghost Rider—a screaming, flaming exposed skull.

Mp5 dude yanks a handgun off his vest, firing wild. He gets me in the legs twice and puts a third bullet past my left ear before I round the shotgun on him and it's fiery game over. Out of spite, I shoot both of them once more. Most of their truck interior is on fire now. Damn good chance these two are permanently dead. I'm not the least bit sorry.

The driver's head crumbles apart into charcoal bits.

I get the feeling he's no longer fit to drive. There's also a bunch of ammo and hand grenades in this inferno, so it's time to get the hell out of here. I spring off the hood into a twisting roll and fly in pursuit of our truck. From the outside, it's scarily obvious how much of a beating it's taken. Silver spots are everywhere bullets shattered the paint. The reason we didn't get chewed up more than we did is a fat steel toolbox in the bed right up against the cabin. It probably stopped most of the bullets that came in below the window line except for the .50 cal machine gun. This giant toolbox is certainly the reason Ashley escaped bullets.

Smoke's peeling out of multiple places, and I think the chemical smell Tilloa mentioned is probably burning anti-freeze. I chase our truck along the 'tree tunnel' of road, struggling to stay in the air due to extreme tiredness. Behind me, the last mercenary pickup drifts into the oncoming lane and keeps going right off the pavement, striking trees with an echoing *whud*. Its cabin is fully engulfed in flames. Good thing everything is wet. Shouldn't set off too much of a forest fire.

There are like eight identical black pickup trucks crashed along a several-mile stretch of this road. Someone's got a heck of a mess to clean up, and it's not going to be me. I'm beat, not to mention a nervous, emotional wreck even though I appear outwardly calm and totally in control of the situation. Wonder if Mom feels like this in court. Inside, total panic, sobbing, screaming, wanting to choke the life out of someone— outside, stoic.

I swing my legs forward and slip in the back window to land seated beside Ashley. Seated is kind of overstating it. I'm slumped, not terribly interested in moving for a few hours.

Ashley peers out the back. "You got them all. No one's behind us now."

"Cool," I deadpan. "About time."

"You okay?" Ashley gingerly squeezes my arm on a spot without any blood.

"I'm seriously in need of a peaches and cream bath bomb," I rasp.

"Ooh, that sounds lovely." She smiles. "I totally need a bath."

Tilloa slows down to about forty-five or so. The truck's starting to shake. Damn. Did they hit a tire? Wait, mercs. Probably got run-flats on this thing. I know we did something really dangerous since driving at a safe, sane speed on this road feels sluggish.

"Uhh, guys?" Ashley flashes a cheesy smile.

"What?" Tilloa and I ask simultaneously.

"There's fire coming from the back of the truck and it's not that guy's nuts." She points her thumb over her shoulder. "I think maybe they hit the gas tank."

Tilloa looks around. "This truck is emitting steam and smoke from places it probably shouldn't be emitting steam and smoke from."

"And fire," adds Ashley.

"Yeah." I sigh. "We should get out before it turns into a fireball. Pull your feet up. I'm in too much pain to bend."

"Huh?" Ashley blinks at me.

"Fuzzies," I mutter.

"Oh. Duh." She shifts around to sit and extends her legs to put her feet in my lap. "Good idea. Fire plus truck probably equals running."

I grab the furry cuffs around her ankles, hoping I have enough left in me to break the chain. Really, I don't. But... this is Ashley. All it takes is me thinking about what almost happened to her and I get pissed off enough for an adrenaline spike. The chain snaps after a moment of me grunting and straining.

"Thanks." Ashley pulls one knee to her chest, then the next, stretching her legs.

Tilloa pulls over and stops. This road doesn't really have much of a shoulder, so she leaves the truck about halfway in the dirt, blocking about four feet of the northbound lane. Can't be helped. As soon as the truck is stopped and she cuts the engine, we scramble out—Ashley kinda lugging me around this time—and stagger down the road away from the smoking vehicle. I feel like one of the guys from that famous American Revolution painting. Just give me a flute, Ashley a drum, and wrap a bandage around Tilloa's head.

It's seriously quiet except for the clap of Ashley's bare feet on the wet road, the dull rattling of broken chain, and my boots scuffing. Yeah, she's holding up more of my weight than I am. This is a sunset ass kicking. What's that mean? Means I'm not gonna wake up until sunset tomorrow.

Eventually, we stop walking, still on the road. It's completely silent now except for Ashley breathing. No other cars. No one else walking. Not even birds have the nerve to chirp right now.

Ashley looks around at the woods. I know it's incredibly dark to her out here, so no idea how much she can see. Since we're on a road with no trees directly overhead, there might be enough moonlight for her to at least make out the path of the road and be aware we have trees on both sides.

"Wow," whispers Ashley. "We're in the middle of nowhere. It's kinda nice. Crazy how it went from so chaotic to so peaceful."

"Yeah," says Tilloa.

I stare down the length of the narrow two-lane road, drinking in the wonderful smell of wet forest. Not sure when, exactly, it rained but it had to be before we started flying south toward the mill. Recent, though. Till and I are bloody messes. Both of us look like we went ten rounds in a boxing ring with a giant weed-eater. Whether or not we won is debatable. Ashley is also a bloody mess but it isn't her blood. Most of it is spray from us and the vampire I shot like nine times while he tried to crawl into the truck.

Ashley's still only wearing a collar, fuzzy bracelets and anklets, and a bit of leash dangling in front of her, yet she doesn't seem to care. She's neither blushing nor trying to cover up.

I start to tug my shirt out of my jeans. "Here, put this on."

She grabs my hand. "Nah. I'm okay. Besides, it's all bloody."

"So are you."

"Not my blood." She brushes bits of glass off her arms, sides, and butt. "And you're shot a whole bunch of times. Wow. All this glass. I can't believe I still have skin."

"It's safety glass," says Tilloa.

I tug at my shirt again.

"Sare. Stop." She pulls my hand away from the fabric. "Keep your shirt. You need to cover those wounds so people don't ask questions. Consider this me taking you up on the streaking dare."

"What if someone sees you?" I ask.

"Then they see me." She gestures around at the woods. "Who the heck is gonna be out here at this hour anyway? What if someone sees *you* guys? You both look like extras from a zombie movie. It's a lot easier to tell someone we all got kidnapped and the bad guys stole my clothes than come up with an explanation for how you have a bunch of bullet holes in you and you're still walking around like it's no big deal."

"She's got a point." Tilloa chuckles.

I sigh at her. "At least let me snap the rest of that stuff off you."

She examines her wrists. "They're just fuzzy bracelets now. Keys are in my bedroom. I can wait."

"We're nowhere near your bedroom," grumbles Tilloa.

Ashley stretches her arms out to either side. "Who cares? They're no more annoying than jewelry now. Save your strength. You barely had the strength to break my legs free and you look like you're about to fall over."

"She's in shock, not processing reality," says Tilloa.

"I dunno. Maybe I am." Ashley shrugs. "This doesn't feel like it's happening for real."

Oh, right. What did Malcolm do to her? I rest a hand on her shoulder and stare into her eyes—and mind. She and Raleigh went up to her bedroom after dinner. They hung out for a little while before it got steamy. Her girlfriend put the cuffs and collar on her a few minutes after seven. I fast forward past the sex part, which isn't really much more than Raleigh lightly groping her for a few minutes. A few blinks forward in time and Raleigh is standing beside the bed, gazing into space. Ashley's stuck on her bed, leashed to the headboard. As she said, she wondered if Raleigh was trying to play some kinky game with her but she eventually got scared and wanted out. Tried the safe word, but Raleigh continued to stand there looking at her phone.

Seems she struggled to escape for a bit over an hour before some of those mercenaries walked in. In utter disregard to the sight of two naked young women, the men pick Ashley up like movers relocating a dresser. She tries her best to resist but can't really defend herself. These guys seem mortal. They carry her downstairs out the front door and dump her in the trunk of that black car. I fast forward the ride. Now she's in the lumber mill watching one of the mercs padlock the leash to the conveyor frame.

There she sits for maybe another two hours before Malcolm arrives. He compels her to read from paper, the same message I got on voicemail. Once he hangs up, he does implant a compulsion. His people apparently hid some white phosphorous grenades in her bedroom. If tonight's plan failed, she's supposed to take them and use them on me while I sleep. However, the compulsion to do that has already disintegrated. It tried to activate as soon as I broke her hands loose… and promptly caused her brain to crash and reboot after purging the poisonous program code. Hmm. That might explain how she remained so damn calm during the chase.

I pull her tight and just start crying on her shoulder, so overcome with relief she's okay and a true appreciation of how deeply she loves me—like a sister. Breaking a compulsion like that from an elder so fast and thoroughly is *not* easy. And yeah, I know not all sisters love each other. Some don't even like each other. But we're almost a shared soul.

Ashley breaks down into sniffles. "Why am I crying?"

"Probably because she is, and I dunno." Tilloa chuckles. "Crying is kind of a normal reaction after being kidnapped, shot at, and nearly killed."

Oh, and yeah, she's indifferent to being out here in her birthday suit because she's too freaked out to care about anything more than being happy she's still alive, I'm okay, and her mother isn't dead.

"Sorry for breaking your toys, but I had to." I collect myself and lean back so we can make eye contact. "I'm emotional right now because that bastard tried to program you to kill me, and it broke. You resisted an elder trying to give you a command."

"Pff." She waves dismissively. "No one makes me murder you. And don't worry about breaking the fuzzies. Being helpless isn't really fun when I'm being shot at and kidnapped for real. I think maybe I'm not gonna be in a real big hurry to replace them."

Tilloa gazes up at the sky. "We best get the heck out of here before someone finds us. You got enough left in you to fly home?"

"Probably. Let's hide somewhere and rest for maybe twenty minutes first? I don't want to drop her." I glance at Ashley. "If you don't mind the delay."

"We're already out here." She flaps her arms. "And I do have a dream about running around the woods like a nymph. Raleigh and I did that the other day for like two hours. So fun and relaxing. You and Hunter should try it sometime."

"Right." I start walking off the road into the woods in search of a hiding spot.

"This umm, nature hike is strictly non-sexy, though," declares Ashley. "Ooh. Ow. Stepped on a rock. Oh, why does it have to be so darn dark!?"

We make slow progress. Tilloa and I are beat and Ashley can't see where she's going, forcing her to wave her arms around, grab trees, and carefully explore the ground with her toes in search of a non-painful place to step. Once we get far enough into the woods where I can't see the road, it's safe to assume no one on the road will be able to see us. There, we sit and collect ourselves. Mostly, I'm waiting for the rest of my bullet holes to close and a bone or two to knit.

Might take a few minutes.

46

CHASING FOREST NYMPHS ALWAYS ENDS BADLY

Other than having blood all over it, my iPhone survived the shootout.

It's 2:37 a.m. Earlier than I thought. In reality, the whole drivey-shooty thing took about twelve minutes. Felt like two hours. Then again, hanging out in an accelerated reflex state that feels like slow-motion time can do that. Ashley's not even yawning yet. Adrenaline is a bitch. We've been sitting in the woods for about twenty minutes in more or less total silence. Just as well. If any of us tried to say anything, it would only be 'holy shit' repeatedly.

Screw it. I hurt. I want to go home. I need peaches and cream.

Again, I scoop her up and limp into the air. My stomach knots up in hunger. It's significant enough to where having Ashley so close to my face is dangerous. The same strong bond we have that let her break Malcolm's kill command is the only thing keeping me from having an Ashley-nom.

Multiple bullet wounds all over my body throb and itch as they heal. A few minutes into the flight, the strawberry scent of Ashley's blood has invaded my senses so badly I expect to hallucinate her into some manner of giant Hostess snack cake in my arms. She's only got a few (dozen) superficial scratches from the safety glass. No way is she bleeding anywhere near enough for the smell to be this strong.

"Sare," asks Ashley in a slightly concerned tone. "Are we going down or am I imagining that?"

"Wake up," calls Tilloa from above.

Ugh, shit. I am sinking. "Yeah... struggling to stay up. I think my gas tank is about empty."

Tilloa descends to my altitude. The effort it takes her to keep flying is pretty obvious on her face as well. "We better land before you crash."

Reluctantly, but knowing it's the wisest thing to do, I cruise down toward the forest floor. The idea of being stuck outside for sunrise sucks, but it beats crashing from a fatal altitude. Unless there's a cave or something close to one nearby, Ash might have to bury us in shallow graves. By the time we reach the ground, the urge to bite her is teetering on irresistible. I hate the thought of it, but if this had happened to Michelle, I'd already be feeding. Don't get me wrong, Michelle is a super close friend... but we didn't spend our entire childhoods together. I wouldn't have been strong enough to resist despite trying to.

I land kinda hard. Ashley slips out of my arms and lands flat on her back in front of me.

"Oof," she grumps from the ground. "You really are in bad shape."

I fall over like a cut tree.

Tilloa crash lands a few feet to my left, mumbles a deadpan 'ow' then sits up, staring at her phone. "I think we're a little north of Buckley."

Ashley rolls over, then crawls closer to where I fell, nudging me. "You okay?"

I put a hand on her shoulder, close my eyes, and rasp, "Ash, you gotta get away from us. So damn hungry right now I'm having to fight the urge to feed on you."

She pulls her hair off her neck. "Okay. If you need to, go for it. Might have to rip the collar off first if it's in the way."

My eyes open against my will. I stare at her neck, focusing on the pulse of her carotid artery above the band of hot pink leather. All the little pink and purple reflective hearts on it catch starlight mortal eyes can't perceive, shimmering and flickering in a hypnotizing display. My vision leaps from reality to waking dream, the nightmare I had about turning Ashley in my bedroom. Had that been prophetic? Am I going to lose control and kill her right now? I'm sure if I taste blood, I'm going to take too much—exactly like Tilloa did after nearly burning to death in the sun. Does Ashley know that there's a damn good chance I won't be able to stop myself before she's dead? Does she want me to? I want her to be with me forever, too. Just like we are now, free to exist in the nowhere land between childhood and adulthood.

We could have fun, no responsibilities, forever.

But... the guilt. Even if she wants me to do it, I'd always be consumed with knowing I killed her. It's so irrational. Ashley gets to be with me forever. Why would I feel guilty about killing her? It's not death; it's rebirth.

I'm torn. I want and can't. She wants... maybe. Or am I projecting my desires onto her, interpreting what she's doing to suit my desires? Can't read her mind... too damn tired. The only thing my mental powers want to do right now is fire the derp cannon so I can start feeding.

I try to tell her no, but only manage a whimper of a non-word.

Ashley twists to look off to one side. "Oh, wait. Hang on. I hear someone. You guys hide. Be right back."

"You don't have any clothes," I say in a sleepy, semi delirious haze.

"I know. That's part of the plan." She stands. "Malcolm used me as bait. I'm gonna use myself as a bait goblin. Wait here."

"Huh?" I ask dazedly.

It's too late. She's run off. I lift my head and catch only a momentary glimpse of a pale form streaking across the dark forest before too many trees are in the way. Bait goblin. Oh... D&D. Dad. She's going to... Ash, no. She's gonna lure people to us. Two starving monsters waiting in the forest. If we kill them, she helped us murder people. She's so damn naïve, sweet, and innocent, she doesn't understand the state we're in.

Tilloa looks exhausted as well, but not quite as badly as I feel. "What's going on? Why do I feel like this?"

"How many times did you get shot?" I ask.

"Lost count. Over twenty. Maybe thirty."

"That's what happened. Healing takes a lot of energy. Takes way more when we rush it along in the middle of getting our asses shot up." I slump down, unable to even lift my head up. "We overextended ourselves. This is like the vampire version of having really low blood sugar."

Somewhere in the distance, Ashley's voice—falsely high pitched and frightened—murmurs something. I think she's telling someone her two friends need help.

"Mm. Blood sugar." Tilloa licks her lip.

My head feels like a bowling ball balanced on my neck.

Next thing I know, I'm flat on my back. There's a man hovering over me, patting me on the cheek. I only see him for a split second before reality flashes forward again. Now I'm kneeling beside him and he's flat on his back, unconscious. I peer down at his neck. When I see it's *not* ripped open and gushing blood, it's such a relief I collapse on top of him. His heart is still beating in a normal, steady rhythm. I must have stopped myself before going too far.

I'm still hungry, but not starving. I don't feel supercharged as if I'd snorted cocaine—bad analogy. Having never actually tried cocaine, I have no idea what it would feel like. That crazy bastard Ruben was a kill-feeder. Drug addict in life, drug addict in death. They say feeding to the point you kill is a rush and it's super addictive. It also tends to make 'civilized' vampires not like you.

Tilloa lifts her face from a second man's throat. Her gold eyes are glowing like firefly butts, her mouth open. Fangs out, blood all over her chin, she looks scary—and I'm a vampire too. Wait. Firefly butt isn't serious enough. Let me try that again. Her eyes are glowing like demonic embers. I get the sense she's forcing herself to stop drinking. One look at the guy she's on is enough to tell me she hasn't taken a lethal amount yet but he's not far from the tipping point.

"We can't kill them," I wheeze. "Nice guys. Trying to help."

"Don't wanna." Tilloa shudders. Her fangs gradually retract. "I'm okay."

Crackling in the undergrowth approaches us from the side. We both whip our heads around to stare in the direction of the noise, growling like feral lions defending their kills.

"Chill, guys. Just me," says Ashley.

She emerges from the trees, carrying a flashlight. She's still wearing the leash, collar, and fuzzy, broken cuffs… but she's added a huge blue flannel shirt to her wardrobe. It must belong to the guy I bit since it covers her to mid-thigh. He is really big. Beefy, too. Tilloa's guy is also unsmall, but not as titanic. Oof. Lucky again. What are the odds of us finding two men out here in a random patch of forest, both of whom are big enough for us to feed sufficiently to get our senses back without it being a fatal amount to them?

I take back what I said before about my luck being generally bad.

Shining her flashlight on the ground, Ashley makes her way over to us, placing her feet with care around roots, rocks, and other potential ouchies. "These guys are camping not too far from here. Didn't think they'd mind me borrowing a shirt."

After closing the fang marks I left on the man's neck, I drape myself across his chest, inches away from sleeping. Good thing I literally cannot sleep at night.

"Probably not." Tilloa sits back on her heels and lifts her plum-colored shirt up to her neck, revealing a black sports bra—and seven coppery 'nipples' scattered around her torso. One by one, the emerging bullets finish exuding from her chest and fall. She helps them along by plucking, grimacing and whimpering each time. "Does this ever hurt less?"

I casually dig a bullet out of my left leg through a rip in my jeans, and flick it aside. "Yeah, but I think bullets only hurt less once you've known real pain."

"Listening to your father sing Karaoke?" asks Ashley.

"Hah." I chuckle. "Nothing that bad. I mean like having your spine broken in half or a coral-encrusted rusty rapier impaled in your chest."

Tilloa stares at me. "I'm not sure if I want to know."

My shoulder lights on fire—metaphorically. I pull my T-shirt sleeve out of the way so the bullet that knocked the crap out of me can fall unhindered to the ground. Rifle shot. Should've known. That one had some stank on it.

"Thanks for the snacks," says Tilloa.

"Least I could do." Ashley smiles. "I'm glad you didn't kill them. I would've felt really bad. They were so nice. I told them my friends and I got attacked and needed help, and they came running."

Wow. I can only imagine what they thought she meant seeing her run up to them. Wait, I don't have to imagine. I hover over the dude and proceed to erase his memory—memory I don't even have—of me feeding. Poor guy didn't even have the courtesy of a derp slap before I went to town on him. He fainted from a combination of fear and the intoxicating effect of our bite. No, a person can't get high from being bitten. It's a sedative effect. Somewhere back in the annals of time, there's probably a more primitive vampire ancestor that lacked the ability to apply a mental derp before feeding, thus needed to rely on a paralyzing bite.

And wow. This is a good dude. He thought some creep abducted three girls for, let's just say 'highly deviant assault.' He'd been ready to beat the guy to death. By the time I'm done with him, he thinks he saw a fleeting glimpse of a wood nymph streaking by, but never caught up to her. Hopefully, it's such a fantastical sight he won't want to tell anyone about it. This guy's urge to help us is pretty strong. And I'm still tired. Swapping a memory is much easier than deleting it.

Sorry, man. You know what they say about wood nymphs. It's dangerous to chase them. They almost always lure men into traps. Tilloa and I lug the unconscious men back to their campsite which is about a quarter mile from where we were. And yes, little me carry-dragging an almost seven-foot-tall, almost-400-pound dude looks absolutely ridiculous. Damn, Ash. You really walked this far in the dark?

She's hovering by the edge of the camp, still holding the flashlight. I can tell she wants to leave it here. Stealing is bad, and stealing from nice people is worse. Wouldn't surprise me if she even felt bad about taking the shirt and considered leaving it behind. I'm almost afraid to look into her head to find out what happened. Did she know how on edge I was, that letting me bite her might have been the end?

We make eye contact.

Ashley seems guilty. She shrugs one shoulder in a 'yeah well, you didn't seem to want to and I don't want you to be guilty for eternity' sort of way. Yes, that's a complex thought to interpret from body language, but it's sitting there right on the tip of her brain for me to read.

Both of us feel like we did something wrong. How messed up is that? I feel like I let her down by *not* killing her.

She walks over and hugs me. "Thanks for saving me from that jackass."

"Thanks for saving me from myself."

Tilloa sighs. "Oh, will you two just get a room already?"

We turn our heads at the same time to stare at her.

"It's not like that," says Ashley.

"I know what it's like." Tilloa folds her arms. "I'm not that oblivious."

Head down, I mutter, "I dunno."

"She doesn't want to turn me," half-whispers Ashley.

"Turn you?" Tilloa blinks. "Oh. Wow. Okay. Never mind. I thought you guys were about to kiss."

Ashley and I burst out laughing.

"I thought you knew us better than that," says Ashley.

Tilloa winks, grinning. "Gotcha. I know exactly what you two are about. You hate not being together, and totally not 'like that.'" She makes air quotes around the last two words.

I peer straight up through the trees at the sky. "I'm good now. Let's go home."

"About time. I've been waiting to ride you all night." Ashley turns off the flashlight and tosses it into the tent.

"You beast," I deadpan. "Come here."

Tilloa snickers.

Ashley hops on my back. It's easier to fly with a passenger on my back. Less tiring than holding someone in my arms.

Flying hurts a little—like running too soon after exhaustion—but it's quite tolerable after a big meal.

We'll be home in no time.

BETRAYAL

We're back at Ashley's house.

Mrs. Carter is sleeping again, but normally—not under the influence of whatever they used on her. We found her in her bed when we arrived, which means she doesn't know anything happened to Ashley. Otherwise, she would've been robo-dialing the police, me, my parents, anyone she could get a hold of.

Ash's house has one bathroom and a toilet closet. Given the late hour, we decided to go full *Starship Troopers* and shower together. All three of us were filthy as hell. Blood, dirt, industrial dust, and so on. I quipped about how it beat the last time we took a bath together. Serious grime is much easier to deal with than skunk spray and dog poop. Ashley helped us out by tweezing flecks of metal out of our sides and back—incendiary fragment bits from the dragon breath near miss.

We eventually end up in Ashley's room, Tilloa and I in borrowed clothes for now: pink sweat pants and white T-shirts. Ashley slipped into her unicorn pajamas. Like three oversized tweens, we're sitting cross-legged on the bed facing each other in a ritual circle. Only it isn't boyfriends and teachers we're gossiping about. We're not even gossiping. Just sorta staring at each other in a 'holy shit, so that just happened' manner.

We also have some friends. Four kittens and a calico cat, their mom. Klepto managed to locate the kitten's mother and brought her here. People say animals are oblivious or dumb. They're wrong. Momcat was visibly thrilled to be reunited with her babies. The four fuzzy cuffs lay unlocked on Ashley's nightstand along with the collar and leash. She's got a red mark around her neck that'll probably take a day to fade.

"Wow." Ashley exhales a sharp puff of air. "Aside from the almost being murdered part, that was kinda exciting."

"You need therapy," I say. "Or memory erasure."

She laughs. "Does anyone know who that jerk is?"

I shrug. "Acheron, but I'm not elite enough to call him that."

Tilloa makes a raspberry noise while giving the middle finger to a random direction. "Whoever he is, he sucks."

"Of course he does," says Ashley. "He's a vampire."

I throw a plush unicorn at her.

Tilloa laughs. "I still can't get over his blasted-off face."

We giggle like kids again. Now, with Ashley safe, I can really laugh. From taking himself way too seriously and being scary as hell to a goofy cartoon explosion in an instant is just too damn much. A moment later, our snickering and tittering peters out to relieved sighs.

A whimper comes from under the bed.

We exchange looks. Ashley tallies felines. All five are accounted for on top of the bed, tiny furballs all cuddled up against Momcat.

"You heard that, right?" asks Tilloa. "Sounded like a ghost girl."

"Mmm!" comes from under the bed.

Ashley glances at the floor. "Umm, I don't think it's a ghost."

The three of us slide off the bed and get down on all fours next to each other. Ashley mouths a silent three count, then lifts the side of her super thick pink comforter.

Raleigh Murphy stares at us, her eyes wide and fearful. She's got black duct tape over her mouth. Her hands are tied behind her back with black plastic riot cuffs; another set binds her ankles... and she's not wearing anything else. Oh wow. She must have been here when Tilloa and I came looking for Ashley before. No wonder her scent was so strong in the room. It hadn't been due to them having massive amounts of sex.

"Oh, hey, Ral," says Ashley. "What are you doing under the bed?"

"Mmm!" says Raleigh, squirming.

Tilloa sniffs. "Chloroform?"

I sniff. "Not exactly sure what it is, but it's the same stuff they used on Mrs. Carter."

Ashley frowns.

I glance at her. "Guessing you didn't do this?"

"No." Ashley shakes her head. "She's not into it. She didn't even want to tie *me* up even though I like it. I might kinda be over it for a bit after tonight, but yeah." She biffs herself in the head. "Really should've known something was wrong when she suggested it tonight. I wasn't even going to mention it. She brought it up and really wanted to use the fuzzies on me. Besides… zip ties aren't comfortable. They pinch. Those aren't mine."

Raleigh's eyes shift from pleading stare to glare and back to pleading stare.

"Why the heck did those mercs leave her here?" asks Tilloa.

"Who knows?" Ashley reaches in and grasps Raleigh's arm at the elbow. "Help me pull her out?"

I grasp her ankle. "The guys who abducted you had to be mortals since the sun hadn't gone down yet."

"Also, vampires wouldn't have needed to use chloroform to knock anyone out." Tilloa—who is between us—glances at Ashley holding Raleigh's arm, me grasping the girl's ankle, and raises both hands. "You got this. I'm not grabbin' her butt."

Ashley and I pull Raleigh out into the light.

"She wasn't the target." Tilloa backs up to make some room. "They didn't have any specific instructions for what to do with her, so they probably just stuffed her under the bed."

Raleigh sits up on the floor, her back to the bed. Her heart rate accelerates. In seconds, her face is as red as her hair and she's squirming, clearly freaked out because we haven't untied her or removed the tape immediately. Totally understandable. In her position, I'd be upset, too. Five seconds later, tears start. Chill out. Gonna let you go in a second, just want to see what's going on in that head of yours first.

And my phone picks this moment to ring. It's all I can do not to smash it. Somehow, I manage to force myself to stretch and grab it from Ashley's nightstand, at least to look at the ID. The list of people who would call me at this hour is pretty small, so it's worth at least seeing who it is before I ignore the call. Oh… it's Darren Anderson. Wow, he's up super early.

"Hello?" I ask, after swiping to answer.

"Mmmm!" yells Raleigh.

"Sarah. It's Darren."

"Yeah. Got that from the caller ID. What's up?"

He chuckles. "In response to your request. The Altoid tin? Is this a good time?"

"If it's not going to be a long story, sure."

Raleigh shifts her gaze from me, to Ash, her big-eyed stare asking 'what the hell is going on'. When she glances at Tilloa, she seems frightened. Our new friend is not in the best mood and those gold eyes make her look fierce.

"Not long." Darren chuckles. "Though, I dare say Landon was somewhat disappointed to find the tin did not contain mints."

I smirk.

"Right then." Darren clears his throat. "You of course understand the art of scrying is not exactly the most reliable or detailed process. However… the bullet you sent us did produce a vision."

"Oh?" I raise both eyebrows, then lower the phone from my mouth to whisper, "Just a sec. This is important." Pretty sure he's going to tell me a guy in black tried to snipe me with some kind of silenced .22 rifle or something.

"In the vision, we observed you approaching the door of a house. You were wearing a long-sleeved sweater of some kind with shorts. Odd."

"Oh wow. I was bringing kittens to Ashley's place," I say.

Ash and Tilloa tilt their heads at me. Raleigh trembles, staring at us like the one girl in the sleepover who's lost a round of 'spin the sacrificial dagger.' No, that's not a real thing, even among vampires.

"A relatively young red-haired woman was hiding in the bushes," says Darren.

"Gee. Wonder who that might've been." I narrow my eyes at Raleigh. *You jealous bitch.*

Sensing my mood, she whimpers, squirming at the riot ties.

"The young woman took a small pistol from her purse, aimed, and tried to shoot you in the back of the head. The bullet seems to have struck a rather ponderously large bee or some manner of insect on its way to you, deflecting its trajectory into your posterior. We did not see anything after the moment of impact."

Oh damn. I *did* feel it, but it hurt so little, I blamed a pain echo from when I'd been shot in the femur during the Chicago chaos.

"Till," I mutter. "Mind checking that black purse over there for a weapon?"

"On it." She scoots across the rug to grab Raleigh's rectangular—and super expensive—purse.

"I'm afraid that's all we were able to see. No indication of why or who she is," says Darren. "Only thing I can say for certain is the shot was not stray. The woman intended to kill… well, perhaps knock you out?"

"Thank you." I exhale. So, so glad I did not ask Sophia to do it. She'd have freaked. "Tell Landon I'll drop off some actual mints as thanks."

"Will do." Darren laughs into a yawn. "Damn lucky bee. Well, not so lucky for the bee, but you…"

"Yeah." I whistle. "No doubt."

"All right then, Sarah. Stay safe." Darren yawns again. "I need to grab some coffee before I go back to bed."

We hang up.

Ashley's soon-to-be-ex girlfriend presses herself into the bed, trying to scoot away from me. She looks frightened enough to make me feel guilty, even though she tried to take me out.

"Bingo." Tilloa holds up a small, silver handgun… as well as a now-detached silencer. "It's a .32. And she's got a sound suppressor."

Ashley gasps. "Ral? What are you doing with a *gun?*"

Raleigh's eyes widen. She squirms and yells, "Mmmm!"

Yeah bitch. You're busted. I glance at Tilloa. "That's a thing? .32?"

"It is. They used to call them lady guns." She rolls her eyes, then pops the magazine out to examine. "Looks like one shot's missing."

"What did you shoot?" asks Ashley.

I pat my butt. "You cut the bullet out of me."

Ashley goes from shocked to furious to despondent to confused so fast she just stares at me without making a sound. "Uhh, she said she wasn't jealous of you."

Before I can snap 'bullshit' at her, my brain decides to do some actual work. Dammit! Malcolm. Why would Raleigh develop a sudden strong urge to have kinky sex when she's been trying to avoid it? She didn't want to tie Ashley up for fun… she gift wrapped her for the mercenaries. "Aww dammit."

Tilloa and Ashley look at me with 'what?' faces.

Raleigh's full-on crying now. Can't blame her. It's super weird we're leaving her zip-cuffed in the nude with tape over her mouth.

"It's okay, Raleigh," I say. "We're not going to hurt you. I just need to make sure you aren't a threat to us or yourself before we cut you loose, okay?"

Tears stop. She stares at me, her expression ninety percent mortified, ten percent clueless.

"Actually." No need to be mad at her. Her clothing is still strewn all over the rug where she'd dropped it earlier. "Let's not be complete bitches to her. It's not her fault."

I stare into her eyes. "As soon as you can, get dressed, then sit on the edge of the bed."

She gazes into the Eighth Dimension.

I pop a claw and cut the zip cuffs off her. They're not cable ties, but legit cuffs like riot police use. They definitely came from those mercs. Like an automaton, Raleigh stands, retrieves her clothes from the rug, and gets dressed, ignoring the tape still over her mouth. After a few minutes, she looks like a model from a Macy's catalog. Or… whatever department store is just a little bit more exclusive than Macy's. White top, black skirt, grey-hued hose, shiny dark grey heels. Yeah, this girl likes clothing the way Ashley likes unicorns.

Once she's fully dressed, she sits on the edge of the bed and rests her hands on her knees. There's a tiny hint of 'eep! What is happening to me?' in her eyes, but she mostly acts robotic.

I pull Ashley's desk chair over and sit facing Raleigh. To be nice, I derp her again so she doesn't feel it when I remove the black duct tape from her face.

"I'm expecting bad news," says Ashley, "but go ahead and Corey her."

"In I go. If I suddenly develop the irresistible urge to shop at Nordstrom's, hold me back."

Tilloa and Ashley laugh.

I dive in.

After fishing around her thoughts—which are mostly freaking out at being tied up under a bed for the past few hours—I discover Malcolm indeed programmed her to get close to Ashley. Her mission had been to spy on me, feeding as much info as possible about me and my daily routine back to him. Raleigh knows all the 'accidents,' shootings, and the backpack bomber were randomly chosen mind-controlled humans used as guided Sarah-seeking missiles. For the past almost month, she's been feeling trapped in her own body, forced to do things she doesn't understand, can't stop, and can't talk about. Poor girl didn't even realize she'd been carrying a gun around. She doesn't understand what vampires are, nor why she's been acting this way.

This is no doubt why Ashley kept sensing something wrong about her. She picked up on the girl's futile attempt to resist the control. Raleigh also knows Malcolm became increasingly pissed off each time one of his minions failed to kill me.

Dig. Dig. Dig. Deeper I go.

It seems Malcolm chose her for being the same age and 'relative cuteness' (his words) as Ash. He's wrong. Ashley is way cuter. Raleigh is more 'pretty.' And here's a bomb worse than anything Ashley suspected. Yeah, she was worried the girl didn't really love her and wanted to break up. That's partially true. She doesn't love Ashley at all. The girl doesn't want to break up because she doesn't consider herself to be dating anyone right now.

The girl is neither a lesbian nor is she bisexual. She has no interest in girls at all. Every time the two of them got close to 'full contact,' her awkwardness at being forced to be with a girl rose up and intermittently stalled the compulsion. It's why all they did was kiss, grope each other, and go nudist hiking while holding hands. Well, I suppose that's quite fortunate. It's going to be much easier to blot out those memories.

Her parents, brother, and friends are unaware she's dating a girl. They think Ashley is just a new friend she hangs out with sometimes. Raleigh couldn't break out of the control but she did have enough influence to keep Ashley at a distance from her family. Hence, Tacoma.

This explains everything about Ashley getting the feeling something went wrong during sex and Raleigh wasn't into her. Oof. Damn. Okay. Malcolm is a son of a bitch. I don't think there's even a word to describe how awful it is to mind control someone into having sex against their will. That's horrible enough, but to attempt making a girl who isn't into girls, erm, 'fully commit' to a relationship with Ashley is unforgivable.

I'm so galled at the cruelty and violation that happened here it kicks me right out of her head.

"That bad?" asks Ashley in a timid voice. "She hates me, doesn't she?"

"You ain't the one she shot," deadpans Tilloa.

"No. She doesn't." I take her hand. "Raleigh is... umm..."

"That creep mind controlled her into dating me," says Ash in a 'yeah, I knew it' tone.

I nod.

Ashley exhales hard. She's almost reacting the way she usually does when someone dumps her, but at only about half the severity. She didn't do anything wrong and it's nothing bad about her that drove someone away. The entire relationship had been a lie from the start.

"It's worse," I say in a somber voice.

"Worse?" Ashley cringes.

I wince. "She's not interested in girls. It's the compulsion forcing her. Raleigh is, uhh... straight."

"Son of a bitch," whispers Ashley, furious. "That bastard."

"Wow. So wrong." Tilloa paces. "We can't walk away without some kinda consequences. That's seriously dark shit."

"Figures. Too good to be true," says Ashley, fading from anger to sadness. "The reason she and I seemed to be on the same wavelength about everything is... he programmed her as a custom spy. She was *too* perfect for me. It should have made me suspicious. Go ahead and erase her mind. It's not fair to her. Anything she said she felt for me wasn't genuine. I'll be okay."

"You sure?" I ask.

"Yeah. I'm sure." Ashley kneels on the floor next to my chair, leaning her head against my arm. "I feel awful for what happened to her. Can you make her forget everything permanently?"

I nod—and go back in.

What's happening to me? asks Raleigh inside her head.

Someone took over your mind and made you do things against your will. I'm going to fix it. Tomorrow, you'll be home with your family and won't remember anything.

Okay. I don't want to remember kissing a girl. Or... touching her.

A person willing to let go of memories makes my job easier. While burrowing around to excise all the related memories of her ever knowing Ashley, I kick up a random thought. She overheard the bastard. Malcolm is definitely aware of Aurélie's protection order. I was right about my thinking a vampire tried to get rid of me and make it look like an accident, just wrong about which vampire did it.

It's easy enough for me to alter her memories of doing sexy type stuff with Ashley, replacing her with a generic imaginary boy. Again, alteration has a much greater staying power than deletion, at least for me. When I attack the compulsion to spy on Ashley and stay in contact with a special cell phone number Malcolm gave her, it's as if I ran headfirst into a wall. I try proverbially kicking the block of thought a few times more in hopes of getting it to budge. Random bits of cognition leak out each time I punt it: her mom saying have a nice time, her driving to a friend's house to swim in their massive pool, shopping trips, and so on. The last time I kick the block of memory, Malcolm appears. Raleigh's standing in a small conference room, 'parked' like a presently unneeded robot servant to one side. He mutters something on the phone about *vrais démons*.

"Dammit. I can't get rid of this." I grumble.

"Huh?" Tilloa purses her lips. "What do you mean?"

"Malcolm's an elder. His memory implant is too strong." I flap my arms. "I don't have enough skill points spent into telepathy to overpower it."

"Drat," says Ashley.

"What the hell did you just say?" Tilloa blinks at me. "I have no idea what that means."

"She's making a game joke." Ashley smirks. "So, what do we do?"

I rub my chin. "What's the proper response to a big gun?"

"Ducking?" asks Tilloa.

"Hah. No. Get a bigger gun." I narrow my eyes. "She overheard Malcolm say something like *vrais démons*."

"Sounds French." Ashley scrunches her nose.

"Exactly." I nod. "This is a job for Aurélie."

Her eyes go wide. "Ooh!"

I grin. "What time is it?"

"About ten minutes to five in the morning," says Tilloa.

"Holy cow." Ashley blinks. "I'm up late. Whew. Good thing it's summer and I'm off tomorrow."

48

VRAIS DÉMONS

Since time is super limited, we cheat.

Ashley insisted on coming with us, so the three of us dragged Raleigh to my place. I picked up Chloe and asked Blix to help us get to Aurélie's apartment via the mirrorverse. Except for the moose-faced octopus, we had an uneventful trip. What's a moose-faced octopus? I don't know. Head of a moose, bunch of tentacles, about the size of a car. It floated across the sky above us... or more like the infinite void of blackness pretending to be the sky. Mirrorverse. Not asking.

Unfortunately, attempting to send a text message from inside the mirrorverse can do crazy things like suck me into the inner workings of the phone. Since I don't feel like getting caught up in a ten-hour long remake of *Tron*, we surprise Aurélie without texting or calling ahead. By the time we're out of the mirrorverse, Chloe is clamp-hugging me, shivering and crying in fear. The ten-foot-tall anthropomorphic mice men who wanted to eat us as a snack freaked her out big time.

I'm going to tell her it's a nightmare and not to worry about it. Note to self: Chloe is too little for this place. Don't bring her in there again except for an extreme emergency.

One nice thing about Aurélie's apartment is the dress room. It has huge full-length mirrors so we can walk right out of them like doors. No awkward climbing. Flying here is usually not bad, maybe eight to ten minutes. Flying here while carrying someone is closer to twenty. Since the sunrise is scheduled around 5:56 a.m., we don't have much time. Taking the mirror took forty-seven seconds. Well, to us, it felt like about a fifteen-minute walk. In the real world, only forty-seven seconds passed.

iPhones don't really like time compression. Apple should seriously get on a patch for that.

"Hello?" I call out. "It's me, Sarah. Sorry to just pop in unannounced. Serious problem."

"That was so fucked up," says Chloe in a slow, whispery voice.

I squat down to her eye level. "Hey, kiddo?"

"Yeah?"

"Can you do me a tiny favor?"

She tilts her head.

"Ease off on the f-bombs? If you can?"

Chloe holds her arms out to either side. "Moose octopus."

"Kid's got a point," says Tilloa. "That's definitely worth an f-bomb."

"Don't encourage her," I whisper. "Mom can't handle language like that. She's brittle. And she really can't handle it from someone this small."

Chloe folds her arms. "That sounds like a her problem, not a me problem."

Ashley giggles. "I love this kid."

"Okay." Chloe flashes a silly 'just teasing' smile. "I'll try, but I can't say I won't make an oops sometimes."

"If it's just us, I don't mind so much." I ruffle her hair. "Just please try to watch it around Mom and Dad?"

The kid nods.

Come to the parlor, says Aurélie's voice in my head.

"Coming!"

I lead my little entourage out of the dress room and down the long crimson-carpeted hallway to the main living room. Swear, the white sectional couch in here is bigger than the entire living room at home. No, I'm not at all jealous. It's possible to appreciate lavishness without wanting it.

Aurélie smiles at us, gives Ashley an ever so slightly different look that gets her blushing, then glances at Tilloa with a simple nod of acknowledgement. Finally, she notices Raleigh and raises an eyebrow. "Who is this, *cheri*?"

"She is the serious problem and the reason we're here so early." I sit on the sectional next to Aurélie. "Time is short. Just please read it out of my head."

On the outside, Aurélie—especially in her overly elaborate doll dresses —looks like the absolute picture of harmless innocence. She is the almost-twenty-year-old noble ingénue who spends all her days in the palace garden at Versailles with not a single clue how the world works. She's the type of girl who would scream and jump on chairs to get away from mice.

Or so anyone who doesn't know her would assume purely from her appearance. The truth is quite far from that.

Under the veneer of a delicate, beautiful innocent is a fearsome being of vast knowledge and power. I have no doubt she could run all of Seattle —insofar as the vampire society is concerned—if she wanted to. However, she doesn't desire political power. That takes time away from relaxing and being carefree.

This outside veneer of placidity evaporates within seconds of her making eye contact with me. I don't know how a woman who looks like the waif-princess from an anime movie can give off *such* a palpable sense of dread, but she does it. I'm expecting full on Akira any second. Like this entire building is going to explode as a massive telekinetic pressure wave consumes a six-block area.

She watches the events of tonight unfold in my mind over the span of a minute or two, as well as the backpack guy, and car accidents. The woman is livid. Mostly because Malcolm tried to kill me... and Aurélie kinda likes me. She's also a little bit peeved at what happened to Ashley. Without a word, she calmly turns to stare at Raleigh. Oh, yeah. She'd be super furious about Malcolm compelling a straight girl to get with Ashley. Aurélie is so old and experienced, she no longer cares about 'petty things' like gender. However, she regards a person's right to have control over their own bodies as sacred.

A moment later, Raleigh faints. Tilloa is closer, and fast enough to catch her.

"Is she okay?" asks Ashley.

"*Oui.*" Aurélie nods curtly. "There is no memory of you at all in her mind. It will be as if none of this 'appened for 'er."

"Whew. You are amazing." I bow at her.

"Someone 'as attempted to 'arm you, Sarah." Aurélie looks at me. She's not asking.

"Yeah. 'Harm' about covers it." I exhale hard. "I feel like I got run over by *all* the buses."

Aurélie examines her fingernails. "You intend to ask me about *vrais démons?*"

"Yeah." I tap my foot on air. "Is it anything meaningful or just him being melodramatic?"

"I have 'eard of zem. They are a sect of vampires."

Tilloa sets the unconscious Raleigh seated on an open part of the sectional. "Bloodline?"

"*Non.*" Aurélie shakes her head. "Merely a sect. An order. They are quite selective in choosing their members, often stalking a mortal for years. They regard themselves as above all others, but in truth, they are merely overly proud of themselves. There is nothing special about them beyond ego. They think that by torturing their new ones, it elevates them above other vampires." She scoffs. "They are nothing more than *psychopathes.*"

"Torture how?" asks Ashley, cringing as if she doesn't really want to know.

She frowns. "When one decides to pass the Transference, they should expect to commit at least twenty years or more to assisting the new vampire as a mentor, perhaps lover, or at least friend. These *vrais démons* abandon their progeny without contact, often leaving them in dangerous circumstances which may even destroy them before they are a day old. They believe only vampires who are strong willed enough to survive with no information and no assistance are worthy of existence as vampires."

Tilloa and I exchange a stare.

"Tainted the purity of the ritual..." Ashley glances at Tilloa. "Sare, you've been teaching her how to vampire."

Tilloa twitches. She glances down at her hands, then over at me. "You think that son of a bitch is my sire?"

"It's the only thing that makes any sense." I flop back on the sofa. "This guy is such a massive douche, he tried to kill me because I 'ruined' his apprentice by helping her figure some stuff out."

Ashley sits between me and Aurélie. "He's going to pick someone else and do the same thing to them so he can have a 'pure apprentice.' Think the mercenaries kept Raleigh because he wants to use her?"

"I doubt it." Aurélie frowns. "Tilloa possesses a set of skills and circumstances he valued. She 'as a distant family with little contact. She already knew how to fight. Athletic. Strong-willed. The girl over there is a socialite who 'as wealthy and moderately influential parents. He would not take her."

"Unbelievable." Tilloa goes wide-eyed. "Oh, shit. He's in my head, isn't he? He knows everything I see and think. No damn wonder he didn't need to send a spy after me."

Aurélie continues studying her fingernails—the same fingernails I've seen cut a man's heart out. "Yes. It is likely."

"I'm too much of a danger to Sarah." Tilloa looks at me. "I guess I'll go somewhere else."

"It's not your fault at all." I sit up. "Just my luck."

"That tracks." Ashley snickers. "Every time Sare tries to help someone, it bites her in the butt."

I roll my eyes. "With six-inch fangs."

"Son of a bitch, I'm so sorry." Tilloa rakes her hands through her hair. "Don't worry about him. I'll stay away so he doesn't know what you're doing. Maybe go to the East Coast."

"Nope." I point at an empty spot of sofa. "Stay. You're a friend. We're not kicking you out of the group."

Ashley offers a hopeful smile. "He's not going to stop just because you move."

"Is there any way to break that link?" Tilloa sits. "I can't stand the idea of a monster like him knowing everything I am seeing, thinking or doing all the damn time. I want him out of my head. Bet the bastard sent those damned squatters who started the fire. Every crazy thing that happened to me must have been him."

"There is a way to break the connection to your sire." Aurélie lowers her hand into her lap and gives us this innocently sinister smile.

I stare at her, knowing exactly what she means.

"Let's go get the bastard," says Tilloa.

"No way." Ashley sits up straight. "He's an elder with a vampire army."

Tilloa holds up one finger. "Correction. He *had* a vampire army."

"He still does." Ashley frowns. "Only like three of them died to the flamey shotgun thing. The others are just knocked out. Wait…" She beams. "Flamey shotgun thing. Maybe we *can* take him? Okay. Let's go."

I grab Ashley's hand. "You can't get involved."

"But I wanna help you roast that guy." Ashley whines at me like she's asking her mom if we can stay up late enough to finish a movie.

"You can help me by staying safe and alive." I sigh at her. "Please. Stay safe."

Ashley tugs on my arm. "I want *you* to stay safe. You know what it will do to me if you die for real."

Aurélie narrows her eyes. "Sarah, this Malcolm 'as attempted to kill you. I cannot leave a matter such as this unanswered. Come. Let us discuss a few details." She floats like a ghost off the couch and glides toward the hall. Those massive dresses plus bare feet make her seem to drift around silently like a life-sized chess piece sliding across the room.

"Someone's getting in troooouble," singsongs Chloe.

Ashley nods at the kid. "Yeah. Big time."

49

FOOLISH YOUNGLINGS

I t's been two days.

Due to the time, I ended up crashing at Aurélie's that night, as did everyone. Raleigh was gone before we woke up. One of the mortal employees took her back to her car, which had been left parked a block from Ashley's house. Not sure how the girl having zero memory of knowing an Ashley is going to go over with her family, but it probably won't be anything worse than possibly an appointment with a therapist to find out why an eighteen-year-old has an imaginary friend.

I slept until almost sunset the first night. Aurélie is awesome, by the way. She knew exactly the state we'd be in and had fresh blood waiting for us. One of the first things we did upon returning home was search Ashley's bedroom for white phosphorus grenades. Good thing: she broke free of the mental compulsion to kill me pretty much immediately. Bad thing: her memory-slash-knowledge of where to find the grenades disappeared with it.

We did eventually locate them in her bookshelf—behind the books— right where she keeps her dongs. Yes, she has more than one. Guess Malcolm figured her mother wouldn't dare look there. And no, we are not mature enough to have such things out in the open together without getting into an epic Jedi dongsaber battle. As for the two white phosphorous grenades, Follows Rules Girl put her foot down. I wound up arranging for a random Seattle cop to find them—as well as the gun we took from Raleigh—just sitting on the sidewalk. No idea where they are now, but they're not going to fall into the proverbial wrong hands.

Speaking of Ashley, I assume she crashed *hard*. She's not used to staying up all night until dawn. Bad enough to be awake for twenty-four hours straight without having the hell scared out of her by an abduction and a bunch of shooting. No surprise she hasn't called or texted me since. It's a *little* worrisome, but my gut isn't giving me any bad vibes. Besides, Mrs. Carter hasn't called me in a panic.

So, yeah, two days after the lumber mill incident, Tilloa and I enter the grounds of a large house out in the woods south of Osceola. Blix helped us out tons by locating the jackass. And by jackass, I mean Malcolm.

The two of us crouch behind an old 1930s era truck, or a rusty shell in the general shape of a 1930s era truck, observing the mansion on the other side of a long tree-strewn front yard. This place looks like the proverbial haunted house in one of those movies where someone inherits an extravagant mansion from a relative they never knew they had, the family moves in, and *maybe* one of them is still alive by the end of the film.

I'm sure there's nothing wrong with the property. It's the presence of an elder vampire giving it the eerie vibes. To say I'm not nervous would be a lie. But I'm more pissed off than nervous. Our plan is pretty simple and it should work. The only real question is how many broken bones am I going to earn. Really, anything short of final death is gonna be totally worth it to do what I came here to do. Also, we're going to permanently break this bastard's mind link with Tilloa.

For obvious reasons, Tilloa is unaware of the true nature of our plan. She thinks Aurélie gave me some of her blood to 'power me up' and we're going in there because I believe I can take him. She thinks we have a chance. I'm not so sure. In fact, I'm sure he's going to kick my ass because she really didn't give me any blood.

But it doesn't matter.

I reach into my jean pocket, pull out a red headband, then tie it on.

"What the hell is that for?" asks Tilloa.

"Tradition." I give the headband knot a firm tug. "Gotta make Dad proud."

"You are a dork."

I grin. "Yep."

With that, I start making my way across the huge grove toward the house. And yes, I feel kinda ridiculous since I'm basically dressed like a background extra from a cyberpunk-themed 1980s aerobics video. It's the headband really pushing me over the edge into fashion crime. Admittedly, a long-sleeved black sweatshirt, black yoga pants, and my 'poop-stompers' are far from normal attire for August, but I wanted to improve my stealth since I'm not the most tan person in the world. The other night when Ashley ran around the forest showing *all* the skin? Yeah, I bet people on the International Space Station were like 'what's that glowing spot moving around down there?'

Ashley's a good sport about it. She knows she's blindingly pale. One of her bathing suits—her smallest bikini—has the phrase 'The beacons are lit. Gondor calls for aid' silkscreened on the top. She printed it herself.

Anyway, it might seem strange for me to know what aerobics videos even are considering they're every bit as dead as payphones, CRT televisions, and David Caruso's acting career. Simple explanation really. My father has a bunch of old television shows that he adored as a kid on video. Used to be on VCR tapes, but he transferred them to DVD. Picture quality is crud but, it's watchable. Know what didn't exist in 1984? Automatic commercial-zapping technology. If my eleven-year-old father wasn't right there to pause recording on commercials, the tape caught all of it. Some of the commercials were for aerobics videos. I can't believe they got people to dress up like that and bounce around to lame music willingly. It's even harder to believe people bought those videos and bounced around in their living room trying to copy the moves.

Then again, different era. People did things back then we consider silly now. Go far enough back and men wore wigs and high heels.

Tilloa's gone less retro. She's channeling a 1990s-era action hero with a black raincoat, tactical pants, and one of those military looking sweater tops. Not that I've said a word about my nervousness, but since she's with me, it's a certainty Malcolm knows we're coming. Now that I know he's her sire, it's obvious he knew we found the lumber mill and just let us walk in. Maybe I'm not so good at sneaking as I thought. He might've ordered his men to ignore us. Explains why they'd arranged themselves around Ashley like the jaws of an enormous bear trap around the bait.

Though, my senses are pretty decent, and Malcolm's an asshole. Maybe we did sneak in after all and he didn't warn his people since he didn't care if we killed any of them.

So, yeah. The Universe's most awesome imp led us here. Wasn't much point to concealing Blix from her since she's already aware of his existence. Let that particular cat out of the bag before we knew who her sire was. Not sure what made me so hesitant about telling her all my secrets—like the hellhound guarding the house—but it's a damn good thing. Besides, if Malcolm is aware of Blix and knows I have a means to find him wherever he goes, it might stop him from trying to sneak away. Then again, this guy is an arrogant jerk. Even if he believes I'm 'powered up' on Aurélie's blood, he'll be completely convinced I'm not a threat.

Hate to say it, but he's probably right about that part.

I don't know the full extent of how much a sire can really 'see' or know over the link. I did, however, discover something of a limitation. Apparently, it can't reach from Washington State to South Africa. Dalton called me the other night to follow up on his having a sense of worry something happened to me. He wouldn't go into detail about what he was doing over there, so I'm guessing he's stealing something. Regardless, he sounded quite a bit worried about me and 'cheesed off' as he put it that someone tried to kill me. Dalton offered to rush back here if I needed help. So sweet of him.

Alas, he's so far away it would take too long for him to get back here. This would be over before he could return to the States. I also think Malcolm is older than Dalton, so my squishy side didn't want him getting hurt for no reason. Yeah, makes it sound even crazier I'm going in here to kick his ass myself, but I, umm… have Aurélie's blood loan.

At least, that's the official story.

We encounter our first obstacle about halfway across the grove: another mercenary. Lucky for us, he's an ordinary mortal using night vision gear. We pounce on him. The fight is about as fair as a pellet trying to take on Pac Man. Wait, no… that analogy implies we ate him. We don't, merely a light thrashing with a side order of sleep compulsion. Much the same way Mom throws our bed sheets into the air and snaps them before letting them settle onto the mattress, Tilloa flung this guy off his feet and whipped him into the ground. I jumped on his chest, grabbed him by the throat with my other hand over his mouth, and derp slapped him.

While I cemented the urge to sleep for at least four hours in his head, Tilloa unloaded his M4 and sidearm, then threw the magazines—plus all the spares—as hard as she could in random directions. It seems Malcolm isn't a complete moron. His people are not walking around his estate carrying hand grenades. No flashbangs either. I wonder if we gave him a phobia. He's probably super pissed off that he allowed me to taunt him into such a state of rage he failed to notice Tilloa chucking it at him. I can't imagine an elder would not have been fast enough to dodge if he saw it coming. He's not going to make that mistake again.

I should expect a moderate-to-severe amount of pain tonight.

After stashing the sleeping dude behind a tree, we hurry along the route of a dirt path leading up to the house. It's picturesque in a 'you're all going to die here' sort of way. Evenly spaced trees, dirt path, fountain at the center of the grove. The place just begs to have people dressed in Jane Austen type attire strolling around. Either that or a pack of men with torches in old timey clothing dragging some innocent young woman out into the woods to burn her as a witch. It's the vibe.

There's another man patrolling back and forth on the porch. Unfortunately, this guy looks like a vampire merc. His eyes are a little too shimmery to be mortal, about at the midway point between, say, mine and Tilloa's. Mine don't do the weird reflective brightness thing at all. I appear to be perfectly mortal. Tilloa's got small battery-powered lights in her skull. It's a pity vampires can't reveal themselves to the public. The combination of her model good looks, dark complexion, athletic build, perfect hair, and glowing golden eyes would make her an A-list action movie star. She could totally play an android or cyborg and save a ton of money on the special effects budget.

Right. Back to the task at hand. Bad Sarah. Focus.

Yeah, I'm nervous. Trying to think about other things.

We hide behind the tree nearest the porch, watching this guy go back and forth along the entire length. It's at least forty yards from one side to the other. Huge porch on a huge house. Most of the wicker furniture is in disrepair. I don't imagine the sort of vampire who owns a mercenary company is fond of sitting out on the porch admiring the moon.

There aren't too many ways to disable a vampire and not make a buttload of noise. Fortunately, I happen to be carrying one with me: my katana. Unfortunately, katanas are pretty ineffective as ranged weapons. The next time the guy walks all the way to the right end, I dive forward into flight, inches above the ground, and 'meat torpedo' my way around behind the left side of the porch. Ivy-covered white wood lattice blocks off a roughly four-foot-tall space underneath. A large 'chamber' under the porch appears to contain only raw dirt and whatever weeds are trying to grow down there. I half expect to see rotting hands burst up from the ground at any second.

Yeah. I've watched too many scary movies.

Slow and quiet, I ease my katana out of its scabbard and wait, listening to the soft thump of boots on wooden boards above me. There are several things wrong with this situation, not the least of which is me wearing shit-kicker boots with yoga pants. For one thing, I'm trying to be a sad approximation of a ninja. Katanas are the blades of samurai. That's like cats and dogs. Stealth attacking a dude with a samurai's weapon is probably the sort of crime that'll get you sentenced to a gruesome death in

Japan. Like... being buried up to my neck in the ground and the whole village surrounds me and pelts me with tiny flaming pickles until it kills me.

Second wrong thing is also related to katanas. Dalton is, as one might infer from his British accent, pasty complexion, and less than perfect teeth, not Japanese. While my wonderful sire did more or less 'upload' a good deal of his sword fighting skill into my brain, his style is entirely different. Ideally, I should have a saber, rapier, cutlass, or even a legit medieval longsword.

However, between Dalton giving me actual skill and my father's love of martial art movies, I'm good enough with a katana to beat someone who has no idea how to fight with a sword—and doesn't even have a sword on them.

Yeah, not exactly fair, but I'm pissed. I'm also not a samurai, so to hell with fair. They messed with Ashley.

The instant the guy's footsteps get close, two things happen almost simultaneously. Tilloa makes a sound like a barn owl arriving back at its nest to catch its mate doing steamy things with another owl... and I spring up into a spinning slash. Her super odd attempt at an owl noise makes the merc vampire spin in her direction and raise his M4.

He doesn't see me coming.

Alas, my aim is a bit off. I miss his neck by about two inches. My blade slices into his face just below his nose. Blood splats in a line on the wall behind him. I put so much power into the swing, I spin like a top in midair three or four times. Only the ability to fly keeps me from eating dirt. When I finally catch myself and stop spinning, I realize the vampire merc is still standing there with only about a quarter of his head remaining. A scrap of his upper lip remains, but the rest of his head above that is lying on the floor like a busted coconut.

Yanno, like a year ago, staring at the exposed underside of someone's brain would have made me scream and faint... unless it was on a video in science class. Then I'd probably have merely felt sick. Now? I shrug.

His body collapses to the porch.

Tilloa emerges from behind the tree, making an 'ooh, nice one' face at me.

I have less respect for these guys than the LA vampires. I sliced a head or two open there, and did them the courtesy of placing the upper part back where it belonged so they only remained unconscious for six to eight hours. As far as I know, severed vampire parts don't sprout legs nor do they telekinetically move on their own to reconstitute. This guy is going to stay asleep until someone puts his cranium back on.

If no one does, he'll lie here and smooch the sun.

He'll probably have a sun bath anyway, even with his head in place. An injury like that is a long knockout. Okay, fine. Fine. Sure, he and his merc buddies were trying to give me a sun bath, but I'm not a psycho murdering bitch. He's just doing his job, even if 'evil henchman' isn't much of a career. Pay's good, but the benefits suck and the healthcare plan is even worse. This guy might not have even been personally at the lumber mill, only works for the same mercenary group. I'll at least drag him into the basement of the house later.

I fly-jump up over the railing onto the porch and step around the body. Might as well keep the sword out for now. Tilloa advances up the stairs and meets me by the door, which promptly whips open. Another mercenary is standing there, pointing a gun at me.

"Hi," I say, making my voice a little higher and kid-like. "Would you like to buy some Girl Scout cookies? Two boxes of Thin Mints are only five dollars."

The guy does a double take.

While he's distracted by my inane question, Tilloa jams her knife at his forehead. He drops his M4 to hang on its chest strap and manages to catch her arm so she only sinks about an inch of blade into his skull above his left eye. Expecting him to scream, shout, or make a ton of noise any second, I jump back, raise my katana, and lunge into a thrust. A strange thing about vampire reflexes: the hundredth of a second it takes him to process the situation is obvious in his eyes. If he lets go of Tilloa's arm to defend against my sword, her knife is going to plunge into his brain and shut him off. If he doesn't let go of her arm, my sword is going to pierce his heart and do the same thing, albeit a bit slower. Heart hits aren't *instant* night time.

Dude comes up with an option three. He wrenches to one side, using his hold on her arm to throw Tilloa into me. I still stab him, but it's in the lung. Either in response to the pain or anger, he lets out a roar and overpowers Tilloa, pushing her knife out of his head. I yank my sword free. He pivots into a disarming arm-bar takedown type maneuver, trying to introduce her face to the floor. Tilloa flings herself around in a levitating cartwheel flip and boots him in the jaw.

He goes flying back into the parlor. She rotates upright, still holding her knife. He crashes to the floor in a slide as she settles neatly on her feet.

I rush after him, sword high. He springs up unexpectedly fast, drawing a knife into a sideways slice at my stomach. Like a matador, I thrust my rear end backward to avoid his attack. He swings his other hand at my face. I fly straight back as if pulled away from him by a guy with a rope around my waist. His fist hits nothing but air, resulting in him spinning like a figure skater for a second.

Tilloa runs in.

The guy pulls a second knife.

We circle around him, trading stabs and slashes, no one hitting anything but metal. He's a margin faster than us, so he's able to keep deflecting my sword with one knife while blocking Tilloa's knife with his other one. Going full defensive is working to keep us from hitting him at all, but the few times he tries to slip in a counterattack are half-assed and easy for me to parry.

Somewhere around the fiftieth time my attempt to slice his head off ends with my katana clashing against his giant knife and me stumbling to the side, a diminutive demonic warble comes from the door.

Blix stands there in a pose like James Bond. He raises a hand and snaps his fingers.

A metallic *ploink* comes from above as the sizable chandelier detaches from the ceiling and lands on top of the vampire merc. He mostly catches it without being knocked over—however, having a 250-pound lamp bonk you on the head is slightly distracting.

Tilloa and I both stab him at the same time.

Blix produces a small pair of sunglasses out of thin air, flicks them open, and puts them on. He then disappears in a puff of smoke.

"Whoa." Tilloa looks up. "That was lucky."

"Just a little home imp-provement," I mutter, yanking my sword out of this guy's chest.

A set of white double doors at the back end of the foyer fling open. Malcolm strides in. He's wearing a dark suit with a fluffy violet ascot thing at his neck. I can't help but snicker a little when I realize there's an oval-shaped patch of skin starting at his hairline, going all the way down to his chin, and stretching to the edge of both cheeks that's noticeably paler than the rest of his skin. It looks like someone pied him in the face with sunblock when he slept on the beach.

"Foolish whelps," says Malcolm. "I had not expected you to make things so easy for me. Yet, here you are, together, right at my door."

I stand away from the disabled vampire mercenary and spin the katana over in my grip. "Nice new face. That grew back fast."

Apparently, I got the number one Family Feud answer on the question 'what's the worst possible thing to say to an angry vampire elder?' I don't even see him move. Next thing I know, my head's stuck through the wall and the bells are ringing. Somewhere behind me, Tilloa gurgles. I push myself out of where I'd flown into the drywall like a human dart. Malcolm's holding Tilloa up off her feet by a one-handed grip on her neck.

"Hey," I rasp. "Isn't that Undertaker's signature move? Copyright infringement."

"You two are such good friends," says Malcolm. "You should spend more time together."

I'm in the wall again. Why? He threw Tilloa at me. We're both in the wall. I think our faces collided. She shifts, falling off me and allowing me to tumble out of the hole. My katana's laying on the fancy carpet a few feet away amid plaster bits. I go for it.

It ought to have been a warning that Malcolm made no move to stop me from recovering my weapon. Roaring a battle cry like I have some chance here, I scramble to my feet, scoop the blade up into a two-handed grip, and charge at him. I feel as if I'm trapped in a slideshow of still images from an artsy samurai movie. Every time I slash at him, I cut only air and there he is leaning out of the way. Again and again, I slash and chop, and Malcolm is always inches away, his body tilted slightly to one side or back.

After nine wiffs, he slaps me across the face hard enough to send me staggering.

Tilloa comes out of nowhere, dropping on him from above. He blurs. I can't say for sure, but I think he does some kind of 'Ryu from Street Fighter' crap, punching up into her stomach as she falls, then side slipping and hammering a fist onto her back, drilling her face first into the floor. It all happens so fast.

Growling, I lunge in, thrusting at his face. He leans aside, grabs a fistful of my hair at the back of my head, and drags me around by it. After everything that's happened to me since becoming a vampire, a schoolyard fight tactic isn't the least bit bothersome. It hurts, but a hair pull has nothing on having my spine snapped in half.

I elbow him in the jaw, knocking him away.

"Really? What are you, a prissy cheerleader?" I snap. "Pulling my hair?"

And I'm on the ceiling... or more accurately, *in* the ceiling.

Damn this guy is fast. Yeah, he *definitely* could have avoided the flashbang if he hadn't been so blinded by anger at my making fun of him. I don't even feel the pain of where his fist hit me before gravity pulls me out of the hole I made. The throbbing starts in my gut when I'm halfway to the floor. Once again, my sword popped out of my hand. It's stuck in the rug like Excalibur waiting to be seized. Tilloa attempts biting him, but he catches her by the back of the neck.

I swoop over and grab my sword.

Malcolm drags Tilloa around by her hair, verbally berating her for being a failure, calling her weak because she needed a teacher, telling her how she's such a disappointment after all the work he put in preparing her for her great moment.

All the while he's swinging her around, I keep trying to get in there and slice him. Doesn't work out for me, though. Again and again, he dismisses me and sends me stumbling or sliding across the room. Most times, he slaps me in the face as a patronizing insult, but he does occasionally slip in a backhand fist.

This is more or less exactly what I expected would happen. I'm not a masochist, so I'm not going to keep letting him get his metaphorical arrogant rocks off toying with us for too much longer. I also hate watching him try to break Tilloa down with a constant stream of belittling comments about how weak, useless, and disappointing she is. Every time she tells him to go F himself, he hammers her face-first into whatever piece of furniture or wall is convenient.

There is at least one thing I want to accomplish before moving to phase two of our plan.

I spend the next maybe two minutes trying to use my katana to pry him off her to no avail. While slapping, swatting, or throwing me across the room repeatedly, he rambles on to Tilloa about how upset and furious he is having to entirely relocate his whole operation away from Seattle because of the problems 'we created' for him in regard to the other vampires here.

"I am going to break you, little Tilloa." Malcolm forces her hands together on top of a banister post at the bottom of an ornate stairwell leading up to the second floor, then rams her knife through them, nailing her to it. "When I am done, you will beg me to forgive you and resume your place as my apprentice. Then, I will destroy you." He smiles.

"Keep dreaming, asshole." Tilloa grunts, attempting to lift her arms to pull the knife from the wood.

He gestures at her. "I was merciful. The edge is oriented outward. Pull back and you'll be loose."

If she does so, her hands would be split in half from wrist to knuckle.

"Make no mistake, whelp," says Malcolm, pacing around her. "Despite knowing I will only destroy you anyway… by the time we are done"—he strikes the knife handle, driving it deeper into the wood, making her gasp in pain—"you will beg me to take you back."

"You have some serious mommy issues," I say in between coughing up blood.

"And as for you…" Malcolm strolls over to me, his gaze focused on my sword.

It's time to do what I came here for.

He's expecting me to use the katana. As he swoops in to grab me, I abandon the sword, extend my claws, and shred his armpits. His back arches, body stiff. Malcolm lets out this anguished shriek of pain like someone clamped his man bits in a searing hot waffle iron. I'd do that if I could, but don't have a waffle iron handy. Also, really don't want to see his man bits.

Did I mention vampire claws hurt? Like an inordinate amount? I may as well have red-hot needles at the ends of my fingers. And armpits are a pretty sensitive place. Snarling, I rake my claws down his sides, leaving multiple slash trails in his skin all the way to the base of his ribcage. The cuts aren't deep or dangerous to existence, but damn are they painful.

"That's for Ashley," I snarl.

He backhand slaps me so hard I'm astonished to remain awake. Somehow, my neck didn't snap. I'm dazed, but not in immediate danger. He can't seem to move much either, gasping in shock, frozen with his arms up a little so they don't brush against the claw wounds. At his age, it's stupid to think he never suffered a claw wound before. However, his reaction is almost as if this is new for him. Gonna guess it's been a while and he forgot how bad they hurt. That's the problem with having a desk job for a century or two. A vampire forgets what it's like out in the street.

Malcolm emits a wheeze.

Behind him, Tilloa continues trying to free herself. She's given up on her arms and is now trying to pull the knife out with her teeth. Almost any vampire should be able to make themselves strong enough to yank four inches of blade out of hardwood. It's a little different when said knife is impaled through both of your hands. Applying enough upward force hurts too much.

Speaking of hurt, Malcolm gasps and wheezes a few more times, jaw open in disbelief.

Much the way a kick to the balls stuns a boy for a moment or two and then they shrug it off, fury returns to his expression. Next thing I know, he's holding me against the wall, his hands clasped around my wrists to control my claws. We're close enough to kiss. The anger in his expression has mutated into unbridled rage. I do believe I have pushed him past the point of wanting to toy with me anymore. Time for phase two... like now.

"What did you hope to accomplish you stupid, sniveling child?" He snaps.

"Honestly? I didn't expect to beat you. I just wanted to cause as much pain as I could to pay you back for what you did to Ash."

He frowns. "How... adorable. Do you have any final words?"

"Wow." I exhale. "This is going to sound like something from one of my dad's cheesy Eighties movies, but yeah. I do have a final word. Let's do the scene right. Start over. Ask me again."

Malcolm glares at me, but for some reason rolls his eyes, huffs out his nostrils and asks, "Do you have any final words, whelp?"

Channeling my best Wesley Snipes from *Demolition Man*, I say, "Yeah. Tag."

This is not what he apparently expected. He stands there for a few seconds in bewildered silence before blurting, "What?"

"Tag. You know, like pro wrestling? Tag team?"

He's giving me this stare like I'm a complete idiot when the front door creaks open.

Eyebrow raised, he turns his head to look behind him.

A young woman walks in wearing a pink T-shirt bearing a white cartoon rabbit print, a rose-colored miniskirt, black leggings, and sneakers with pink soles. Her hair is past her butt, snow white and perfectly straight. Her skin is almost the same shade of pure white. Large eyes of bright cobalt blue take in the scenery, a note of somber loneliness in her expression. Glimmering pink heart-shaped earrings dangle on either side of her head. From a distance, the outfit makes her look sixteen.

It's so damn bizarre to see her in ordinary-ish clothes.

5 0

TAG

Malcolm looks back at me, frowning.

I smile at him. Bye bye, asshole.

"What is this? Another little high school girl?" asks Malcolm, his tone dripping with annoyance.

"Hah." I flash a sarcastic smile. "Hardly."

Aurélie's eyes change from blue and innocent to red glowing embers, yet she keeps her gaze downcast as she creeps closer. Yeah, she does the super creepy anime waif thing well. "You 'ave tried to kill a young vampire under my protection." She drifts toward him. "For this, you forfeit your right of existence."

Laughing, Malcolm casually snaps both of my wrists, then drops me. Ow, you motherf— I curl up cradling my arms to my chest. He's stupid, but he's not a moron. Doesn't want me clawing him again while he 'disposes' of this new annoyance. He leaves me slumped on the floor and turns to face Aurélie.

"Come, little girl." Malcolm raises a hand in a beckoning gesture. "If you dare face the *vrais démons*."

"*De vrais démons?*" She scoffs. "*Vous êtes à peine lutin.*"

Malcolm's expression starts to change to the gawping, indignantly offended sort of face one might make while watching someone dump ketchup on a filet mignon, but doesn't fully get there. Aurélie snaps her head up to glare directly at him—and she lets her charm power off its leash. The woman is so furious I swear the damn air turns purple like colored stage lights just came on. He really shouldn't have snapped my wrists like that right in front of her. The whole mood in this room plunges into an abyss of doom. Maybe I'm hallucinating the purple, but daaaaamn.

Know how when you're a little kid and your mom or dad gets extremely furious at someone else. You're not at all related to the problem or in trouble, but still scared to make so much as a tiny sound in case Angry Mom notices you exist and you catch some portion of tangential hell? Yeah. That's me right now. I'm just gonna sit here curled up in a little pain ball waiting for my wrists to un-break.

There's about a one-point-eight second window where Malcolm's face is a mask of fear.

Aurélie's on him in a blur. It's as though I'm watching a live action cartoon, just smears of motion rocketing back and forth across the room, crashing into walls, smashing holes, splintering the furniture.

Whoa. I know she unintentionally looks like an anime character, but I didn't realize Aurélie likes—or even knows about—it. The ridiculous kinetic crap going on right now is straight out of every over-the-top fight scene in *Fist of the North Star*. It's even more pronounced since she dressed up to look like a harmless teenage girl. For some reason, that's like really big in anime. Some innocent young person—not always a girl, but usually —has unimaginable power stored in their little body. I'm not saying Aurélie is tiny. She's short and petite, but clearly not an atomic preteen like the anime trope. Hey, people were shorter in the 1600s.

No, 'atomic preteen' is Sierra, thanks to Sophia's magic.

Anyway...

Aurélie whips him across the room, slamming and smashing things. At one point, the blurry smear sails over Tilloa and the knife disappears with a faint upward spurt of blood. She gasps and slumps to her knees. I think the sound of repeated stabbing is coming out of the blur. Also, bone crunches. Malcolm's face print is appearing in the walls here and there. The two of them have become a cloud of distorted light. This is Fight Cloud. First rule of Fight Cloud is we don't talk about Fight Cloud.

Tilloa scurries over to take cover next to me. "You okay?"

"Couple of broken bones. Totally worth it." I bite my right middle finger and tug the hand into a more natural position. A crunching crackle comes from the wrist. Pins and needles follow.

Malcolm manages a confused, anguished scream before two pieces of him go flying in different directions, leaving Aurélie in the middle of the room with her arms extended out in two directions. Whoa. She totally 'Bishoped' him, like from *Aliens*. Waist up goes one way, hips and legs fly the other. Malcolm's upper half bounces once, rolls face down, and gurgles. His skull's been shattered so badly it has no solidity left whatsoever, merely bone chips suspended in a gelatin mold. His face deflates to resemble a blob fish.

Aurélie lowers her arms, standing there placidly, looking like a fairly normal, somewhat emo, young woman… except for having blood up to both wrists and a twitching raisin of a heart clutched in her right hand.

Tilloa closes her eyes in a hard cringe as if struck with a sudden, intense migraine. Her entire body shudders for a few seconds before whatever spell came over her passes. When she looks at me again, she appears to be okay… and a touch confused. If I had to guess, she probably *felt* Malcolm's destruction. Well, it's official. There *is* a way to break a sire's mind link with their vampire offspring: destroy them.

"I'm legit not sure what shocks me more." I bite my left index finger and tug my hand back into position with a faint *crack*. "Seeing Aurélie in ordinary clothing or this display of supernatural power."

Tilloa's not trying to hide her 'holy shit' expression. She leans her head toward me and whispers, "I'm most impressed at how she didn't get a drop of blood on her outfit."

"It is simply a matter of practice," says Aurélie.

The weird dissociative emo act stops in an instant. Aurélie smiles at us. The pall of freakish dread in the room disappears. She approaches, tossing the heart aside. It hits the floor with a thud as loud as if she'd dropped a bowling ball. "Come. Let us leave this place."

I stand, as does Tilloa.

Aurélie glances down at her outfit, then at her bloody hands, then us. "What is it we are supposed to do now? If we are pretending to be *lycéennes*? Do we go out for ice cream?"

"Umm, what?" asks Tilloa. "Lee see en?"

"Oh, *oups*." Aurélie grins. "I sometimes forget the young only know one language in this country. High school girls."

Can't say I know the proper etiquette for teenage girls to follow after tearing a vampire elder in half, but I suppose this is comparable to hitting the mall on Black Friday. The level of violence is roughly the same. "Yeah. Ice cream works."

"Umm, we can't eat it," whispers Tilloa.

Aurélie winks. "We are not *lycéennes*, yet I pretend to be. We can pretend to enjoy our *crème glacée*."

"I dunno about you guys, but I plan to do more than pretend." I grin.

"So jealous," says Tilloa in a teasing tone.

WEIRD IS IN

I wake up.

I'm in my bed at home. It's been a day since Malcolm decided to split. I expect to have a tiny person curled up next to me. I do not expect to have a less-tiny person curled up on my other side. Before I even open my eyes, I know it's Ashley from the way she's tucked up against me with her head on my shoulder, not to mention her scent is familiar.

No idea what she's doing in my bed, though. I mean, we used to do this all the time on sleepovers. Her being here at all isn't weird to me. Her being here as I wake up but not when I first went to sleep *is* a bit strange.

I open my eyes.

Ashley's on her side, her hair draped over her face. She's wearing a pink PJ top with smiling unicorn faces and matching PJ pants—like little kid ones with elastic ankle cuffs. A strip of bare stomach where her shirt crept up is a tempting target. Whenever we co-slept as tweens, I'd always wake up first. Not sure what started it, but tickling her awake became something of a habit. She usually squeals and demands I stop. The tone of her laugh—it's a fairly unique and bright laugh that only seems to come out of her when she's tickled—says she doesn't hate it. Yes, she wants the tickling to stop, but only right then. It's not a 'never do that again' demand. Did I mention she's crazy ticklish?

I don't bother her now, though. She looks too peaceful and happy.

Chloe's in a ball, wedged between my chest and right arm. She's taken to my habit of going to bed in a giant T-shirt. Only, she's presently wearing one of my normal-sized ones. On her, it's a shin-length nightgown. She's tucked her knees up inside the shirt. Only a hint of her toes peek out the bottom.

Aurélie has done two giant favors for me recently, and the one I'm more grateful for isn't destroying Malcolm. Vampires are stuck pretty much as they were at the moment of death. For example, if I cut my hair, it's going to grow back to the exact same length it was when Scott stabbed me. If I concentrate and force it to grow longer, it will shrink during the day as I sleep. If I cut it, it will grow out. My knife scar isn't going anywhere. Thankfully, it's only a small white line. People don't even notice the scar if I'm topless unless I point it out. So yeah, our bodies are a snapshot of the moment of death. Ugh. Ashley talking me into getting a Brazilian—mostly because she didn't want to go alone—had some really unfortunate timing. Two days before my death. 'Try it and if you don't like it, don't do it again' has become forever. Could be worse. I could have a gaping bullet hole in my face every night. Shouldn't complain about trivialities.

Anyway… little Chloe's piece of shit father beat her to death after violently abusing her for years. The girl had bruises on top of bruises, recognizable handprints where he grabbed her. Looking at her when she slept used to make me just want to curl up and cry, disavow myself from ever having been part of the human race for being capable of such cruelty. Except for not having her head cracked open, she looked like a tiny little murder victim… just like the cops might've found her the following morning if her sire hadn't been there.

Thanks to Aurélie, Chloe no longer reverts to appearing severely beaten and abused when she sleeps. She looks angelic. Pure. Not a mark on her. I'm a little fuzzy on the mechanisms involved, but the simple explanation is she basically updated the kid's system BIOS. No, she's not a computer or robot. I mean, Aurélie exploited their age gap. Vampires who are sufficiently older than other vampires can read the younger one's mind. Because Chloe is *so* new and Aurélie almost 400 years old, the kid is susceptible to the full range of vampiric mind powers. As in, she can be given command compulsions the exact same way Malcolm turned people into ticking time bomb assassins.

It's a little more complicated than Aurélie giving her a 'stop that' command. Think of vampires in a computer sense. When we sleep and wake up, it's like a reboot. Everything resets, reformats, and begins loading the vampire.exe program. Part of that 'startup routine' is resetting our body to what I'll call 'state zero.' That's our moment of death. Aurélie managed to edit Chloe's 'programming' so the lines of code responsible for making all those bruises come back are gone. She reset Chloe's 'state zero' to be immaculate.

It may even have something to do with her being so little. Her mind is much more pliable than an adult's, or even mine. Her sense of self isn't as strong, so it's possible to shape it at a subconscious level.

Whatever. I really don't care how it worked. It worked. I never have to see Chloe looking so battered again. It had been tempting to ask Aurélie to make me forget ever seeing her like that, but I didn't. It motivates me to protect her as well as not feel the least bit bad about her being a vampire.

Chloe, I expect to sleep here. Ashley not so much.

Uh oh. She's been kinda radio silent for the last three days. Yeah, she's freaking out over the abduction. Can't blame her, but I'm still slightly worried.

"Oh, hey," says Ashley in a sleepy voice. "Sorry. I didn't mean to pass out."

"It's fine. You okay?"

"Mm hmm," she says, eyes still closed.

I lightly trace one finger over the strip of bare stomach.

She grins, squirms, and pulls her shirt down to cover it. "Staaahp."

Smiling to myself, I stretch. Chloe snuggles in tighter, still not quite awake. She's in between, though. Not stiff and corpselike as we become when deeply out.

"Is it okay if we hang all day?" asks Ashley.

"Absolutely. Let me try again. Are you okay?"

She yawns, then sits up, futilely puffs at hair draped over her face, then yawns again. "Fine. I'm thinking I should probably stop going out of my way to find a date and just enjoy life for a while."

"Might not be a bad idea. Try letting someone come to you instead of throwing yourself at the first person to say two words."

She tickles my side, making me draw my knees up. "Ack!"

"I didn't *throw myself* at Raleigh. Or River. Or Tabitha. Or Melanie Francis. Or..." She blinks. "Okay... maybe I did."

We exchange a look before bursting out in laughter.

"I'm worried about you." She stops trying to tickle my ribs and shifts to sit cross-legged with her back to the wall.

"You're worried about me?" I grin.

She nods. "Yeah. You're a powerful immortal with unlimited cosmic power, but you're not invulnerable."

I roll my eyes. "I'm hardly in possession of unlimited cosmic power."

"Still." She picks up my lone plush rabbit and bonks me on the head with it. "It's so stupidly lucky none of those guys managed to hurt you."

"Which guys? The mercenaries who threw a few thousand bullets at us that night?"

She shudders. "No, I mean the accidents and stuff before that. Especially the coffee survey guy."

"Oh, yeah." I bite my lip. "I feel so bad for them, too. They're victims."

"Yeah." Ashley bows her head. "I'm glad Malcolm paid for what he did to them, and to Raleigh, even if she doesn't remember me."

I think about all the near misses. The thousand bullets thing is pretty incredible, too. How easy would it have been for one bullet to catch me in the face or the heart? Lights out. At last count, I'd absorbed twenty-six bullets during that chase. Not one of them hit me in the two off switch spots.

"Yeah. Lucky…"

What are the odds a fat bee happened to collide with the bullet Raleigh tried to put in the back of my head? Probably about the same as a baseball pitcher killing a pigeon going by.

"Yep." She nods hard, deliberately throwing her hair over her face like a goof.

Lucky. Hang on. I glance over at my desk. My hairbrush is suspiciously clean. Not a single strand of stray hair caught in it. Sophia appears in my memory with her four extra magical arms, cleaning the kitchen counter. Her impish little smile hits me just right and I break out laughing so hard I'm crying.

This wakes Chloe up. She sits up, one eye wider than the other, scrunches her nose at Ashley, and blurts, "The eff time is it?"

Yes, she says 'the eff.' Didn't drop a real bomb. She's trying.

I get a hold of myself and point at the brush. Ashley looks at it, wondering what I'm trying to say. Chloe scrambles off the bed, grabs the brush, and runs back to sit next to me with her back turned, brush extended over one shoulder.

Sigh. Okay, kid.

I sit up, pull her a little closer, and proceed to start brushing.

"What?" asks Ashley. "How is a hair brush so funny you laughed so hard?"

Smiling, I work the brush through Chloe's long, jet-black mane. Swear this girl is part cat. She adores this. "Just remembering something Sophia said when I found her cleaning the kitchen the other day. She used magic to give herself some extra arms. I said something about her maybe overusing magic for such a small chore. She said magic didn't always have to be 'world exploding,' sometimes it's for small things... like luck spells."

Ashley glances at the brush. Her eyes light up. (Not literally). "Ooh. She did!"

"Yes. She did." Remind me to go squeeze her. That luck spell is probably why I survived the backpack bomb... and Raleigh trying to shoot me, and the window-washing rig falling at us, and who knows how much else. Sophia saved my unlife... and she came close to killing Malcolm through sheer frustration."

"Why are you wearing kid pajamas?" asks Chloe.

"Because I like them," says Ashley.

"She's eighteen going on nine," I mutter.

Ash bonks me with the bunny plush again.

I glance at her. "Are you okay? Really? After Raleigh, being stuck in an umm, 'uncomfortable costume' for like six hours... shot at?"

"Yeah." Ashley nods. "I'm fine. Totally over it." She tilts her head. "Is that weird?"

Here I sit, a vampire, brushing the hair of a vampire child, in my basement bedroom that keeps us away from the sun. "Maybe a little weird. But weird seems to be in lately."

"Seriously," says Ashley.

I stop brushing Chloe's hair as my brain jams to a hard stop on a reality error worthy of a Bethesda game. Hang on. The only window in my bedroom is a giant printout. My room has no real windows. Not that I notice, but it's technically pitch black in here. Zero light. Ashley should not be able to see a damn thing. She's looking at me. She looked exactly where I pointed at the hairbrush on the desk. My heart nearly stops. I slowly turn my head to face her.

"Ash?"

As if she can sense exactly the reason why I've frozen to stare at her, she flashes a knowing smile—and bares her fangs. "What's up?"

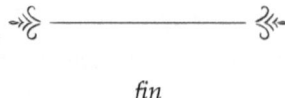

fin

ACKNOWLEDGMENTS

Thank you for reading the fourteenth installment of the *Vampire Innocent* series! I am truly grateful for all the support and wonderful feedback you've given me in regard to this series over its course thus far.

Sarah's story will continue in book fifteen.

Additional thanks to Lee Sheridan for editing and Alexandria Thompson for the cover art.

Also, many thanks to David Lee Cox (no relation) for proofreading!

ABOUT THE AUTHOR

Originally from South Amboy NJ, Matthew has been creating science fiction and fantasy worlds for most of his reasoning life. Since 1996, he has developed the "Divergent Fates" world, in which *Division Zero, Virtual Immortality, The Awakened Series, The Harmony Paradox, and the Daughter of Mars series* take place. Along with being an editor at Curiosity Quills press, he has worked in IT and technical support.

Matthew is an avid gamer, a recovered WoW addict, Gamemaster for two custom RPG systems, and a fan of anime, British humour, and intellectual science fiction that questions the nature of reality, life, and what happens after it.

He is also fond of cats.

Visit me online at:
    Facebook: https://www.facebook.com/MatthewSCoxAuthor
    Pinterest: https://www.pinterest.com/matthewcox10420/
    Goodreads: https://www.goodreads.com/author/show/7712730.
Matthew_S_Cox
    Email: mcox2112@gmail.com

OTHER BOOKS BY MATTHEW S. COX

Divergent Fates Universe Novels

Division Zero series

- Division Zero
- Lex De Mortuis
- Thrall
- Guardian
- Harbinger
- The Shadow Fixer
- Neuroshock

The Awakened series

- Prophet of the Badlands
- Archon's Queen
- Grey Ronin
- Daughter of Ash
- Zero Rogue
- Angel Descended

Daughter of Mars series

- The Hand of Raziel
- Araphel
- Ghost Black

Virtual Immortality series

- Virtual Immortality
- The Harmony Paradox

Prophet of the Badlands Series

- Prophet's Journey
- Prophet's Mercy

Divergent Fates Anthology

(Fiction Novels - Adult)

The Roadhouse Chronicles Series

- One More Run
- The Redeemed
- Dead Man's Number

Faded Skies series

- Heir Ascendant
- Ascendant Unrest
- Ascendant Revolution

Temporal Armistice Series

- Nascent Shadow
- The Shadow Collector
- The Gate to Oblivion
- The Queen of Discord
- The Burning Alchemist

Vampire Innocent series

- A Nighttime of Forever
- A Beginner's Guide to Fangs
- The Artist of Ruin
- The Last Family Road Trip
- The Phantom Oracle
- How Not to Summon Demons
- Ordinary Problems of a College Vampire
- A Vampire's Guide to Surviving Holidays
- An Introduction to Paranormal Diplomacy
- A Vampire's Guide to Adulting
- How to Stop a Vampire War in Six Easy Steps
- Ancient Vampire Death Cults and Other Annoyances
- Hunting Vampires for Fun and Profit
- A String of Seriously Unlucky Events

- The Summer of Completely Usual Strangeness
- Demonic Crisis Management for the Modern Vampire

Standalones

- Wayfarer: AV494
- Axillon99
- Chiaroscuro: The Mouse and the Candle
- The Spirits of Six Minstrel Run
- Sophie's Light
- The Far Side of Promise anthology
- Operation: Chimera (with Tony Healey)
- The Dysfunctional Conspiracy (with Christopher Veltmann)
- Of Myth and Shadow
- The Girl Who Found the Sun

Winter Solstice series (with J.R. Rain)

- Convergence
- Containment
- Catalyst
- Catacombs

Alexis Silver series (with J.R. Rain)

- Silver Light
- Deep Silver
- Silver Quarrel
- Silver Crucible
- Silver Heart

Samantha Moon Origins series (with J.R. Rain)

- New Moon Rising
- Moon Mourning
- Haunted Moon

Vampire For Hire series (with J.R. Rain)

- Moon Master
- Dead Moon

- Lost Moon
- Vampire Destiny
- Infinite Moon
- Vampire Empress
- Moon Elder
- Wicked Moon
- Moon Blade

Maddy Wimsey series (with J.R. Rain)

- The Devil's Eye
- The Drifting Gloom
- Dark Mercy
- Primal Wrath

Samantha Moon Case Files series (with J.R. Rain)

- Blood Moon

Immortal Operative (with J.R. Rain)

- Broken Ice
- Broken Wing

Four Elements series (with J.R. Rain)

- The Elementalist
- The Black Rose
- The Wakefield Curse

Witches series (with J.R. Rain)

- The Witch and the Hangman

Zeb Clemens series (with J.R. Rain)

- The Beast of Devil's Creek
- Wanted: Undead or Alive

Young Adult Novels

The Eldritch Heart Series

- The Eldritch Heart
- The Cursed Crown
- The Sapphire Soul

Evergreen Series

- Evergreen
- The World That Remains
- The Lucky Ones
- Nuclear Summer
- The Nuclear Frontier
- The World We Make
- The Threat Unseen

Progenitor Series

- Out of Sight
- Out of Mind

Diary of a Teenage Fey
(Short story series)

- Elder Horror
- The Hag of Barrow Falls
- Babysitter's Nightmare
- Lharakki
- Bauble for a Soul
- Simulacrum
- Amorphous
- Manticore

Standalones

- Caller 107
- The Summer the World Ended
- Nine Candles of Deepest Black
- The Forest Beyond the Earth

Middle Grade Novels

The Adventures of Ubergirl series

- My Dad is a Mad Scientist
- Aliens Ate My Homework
- The End of all Halloweens
- Dr. Infinity and the Soul Smasher

Tales of Widowswood series

- Emma and the Banderwigh
- Emma and the Silk Thieves
- Emma and the Silverbell Faeries
- Emma and the Elixir of Madness
- Emma and the Weeping Spirit

Standalones

- Citadel: The Concordant Sequence
- The Cursed Codex
- The Menagerie of Jenkins Bailey

www.ingramcontent.com/pod-product-compliance
Lightning Source LLC
Chambersburg PA
CBHW051948240626
47153CB00005B/1677